OUT OF THE BLUE

KATHRYN NOLAN

Editing by Faith N. Erline
and Jessica Snyder
Cover by Kari March

ISBN: 978-1-945631-76-4 (ebook)

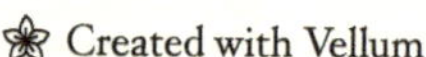 Created with Vellum

For those who refuse to stay in their lane.

COPE

My client had made the barista cry.

Again.

"You are well-known for providing the most expensive and sought-after coffee in San Diego," he said. "Yet what I'm currently holding in my hand is nothing but pure disappointment served at room temperature."

I clasped my right hand around my left wrist, feet planted six inches apart. It was the classic posture of protection agents everywhere, but I was only using it to control my irritation. I'd been unlucky enough to be placed on Arnold Sheffield's security detail for six months now. He'd come into this world with a trust fund, and over the years he'd acquired a flashy lifestyle, fueled by the Fortune 500 company he ran in name only.

That meant Arnold Sheffield was a total and unrepentant douche. We were currently fielding a dozen kidnapping threats a week on him.

Mostly from his adult children.

While Sheffield continued to berate the barista, I leaned

over to whisper at Falco. "I kind of hope one of his kids actually goes through with those kidnapping threats, you know?"

Falco remained stone-faced. We'd worked together at Banks Executive Security for years, and he was a rule follower to his very core.

Sheffield dropped the cup of coffee back onto the counter and whirled around to take a phone call. The barista was pink-cheeked and watery-eyed. I shot her a sympathetic smile.

Meanwhile, my client paced back and forth dramatically, aware of his audience. He was in his early sixties, pale with gray hair and a mustache he thought made him look distinguished. He ended his call, exasperated, then pushed open the front door. Falco dutifully followed at the prescribed three-foot distance. With one eye on the street, I walked to the barista and reached for my wallet. I had all of forty-two dollars in crumpled bills, but I shoved them into the tip jar just as she was turning around. "If it's any consolation," I said, "I really think he's going to be kidnapped soon by one of his own children."

Her brow furrowed. "What the hell?"

I nodded, sliding on my aviator sunglasses. "My thoughts exactly. Have a nice day, ma'am."

I backed out through the door and onto the sun-drenched sidewalk. Falco was waiting for the valet to return the town car while Sheffield fumed. The man's three adult children were a pack of money-obsessed hyenas who'd stab each other in the heart with a salad fork if it meant they got one extra penny. And they were privileged enough to believe they could orchestrate a kidnapping plot against their dad for the ransom money without consequences.

Personally, my odds were on Arnold Jr., who had three yachts, zero compassion, and the personality of a houseplant.

"Do we know why the car is taking so long?" Sheffield demanded.

"No sir," Falco said. "I'm sure it'll be just a moment."

There was a sharp, piercing squeal of tires on asphalt. Then a black van with tinted windows slid right in front of us, slamming on the brakes so hard I winced. But that wince became a grin when the side door peeled open, revealing an average-sized guy in all black wearing a face mask that disguised his features.

"Well, whaddya know," I said, reaching down to adjust my cuff links. Falco sprang into action, shoving Sheffield behind him and radioing for help on his walkie-talkie.

I stepped gracefully in front of them both to greet the situation.

The guy in the face mask saw Sheffield, then saw me, and made the wrong choice. He ran at me like a flying squirrel. I shrugged, dropped low, and hit the guy in his mid-section. He went hurtling over my shoulder, landing with a thud on the ground.

Falco was still barking orders into the walkie while Sheffield wailed, "*Am I being kidnapped?*"

The guy on the ground scrambled up. I punched him in the jaw, and he dropped back down. "Don't worry, sir," I assured Sheffield. "Falco and I have been on the receiving end of plenty of attempted kidnappings. And they haven't gotten us yet."

Guy-on-the-ground tried to sit up, woozily. I grabbed a fistful of his sweater and dragged him to the wall. "You see, your average kidnapper these days is pretty fucking incompetent."

Falco hustled over to restrain our attacker. "If that guy doesn't kill you, Cope, I swear to god I will," he hissed.

I arched my eyebrow. "Which guy?"

"*That* one."

I spun on my heels as the second kidnapper lunged at me. His arm arced back in a wide attempt at punching me in the head. But I ducked free, clocked him under the chin, and followed it with a swift knee to the stomach. I shoved him to the ground, slightly out of breath. When he tried to squirm away, I dropped to my knees and pinned him to the sidewalk.

"Backup is on its way," Falco said through gritted teeth. "Mr. Sheffield, sir, you need to stay behind me."

Our client was, literally, pulling his hair out. "Do you... *Jesus Christ*... do you think one of my kids is behind this?"

Falco and I shared a conspiratorial look. "*Arnold Junior?*" I mouthed. He shook his head and went back to securing the first attacker.

Whistling, I tried to get my own bad guy under control. Today was a lot more fun than Sheffield's usual security detail, which consisted of driving him from high-profile meeting to higher-profile meeting, watching him yell at his staff like they were worth less than dog shit on the bottom of his shoe and having a front-row seat to family dynamics so fucked up *I* probably needed therapy.

So sometimes a little action was nice. I wasn't put on this earth to protect people from harm just to make sure guys like this had access to their favorite hundred-dollar cup of coffee.

My attacker was trying to yell something at me, but his face was muffled by the sidewalk I was grinding his cheek into.

"Sorry, what was that?" I asked.

More garbled noise followed. I shook my head and sat back on my heels. Falco cursed and Sheffield gasped. Then I heard the all-too familiar sound of my partner cocking his weapon.

Cold metal pressed to the back of my head.

"Drop it, or I'll shoot." The voice behind me was thin. Nervous. I didn't like nervous. Give me a skilled, confident kidnapper any day. Nervous ones made mistakes, like shooting a man in broad daylight in downtown San Diego.

"*Now* I know what your friend was trying to say," I drawled. "*Watch out for the third asshole.*"

"That was stupid of you not to bring a gun." The nervousness had transformed into a false bravado that raised the hair on the back of my neck. Memories of the last time I'd been at the receiving end of a gun barrel beat at the edges of my thoughts. But I muscled them back and locked them away.

"I hate guns," I said smoothly. "Never use 'em. Besides, in most courts of law, my hands would be considered dangerous weapons."

"You got a lot of jokes for a man with a gun to his head."

"A habit I haven't been able to break."

I cast my eyes down to the side. His boots were within striking distance. Complicating things was the guy I'd been restraining on the sidewalk, slowly catching his breath and turning over. Two against one meant I was done for. I mentally ran through a catalog of low takedowns, but they'd have to be fast. And a surprise.

"Put the CEO dude in the car," he said. The cold metal dug into my skin.

"You know I can't do that." I flexed my fingers, just slightly. Felt a corresponding *zap* of adrenaline.

"I'm not asking—"

I grabbed his booted ankle, yanking forward as I stood. I knocked the gun from his hand with my shoulder, swiped the back of his knees, and sent him tumbling down to the hard ground. With the first guy restrained, Falco was next to me and on the other man immediately.

I stood all the way up, hands on my hips and head tilted back. Chest still heaving, I let out a slightly pained laugh.

Then I gave the third guy a petty little kick in his side. "That's for bringing a gun."

"Fucking *ow*," he cried.

But now that I was surveying the scene around me, I was less in the mood for snappy one-liners. Because the nervous-sounding dickhead laying on the ground had gotten the drop on me.

And that wasn't good, evidenced by the scowl on Falco's face when we made eye contact. Marilyn, our boss, had already professed her sincerest disappointment in my performance a few months ago. *Chatty and overly familiar with clients. Seems bored and disinterested. Makes risky choices that go against protocol.*

Sheffield stumbled over, frazzled and rumpled. "That man could have *killed you*."

Falco muttered, "Or the boss will."

Ignoring him, I flashed a grin and brushed a few pebbles from my suit sleeves. "Not in the cards for me today, sir. But your concern is appreciated."

The door to the coffee shop creaked open. The barista from earlier stood there, eyes wide, jaw dropped open.

"See?" I said, indicating the bodies on the ground. "Karma's a bitch."

2

SERENA

The marketing team in the conference room at Aerial's headquarters was absolutely silent as they watched the tiny figure being towed out by a jet ski to surf giant waves. The video was projected up on a wall made of natural-looking wood. Above it, the words *Invest in Planet Earth* were painted in teal and yellow.

I re-crossed my legs and settled my hands in my lap to keep from twisting them nervously. I'd gotten dressed up for this meeting. Or as dressed up as was physically possible for me. My wardrobe consisted of board shorts and wet suits, but I'd dragged a slightly wrinkled dress from the back of my closet and thrown it on before racing out the door.

The guy sitting next to me had the wiry, muscular forearms of a rock climber. "Were you scared shitless out there?" he asked.

"I'm always scared shitless," I admitted. "Going over the lip of a forty-foot wave pushing you at fifty miles an hour is terrifying." I glanced back at the video, where I was waiting patiently on my board for the right set. The Jaws Invitational only went when Maui's infamously big waves were perfect. And it hadn't been called in years.

Every surfer that day understood the waves at Jaws to be a class onto their own—they were heavy, loud steamrollers of water. The slabs of white foam curling up and over the heads of those tiny human beings shook the sand, carved canyons into the ocean floor, sent surfers tumbling end-over-end into a dangerous maelstrom of currents and riptides.

And I loved every second of it.

My gaze flicked back to the man next to me. "It's also the gnarliest thing I've ever done. Would do it again in a heartbeat."

Reaction sounds bubbled up from the front of the room. Even now, my stomach hollowed out as I watched my hands let go of the rope towing me behind the jet ski. My board skimmed across the top of a wave I later found out measured forty-six feet high. It was a beauty of a bomb—turquoise blue, clear, and shimmering. I dipped down the face, gliding across the water with spray flying up all around me. The only thing I remembered was the absolute roar in my ears, the saltwater stinging my skin. And the all-out adrenaline of being shoved forward on a board by the power of an epic wave.

The lip curled up and over, obscuring me from view. There were hushed gasps, some nervous-sounding laughter. At that point, I was one with the wave, and that tight green barrel hadn't scared me one bit.

A row of bumpy water *almost* had me tumbling off, but I caught myself. I bit the tip of my thumb and smiled as the audience reacted with cheers. Cheers that grew louder as I caught the path back up the barrel. With the momentum of the water behind me, I shot off the top of the wave, hands down to grab my board, before diving into the ocean.

The lights came back on, revealing the five executive

members of Aerial's marketing team. And at the head of the table stood David and Marty Lattimore, the brothers who had founded the company in the seventies, with the goal of creating an outdoor clothing and gear brand that protected the environment at the same time. Standing next to each other, they didn't look like the leaders of a billion-dollar business. They were both white with shaggy hair and the kind of craggy, wind-burned faces common among San Diego's population of surfers and rock-climbers.

"Well done, Serena," David said, shaking his head. "We've watched that video a dozen times, and it never gets less impressive."

Marty slid his hands into the pockets of his hiking pants. "When I heard you'd qualified for the ISC, I ran right to Dave's office and said, 'That's her: Aerial's next brand ambassador.'"

I smiled in response, wanting to pinch myself. "Thank you so much for saying that. This opportunity is a literal dream come true for me. When I started surfing at twelve, my very first board was an Aerial one. And I'm proud to say I still only use yours."

"Happy to hear it," Marty said. "And that's one of the many reasons we chose you to represent us. You are *the* surfer to watch at this year's ISC events. You're outspoken. A maverick. Passionate. These are the qualities this company has always embodied, both in spirit and in practice."

"Our team is very excited," David continued. "We partner with *Heavy* magazine whenever we have a new ambassador to officially launch them as the face of our company. Your interview is in two days, and the photoshoot is the week after."

"And from there?" Marty said. "We've got press scheduled at your next three competitions to start and even more photo shoots to model gear and clothing. And all of this is to prepare for next year's Olympics in Barcelona. We want you front and center in promo, ads—"

"Speaking up, speaking out," David interjected. "We want you to be *you*, Serena."

My smile widened. "I think this is going to be a perfect fit."

I had waited a long, long time to compete at the international level. And while I was surfing at twelve and began competing at fourteen, it wasn't until the infamous wave at Jaws that I qualified for the elite events. And that was only after years of grueling training and an intense competition schedule.

So when my agent had called to say that Aerial wanted *me* as their newest brand ambassador, I'd been shocked. They were the most respected eco-conscious company in the world —and one I had always admired. I wore their wetsuits and clothing, used their surf wax and safety gear. Their activism was bold and ground-breaking, and they stood on the forefront of climate justice and sustainable practices, setting an example for other companies to follow.

"We think it's perfect too," Marty said. "Before you head out, do you have some time to talk a little bit with the marketing team about what you'll be focusing your spotlight on?"

"I can do that, yeah," I said, facing the marketing team at the end of the table. "David, Marty, and I have already chatted about what I'd like to raise awareness of within the surfing industry since I'll have an even bigger platform now. And that, of course, is sexism. Inequality that's been prevalent in this sport since it began and all the ways it negatively impacts the lives of fellow athletes."

I watched my surfing video, playing on a loop against the wall. I could just make out the very first comment beneath it: *This bitch can't surf for shit.*

My face went as hot as the mid-day sun outside, but I tried to restrain my anger. In surfing, women were viewed as bikini models first and athletes second. And I *was* outspoken and passionate, like Marty had said, but those weren't the words a lot of male surfers used to describe me.

"Anything Aerial can do to combat sexism and other forms of discrimination within surfing will make a huge difference, I just know it," I said, thankful my voice was steady. "You could use your website and magazines to elevate the voices this sport ignores or leaves behind. The company could sponsor forums and events that highlight this issue but also propose ways for real change. You could push for pay equity and representation in leadership. Really, with the size of your platform, there's no limit to what can be done."

I lifted my chin, expecting at least a little pushback. But the marketing team was all encouraging smiles and nods.

"I love those ideas, and we can start implementing them right away. Change is what we're all about," the rock-climbing guy said next to me. "We want to do the work."

I let out a slow sigh. "I want to do it with you. Women in this sport deserve to be amplified and celebrated, not hyper-sexualized and diminished."

"And we agree," Marty said. "You're the perfect role model to embody that change, Serena. We're proud to stand with you on these issues."

My fingers stopped twisting in my lap. I grinned, confident. "Then let's do it together."

David looked at his brother, who was absolutely beaming. "I heard Trestles is going to get called any day now. Are you ready to get out there, represent this company, and win?"

Behind him, I could see the determined expression on my face as I sailed confidently down a wall of water. I looked more than just *ready* on my surfboard.

I was unstoppable.

I leaned forward on my elbows. "There's no doubt in my mind that I'll win."

The room erupted into happy, celebratory clapping.

"Then welcome to Aerial," Marty said.

My cheeks ached from smiling, my anger forgotten in a moment I'd been dreaming of since I'd caught my first wave. My older brother, Caleb, had lied to our parents about an after-school activity so we could go to the spot on La Jolla beach where all the surfers our age hung out. There had been no hesitancy on my part as I stepped into those waves that afternoon. No reluctance, and not an ounce of fear.

I was welcoming myself home.

"We'll let you get back to your full day of training, but we'll be in touch about all of this. And the *Heavy* interview will take place here. Thought that would make things a little easier for you since you'll be so busy the next few weeks," David explained.

"I can't wait," I said. "And there will be some phenomenal women competing alongside me at Trestles. I hope they'll be given an opportunity for media too."

"Absolutely," David said, emphasizing the word.

Nodding, I grabbed my bag and dropped it across my chest as I walked toward the door. I didn't expect to feel so listened to in this meeting, although I'd hoped for it. Aerial had shown, over the years, that they were dedicated to having a real impact on my community, so I was trusting that they really cared.

"Oh, Serena?"

I turned to Marty, my hand on the doorknob. "Yes?"

"We forgot to mention that, with the announcement of Aerial being an Olympic sponsor, we expect a heightened attention around our company, including our newest ambassador. That's why we'll be placing you with a security detail."

My nerves flipped from elation to panic. "Like... a bodyguard?"

"Exactly," he said warmly. "We're also the lead sponsor of the next three ISC events here in southern California, which means you'll be extra exposed to the public while traveling with a raised profile. We've had a few close calls over the years—erratic fans, press that's too nosy. We might be a bunch of crunchy-granola types, but we've learned you can never be too safe, especially in the world of extreme sports. The last thing we want is for you to feel uncomfortable when you need to focus on the task at hand."

I gripped the door to steady myself, legs shaking. My body's flushed, uncontrolled response to those words was irritating, as were the memories I worked to avoid every day. Sometimes every hour.

"We need to focus on the task at hand, sunshine," he said, clicking his tongue like I was about to get in trouble. His firm lips glided along my inner thigh. Big, calloused palms skated up the backs of my legs, squeezing my ass. "Because I only have fifteen minutes before I need to get to work, and I intend to spend every single second with my—"

"Serena?"

David's calm voice dragged me back to the conference room.

"I'm so sorry." I laughed, hoping it sounded carefree. "I'm already thinking about the competition."

He tapped his forehead. "We love that winner's mindset. And we'll be in touch about your security detail. You'll be meeting them tomorrow night, here at our offices."

"Great," I said, much too brightly. "I'll see you then."

I slipped out into the hallway then walked quickly, distracted, back through the open-air lobby filled with plants and big windows and outside into the heat. I blew out a slightly shaky breath.

The odds of it being him, of all people, were essentially zero to none.

Right?

I walked even faster around the side of Aerial's offices, heading towards my pink surf van. A person barreled into me. It sent my bag flying to the ground, a few of my things scattering out—sunglasses, sunscreen, mango-flavored lip balm. I managed to stay upright and grabbed the person by their shoulders.

"Oh my god, *I'm so sorry*." It was a woman, shorter than me, but about my age. She had long black hair, light tan skin and expressive, dark eyes. "I bumped right into you, I'm so embarrassed."

She dropped down to scoop everything up, and I noticed her hands trembling as she did so. I mirrored her pose, knees on the asphalt, and lightly touched her shoulder. Her smile, when she looked up, was strained.

"Don't even worry about it," I said. "I get knocked over by giant waves literally every day. I'm used to it." I extended my hand. "I'm Serena, by the way."

She shook it. "Catalina Flores. And I know who you are, and I'm a *huge* fan." I stood and helped her up. She swept her hair from her face before handing me my bag. "I'm a lawyer for Aerial. In-house counsel. But in my spare time, I'm a wanna-be surfer. A total newbie."

I waved off her comment with a smile. "All it takes is a little practice, I promise. I surf every morning with a bunch of badass women at the northern-most point on La Jolla. We're dawn patrol all the way, so if you wanna get up early, come hang out with us."

I slid my bag back over my head and caught her staring at it. "That's so kind of you, thank you. My parents are from Mexico, and when we visit family in the summer, I surf at Playa Hermosa in Ensenada."

"That's totally rad," I said, slipping on my sunglasses. "Have you tried the waves at Isla Todos Santos yet?"

She bit her lip. "Not yet. I want to, but I'm scared."

I touched her arm. "Come find me if you join us at our surf spot. We can start practicing if you want. The more the merrier, right?" I started walking towards my van. "It was really nice bumping into you, Catalina."

She laughed, still sounding nervous, but I hoped she came out with us. If there was one thing being a surfer had taught me, it was that we were *all* newbies when it came to the mercy of the ocean.

And the world needed as many fearless women as possible.

3

COPE

I held my palms up and gave Marilyn my most charming smile. "You know, Falco said you were going to kill me. But I see no evidence of that."

Marilyn's lips twitched. "If I wanted you dead, Copeland, you'd be dead. And, trust me, you wouldn't see it coming."

I pointed at the coffee pot. "Poison my drink, huh?"

Another secret smile. "How pedestrian. And no."

"Then how?"

"Secrets like that are for keeping," she said. "And you are currently here not to make jokes but to listen to me tell you, yet again, how gloriously stupid and reckless your actions were today."

I dropped my hands, dropped the act. Marilyn Banks had hired me four years ago, when I was heartbroken and directionless. She was as fair a boss as you could get, easily earning and keeping your respect. She was a fifty-year old Black woman with short gray hair and an addiction to tailored pant suits that cost more than my salary.

And she was right. If she wanted to kill me, I'd never see

it coming. Whatever skills I'd developed in this line of work were amateur compared to her decades of experience.

"Marilyn," I said. "We stopped one of our most elite clients from being kidnapped in broad daylight. That's my job, and I did it."

Her eyes blazed with irritation. "You made a basic mistake and assumed you had visual confirmation of the number of attackers when you did not. You're a highly trained guard, with an extensive hand-to-hand combat background, and yet an amateur kidnapper had his gun to your head while you knelt on the ground."

I exhaled slowly, still pissed off. Being outsmarted by anyone in a fight wasn't something I was used to.

"According to your partner, you were distracted all day. Not paying attention. And then almost got yourself shot in the process." She paused, mouth pursed. "And this right after Arnold Sheffield had already complained to us about your attitude."

I rubbed the back of my neck. "I'm sorry, really. There's no excuse for not handling the situation the way I've been trained to. But, for the record, I'd like to say that spending hour after hour of watching Sheffield humiliate people while making a gargantuan amount of money isn't exactly engaging." I shrugged. "Or heroic, for that matter."

"That's interesting," she said. "Because last I checked, I don't pay you to be heroic. I pay you to take your job seriously and to take the safety of your client seriously. I pay you to know your routes, do your background checks, and be aware of the movements of every single person in the room."

I swallowed a frustrated sigh. "Ask anyone I know. Hell, ask my mom and little sister. I take *everyone's* safety extremely seriously. In fact, my family and friends would call it my most annoying trait."

The subtle arch of her eyebrow let me know I was tap-dancing on thin ice. Working for Marilyn was a professional privilege—her leadership and mentorship had allowed me to level up in my career. But I didn't have a clue about what to do with her recent frustration with me. I fully believed protecting people was my actual birthright. And, quite frankly, thought I was pretty damn good at it.

My boss stood up, walked around her desk, and perched on the edge. She handed me a thin file and said, "I'm pulling you and Falco from Arnold Sheffield's detail and placing you with a new client. Falco has already been asked to keep an extra sharp eye on your performance. It's an easy client, to help me decide your fate."

I paused in the act of opening the folder. "My *fate?*"

She crossed her arms. "I'll start by saying this, and you'd be smart to listen. You're unhappy with this job, and it shows. It's been showing, especially these past few months, but I've been noticing it for an entire year."

My chest tightened painfully. *That couldn't be right.*

"Do this next assignment well, and then we'll talk. Do you understand me?"

"Yes, ma'am," I said.

Her gaze softened *just* a little. "What happened today could have ended a lot differently. I know you know that."

I flashed her a grin. "I'm indestructible, Marilyn. I'm here to stay until I annoy you so much you send my ass packing."

But she didn't return the gesture. "Just because you believe it is your duty to protect those around you does not automatically make them *helpless*. And it does not automatically make *you* indestructible. There's a line between acting on behalf of the client and recklessly seeking out danger, and you obliterated it today."

I didn't have a quick retort for that. I was indestructible because I had a calling.

And if I wasn't? Then my father died for no reason.

"I'm really, truly sorry," I said, sincerely. "I understand what you're saying, I promise."

She held my gaze until I wanted to squirm. Then she said, "I'm placing you at the outdoor clothing company, Aerial. Their headquarters are downtown, and they need two agents to cover their new brand ambassador for the next three weeks. This time of year, there are three popular competitions—"

"Trestles, The Wedge, and Huntington," I said automatically.

She paused. "That's right. You're familiar."

"If you're from here and were the child of a pro surfer, then you know the competition schedule better than your own math homework." I lifted a shoulder. "Not that I ever did my math homework."

She nodded, tapped the file. "Then you understand that they're high-profile events with huge crowds that aren't controlled."

"Security's usually lax, yeah," I said. "Who's the client again?"

I opened the file in my lap. The face that stared back at me was a white woman with wavy, dark-blond hair in a messy braid. Dark brown eyes, freckles covering her entire face. A sexy smirk on her full lips. And a scar that cut across her cheek from the time her broken board sliced her on a bad wipe-out. Later, after a couple stitches, I'd sat with her in our kitchen and held a towel wrapped in ice against her swollen cheek.

"Do you think the scar will make me look like a badass?" she'd asked, eyes bright with mischief.

I'd grinned at her. "You already are a badass, sunshine. I think it makes you look more beautiful."

My fingers crushed the edges of the folder. Seeing the love

of your life without fair warning was like taking a hard punch to the solar plexus.

Breathe, I commanded my lungs. *Just keep breathing.*

Through sheer force of will, I dragged my attention away from a face I never thought I'd see again.

"Her name is Serena Swift," Marilyn said. "She's a professional surfer, recently signed as Aerial's new ambassador. The face of the company. They're investing a lot of money and media attention into her career and want to make sure she's protected."

"She signed with Aerial? Are there any active threats against her?" I managed to keep the note of shock out of my voice. Just barely. And I didn't miss the scrutiny on Marilyn's face. But she walked back to her desk, picked up a tablet, and handed it over.

"There aren't any active threats, no." An immense wave of relief washed over me. "The company has had a few issues in the past, though. One of their ambassadors had a persistent stalker, and there was a confrontation on a beach during a competition. The man was ultimately fine, but they've been working with us for protection ever since. Also, our new client does have a bit of a reputation."

Marilyn had pulled up Serena's Instagram page on the tablet and selected a recent post. I narrowed my eyes, taking it in, then covered my mouth to hide the smile I couldn't suppress.

Fucking Serena.

"She's a bit of a troublemaker, huh?" I said, clearing my throat. The picture was of Serena and a few other surfers I recognized as friends, all wearing hoodies and sweatpants on the beach. Her long, curly hair whipped around her face while she displayed not one but two middle fingers for the camera. Behind her was a roaring bonfire of what looked to be... *magazines?*

"This is from a few months ago," Marilyn said. "A popular magazine, *Men's Workout Journal*, had a big hit after releasing a list of the top women surfers in the world, ranked by attractiveness."

My jaw clenched. "Assholes."

Her brows raised in question.

Sighing, I shifted in my chair. "Women surfers get treated like this all the time. It's atrocious."

Marilyn re-crossed her arms. "You mean a sport dominated by men has a toxic culture? Why am I not surprised?"

I enlarged the caption on the screen. Serena had written: *Dear Men's Workout Journal: Please accept this message from some of the world-class athletes you recently objectified and critiqued. Here's a pro tip: Women belong on these waves just as much as men do, and we'll be out here whether you deem us "hot" or "not." If you need convincing, we'll be waiting on our boards to show you how we surf. Don't worry, we'll go easy on you.*

I tamped down my own rage on her behalf and set the tablet back on the desk.

"She's right to be furious. I would be and have been myself," Marilyn said. "Unfortunately, you and I both know there are certain types of people—including sports fans—that don't approve of women speaking their minds. We want to make sure Serena is safe from something like that."

I nodded silently, afraid I'd be unable to censor myself. Fearing for Serena's safety was a feeling I understood deeply, and it always left me rattled. So instead, I pretended to study Serena's report like it held new information. My connection to this woman was buried in my personnel file. There was no way I'd be gazing down at a picture of Serena if Marilyn knew the actual truth. That meant she was either testing my trust —in which case I was already failing—or this was a rare mistake. An oversight.

Or, possibly, a fucking curse.

"Do you foresee any problems with this assignment?" Marilyn asked.

Was it a *problem* that I still dreamed of Serena every night? And that those dreams were so dirty I woke up to my hips punching into my mattress, grinding away my frustration?

"Problems?" I repeated with a frown. "I don't think so. It seems pretty straight forward."

"Excellent," Marilyn replied.

All the voices in my head began panic screaming.

I'd just been assigned as Serena's *bodyguard*. That meant watching her all day. Following her around everywhere. Listening to her talk and laugh, breathing in her mango-and-saltwater scent.

Catching the sun glint off her golden hair as it set behind the ocean.

"And I think it's straightforward as well," Marilyn said curtly. "But if Aerial has their concerns, we're smart to listen." She leaned over and tapped Serena's picture. "Protect this client, Cope. Do not do anything reckless to put her life at risk."

As if I could do anything less. I'd rather chew my own arm off than put Serena's life at risk. Every protective instinct in my body surged to the surface. Although these same instincts weren't enough to protect my *own* heart four years ago.

I closed the file and placed my palm on top of it. "You have my word," I said. "No fuckups, I swear."

Protect Serena. Of course, I'd protect her. I'd do it even if I *wasn't* hired as her protection agent. Because if she was truly in trouble, I sure as hell wasn't going to let someone else do the job I was made to do.

I was still her husband, after all.

4

SERENA

I hauled open the side of my van and stepped barefoot onto the cool sidewalk. With a bobby pin between my lips, I dipped my head down, gathered the unruly mess of my curls, and twisted them into a bun on the top of my head. I slid the bobby pin into the back and smiled at the scene in front of me. With the exception of San Diego's rare rainy days, this was the same view that greeted me every morning: a dawn sky painted in twilight purples and peachy-pinks, glossy barrels of waves, a beach filled with surfers and a long line of surf vans just like mine. Someone was cooking coffee over a bonfire. Soft reggae spilled out of a van painted in tie-dye colors. I picked up my own thermos and perched on the van's ledge, listening to the surf report on my radio.

Extremely rideable waves at La Jolla today. Swell over head height. Eight to ten feet, some at twelve. Get out and catch 'em early if you can, folks.

I reached behind me for the surf wax and started dragging it across my board. At the sound of cheering, I glanced up in time to see my friend Kalei Peleke catch a gorgeous wave.

The sounds and sights of surfers at dawn were imprinted

in my DNA and marked in my fingerprints. I'd set my internal clock to these rhythms at the age of twelve, and now beginning each day like this was a necessity.

There was no better way to learn to be present in the moment than by being a surfer. Because the ocean didn't owe you a thing, and while you could be predictable, the ocean *never* was. We waited for waves to break while holding our breath, sat on boards for hours for the lure of a decent set. In the ocean, nothing was promised, and everything was in flux.

So it didn't matter if you woke up tired or cranky, if your mind was filled with worries or stress. If the surf report declared the day to be *extremely rideable*, you pulled on your suit, grabbed your board, and you showed the hell up.

"If you give me some of your coffee, I'll make you do ten less squats."

I twisted at the waist and handed Dora the thermos. "You can always have some coffee, but I demand *fifty* less squats, thank you. Ten's basically nothing, and you know it."

My trainer—and mentor—carried a board under her arm and wore a full wetsuit. Her buzz-cut was purple and fading, but her smile made her look twenty years younger. In her mid-fifties, she had light blue eyes and the kind of deep tan that came from spending her entire life on the beach.

"Fucking hell, kid. Who taught you to negotiate?"

I leaned my elbows onto my knees and cast her a wry smile. "You did, of course."

She shrugged then proceeded to drink all my coffee. "You missed me earlier. Showed a few newbies what this old girl can do."

"Oh, yeah? You make anyone cry?"

"Hard to tell." She frowned. "But there were a lot of wet faces after I left them to stew in their own disappointment."

I stood up, laughing, and pulled my long-sleeve top on, zipping it over my bikini. I lifted my board up and Dora closed the van door behind me. "You're gonna scare them *away*."

She snorted. "I didn't scare you away, did I?"

We walked down the beach, the sand cool on my toes. "I don't know," I teased. "Maybe it should have."

Theodora Frances Tilden was something of a legend in the San Diego surf scene. She came from political royalty and had been expected to wear a polite smile and a string of pearls while acquiring a husband who could help her father's political career. She'd said, "Fuck it," moved into a van, and spent her days on a surfboard instead.

A fierce competitor back in her day, she'd taken me under her wing when I was a newbie myself—twelve years old with an older brother trying his best to help me and two parents we were both desperate to avoid. She'd seen me on the water with my clumsy limbs, already trying to surf waves much too big, and asked my brother if I needed a trainer.

"How was it at Aerial yesterday?" she asked, running a towel through her short hair.

"It was good." I stared out at the oncoming set from under my hand. "Great, actually. I think we're going to do a lot of important work together. And they obviously expect a win at Trestles."

"You will win." She tossed her towel on the sand. "We've been training for this day for a long time, my dear."

I wrinkled my nose. "Think I can handle these little baby waves out there?"

She plopped down on the towel and leaned back on her arms. "Such a showoff."

I hefted my board over my head and started towards the water. "I was taught by the best," I said over my shoulder.

My feet reached the cold waves, breaking against the sand. A crab scuttled quickly away. Seagulls circled overhead. Surfers and bodyboarders dotted the horizon, bobbing up and down in the morning light. I waved to Kalei and her wife, Prue Dorsey. Kalei was native Hawaiian, raised chasing the famous waves on Oahu. Prue, a well-known goofy footer, was white, with a bleach-blond pixie cut. They were only a few years older than me—we met when I was eighteen and lonely on my first tour, and over the years, the three of us had worked to bring together a lot of the women who showed up to surf at dawn.

"Bitchin' ride," I called out to Kalei.

She tossed her long, black hair with pure confidence. "I know, right? Now it's your turn, babe," she called back.

Feeling amped, I pushed onto my board and began paddling to the barrels farther out. I concentrated on the feel of my arms diving into the ocean. The board beneath my chest, the morning sun warming my back. When I reached a spot that felt right, I sat up, legs in the water, and turned toward the oncoming set.

What I *didn't* do was think about meeting my security detail later that evening. Because that train of thought was more dangerous than the sneaky rip currents this part of La Jolla was known for. Just because I happened to *unfortunately* know one bodyguard didn't automatically mean it'd be him.

You think I won't protect you forever, sunshine? Because I will, and happily, for the rest of our lives.

"Oh, look, Swifty's here."

My eyes were already starting to roll at the annoying nickname as Kyle paddled into view. He was the epitome of hyper-macho, surfer-dude sexism and absolutely the last person I wanted to be out here with.

"Listen," I said, "I'm about to catch this wave, so I don't really have time for you this morning. Can we jump to the part where I tell you to fuck off?"

He pulled his board right up to mine. I could *feel* him eying the same wave. "I heard you got mega lucky at Jaws."

"Really?" I started to turn my board, only half paying attention. "I heard the wave I caught was the biggest one that day. Even bigger than the ones caught by the guys."

"Bullshit," he said. "You caught a lucky break, and the whole world's gonna know it at Trestles."

"Sure, whatever, Kyle," I yelled over my shoulder. The next wave—the one I wanted—was coming in hot now, and I wasn't about to lose it arguing with this asshole.

"I'm calling this wave," he yelled.

"No way," I muttered to myself. I paddled as fast as I could, aware that Kyle was right behind me. This kind of stand-off between surfers as they charged a wave was a sure-fire way to cause an injury, but I was past rational reasoning.

"Swift, I'm *calling it*," he said. The wave rushed to the side, barrel starting to curl, so I stopped mid-kick and let Kyle sail right past me. He spun around, momentarily confused, which allowed me to push up onto my board and drop right beneath him. For one terrifying second, I thought his giant board was going to fall on top of my head, but he rolled away from me and into the foam.

I should have been focused, but my vision was already turning red. It didn't matter how many times women crushed bigger, better waves. The constant insinuation was always some bizarre stroke of luck, delivering us to victory. Not that we were just as strong, just as talented, just as deserving. So I was late pushing up. Late and unbalanced, a rookie mistake if I'd ever made one. As soon as I stood, I over-corrected, tilted too far to the right, and lost my footing. And I didn't bail with any kind of grace either.

I ate absolute shit.

My body hit the water at an awkward angle, the heavy saltwater like a slap to the face. I got stuck in the barrel, whipped around and disoriented in the dark. I scrabbled for calm, attempted to access the years of dedicated training that was supposed to help me emerge safely from a situation like this.

Instead, I was pissed. At Kyle. At that comment on my *Jaws* video. At myself for letting my anger put me in harm's way. When I finally surfaced, I was sputtering and dizzy, my board tugging me to shore by the leash strapped to my ankle.

I floated as the waves pushed me along, coughing. My nose was on fire. Salt stung my eyes. It was a hard and *stupid* wipeout. Dora watched carefully but knew me well enough to leave me be as I hauled my board onto the beach and dropped to the sand. I did what I'd been taught: feet flat, knees bent, head between them. I'd inhaled a lungful of water that burned like hell and had that panicky, *can't-take-a-full-breath* feeling.

You caught a lucky break, and the whole world's gonna know it at Trestles.

I gripped my ankles. Coughed. Dimly, I heard footsteps on the sand, then felt a hand on the middle of my back.

"You have enough breath. Your lungs will take in air. Your lungs will take in *enough* air."

I managed a smile while still coughing.

Caleb, of course.

"You have enough breath," he repeated. "Your lungs will take in enough air."

I latched onto the mantra and did as he'd taught me—visualizing my lungs functioning properly, the air inside, the sensation of *enough*.

"With me now, Serena," he said. "One... two..."

"Three..." I panted. "Four."

I exhaled a long, full breath. *Finally*. When I turned, my big brother was crouched next to me in his running clothes with a white shirt that said *Coast Guard Search and Rescue*.

"Thank you," I said.

He nodded like it was no big deal. "Bad fall?"

"Asshole got in my head."

He nodded again before turning to sit next to me, mirroring my pose. We shared the same dark blond hair and brown eyes, but he hadn't inherited the gene that gave me freckles all over my body.

"You out for your morning run?" I asked. I surfed at La Jolla, and Caleb was—among many things—an ardent fan of running on the beach. And more days than not, our mornings ended up colliding.

"Yes, but when I see a person gasping on the beach, I have to do the whole rescue thing," he said with a grin. "Kind of my job. *Especially* if it's my sister."

I snorted, bumped his shoulder with mine. Growing up, our parents kept our house strict, cold, and joyless. They preferred children to be seen and not heard and for their son and daughter to be placed neatly into the gender roles prescribed to us. It was not a surprise that Caleb and I had sought out more extreme careers—bold, somewhat dangerous jobs that required us to take up as much space as possible.

"I might be a little more nervous about my next competition than I'd care to admit," I said, still out of breath. I plucked a cracked bit of shell from the sand. "It's the Aerial thing. They're not my first sponsor, but they're the biggest with the best reputation. Before, it always felt like I was competing for myself—competing to win, for cash prizes, to score more points and qualify for more events." I let the shell fall and looked at Caleb. "Yesterday, they said I was *the* surfer to watch this year. So then, out there..."

He winced. "Ouch. Nothing like the heavy weight of enormous pressure to make an athlete freak out."

"You drop out of helicopters and into waves scarier than the ones I'll see at Trestles to save people's lives," I said. "How do you deal with the pressure?"

I had a sneaking suspicion of what he was going to say.

The same thing Dora had been gently—and not-so-gently—telling me as soon as my career started taking off. *Quiet your mind. Let your anger go. The only thing that matters on the water is staying alive.*

"It's a lot of mental practice," he said softly. "You develop a relationship with adrenaline, which has the ability to intently focus you or send you panicking. It doesn't come overnight. And I know you already have this skill." He nudged me again. "I've seen you focus out there, even when you're in a mess of a wave or need to bail."

Kyle walked out of the water fifty feet away, shaking out his hair and glaring at me. When we made eye contact, he flipped me off, striding over to a small circle of other surfers. Within seconds, they were peering at me like I was an animal in a zoo. The annoying, loud animal they wanted to shut the hell up. Which was infuriating. I'd seen women have wave after wave stolen from them by men like Kyle. We'd been knocked off our boards, harassed out of the water, threatened off the beach.

"I get distracted," I finally said, dragging my eyes away from the pack of dickheads scowling at me. "Still. Dora says—"

"What does Dora say?"

We turned to the woman in question, who handed me my water bottle and my cell phone. "It's been ringing, by the way. And nice form out there, Caleb. Your running stride's lookin' good."

"Aw, shucks," he said. "Thanks, Dora. I've got a few days off, but you know me."

"Can't keep still to save your damn life," she said. Dora hadn't been part of Caleb's training in years—the Coast Guard had seen to that. And even though he was one of the most elite swimmers in the world, she never hesitated to give him pointers when he stopped by her gym. And my brother, being who he was, always graciously received them.

I glanced at the screen. It was a message from someone at Aerial, reminding me about my meeting tonight.

"Um..." I turned the screen down and looked up at my mentor, squinting against the sun. "You know. What you always say. I've got to clear my head when I'm out there."

She nodded thoughtfully before sinking down next to me. I was briefly comforted by the brother to my right and the mentor to my left—the little found family that had kept me afloat. When Caleb had finally escaped our house at eighteen to go to college, he'd had the foresight to take me with him. And Dora, who had never married or had children of her own, had made sure we were fed and cared for, had holidays together, and had a person who showed up to our school events.

She reached for my hand. "You pissed off at that guy out there?"

I bit my lip, nostrils flaring. "Yeah. I fucked up."

She released me, but her face was serious. "You can't do that at Jaws. You can't do that at Mavericks or Trestles or Huntington. You can't do that out *there*, but at least it's easier to rescue someone falling off eight-foot waves. I don't need to tell you the difference when that wave is forty-feet over your head."

She did not. Because, like all surfers, I *had* wiped out on a wave that size, and the only thing that got me through it was dedicated training and precise focus.

"I'm angry too, all the time," she said. "You can't be a woman who surfs and not be. Assholes like that guy are going to continue to dismiss your talent because of their own insecurities, no matter how well you perform. The question is, the question *always is*, will you let the anger eat you alive? Or will you use it to accomplish something useful?"

I squeezed my knees to my chest. "Like what I'm going to do with Aerial," I said, reminding myself. "Changing the world. Saving the planet. Leading by example. That would be an accomplishment."

"Exactly," she said. "You know what you're doing, Serena. You always have. You just have to listen to yourself sometimes."

As my brother stood up, stretching his arms overhead, my attention landed on the appointment reminder on my screen. I hid a grimace. "I'm getting a security detail for the next few weeks. Courtesy of Aerial wanting to keep their new ambassador safe at these events."

Next to me, Dora went still. Caleb paused mid-stretch, slowly releasing his foot to the sand. He was trying to stay serious, but the happy smirk on his face couldn't be contained. "What kind of security?"

"I don't know," I said breezily. "And to answer the question I know you're dying to ask, it's not him."

Caleb bent down to give Dora a peck on the cheek. He squeezed my shoulder before bouncing on his toes, checking the time on his watch. "Much as I'd love to stay here and keep grilling you, I've got to finish this run. Don't forget to breathe, and call me if you need anything."

I stuck my tongue out at him. "I love you. Stay safe out there."

He nodded, running backwards. "I love you too. Stay safe out there."

A second later, he was moving back down the beach. Between what we'd survived with our parents and our similar careers, my brother and I were more than siblings. He was my best friend. The elements of danger and injury inherent in both of our jobs had built an extra layer of trust. We understood that certain risks couldn't be controlled, but we trusted each other to come back home.

Not everyone in my life had been like that.

"Are you sure it's not him?" Dora asked, running a hand through her purple hair.

"Positive," I said. "How many bodyguards are employed in this city anyway? It would be some kind of freaky-ass coincidence if it was him."

She hummed beneath her breath like she didn't believe me. "Either way, I need you focused out there, alright?" She wrapped her arm around my shoulder and squeezed until I laughed.

"I'm focused, I promise," I said. The next set was rolling in, and we instinctively turned toward the oncoming waves.

I arched an eyebrow at my trainer as she released me. "You ready to keep surfing?"

But she was already heading back for her board. Kalei and Prue appeared a second later, both looking wild and windswept.

"Come on, goddesses. The ocean awaits us," Prue said, tugging her wife across the wet sand and into the water. With a grin, I followed, feeling the bite of chilly spray against my legs and the buoyancy of my board. The three of us paddled out together, with Dora close behind, and we spent the morning flying across foamy breaks beneath the dazzling California sun.

I maintained my focus with an iron grip. Because Dora was right, and I had faith that the universe wouldn't screw me over like that.

Having an ex-husband for a protection agent was the last thing I needed before the most important competitions of my career.

❄ *5* ❄

COPE

I was early to my meeting at Aerial. Like, *way* early. But I wanted to give myself time to stand in the parking lot—in my usual black suit and sunglasses—and pretend I wasn't hoping to see my wife before heading inside.

I had no idea what the hell we'd say to each other. Like everything that we did, our breakup had been the result of stubborn recklessness and too much passion. We absolutely *did not get* closure. Which was odd for two people united in their greed for adventure, for spontaneity and fun, for grabbing all that life had to offer and running with it.

We only had silence at the end. The cold, hard kind that gets harder and more awkward the more time passes.

I ran my thumb across my lip, then shoved my hands in my pockets when I saw my fingers were trembling. My mind insisted on feeding me one super-hot memory after another. And even though I'd just told Marilyn I wouldn't mess this up, I'd stumbled around my house last night, bumping into furniture like a clumsy teenager.

The memories of our honeymoon night had become a constant distraction. Once we'd finally made our way into that hotel room—tipsy, exhilarated, horny—we only left that bed to fuck on the dresser. Then fuck in the shower. And then we fucked on the closet floor before climbing back into that bed.

"I won't stop until my new wife is satisfied," I growled, licking the beads of sweat sliding down her neck.

Serena only purred in response. "Then you better get to it, husband."

My phone rang. I smiled when I saw the name pop up. "Well, if it isn't Quentin Abernathy the Third."

"Good evening, Copeland," he drawled. "I'm merely a simple country man responding to a bizarre text message I received from you indicating that your new client is... let me check my notes here... your beautiful wife who broke your heart into a million pieces. Now did I get that right?"

I rubbed the center of my forehead. "Off the record, I'm assuming?"

"Not at all," he said. "This'll be front page news tomorrow as long as you're okay with me recording this conversation."

Quentin was a true Southern gentleman who'd come all the way from Memphis, Tennessee, to attend San Diego State. He'd been my randomly assigned roommate, but our friendship had solidified fast and stayed strong even seven years after graduating. While I was learning advanced driving tactics, Quentin had pursued his dream of becoming an investigative journalist and was now a reporter for the *San Diego Times*.

"I've always yearned to have my heartbreak and humiliation immortalized in some kind of public setting," I said, scanning the parking lot for a gorgeous blonde with a smirk that sent me to my knees.

"What are friends for?" he replied. "The bigger question is, did you come clean to Marilyn about any of this?"

"Nope," I said. "And I already feel guilty about that, so

you don't need to lay it on me. If she knew, she'd have pulled me off the case before I'd finished speaking."

Quentin didn't push for more because he was a good friend and familiar with my own brand of unique bullshit. I'd already badgered myself enough for two lifetimes. Because I didn't need to do any of this. In fact, I could have said, 'So sorry, this woman is my wife,' and been free to go. Marilyn would have found me another easy job to test my merit.

But I'd been a special kind of fool around Serena since day one. And *learning lessons* wasn't my thing.

"Did you at least give Serena a heads-up?" he asked.

I pressed my palm down my tie to bide myself time. Then I said, "Well... no."

"You're going to let that sweet woman get ambushed?" His voice was muffled. I could hear pages shuffling around, keyboard sounds.

"It's been four years, and I don't owe Serena a damn thing," I said. "Wife or not. She's my client; she doesn't get any special treatment." I slid my hand into my pocket. "Also, have you met her? She's more *fire* than sweet."

He chuckled. "Sure, she's a damn force on those waves, and she does frighten me a bit. But you're forgetting I had a front-row seat for your two-year courtship, and the two of you were sweet as candy. Oh, *hell*, I just spilled coffee all over my desk."

"Are you working on something?" Quentin's investigative instincts were legendary. He had a penchant for sniffing out injustice and always stood up for the little guy. That meant he went after scandalous billionaires, corporate liars, creepy politicians.

There was a reason I'd stormed over to his apartment two years ago and installed a high-tech security system for him. Quentin was on an endless search for bad guys who believed they were untouchable—and then he basically launched a rocket at their face. He made making enemies look easy, and that made *me* want to put barbed wire around his block to protect him.

"Kind of," he said, still muffled. "Since you're now working with Aerial, I thought I'd do a little digging just for fun, see what skeletons I can unearth."

I grinned, surprised. "Wait, you never did that when I was with Sheffield."

"Arnold Sheffield isn't hiding anything. He puts his atrocious crimes out in the open." I heard water rushing, something clanging in the sink. And then his voice came back on more clearly. "But Aerial is intriguing."

I studied their building. "They were doing the eco-conscious, sustainability thing before it was trendy. I think you can relax, Quent. They're one of the good guys."

"In the world of big corporations there are no good guys, only guys that are good at lying."

I laughed because it was so utterly Quentin. "Okay, my friend. Have fun with that."

"I'll update you when I've found something," he said. "And *you* update me after you reunite with Serena."

Falco pulled up next to me and got out of his car.

"Will do," I said.

I hung up the phone and turned to my stoic partner. He was a big, beefy white guy with a shaved head who almost never smiled. "Good evening. Ready for a new assignment?"

He grunted in response, but wariness flashed in his eyes. I felt guilty again—for keeping my relationship to Serena a secret from my partner and for not addressing his own understandable frustrations with my attitude. We weren't fully friends. I mean, I sometimes grabbed a beer after work with him and some coworkers, and I'd met his boyfriend, Connor, a few times. But still. We'd worked together for years, and I felt shitty about the Sheffield job.

"Hey, Falco," I said, hands back in my pockets. He turned around. "I am sorry about how the whole kidnapping threat went down the other day. And I'm sure having to babysit me on this easy assignment isn't your idea of a good time."

He shrugged, then admitted, "It's not. But it's my job, and I'll do it."

Marilyn's words came back to me: *You're unhappy with this job and it shows.* Was Falco happy? And did it matter how I felt if I knew I was always meant to do it?

"I'll be more focused and professional," I said, which had me breaking out in a cold sweat. As if my feelings towards the woman we were about to meet had ever come close to *professional.* "I won't let you or Marilyn down."

Falco nodded, turned on his heel, and walked to the building with perfect posture. I'd known him long enough to understand he'd non-verbally accepted my apology.

"Well, alright then," I sighed. Checking my appearance one last time, I followed him into a brightly lit lobby. There was a rock-climbing wall on one side and bikes parked in the corner. All of the staff walking around looked young and hip and effortlessly outdoorsy. Aerial was well known and had devoted consumers—something I knew personally because Serena had sworn by their surfboards and refused to purchase anything else.

An older man walked up to us, dressed like he was about to embark on an afternoon hike. "Mr. Falco? Mr. McDaniels?"

We stepped forward to shake his hand. He seemed friendly. Approachable. And he surprised me when he said, "I'm Marty Lattimore, one of the CEOs for Aerial. Come on back."

Falco and I exchanged a glance. Not that I didn't consider myself to be a big fucking deal, but CEOs didn't usually come out to greet us.

We followed him down a hallway into a smaller room.

"Sit, sit," he said, indicating two chairs. He perched on the end of the table, relaxed and loose. "We've worked with Banks Security before and have always had an excellent experience with their bodyguards. My brother and I take the role that Serena Swift now has very seriously. She's representing us out there, in the real world, showing off our products and exciting our fans. We want to make sure she feels happy and secure. And focused on winning."

"Yes, sir," Falco said. "We'll do everything we can to make Ms. Swift feel safe and comfortable."

I leaned back in my chair and hooked my ankle over my knee. "In the past couple days, have there been any threats made against Seren... excuse me, Ms. Swift? Or are we still being called in out of an abundance of caution?"

"Abundance of caution," Marty said. "I know you've been brought up to speed on some of our incidents and close calls in the past. And after one of our ambassadors was stalked and then threatened, we got serious about personal protection. Serena is well-known in this industry, but her profile is about to be amplified and raised tenfold, especially with some of the media spotlights we have planned for her. I'm sure I don't have to tell either of you that the higher profile the client, the more they attract an *unsavory* audience."

My body flooded with a furious adrenaline.

"Now obviously this is a little delicate," he continued. "But Serena is clearly an extremely... *striking* woman. Outspoken as well. That combination is why we wanted her. It's also the kind of combination that draws unwanted attention."

I was pretty sure I caught the *fastest* glimpse of smug delight in Marty's eyes. A *yeah-she's-super-hot* look that sent a tendril of unease through me. And a somewhat immature desire to punch him in the nuts.

"Aerial made the smart choice for brand ambassador," I

chimed in. "She's one of the best surfers out there, hands down. Her talent is unparalleled."

His expression turned sincere, and I loosened up a little. "I think Ms. Swift has a long career ahead of her for just that reason." A spark of recognition flickered across his face. He tilted his head. "Sorry, this might be rude, but you seem so familiar to me. Have we met before?"

I hid a wince, even though I should have expected it here. "I'm Copeland McDaniels... the second."

His face shifted. "Oh. Oh, you're his *son*, right?"

When I nodded, Marty beamed. "I should have known right away. You are the spitting image of your father."

"I've heard," I said, throat tight.

He stood up, passing his hands quickly over a wall of athletes photographed mid-action. Falco's face was all craggy questions, but I only shrugged. "You never asked."

"Yes, here we go." Marty handed me a framed picture in eighties-Kodak tones. It was of my father with his arms around a few other surfers—family friends I remembered from when I was a kid. He was smiling wide, holding up the two pieces of his board. I knew this story. He'd wiped out on a big wave, surfaced, and then found these pieces more than a mile down shore.

"I didn't know your father personally, but like most surfers in San Diego, my brother and I greatly admired him," Marty said. "His talent but also who he was. He really cared about building community."

The skin around my eyes got hot. I swallowed a couple of times and then set the picture down on the table. Seeing him like that was always hard for me. My mother, Helen, and younger sister, Billie, got comfort from looking at old pictures and watching videos. But I hated feeling like I'd seen a ghost. Never liked seeing him in the midst of being so alive when he was dead and had been for thirteen years now.

"Yes, sir, he really did care," I finally said. I faked a smile. "I'll tell my mom that my new client is a fan. Was a fan, I mean. She'll appreciate it."

He hung the picture back up on the wall. "You must be excited then for these competitions. And it helps that you understand these events. We're the title sponsors for the next three in the ISC and have beefed up security a bit. But there's still a chance that something can happen."

When we were little, Billie and I had loved competitions. Had loved hanging with my dad's cool surfer friends while getting sunburned and sun-dazed surrounded by cheering fans. I certainly never thought of them as occasions for potential threats. But that was well before I understood my dad's career was dangerous.

"Of course," I said. "Being overly cautious is always the smartest option when it comes to personal safety."

Falco gave me another slightly shocked look. Probably because he hadn't seen me take anything seriously in a long time.

Someone knocked sharply at the door. My heart sped up so fast it was painful. But it was only one of Marty's staff. "Do you have, like, five minutes to talk to Jane before Serena gets here?"

"You betcha," he said. "Are you two okay waiting for a few minutes alone? Or do you want to head to our kitchen and grab some coffee or tea? All fair-trade of course."

Falco stood up so fast his chair almost fell over. Dude was *hooked* on caffeine, and he needed to stay wired to work the night shift. He followed, hot on Marty's heels, and I barely got out "Yeah, I'll take a decaf coffee too, thanks," before he slammed the door shut.

I sighed, let my head tip back, and pinched the bridge of my nose. Then I stood up to pace the room, passing over my father's photograph to examine the rest of the framed athletes. Almost all of them were men. And there were no women surfers.

The door creaked back open.

"Did you get me a coffee, or did you forget as usual?" I asked.

There was no answer, so I turned around, hand in my pocket, and came face-to-face with my wife.

The door shut behind her as she stood there, frozen in place, lips parted. That soft *click* faded the world away, hushed the sounds of a busy office in downtown, brought Serena into sharp, precise focus. Our eyes connected. Held. My brain went fuzzy. My skin went electric.

I got hard as a rock.

"Cope?"

Serena's voice saying my name again after four long years was already my undoing. But the emotion etched into it tipped me right over the edge. It was raw, painful yearning, and the force of it had me touching the wall to steady myself.

Serena wasn't doing much better, swaying lightly like grass in the wind. The motion told me everything I didn't *want* to know about her feelings.

Surfers weren't unsteady on their feet.

"Serena," I said on an exhale. Her eyes closed. My voice sounded just as exposed, utterly naked to the elements. She was, even after all this time, achingly beautiful, all muscled, tan legs and wild, untamed hair that fell halfway down her back. Her jean shorts were tantalizingly short. Her gray sweater hung loose over her shoulder, exposing the delicious curve of her throat.

I contemplated a thousand different courses of action—running away for good, begging her to take me back, locking the door and bending her over this table. And then all the way back to *running away for good.*

My gut instincts were spot-on, as always. Because the

second she opened her eyes, blazing with anger, I knew this emotionally charged truce had come to an end.

"Let me get this straight. *You're* my bodyguard?"

"One of two bodyguards. But unfortunately, yes," I said. "And before you get on your high horse about it, I'm pissed off too."

"It's not going to happen."

"Serena."

"Do not *Serena* me. This tops the list of worst ideas of all time, and I can't have this kind of stress in my life right now."

I took a step closer. "You think I don't know this is the fucking worst? You think I've somehow forgotten what happened between us?"

She crossed her arms, preparing for battle. "Then why are you here?" She pointed behind her, over her shoulder. "And does your work know? Does anyone—"

"No," I said. "Of course not. Wait, does Aerial know?"

She shook her head firmly. "I don't talk about it anymore. The only people who know are—"

"Our family members and closest friends?" I interjected, hating the low tone of hurt in my words.

Her nostrils flared. "Well, do you go around talking about it?"

"No, I don't." I said, jaw tight. *But I go around thinking about it constantly.*

"Great," she said sharply. "Then we can stop whatever's about to happen, no questions asked."

I leaned closer, dropped my voice. "For the record, and I *despise* telling you this, but I'm on thin ice at my job right now, and I could use the win because I really don't want to get fired. It's three weeks, maximum. If we can be *civil* to each other for twenty-one days, then I'll be out of your hair, and you'll never see me again."

She stepped one foot closer. I could see the freckles that

covered her face. The freckles that I knew covered her entire body.

"Civil?" she said, with a smirk. "You think I can't be civil? I'm more concerned you'll spend the entire time trying to control my actions and telling me what to do like always."

I held up my finger. "First, I know you better than you know yourself, sunshine. I have no delusions of you actually listening to me or trusting that I'm an expert in keeping you safe from harm. Which isn't *telling you what to do.* It's protecting those you—" I tripped over the word *love.* "—used to care about."

I ignored the pain that flashed across her face.

"And two, I know you're only going to fight me tooth and nail the whole time."

Serena moved right into my personal space. So close. So *goddamn close.* She held herself like she always did, like she'd been born a warrior-goddess of the sea who never felt fear.

She raised a single finger, mimicking me with a smug expression. I was so annoyed right now, and *Jesus Christ* I wanted to kiss her. Those pursed, full lips were an obnoxious temptation.

"First," she said. "Do not, under any circumstance, call me *sunshine.*"

"My memory is you actually used to love it—"

"And secondly," she said right on over me. "I don't care how good of a bodyguard you are because I will evade you at every turn."

My eyebrows shot up. "Funny because usually the protection agent-client relationship commands a certain level of respect."

"Bodyguards that are ex-husbands of mine don't command jack shit." Her chin tilted up in full defiance.

She thought she had me.

Making sure I held her gaze, I bent down until our noses

were barely two inches apart. Her pretty eyes darted down to my lips, and I smiled—slow, confident—to let her know I caught the mistake. Her cheeks were pink, her pupils were dilated, her chest rose and fell rapidly.

"I'm not your 'ex' anything," I said. "That would imply either one of us had filed divorce papers, and we surely haven't. Legally, you and me? We're still married as hell."

❧ 6 ❧

SERENA

There were two things I really didn't need right now.

My annoyingly hot *ex*-husband being my bodyguard.

And that *same* ex-husband reminding me of the many legal ways our lives were still bound together.

I didn't need that smile of his either. Charming, smug, quick as lightning. He'd wielded that smile with meticulous accuracy when we were together: softening me up when he wanted to win an argument, curling my toes when I'd catch him staring at me with hunger in his eyes, making me laugh while we cooked dinner over campfires.

The tension strung between us right now was taut and electrifying. It was unfortunate that the past four years had been good for Cope. He was well over six feet tall, and his background in mixed martial arts had given him a shredded physique. But he'd bulked up a little, grown even broader, and now had a short beard to match his thick, dark brown hair. He was white with skin that blushed easily and blue eyes that never missed a thing.

Against my better judgment, I reached forward and

tapped him in the middle of his tie. "We haven't seen or spoken to each other in four years. I don't give a flying fuck what the law says. You are my ex, and we are broken up, and you can be my bodyguard, but there is *nothing* left between us."

"I happen to agree," he drawled. "Right after we're done with this clusterfuck of a situation, we can finally file those divorce papers and do the damn thing."

"Sounds good to me," I said. Less than an inch separated us—chests heaving, voices strained. "I'm looking forward to it."

He was openly gazing at my lips now. "I'll probably throw a party after."

I shrugged. "Given the circumstances of how it all went down, I doubt it'll even register for me."

My words came out as nothing more than a *purr,* a physical reaction to Cope's nearness I could never, ever control. And from the satisfied twist of his mouth, I knew he saw right through my hastily constructed lie. *How it all went down.* He knew, as well as I did, that we'd barely contained ourselves during the ceremony. And the second the elevator doors closed, my new husband pinned me to the wall with ease so he could slip his hand beneath my wedding dress. He'd finger-fucked me to a quick, intense orgasm before we'd even made it to our floor.

The door opened, and we flew apart—Cope, to lean against that wall like he hadn't a care in the world. My legs bumped into the back of the table, but I steadied myself as I found Marty and, I assumed, the other agent, walking into the room.

"Serena, so glad you could make it," Marty said, giving me a vigorous handshake. "Looks like you've already met Cope McDaniels, your daytime personal security."

I turned and gave Cope a fake polite smile. "Nice to meet you."

"Howdy," he said, brow arched.

I fought an eye roll before turning to the other man, who was about Cope's height but even bigger. "This is Lee Falco, and he'll be your evening security. Someone will be posted outside your residence every hour for the next few weeks. Another team of agents from Banks Security will relieve these two as needed, but they are taking the lead on your assignment."

I shook Falco's hand. "It's very nice to meet you."

He nodded before taking a seat and I settled in next to him. Cope stayed standing. Marty was his usual buzz of kinetic energy around the table. "Is this your first time working with a private security team?" he asked.

"It sure is," I said. Being married to a bodyguard certainly didn't count for anything.

"Wonderful," he said. "We've worked with Marilyn Banks for a long time, and she assured us she'd sent over her best."

I refused the urge to look at Cope. What had he said? *I'm on thin ice at my job right now and could really use the win.* He saw being a protection agent as his destiny, channeling his grief over his father's death into a career that made him feel helpful.

It was also a career that only added to his feeling of invincibility, an issue he refused to acknowledge even after his incident.

"I'm grateful for the added safety and protection," I said.

Marty rubbed his hands together. "We can't do much in keeping you safe on the water. But we can do our best to make you comfortable while on dry land."

I propped my chin in my hand. "Don't worry. I've got the surfing part down, so no help needed there."

He laughed, rapping his knuckles against the table. "Now that I've been here for the introductions, I'll need to scoot out to my next meeting. Cope, why don't you give Serena a rundown of what a standard security detail entails, answer any questions?"

"Happy to," my ex-husband replied.

"Wonderful," Marty continued. "I'll let you three get acquainted and will send over the details for your interview tomorrow with *Heavy* magazine. And we've got your new wetsuit for you. Neoprene-free, fair-trade of course."

"I love it," I said. Aerial was the first company to invest in wetsuits without neoprene, which was both dangerous to manufacture and completely toxic to the environment.

"We love *you*," Marty said. I waved to him as he left, and a corresponding lightness spread through my chest.

Cope moved to the chair directly in front of me, evaporating that lightness.

He unbuttoned his suit jacket with one hand then sat down a few feet away. This new mountain-man-in-a-suit vibe of his was stupidly sexy and therefore aggravating. But Falco was looking directly at us, so I mirrored Cope's fake professional expression.

"Both Falco and I have been in the private security business for a long time," he said. "And have worked with dozens of high-profile clients like yourself. You can trust that, no matter what, your safety will be a priority."

I got the message. In *no way* was it even close to a cease-fire between the two of us, but Cope's ability to protect me—even when I felt frustrated by it—couldn't be called into question. He'd do it gladly and very well.

Even if he never wanted to see me again.

"Like Mr. Lattimore said, Falco will be posted outside your house for the seven p.m.—seven a.m. shift, usually in a town car, and with the ability to radio in to Banks Security if he needs back up for whatever reason. I'll reiterate what we were told earlier, that Aerial has dealt with security issues with their ambassadors in the past, which is why they take it so seriously now. There are no active threats against you, though." His throat worked. "Hopefully, that helps you rest a little easier."

"It does, thank you," I replied, feeling relieved it wasn't Cope outside my house at night. While I slept in a bed we'd once shared together. Like big waves and adrenaline, some things in life were too tempting to resist.

"I will be with you every hour of the day when Falco's not on duty," he said. His jaw tightened. "The intent is for you not to notice my presence but to feel comforted knowing I'll be about three to six feet away from you at all times, depending on the situation."

A hot, delicious flush worked its way up my body. "I understand."

"And I'll have my eyes on you at all times," he continued, voice hoarse. "As long as there are no confidentiality or privacy concerns, I'll be privy to your conversations, your phone calls, where you travel to and from every day." He cleared his throat, fingers clutching at the arm rests with barely restrained force. "Of course, if you're... dating anyone right now or have a boyfriend, he should probably be made aware."

The question surprised me, and a long enough beat passed between us to have his nostrils flaring. "I don't," I said. "Don't have a boyfriend, I mean. And I'm not dating anyone."

Cope was wound so tight I worried he'd break right apart. "That's great news," he said. "What I mean is, it makes it easier if your social circle is small right now. Can I get a list from you of your closest friends, family members, and anyone else you'll be around that we need to be aware of?" He took out a small notebook and pen, then studied me expectantly, even though he knew exactly who was on that list.

"Theodora Tilden, my trainer," I said. Cope paused before writing her name down. They'd grown extremely close while we were dating. It helped that Dora had known Cope's father.

"Caleb Swift, my older brother. He's in the Coast Guard. Search and Rescue."

Cope's head was down, writing, but I caught his shoulders twitch at my brother's name.

"What about your parents?" Falco asked—the first real words he'd said. Cope's movements stilled.

"We don't talk," I said firmly. "I actually emancipated from them when I was fourteen."

His brow furrowed, but he gave a short nod.

"I can get you a list of the surfers I see at the beach where I surf every morning," I said. "And the events should have the competitors registered. My closest friends are also pro surfers. Kalei Peleke and her wife, Prue Dorsey."

Cope coughed at their names.

There was a picture I kept hidden behind ten others on my bookshelf, a photo that Prue had taken. In it, Cope is shirtless and barefoot, on a chair in the sand, and I'm curled up in his lap, laughing at something he'd said. We were twenty-three, and it was the usual bonfire-on-the-beach party: coolers of beer, a few joints, faded lawn chairs, and music that blended with the waves. That picture always plunged me into an aching nostalgia of yearning for bonfire sparks, cool sand between my toes, and the warmth of Cope's bare skin.

"That's a good start," Cope said, interrupting my memories. He slid his notebook and pen over to Falco. "We'll be finalizing the routes you'll be taking to the competitions, conducting background checks if necessary, and fielding anything that Aerial brings to us that we believe could put you in harm's way." Raising his gaze to mine, he asked, "Do you have any questions, Ms. Swift?"

His face was unflappable, mouth set in a hard line. There was no mischievous humor, no sly half-grin, no rumbling laughter. Every scrap of intimacy from our argument, just minutes ago, had been scrubbed clean from his body language. And even though we were pissed at each other, I didn't like how desperately I wanted *that* man back, over this serious robot in a suit.

"Not at all," I said. "Thank you, Mr. McDaniels."

Falco stood up, checking his phone. "It's just about time for my shift to take over then. One thing Cope forgot to mention was that we'll be the ones driving you from now on, once you get home tonight. We have a series of secure cars, and you can rest assured that we've both been highly trained to keep clients safe on the road."

My eyes flicked to Cope's and the flash of unexpected lust there had my pulse racing. Being locked in a car with my ex-husband while he drove me up and down the coast of California wasn't a smart idea.

"Excellent," I said. I locked my knees when I stood and straightened my spine. I grabbed my bag and extended my hand to my new protection agent. "It was nice to meet you, Mr. McDaniels."

With a curt nod, he shook it, and the gesture was entirely professional. Except this was the first time we'd touched in four *years*, and the slide of his palm against mine unleashed a cascade of emotion.

"I'll see you bright and early, Ms. Swift," he replied.

I moved right past him and waited for Falco out in the hallway, who was having a brief exchange with Cope. But once he joined me, I trained my eyes forward. Resisted the strong desire to turn around and look at Cope one more time.

That man had *always* been a force of nature in my life. And even though my job was utterly terrifying to most people, it was the power my ex-husband still had over my heart that frightened me the most.

❧ 7 ❧

SERENA

The next morning, I woke up right before my alarm went off at 5:30. Pulling my hair into a ponytail, I leaned over to check my phone on the nightstand. A white message notification said: *Officials from the International Surf Competition have called the Aerial Big Wave event at Trestles Beach for tomorrow morning.*

Beneath that was a message from Dora: *I heard about Trestles. You got this, kid. I'll see ya at practice in a bit.*

Prue and Kalei had sent me separate *we're freaking out* messages that had me squealing softly in my bed, phone pressed to my chest.

My body filled with the familiar glow of adrenaline, a sensation of anticipation I craved as much as the sharp thrill of speeding down a wall of water on a board. The ocean was permanently unpredictable, and therefore every competition contained the glittering possibility of the best ride of your life.

You caught a lucky break, and the whole world's gonna know it at Trestles.

Red-hot anger spiked through that adrenaline, turning my

nerves panicky. Before it derailed my happy mood, I took six long inhales and six even longer exhales. Tomorrow, I was officially representing Aerial, a company I believed in. But at the end of the day, I was still just Serena Swift, a woman who spent her life training to compete as an elite athlete. Luck played a role in any surfer's life. Sheer dedication played an even bigger one.

Shaking it off, I threw the covers from my bed and pulled on cropped running pants and a sports bra. Outside, the sky was a dark, pre-dawn twilight, my absolute favorite time of day. Spending my life as a surfer had turned me into the ultimate morning person and deeply appreciative of this purple-tinted peace. I had no stamina for night life, but there wasn't a single part of me that really cared. Stepping into morning waves while the rest of the city slept was worth the early bedtime.

I filled a backpack with my water bottle, two bananas, and almonds. Then, running shoes in hand, I crept out the side door of my house as quietly as I could. Based on the time, Falco would still be here, and I was pretty sure he wouldn't mind if I—

"Going somewhere?" Cope said.

I yelped, falling back against the side door and clutching my chest. "Holy *shit,* is giving your client a heart attack part of your protocols?"

My ex-husband leaned against a tree with his arms crossed, jaunty and fresh even at this early hour. "At Banks Security we believe in keeping our clients on their toes. It's even in the bodyguard handbook. Oh, and good morning to you too, *Ms. Swift.*"

Scowling, I perched on the step and tugged on my running shoes, tightening the laces. "So did you send Falco home, or did you sleep out by this tree like a weirdo?"

His eyebrow arched. "Sent him home, of course. You

woke up at this time every single day when we were together to either train or surf. And since you're a royal pain in my ass, I had to get here early to foil your plans to give me the slip."

Laces tied, I jogged down the steps and bounced lightly on my feet. Warming up, stretching my muscles. I needed to be strong for tomorrow, loose and flexible, focused and prepared.

I did not need Cope in his running clothes, showing off his giant biceps *or* his rough, gravelly, just-woke-up voice either.

"Do you talk to *all* of your clients like that, Mr. McDaniels?" I asked, tapping my chin. "I can't imagine they enjoy being called a pain in the ass."

"Nope," he said cheerfully. "I only talk like that to the ones I'm married to."

I spun on my heels and broke into a run. "We're *not married*," I yelled over my shoulder.

"Tell that to the state of California," he yelled back, but he caught up to me quickly. I didn't have to tell him where we were going. Because the little blue beach house that I lived in had been our house. And the route I was running was the same one we ran together on the mornings I didn't surf.

"Oh, yeah," I said. "This kind of charming interaction is really convincing me to respect that client-bodyguard rela-tionship."

He *tsk*ed behind me, slowly moving up until we were shoulder to shoulder on the sidewalk. "Try as hard as you'd like, but you'll recall just how determined and dedicated I am. At everything."

My feet faltered for a second, but I pushed past it. "I don't recall, actually."

I heard the soft growl of frustration in his chest and the steady sound of his breath.

"You stayed in the house, I guess?"

I trained my eyes straight ahead. "I was traveling a lot, still am. It's been easier to stay, to not have to pack up everything and move. You know I always really—"

I stopped, surprised at the admission. But Cope said, "You always loved that house."

It was bright and sunny and close to the beach. And it had been filled to the brim with our love once. Given that love was absent from my house growing up, it felt impossible to leave.

"I do love it," was all I could say. Our feet pounded against the pavement in perfect sync.

"I heard about your win at Jaws. Congratulations."

I shook my head, panting slightly. "You don't mean that."

"You don't know *what* I mean, actually."

I picked up the pace out of sheer irritation. "So... how have the past four years been?"

"Spectacular."

"Yeah?"

"Oh, yeah," he said. "Four best years of my life probably."

"Well, good for you," I said. "Since you asked me like a hundred times yesterday if I had a boyfriend—"

"Oh, *bullshit*. I was doing my job—"

"—do you have someone? A girlfriend or anything?"

"Of course not," he said. He turned, saw the amusement on my face. "Obviously, I receive a lot of attention and *requests* from, like, literally hundreds of women wanting to take me out on a date every day."

Our shoulders brushed together, and we both bounced away instantly.

"Hundreds, huh?" I said. "Your inbox must be agony."

He waved his hand over his face and chest. "This body is basically a liability."

I felt the very beginnings of a traitorous smile, so I picked up the pace *again* until I noticed a distracting burn in my calves. "I'm so sorry for you," I managed.

"Heavy is the head that wears the... super hot face and stuff," he replied.

I smiled—*goddammit*—but covered it by wiping my arm across my mouth. "Are you going to tell me why you're on thin ice at your job?"

I heard his grunt of annoyance. I snuck a sideways glance and caught the clench of his jaw. "My boss, Marilyn, who I genuinely respect and appreciate, is pretty pissed at me right now. Clients complaining about my..." He paused, breathing heavily. "Attitude. Lack of focus. Apparently, I'm not taking things seriously, and I often come off as *chatty* and *overly familiar*."

"Wait, *you?*" I said with as much sarcasm as I could muster.

"Not everyone appreciates my unique work style or sense of humor," he replied.

"You referred to me as a royal pain in your ass not one minute into being my bodyguard," I said.

The corners of his mouth twitched. "I'd like to think the other agents are jealous that I'm so funny."

I shook my head, not buying it. Cope's lightness and silly jokes had been one of the things I *used to* love about him. But he also used it as a shield when things got too intense. And in the months after the incident, when I begged him to open up to me, to acknowledge how scared I'd been, he used that lightness to shut down. To shut *me* out.

Sometimes I worried he used it to avoid his grief.

"What?" he pressed. "You don't believe me?"

"What exactly were you not taking seriously?" I asked. I could feel the threads of our past arguments drifting into this conversation and didn't like it. But there was no escaping my morbid curiosity.

Cope went quiet. We reached the outside of Dora's gym and slowed to a stop together. I propped my hands on top of my head as I breathed heavily. He leaned against the wall, one hand up, and stretched his right quad.

"There was a kidnapping attempt on my last client," he finally said. "I messed up, wasn't paying attention. Got myself in a sticky situation, as it were."

I narrowed my eyes. "Define *sticky*."

He shrugged, ran a hand through his hair. "I miscalculated the number of attackers. Ended up on my knees, restraining a guy, when a third guy stepped out." He shrugged again. "He held a gun to my head."

I gripped my hips, focusing on my breathing to keep from being pulled under by bad memories. "Someone got the jump on you?" I asked.

"I had him on his ass, gun in my hand, thirty seconds later," he said. "It was fine. I was *fine*. Most importantly, the client was fine. Arnold Sheffield will live to swindle people out of their money for another day. It's not that big of a deal. And no one got the *jump* on me, thanks."

I marched right up to him, angry. "You, Cope McDaniels, were reckless on purpose."

His answering grin was all charm. "I was never in any real danger."

"If *I'd* done what you did when we were together, you'd be giving me a lecture right now."

The grin vanished. "*If?* Serena, you put yourself in danger every goddamn day."

I blew an irritated breath out of my nose. "You had a gun to your head. I happen to think that men with guns are scarier than Mother Nature."

He pointed at the ocean to our left. "You're surfing thirty-foot waves tomorrow, *and* you tried to escape from a body-guard being paid to protect you right now."

I glared down at the ground, tapping my foot. "Four years later, and we're still going 'round and 'round."

He crossed his arms. "For the record, you picked the fight right now. I'm just the bodyguard, remember?"

"Really? Because earlier you were so sure you were my husband."

His gaze filled with anger and lust. "And you've made it perfectly clear that I'm not."

"Good."

"*Great.*"

"And I don't need your protection, by the way," I said.

A shaggy-haired guy with a strip of sunscreen down his nose suddenly walked right between the two of us, carrying his board over his head. Cope and I maintained pissed-off eye contact the whole time, both refusing to back down. But when the surfer turned, the heavy end of the board swung hard right at my face.

Before I could even blink, Cope reacted. He reached out and caught it a mere inch from hitting me square in the forehead.

"Oh, *bro*, sorry about that," the guy said in his SoCal drawl.

Cope still held the end of his board, which had the veins in his forearms standing out. "Hate to break it to you, *bro*, but the board goes in the water not onto people's faces." His voice was mild, but his grip was still strong.

"Right on, right on," the guy said. He struggled to break Cope's firm hold, and when he did, he laughed nervously while Cope watched. "Thanks for the pro tip." As if finally realizing I was standing there, the guy gave my body a comically long perusal. When his eyes reached my face, he bobbed his head. "What's up, beautiful? You doin' anything later?"

"Competing as one of the most elite surfers in the entire world," I said.

"*Damn,* that's hot." He laughed, took a step closer, but I wasn't in the least bit concerned.

Cope had his palm on the guy's chest a nanosecond later. "Watch it," he snapped. "I only had a few fucks to give this morning, and unfortunately for you I'm now bordering on *zero.*"

The guy gulped, audibly, before walking away backwards. "Okay, *geez.* See ya later or whatever."

The moment he was gone, Cope and I exchanged a much too intimate look. I stepped back, shaking my head. "I need to get to my workout. Are you coming with me or not?"

His grin reappeared. "Of course. Three feet behind as the handbook says. Oh, and *you're welcome* for protecting you from getting your face smashed in."

Rolling my eyes, I flounced toward the door before I could get sucked into his frustrating orbit. "I could have handled that myself," I yelled, sounding pissy.

"I'm so glad we're going on this journey together!" Cope yelled back.

$ 8 $

COPE

Silently fuming, I followed Serena into her gym and was sucker-punched with nostalgia. Run by Serena's long-time trainer, this gym had become an oasis for mostly women athletes—a majority of them surfers and swimmers—and the two of us were here, together, most days in a week. Large garage doors rolled up to let in the outside air, the crashing waves, the San Diego traffic. Music blared over the sounds of jump rope, boxing, and treadmills.

I stretched my neck from side to side, attempting to soothe my irritation with my client-wife. Serena stopped in front of me to toss her bag on the ground and grab a bottle of water.

I allowed myself four seconds of watching her.

Which was part of my job now. It wasn't my job to linger on the nape of her neck and the sweat that clung there, or to admire her taut stomach or her firm ass in those tight workout pants.

I used to bury my face in every inch of that luscious, tan skin, lick every curve, scrape my teeth right where her neck met her shoulder while I tangled my fingers in that ponytail and *yanked*—

"Well, holy hell in a hand basket," Dora said, walking over to us wearing a gray tracksuit and an expression of bemused shock. "Now isn't this a *freaky-ass coincidence*."

"Theodora," I said, opening my arms. She stepped right into them, as small and wiry as ever.

"How you doing, big guy?" she asked, voice muffled. When she stepped back, she threw me a few shadow boxes. I ducked and dodged, laughing.

"My reflexes are *still* faster than yours, so I'd say I'm doin' mighty fine."

Dora planted her feet wide, hands propped on her hips. She contemplated the two of us, desperately trying—and failing—to stay serious. "So, uh... this is your new bodyguard, huh?"

Serena reached up to tighten her ponytail. "Unfortunately, yes, and if it's not obvious, I'm not happy about it."

I held up my finger. "Nor am I."

She tossed me a scowl before strutting towards the front of the mat. "I'm starting with weights and jump rope to warm up."

Dora watched her over her shoulder. "A *light day*, Serena. So help me god, I'll smack those heavy weights right out of your hands. I want you loose before we get in that pool."

I took a second to scan the room, noting the three entrances and two exits I knew well, plus the pool off to the side. There were no weird vibes, no sudden movements, just the usual steamy gym environment. I tracked back to Serena, dipping into a squat with a barbell on her shoulders. Sweat shone on her stomach, and her cheeks were flushed.

Light day, my ass.

She dropped the weight, caught me staring. I mouthed, "It's my job."

She gave me the finger.

And then she picked up the jump-rope and faced the mirror.

I swallowed a growl of irritation.

"Well," Dora said next to me. "This is fun."

"Compared to what? A fucking root canal?"

Dora pinned me with a look I knew well—one part maternal, one part asshole. It was her whole vibe. "It's gonna be nice, watching you two swear up and down to anyone in hearing range that you aren't secretly happy about this."

"*Happy?*" I huffed out a sarcastic laugh. "No way."

Yeah, sure I might have woken up this morning with an interesting lightness in my chest at the thought of seeing her again. And there was the requisite 24/7 erection situation I always had around Serena. But none of that qualified as *happy*.

Dora ignored my flustered sounds, sipping from her coffee cup with mirth in her eyes. "You look good, Cope," she said. "Really. It's nice to see that mug of yours. I thought I wasn't going to see it again, to be honest."

I opened my arm and pulled her in for another side hug. "Nice to see you too. I've missed you a lot."

"Yeah?"

"Don't tell anyone though," I said. "Don't want to ruin my hardened agent reputation."

She eyed me carefully. "Did you put on some weight?"

I winked. "All muscle, of course."

The first time I met Theodora, I'd been dating Serena for a few weeks. I'd walked into this gym, and she'd stared at me like I was a ghost. Like most local surfers her age, my father was her friend, her surfing buddy, and her mentor. Even as I knew, deep down, that Serena's chosen career had the potential of breaking my heart, there was a part of me that couldn't stay away from this town's surf culture. It had been ingrained in me so deeply that not even my grief could smother my connection to it entirely. Having lost people herself, Dora understood the complicated gray area that left me in.

"You should come by my mom's house," I said. "See Billie. I can cook us all dinner, and we can catch up over—" I checked an imaginary watch on my wrist. "—the past four years."

She snorted. "Things weren't exactly great there at the end between you two, and it's not like there's a handbook for keeping in touch after a breakup. I would have stayed away too."

I swallowed, directing my attention back to Serena. Her ponytail swung back and forth as she moved seamlessly with the rope.

"Your understanding is appreciated, but my mom and sister really *would* love to see you. It can be like old times. We can drink some beers on the beach. You and mom can tell stories about dad that'll make me and my sister uncomfortable."

Old times, but without the addition of Serena teasing my sister about school. Or Serena washing dishes next to my mom in the kitchen with a beaming smile.

Dora started laughing—and then grabbed the whistle around her neck and blew on it.

I winced, finger in my ear.

"*Did I not say a light day?*" she yelled.

Serena stopped jumping rope with a glare.

"I'd love to get dinner as long as that ex-wife of yours doesn't send me to the hospital with high blood pressure."

I crossed my arms over my chest. "I fully expect to be there too. Maybe we can bunk up together."

She sighed, frustrated. "I need to go help her stretch before the pool. But I'm not done with you yet."

"Yes, ma'am," I said with a nod.

Serena's eyes flicked over to mine and held for a fleeting

moment. *You, Cope McDaniels, were reckless.* I broke away from her gaze first, trying to forget she'd said that. Trying to forget Marilyn's insinuation of the same thing.

I hated that Serena was right, that four years apart hadn't given either of us more clarity on our issues or made us less obstinate.

She was wrong about one thing though. Given the death of my father, risking my life didn't factor into my decision-making. Ever. Meanwhile, I'd gone ahead and fallen in love with a big wave surfer who put herself in harm's way for fun. In slow-motion videos of Serena, you could see her smiling as she glided through massive barrels.

The woman I married looked danger right in the face and *fucking smiled at it.*

My phone buzzed in my shorts pocket. Taking it out, I checked my messages as discreetly as possible.

Quentin had texted: *The next time we get a beer, let me fill you in on what my amateur sleuthing uncovered about Aerial.*

I glanced back at Serena, made sure she was safe. She was nodding with Dora, listening intently. Then I read the rest. *The company has been tied up in private arbitration for years. A corporation all about public transparency hiding a bunch of lawsuits is fishy.*

I didn't really know what the hell that meant, except that my best friend wouldn't have mentioned it if it didn't make him concerned. I typed back: *Dangerous?*

Dora blew a short whistle at me before waving towards the pool. I slid my phone back into my pocket and followed with a feeling of dread in the pit of my stomach. Not because of Quentin's poking around. Because I knew the real threat was about to happen next.

I posted up by the pool—feet apart, hands clasped—while Serena changed quickly into a black bathing suit. She slipped into the water with the grace of someone more comfortable there than on dry land.

I distracted myself with a brief check of the exit to my right, the locker room doors to my left, and the entrance behind me. That took ten seconds max, so by the time I reluctantly dragged my attention back to the pool, Dora was bent over handing Serena a weighted medicine ball.

She stood back up, staring at the black-and-white clock high on the wall. "Biggest breath of your life, okay, kid?"

I recognized the intently focused look on Serena's face. She inhaled audibly, squeezed her nose shut with her fingers, closed her eyes.

Muscle memory had me taking in my own breath.

She dropped beneath the water, leaving behind a tiny circle of air bubbles.

"Counting down from four," Dora called out.

My father practiced apnea training when we were growing up, which Billie and I thought made him magic. And it was magic, in a way—pushing the human body past its natural limits, clinging to that slippery edge, was a kind of alchemy. Surfers understood how important it was to be able to withstand holding your breath for impossibly long stretches of time—to stay calm, equalize your ears, manage your precious oxygen.

Still.

This vital technique had not saved his life.

A slight panic started to beat at the edges of my vision and Dora, being Dora, must have sensed it. She was suddenly by my side giving me one light touch on my arm before letting me go.

"You probably never saw her do this before, did ya?"

I shook my head, staring at the place where Serena'd just been. "I avoided it."

"It's pretty scary for me still, imagining my students

sitting at the bottom of that pool while holding their breath. Doesn't feel quite right. Always makes me nervous." She blew a short whistle and yelled, "*From three.*"

Serena had already been holding her breath for sixty seconds.

"Do you sneak a bottle of vodka in here to help with the nerves or what?" I asked. She was distracting me on purpose, and I wasn't going to turn down the life preserver she was tossing me.

"I've always been a tequila lady, and you know that, Cope." Her smile was quick. "But no. I sit with the discomfort. Sit with it and respect it. Speaking as a surfer myself, fear is like a radio station you hate tuning into because the DJ sucks." She cast me a sideways glance. "But that same DJ is gonna save your life when you need it."

I rolled my shoulders, stretched my neck, and didn't respond.

"I sit with it," she continued. "And remember Serena has trained her body to do the impossible because she takes the risk of her job seriously. Will do literally anything to protect herself out there."

I kept staring straight ahead, remembering words my mother repeated to me often, especially when I was with Serena. *Your father's death was a tragic accident. It was not your fault. You cannot always protect the ones you love from harm, much as I wish you could.*

Dora blew her whistle, startling me. "*From two, Serena.*"

She was only halfway done.

"It doesn't always work," I said quietly.

I didn't have to explain myself.

"I know it," she replied. "Don't I know it."

Now it was my turn to place my hand on her arm for a brief squeeze. Besides my father, she'd also lost two friends in a boating accident five years ago.

"But you have to trust that I wouldn't send that girl out into *those* waves unprepared," she said. "And, for what it's worth, I think she wants you to trust her too."

I crossed my arms. "Trusting her has never been my problem."

You put yourself in danger every goddamn day.

"If you say so." She sighed. "Let me tell you this. You haven't been around the last four years, so you don't know jack shit about the sacrifices she's made to be the best. Tomorrow is only the beginning of a long career for her competing at an elite level. She's ready."

Dora walked away, back to the side of the pool, and crouched down to peer into the water. She blew her whistle three short times. "*One minute left. You can do it, kid.*"

I plucked my phone out of my pocket to give my hands something to do. An alert from Quentin caught my eye.

Call me pessimistic, but I tend to think any billion-dollar company with something to hide is dangerous.

I texted: *I think you might be reading into things a little too much, buddy.*

Serena reappeared, gasping, and a significant amount of tension left my body. I rooted myself to the spot instead of doing what my instincts demanded of me. Run to her. Pull her from that water and clutch her to my chest. Never let her out of my sight again.

Slicking her hair back, she grabbed Dora's hand, who pulled her over to the ledge. Panting, she rested her cheek on her arms, legs kicking slowly in the water behind her. Dora was coaching her through a breathing exercise to help her regain control.

Our eyes caught and held, and I was shocked to see the compassion there. I cleared my throat, stared back at the ground. She understood more than any person in my life how seeing her train made me feel. *We're still going 'round and 'round.*

The end of our relationship was already apparent after our second date, where we'd spent an entire afternoon sitting on the low wall that faced La Jolla Cove. Over coffee under bright blue skies, she had me charmed, dazzled, elated. And desperate to freeze time to escape our reality.

I'll always be a surfer, she'd said, biting her lip with regret in her voice. *And given what happened to your dad, I completely understand why you wouldn't want to date me.*

I understood too. God help me, I understood. I should have walked away as fast as I could. Instead, against my better judgment, against *every warning*, I slid my fingers into her messy, golden hair, tipped her face up toward mine, and kissed her.

She tasted like sunshine.

Quentin texted again. *Oh ye of little faith! I'm hooked in now, so I'm going to keep reading too much into everything. But only 'cause you're my best friend. Keep a close eye on Serena. Just a gut feeling.*

My fingers tightened around the phone. *Just a gut feeling.* Quentin was many things, including an ace investigator who took shit like this seriously. He wouldn't have said those words if he didn't want me to read into what he was implying.

Happy you've got my back, I replied.

And then I looked up just in time to see my wife's head slip beneath the water.

9

SERENA

As soon as I hit three minutes beneath the water, I thought of my parents. The helpless rage I felt as a child—the fear, the confusion, the hunger—acted as a golden light in the crushing, cold darkness. As the heavy weight pressed down on my shoulders and the top of my head, I clung to that light with every fiber of my being.

There was a smug satisfaction in using them as motivation when I needed to monitor my breathing. They had, after all, introduced me to the discomfort of keeping my mouth shut, forcing me to access quiet parts of my inner self at a young age. My father's strict style of parenting meant careful movements to not incite his sporadic temper. It meant being sent to my room with the door locked when I did anything my parents did not believe girls should do: speak my mind, share an opinion, scrape my knees, or raise my voice. When I was especially bad, the door was locked all night long—no food, no water, no bathroom.

I had, give or take, twenty seconds left now. This was my third four-minute stretch, and I was *this close* to hitting my own limit, which Dora understood. I needed my lungs warm and oxygenated for tomorrow—but not sore or tired.

Fifteen seconds now. Ten. The burn in my muscles was hot as a forest fire, so I hung on to my anger and counted down the final seconds.

It didn't matter how often Caleb and I would turn to our mother for comfort or safety. In the end, she was as bad as our father. And while I often bore the brunt of his frustration, Caleb bore the brunt of hers. *Don't cry, don't be soft, don't be emotional, girls won't like you.*

Slowly, deliberately, I moved toward the surface, pushing the weighted ball ahead of me. I emerged, *finally*, sputtering. My lungs seized up. I wiped the water from my eyes and grabbed Dora's hand. She hauled me out of the water a second later onto a towel where I lay on my back and forced my lungs to take in smooth, steady gulps of the most exquisite air imaginable.

She still held my hand, tethering me back to dry land. "That's it," she said. "You did it. The final four minutes, like the champion you are."

I nodded that I heard her, still unable to speak. Coughed, gasped in a breath.

"Thumbs up if you're okay?"

I gave her two while managing a weak smile. "Need a sec," I whispered.

"Take your time," she replied. "I'll grab your water, how about that?"

I closed my eyes. My lungs gradually filled all the way up, feeling bigger, broader. Even my ribcage buzzed with a sense of expansion.

Smiling to myself, I opened my eyes and found Cope standing over me. He looked deeply worried before smoothing it away. I knew why and felt like shit about it. Having to be around me all day meant seeing all the risks and intimacies of what I did, maybe even more than when we were together. As my bodyguard there was no haze of love or passion obscuring how my job and Cope's loss intersected at all the most painful angles.

"You okay?" he asked, a little hoarse.

"Yeah." I pushed up on my elbows. "Yeah, I am." I held out my hand, and he took it without hesitation. I was gently lifted to standing, although our fingers disengaged after only a second. "I'm sorry about..." I waved at the pool, still out of breath. "I should have told you. I know it's not easy to see."

His eyebrows knit together. "It's really fine. Just doing my job." His mouth twisted into a tiny Cope-like smile. "If you think this is hard, you should try being personal security for Arnold Sheffield. The guy grossly underpays his staff while forcing them to skip their kids' birthday parties. Then uses a company helicopter to go commit, I don't know, crimes against humanity while playing tennis."

I leaned to the side to wring out my hair. "Wow. So am I still a bigger pain in the ass than him or...?"

"Like, fifty times more a pain in my ass."

I laughed before I realized what I was doing. I jumped back in surprise. Cope's eyes went wide.

"Anyway," I said, voice flat. "I'm not, you know, apologizing for what I said out front. Because I still mean it, and I'm still pissed about it."

He brightened. "When I saved your life from that surfboard of doom?"

I strutted past him and toward the locker room. "Still could have handled it myself." I checked the clock on the wall. "I've got the—"

"Interview in two hours," he said. "I have your schedule and will drive you there and back and anywhere else you need to go today. Oh, and to be clear, I'm also not apologizing."

"Amazing. Can't wait to be locked in a car with you."

His answering smirk was *almost* flirtatious. "The dread is mutual, Ms. Swift."

I shouldered open the door to the locker room and changed back into my running clothes. When I glanced in the mirror to braid my hair, the dreamy smile on my face startled me.

I recognized the source of that smile, so I scrubbed my hands down my face and removed it.

"Do not give in to him," I whispered beneath my breath. "You know where this goes."

Confident that I had my emotions—and hormones—under control, I marched out into the humid pool air, breezed past Cope, and found Dora in the lobby.

"Thanks for today," I said. She held up both hands, as usual, and I high-fived them both. Then she pulled me in for a swaying, side-to-side hug that had me giggling. "I'm excited to make you proud tomorrow."

"I'm already proud, duh," she said. "But I'll be extra proud *regardless* of what happens."

"Well, I'm definitely going to win," I said, scooping up my bag and cinching it over my shoulders. "You'll be watching from here, right?"

"Absolutely."

She walked over and punched Cope in the arm.

"*Easy.* Damn, Dora, I use this arm." He winced, but his eyes were sparkling. This—this feeling like no time had passed, like this was a typical Saturday for us, laughing with Dora—was the most confusing déjà vu sensation of my life.

She pointed at him. "You keep an eye on her."

"Yes, ma'am," he said, gaze finding mine. I didn't like that either. As frustrating as his overprotective nature could be, it was hard to deny the swarm of butterflies it used to give me.

You think I won't protect you forever, sunshine? Because I will, and happily, for the rest of our lives.

My cheeks flushed. I fiddled with the straps of my bag before heading towards the door. "I'm running home if you can handle it."

"*Handle it?*"

But I was already outside, the sky brightening with the dawn, and starting to run.

Cope—*dammit*—appeared next to me, stride matching my easy, cool-down pace. "For the record, I can always fucking handle it."

The coarse scrape of his voice had me shivering. "If you say so."

"You've got an event tomorrow, so I'm not going to challenge you to a race," he said. "I'll just allow both of us to *remember* who the faster runner is."

Sheer force of will kept me at this cool-down speed instead of sprinting ahead like I wanted to. We ran in silence most of the way—part awkward, part companionable. I was much too tired, and my brain was fuzzy from holding my breath. Speaking right now made me nervous I'd say something I'd regret, like *How come you left me without saying goodbye?* or *How come you never filed for divorce?*

Or the question currently floating around in my head: *Were your shoulders always this lickable?*

"Can I ask you a work question? As your protection agent, I mean?"

I gaped at him. "Am I in some kind of danger right now?"

He shook his head, brow creased. "I told Quent about being posted at Aerial."

We rounded onto the street that led to our house. My house. "You talked to Quentin?"

"Yeah." He slowed to a stop on a patch of my neighbor's grass.

I followed his lead, confused. "What's going on?"

He peeked over his shoulder again. Then he took a step closer.

He smelled *delicious*.

"You know how he is," Cope said in a low tone. "He looked into Aerial, just curious about their reputation, seeing if anything weird came up."

I felt the first pinprick of alarm. "And?"

A shrug of those broad, lickable shoulders. "I don't know. He said they were tied up in some... private lawsuits. Had been for years. It struck him as odd. 'Fishy' was the word he used. He wanted me to be extra cautious."

I propped my hands on my hips. "Much as I appreciate Quent looking out for me, I think this might be one time he's actually barking up the wrong tree." I pushed the sweaty hair off my forehead. "They've got the best reputation. The best environmental practices. Tons of corporate philanthropy. No scandals."

"You're sure?"

"I did my research," I said. "I have to represent them for the next three years. I didn't want my name to be tied to some skeevy corporation. I *wanted* Aerial because I'll be in the perfect position to work on real issues within the surfing industry. Issues they care about too."

Cope sighed and linked his hands over his head. His biceps bulged with the motion. "I think you're probably right. Anything give you bad vibes?"

"Nothing comes to mind."

"Okay." He nodded. Rolled his shoulders. "Then I'm probably taking a cue from Quent and reading into things."

He started running again, and I joined him. "It's your job though, reading into things. So. Thanks, I guess."

We reached the house, slowing again.

"*Thanks?*"

I grabbed the key from my bag and jogged up the steps.

The door was still painted a light, dusky pink we'd done ourselves. I slid the key into the lock or attempted to. It was his body heat, his scent, his closeness that made my fingers clumsy.

"Yeah. Thanks," I said, teeth gritted. The key finally slid home, and I shoved the door open as wide as I could, putting quick distance between the two of us.

"Well, look at you respecting the agent-client relationship." He folded his arms across his chest with an amused expression.

I gripped the door. "Speaking of. I'm going inside to shower, and you're...?"

He cleared his throat. "Checking inside to make sure you're safe."

"Seriously?"

"It's for real protocol."

"Not the other fake protocols you've been telling me?"

I was stalling. Not much in the house had changed since we'd broken up, and him wandering around in it was not a smart idea.

"May I?" His tone had grown as somber as his expression.

Swallowing around a sudden lump in my throat, I opened the door all the way and let him inside. The short hallway felt overly confined and filled with memories. Especially since, more often than not, we'd come in post-workout—sweaty, happy, full of endorphins—and the man standing in front of me would have his palm on my chest and my back against the door immediately. He'd even taken me on the small end table once, which usually held keys and sunglasses, spare change and ticket stubs.

They'd been knocked to the floor to make room for me.

The first deep stroke of his cock already had me moaning, fingers clutched in his shirt, our foreheads pressed together. The table smacked against the wall—smack, smack, smack—and I didn't even mind that we'd probably have to patch it. It was worth it for this.

I didn't dare make eye contact. I walked into the wide-open kitchen and living room. Desperate for water, I turned on my heel to head to the fridge. Cope stopped me with a hand wrapped around my wrist. His throat worked as his fingers tightened on my skin.

It would be so easy to give in to him here, without anyone watching. In this home we'd filled with as much lust as love, as much ecstasy as romance.

He let me go. "Sorry. Let me check first."

I dropped my bag on the floor. Toed off my shoes. He moved effortlessly through this space he'd once lived in, fingers dragging down the island in the center of the kitchen.

"Can you believe we live together?" Cope said, dipping fries into a little cup of ketchup. We'd moved that morning and still had no furniture. So we sat on top of the island, cross-legged and exhausted, eating our first meal of cheeseburgers in our new house.

He checked the windows there and the lock on the patio door. He walked into the living room with a clenched jaw. Examined the windows, pulled open the coat closet. He noted our yellow couch before turning towards the stairs.

The rug was soft beneath my knees. Cope's cock was the exact opposite—ridged, hard, magnificent. His hand held the back of my neck as I gripped his shaft, taking him between my lips, swirling my tongue just the way he liked it.

"I love how horny you get when we watch movies together," he gasped, head tilting back.

I followed him from a safe distance. There was another bathroom up here, a lofted sitting area, and our bedroom. A deck opened up from the sliding glass windows, overlooking my neighborhood. Past the trees was the sweetest glimpse of the ocean on the horizon.

"Is it... may I check the bedroom?" he asked.

I shrugged. "Go for it."

He double-checked the lock on the doors and peeked under the furniture for intruders. He grasped the edge of the bed, *our* bed, and left his hand there.

I twisted my fingers together. "Are you okay? You promised to be chatty and overly familiar, and you've barely said a word."

I was giving him a conversational out. A pathway to a joke or some snarky observation. Not that I cared. Really.

Cope sat back on his heels with a deep sigh. He looked like himself, like my husband and not my bodyguard. My heart pounded in my chest as I was unsure now if I wanted this intimacy. *I shouldn't have said anything. I shouldn't have—*

"This is fucking weird, isn't it?" He gave me a lopsided grin that only sped up my heart rate. "Because I used to live here, you know."

I smiled back before I could help it. "Is it weird? I would have thought there was a section in that bodyguard handbook of yours. *How to Handle Your Ex-Wife as a Client*. Dos and don'ts. Tips and techniques."

"I wish," he said, elbow resting on the bedspread. "There's tips on how to handle when your client is acting like a real Bond villain. But because protection agents aren't supposed to have emotions or personalities, the complication of an ex-wife isn't addressed."

I sealed my lips together so I wouldn't fall into the temptation of this conversation. I felt a tug behind my belly button, some primal emotion, driven by memory, urging me to drop to the floor beside him. To keep talking until the sun set and all through the night. It had been so much easier when he wasn't inside my bedroom.

There the words sat, on the tip of my tongue: *I miss you so much I can't stand it.*

"Can you, um, finish up?" I asked. "I need to get ready."

His grin, this time, was resigned. "Of course."

He stood up and then moved past me, avoiding eye contact. We'd made more memories in that bed than I could count.

"Everything is good here," he said, indicating the sitting area. "I'll just check the bathroom and shower before you use it."

"The shower?" I asked. "Really?"

He ducked past the low door frame. "It'll only take a second."

I waited outside with my back to the wall, toes curling up and down into the rug. "Your dedication to my safety is admirable," I called inside.

He reappeared, standing much too close. "If you think I'm on thin ice with my boss now, letting my brand-new client get kidnapped through some secret portal in her shower would definitely get me written up. Maybe even a slap on the wrist."

I arched my eyebrow. "My imminent kidnapping barely warrants punishment, huh?"

He lifted a shoulder. "You'd be so annoying to your kidnappers, I'd give it an hour, tops. They'd send you right back to me."

I strutted past him with a huff, hiding my amusement. I turned on the water then popped my head back out. "There's no portal in here by the way."

"Yeah," he said. "Because I *checked*."

I closed the bathroom door before that crooked grin of his got us both into trouble. With shaking fingers, I tore off my sweaty running clothes and stepped under the perfectly hot water. Sighing, I tipped my head back, water sluicing through my hair.

Cope's presence was the opposite of what I needed. I needed to focus on this interview, organize my thoughts, prepare for tomorrow's event. I squeezed shampoo into my palm, frustrated.

Cope, pressing me against this glass as steam billowed. Cope, on his knees and spreading me roughly with his hands, fingers working magic, tongue licking through my folds as hot water cascaded down our naked bodies.

The bottle clattered to the floor.

I rested my forehead against the wall. Without realizing it, I was already accessing my apnea training—scanning my muscles, filling my lungs with air, quieting my mind. And it was working. Ease and calm spread through my body. I pictured myself on a record-breaking wave tomorrow, gliding through the barrel like I was born to be there.

It wasn't the weight of the ocean pressing down on me that triggered this response.

It was Cope's sudden return in my life. A return I was not in any way prepared for.

❦ 10 ❦

C O P E

I drove Serena to her interview with *Heavy* magazine at the Aerial headquarters in total and complete silence. Whatever ease had developed between the two of us while inside our house—*her* house—had evaporated just as quickly. She sat in the back seat of the town car, chewing on her lower lip while scanning documents and taking notes. At every stop light, I checked the rearview mirror, hoping to catch her eye.

It never happened.

I pulled into the parking lot slowly, since we had ten minutes to spare. My fingers throbbed from where I gripped the steering wheel. Probably had something to do with standing outside of her house for an hour, waiting for her to get ready, and clenching my fingers into tight fists of self-control. Staying calm and restrained while strolling through our house, our memories, had required a discipline I didn't know I possessed. As had spending sixty straight minutes remembering what her skin tasted like, how her naked body looked with water droplets beading everywhere. Remembering all the filthy, *filthy* things I'd done to her in that shower.

I'd used the bathroom on the first floor to clean up after our run and change back into my uniform before driving us over here. After double-checking my cufflinks, I glanced one more time into the rearview mirror.

"Are you nervous?" I asked.

She was shoving papers into her bag and messing with her phone. "Not at all. Should be a piece of cake. I've done interviews before."

If there was anything my wife hated, it was showing vulnerability in the face of a challenge.

"This one's pretty important though," I said evenly. "I'm just saying, you know, it's okay to be nervous. All the cool kids are doing it."

Her hands paused. "I'm fine. Can we go inside?"

"As you wish, Ms. Swift." I stepped into the balmy, late morning heat and walked around to her side, scanning the parking lot for anything suspicious. Satisfied, I opened her door, and she stepped out of the car directly in front of me.

Her hair was unusually tamed in a low bun, and she wore a long dress with pink and white flowers that tied at the neck. The sun glittered off her gold earrings.

She was unbelievably beautiful.

My hands clutched the door as I drank her in. I was going to have joint damage by the time this assignment was up.

"You look very nice," I blurted out.

Her brows raised in surprise. "Thank you?"

I slammed the door shut, a little embarrassed, and buttoned my jacket. She breezed right past me and towards the offices. "Is it in your bodyguard handbook to compliment your clients on their appearances?"

I hid a relieved smirk. "I started each morning by telling

Mr. Sheffield he was a walking thirst trap, which he appreciated."

Her full lips curved into a real smile, a Serena smile, which had my naive heart spinning like an ice skater in my chest. She didn't laugh, but I still considered it a win.

And why are you trying to win right now?

I slid my sunglasses into my pocket and grabbed the front door. Being with Dora this morning, seeing our home, seeing that *dress*, was creating irrational feelings of lust and longing that crowded out the reminder I needed to slam on the brakes. Hard. And then slam on them again.

There was no denying the electrifying pull that existed between the two of us.

There was also no denying that we broke up because of our insurmountable differences, evidenced by our fight outside the gym just this morning. If there had been *any* way past it, both of us would have crawled towards reconciliation on hands and knees if we had to.

Once inside Aerial, we walked across the front lobby, and I tracked the stares she garnered from the various surfer-looking dudes hanging out in hoodies and flip-flops. I'd seen that specific look when it came to Serena a thousand times when we were together. It was attraction, of course, but an ugly kind—a kind that was deeply jealous and angry.

Their eyes stalked her movement toward the elevator, but the moment they saw me, I gave them my best *hey and fuck you too* glare.

They stopped staring immediately.

I stood three feet behind Serena as the elevator lights blinked slowly down to lobby level. She stood in her usual ocean goddess stance—chin lifted, spine straight—but I caught her tell. Her fingers, decorated with silver rings, were twisting back and forth in front of her. So slowly her arms didn't seem like they were moving.

The elevator still hovered on the fourth floor. Once we were alone, I dipped my head down, close to her ear. "Remember when we drove all the way to Venice Beach that one weekend so you could meet that group of high school girls with their own surf club?"

She smiled immediately, then turned to me like she used to, like the gesture was only for me. "I forgot all about that. They were so badass, and they were only fifteen."

"They said you were their hero. They said women like you were an inspiration."

She touched her fingertips to her lips. "Oh, yeah. We went out on the waves later, and I showed them my gnarliest tricks."

"And they loved you for it," I said.

They'd gazed at Serena like she was the glowing god they worshiped. Later, in the car, she'd turned her face to the window and cried, and I'd given her as much privacy as she needed. Her parents were totally fucked up and had really done a number on her and her brother, so crying in front of people wasn't easy for her. But it wasn't the girls' worshiping that had made her emotional. It was meeting young women just like her—bold and unafraid to take up space, strong and dedicated. Fearless on the water.

I think it made her feel less alone.

"Anyway," I said as the elevator slid to the lobby. "I'm not saying that you're nervous, but if you were and needed a reminder that you're a motherfucking badass..." I shrugged. "Could work."

The doors opened as Serena stared at me with pure gratitude. Her fingers were still. I nodded towards the empty elevator, arm outstretched, and followed her inside.

"Cope," she started to say. "That was really nice of you—"

A veritable army of Aerial staff appeared, dressed for a picnic or a hike or both. They were talking, staring at their phones, balancing reusable water bottles and earbuds. A few acknowledged Serena, but then the doors shut, squishing us tight. There was a big shuffle of bodies at the front, and we were forced into the back corner, boxed in on all sides. A protective instinct that was more *husband* and less *hired security* had me tugging Serena against me.

"You okay?" I whispered.

"Yep." Her attention darted to the numbers as we climbed to the fifth floor. The elevator shook. The perfect curve of her ass fell against my cock. My hands flew to her hips to keep her steady, but I let them drop. This close I could smell her mango shampoo, her sunscreen, the saltwater scent imprinted on her freckled skin.

Right after our spontaneous wedding, we'd stumbled into an elevator happy-tipsy and flushed with love. I had my hand beneath the skirt of her thrift store wedding dress the second the doors closed.

"You're going to come for your new husband, aren't you?"

"Here's our floor," Serena said with a shaky voice. The Aerial employees spilled out and let us leave, where we stood awkwardly for a moment, avoiding eye contact. Glancing over her shoulder, she whispered, "I was nervous. I *am* nervous. Thank you for the story."

"You'll kick ass in there," I said, indicating the closed office. "You always do. And I'll be right outside if you need anything."

An older white man with sandy-blond hair suddenly stepped out into the hallway. "Serena Swift, what a pleasure to finally meet you. I'm Chase Riley." The guy shook her hand. He wore board shorts and a blue, linen shirt and had a sunglass tan around his eyes.

"It's nice to meet you too. Thank you so much for talking to me today," she said. "And for doing it at Aerial. I've loved your magazine for years. It's an honor."

"Well, we've been big fans of yours for years, so the feeling's mutual. And I'll be chatting with Marty and Dave after this for another piece, so it worked out perfectly." He held open the door with a welcoming smile. "I'm assuming your security guard will stay out in the hallway?"

My dude Chase hadn't even acknowledged me yet, which I was used to. For a lot of clients, I was like a nicely dressed piece of furniture with knowledge of hand-to-hand combat.

You're unhappy with this job, and it shows.

I dodged that unpleasant thought but noticed Serena's body language was still jumpy.

"He goes where I go actually," she replied.

A frisson of connection ran up my spine.

"My client is correct," I said to Chase. I didn't miss the disappointment in his eyes, so I was even happier to stand like the Hulk in a corner and intimidate him a bit.

"Everyone seems to need security these days, huh?" he said evenly.

"They sure do, Chase," I grinned, sliding right past him. They followed me inside, and as the interviewer got busy setting things up, Serena shot me another grateful look.

I got comfy in the corner and tossed her a wink. Her cheeks flushed before she turned toward Chase.

Chin lifted, spine straight. Fingers still. She was transformed back into the woman who conquered the ocean with courage in her heart.

I, on the other hand, had been back in her life for less than twenty-four hours and was the hottest fucking mess about it.

I faced the reporter and felt ready for the first time all day.

Cope, standing behind me in that corner, caused a prickle of welcome awareness on the back of my neck.

If you needed the reminder that you're a motherfucking badass...

"Let me give you a rundown of what we're doing today," Chase said. He had the typical surfer's build and was maybe twenty-five years older than me. "At *Heavy*, we always work with Aerial when they have a new brand ambassador. It's no secret that they're one of our biggest ad clients. And let's face it—everyone at *Heavy* buys their products almost exclusively. To us, this is a really great partnership. And a great way to profile a surfer like you."

My nerves settled even more. Just because this was a bigger opportunity than I was used to didn't mean I couldn't handle it.

"Right on," I said, crossing my legs beneath my skirt. "I've been buying Aerial surfboards and *your* magazine from the time I had my own money to spend."

He took out his notebook and pen and pressed *play* on his

recorder. "I know you've been on the circuits and the tours for a long time, and you've always had the talent. When did you start pursuing pro surfing as a career?"

"I was fourteen, although I started surfing at twelve. My first real win was at fifteen. I was hooked after that first trophy. It was the Oceanside High School Champs event, and the waves that day were sharky as hell."

He was scribbling with his pen. "You still remember that?"

"Oh, yeah. You definitely don't forget your first time being on your board and knowing there are sharks beneath you."

"You weren't scared?" he asked.

"Oh, I was scared out of my mind." Chase laughed to himself as he wrote something down. "But I wanted to win more."

"What'd you do about the sharks?"

"Avoided them." I grinned at the memory. "Stayed out of their space, and they stayed out of mine."

"You ever see sharks again?"

"Sometimes," I said. "And it does make you think twice when something brushes against your leg in the water. The worst was when I was training at Hout Bay in South Africa. Those are great whites sharing the water with you. Getting out of their way isn't really an option."

He was nodding, checking a pile of notes. "You were out training on big waves, right?"

"I was, yeah." I leaned forward, excited. "I've spent time at Torquay in Australia. Nazaré in Portugal. Bundoran in Ireland. I've trained with Kalei Peleke in Oahu, where she's from. I really focused on skill and technique the past few years, and I think it's why I won at Jaws."

"Wait, you surfed at Nazaré?"

"Not at the competitive level, but I spent a few months there with my trainer, Dora."

Those waves in Portugal had chiseled themselves into my

very bones. They were large as skyscrapers, frothy black and cold, unpredictable, and mean.

"I didn't realize," he said. "And sorry for my surprise; you don't see a lot of women out in Nazaré given how dangerous it is."

I frowned. "I was there for three months surfing with other women every day. And it is dangerous, but we worked with a highly trained safety crew. Prioritizing some of the newer safety guidelines in big wave surfing is a passion of mine."

"Like what?"

"Mandatory life vests. Helmets. Continuing to use a jet ski to tow you out instead of paddling. Making sure there are trained medical crews on the beach and rescue volunteers in the water."

There was a long pause while he finished writing. "You don't think that's cheating a little bit?"

"How so?"

His tone was just shy of patronizing. "You don't think towing out, wearing all that gear, is cheating? Before this stuff was invented, people were riding big waves without any kind of assistance."

My pleasant, polite smile froze on my face. Because when he said *people*, he meant *men*. "To be clear, and you can make sure this goes in your article, proper safety precautions are not cheating, and I will always utilize them."

Chase made a frustrated sound in the back of his throat. "Towing makes it easier. If a jet ski pulls you to the wave and you don't have to paddle, you're not working as hard."

"Have you ever surfed the waves at Nazaré?" I asked with feigned innocence.

He glanced away. "Uh, no. I'm only repeating the water-cooler talk in the industry."

"Gotcha." I cocked my head. "So how do you know I

wasn't working as hard if you haven't surfed waves as gigantic as I have?"

I'd poked him hard, right in his ego, before I could help myself. I couldn't *believe* that sitting here, talking to the most respected surf magazine in the world with a billion-dollar company supporting me, I still had to prove I was just as good.

His gaze hardened. "You know what, I think that came out wrong. But let's move on to a happier subject, okay?"

My eyes narrowed, thoughts in sudden disarray. His line of questioning wasn't technically a shock. I'd heard some version of his ideas my entire life. It was jarring though—Aerial put their trust in this magazine as a partner, as a media source responsible for launching this next step in my career.

Should I trust this guy if a company as good as Aerial did?

"Okay," I said slowly, still wary. My spine was straightening, my body pulling back into my chair. "What's your next question?"

His posture seemed to loosen as mine only tightened. "How about we talk about your incredible win at Jaws? That video of you was all any surfer was talking about for a while."

I could hear the curt edge of my tone when I replied, "That was the culmination of fifteen years of dedication and hard work."

His writing stopped for a second before resuming. "Did you get a lot of praise from other surfers in the industry? Anyone you want to share with us?"

I relaxed, just a little. "I did, yeah. Kalei Peleke and Prue Dorsey, who I've known since my first tour. And other big wave surfers who really paved the way for women like me: Maya Batista, Arya Young, Malia Kim. The sisterhood and camaraderie among women in this sport is really powerful."

He nodded as his pen moved. "Finn Travis wrote a really nice piece about you online, didn't he? He's a super nice guy."

Super nice guy was downplaying it. Finn Travis was famous and highly respected, and he *always* supported women, our talents, and our ability to ride the biggest waves. An hour after I finished at Jaws, there was a text on my phone from Finn that read: *You're a fucking superstar, Serena!*

He and his wife, Avery, had opened an eco-friendly, sustainable hotel in Playa Vieja a few years back, so when he wasn't crushing the gnarliest waves, he was saving the environment in his free time. I'd always admired that about him. In fact, Finn's intertwined careers of surfing and activism was the first thing I thought of when Aerial called.

"That was a dream come true," I admitted. "Finn is a surfer I really admire."

"Must be cool to see that kind of encouragement from your community," Chase continued. He looked at me expectantly, and I knew what he wanted to hear.

What he wanted to hear wasn't the truth though, and if Aerial had brought me on to raise awareness of disparities in my sport, I wasn't going to censor myself.

"Yes and no," I said. "I received a ton of support, yes, but the majority of that support came from other women. You'll recall a few of my male colleagues, even more famous than Finn, had very dismissive things to say about me online and in public."

His forehead wrinkled, but I didn't buy the act. "That doesn't ring a bell for me."

I maintained his eye contact. "They said I didn't deserve the win because I'd been reckless, putting other surfers at risk because I couldn't handle those sets."

"Do you think you were being reckless?" he asked in an *I'm only playing devil's advocate* tone of voice.

"No, and if I was, I was no more or less reckless than any surfer out there attempting to level up in their sport. They don't get publicly criticized by their peers, though."

He fiddled with his notes, looking annoyed with me. "Listen, Serena—"

"They said I got lucky," I continued, speaking over him. "That I wasn't ready. And, believe me, their public statements were more diplomatic. I saw way too many comments on the YouTube video that will haunt my dreams." I swallowed hard. "And have had way too many things said to me, face-to-face, right on the beach."

He placed his pen down, like he was dealing with an unruly teenager he wanted to keep quiet. "What's your point then?"

Fiery red flashed at the edges of my vision, but I tamped it down as best I could. If this was getting written about, it was extra important that I chose my words carefully. "My point is that we cover up and ignore the ugly truths of this sport because it's always been viewed as a group of athletes who are chill, who are into *good vibes*, who just want to hang on the beach all day. That's never been the reality though. Sexism, toxic masculinity, racism, bigotry in all of its forms are all alive and well within surfing, and we all need to be working together to do something about it."

Behind me, Cope shuffled his feet, and I'd known him long enough to decipher his tiny cues of support.

Chase closed his notebook and settled back in his chair. "Isn't that everywhere, though?"

"So?"

"*So*, seems to me that kind of stuff eventually goes away on its own."

I arched my eyebrow. "You just described entrenched discrimination the way a doctor talks about a random rash on your arm."

He dropped his elbows to his knees. "What I'm saying here is that surfing is *fun*. It's the happy sport. The more you talk about it, the more you shine a light on... *stuff* like that...

the worse it gets, right? And besides." He flipped open his notebook again. "I'm not really here to talk about sexism. I'm here for a lifestyle story. What do you put in your smoothies? Best playlists to work out to? Things like that."

Dread and anger spread through the pit of my stomach. "That's not what Aerial wants with this interview. They're pioneers. They talk about real things, things that matter."

"I'm sorry to say this, but it *is* what they want."

His tone was definitely patronizing now.

My lips pressed into a thin line. I was pissed and *so over* being careful. "If *Heavy* isn't willing to write about and elevate these issues, to be a part of actual change, then you haven't been listening to the communities who have been shouting about this for years. I'm only talking about *my* experience. There are other experiences we need to listen to—stories from queer surfers, non-binary folks, Black surfers, surfers of color... basically any athlete that *isn't* given sponsorships or platforms or financial backing to compete. It means they're locked out of the tours and the circuits. Their contributions are completely erased or ignored all together." I reached forward and tapped his notebook. "This isn't *new*. It's always been there."

I watched Chase become more and more uncomfortable the longer I talked. But I wasn't uncomfortable at all. It was what I'd said at the end—about money and sponsors—that had tiny sparks, the first beginnings of an idea, going off in my brain.

"Serena." He turned off his tape recorder, and the reality of what I'd done came storming back in. My cheeks got hot, my neck flushed. "Maybe we should reschedule this for next week, give you some time to think about your answers."

I reared back, surprised. "You're ending the interview? We just got started."

"For next week," he said mildly, "I'll bring more specific

lifestyle questions like we talked about." Another flash of that placating smile. "Listen, and I don't mean this to be offensive, but think of it as a puff piece. It's fluffy, it's fun, it's light-hearted. Okay? I won't tell Aerial, and we can redo the whole thing."

He was being nice, but not in an actually nice way. Nice because I got the distinct impression he pitied me. He shuffled his tools back into his bag before standing with his hand outstretched. I shook it, feeling slimy.

But then I stood up—I was almost as tall as he was, and I enjoyed that he couldn't physically look down on me. "Every day women are treated unfairly in this sport. I think my favorite smoothie recipes can wait, don't you?"

"I think I know what my readers want to see more than you do," he said with a shrug. "Can I offer a word of advice?"

My molars were already grinding.

"Aerial wants this piece to do well and officially launch you as their brand ambassador. It would behoove you to do what they're asking."

Chase stepped past me as my hands curled into fists, and I restrained a howl of frustration. Plus a new anxiety, brought on by Chase's *advice*, that I needed to play by the rules if I wanted to keep my *own* financial backing. I rubbed my forehead, confused about the game I was playing. Because I didn't know the rules, and Aerial was supposed to be on my team.

"I'll escort you to the car, Ms. Swift." It was Cope, right behind me, kindness in his voice. His hand barely grazed the small of my back, but it felt like a lifeline. I walked out of the office and passed Chase, who was holding the door open. His eyes narrowed as Cope walked by, then his face lit up in recognition.

"I can't believe I didn't notice it before," he said, staring at my bodyguard. "You're Copeland McDaniels's son, right?"

I touched my hair and tried to discreetly make eye

contact with Cope. He wasn't looking at me though. He was looking at Chase like the guy was a new punching bag at the gym.

"I am his son," he said.

"Wow." Chase shook his head like he couldn't believe it. "What a legend your dad was. I wish I could have known him."

Cope took a step closer to Chase and dropped his voice. "I wish you could have known him too. And it's such a weird coincidence, what Ms. Swift was talking about, because my dad was a huge proponent for equality and standing up for what's right. He taught me and my sister to do the same. Always." Cope slid his hands into his pockets with an easy grin. "Can I offer a word of advice? If you really think my dad was a legend, then you'll include everything she just said in your article."

❧ 12 ☙

COPE

Serena and I were halfway down the hallway, heading toward the elevators, when Marty Lattimore appeared out of nowhere.

He startled us both, but that was to be expected. After spending the past half-hour watching that douchey shithead dismiss Serena's experiences with a condescending smile I wanted to smack, we were both on edge.

"Serena, Mr. McDaniels, how nice bumping into you here," he said, clapping his hands together. He nodded to his left. "This is my office. My brother's is two doors down. This is a lovely bit of serendipity in the middle of a busy day."

Serena caught her breath and managed to say, "It sure is." But there were lines around her mouth and a tightness around her eyes. "We were just heading—"

"How was the interview? He's coming to speak with me next. He didn't grill you, did he?" He laughed at his own joke. Meanwhile, Serena paled.

"I'm hoping it turns out okay."

"Oh, I'm sure it will," he said. "Listen, this is actually perfect timing for another reason. A reason that's... a little bit embarrassing, a little bit sensitive." He made a face as he said *embarrassing* and *sensitive*. All the hair on the back of my neck stood straight up. "Do you mind stepping into my office?"

"Of course, not a problem."

Marty held open the door for her, but she turned to me and said, "After you, Mr. McDaniels."

That was twice now that she'd looked to me for comfort or soothing, and my foolish heart wanted to read between the lines.

"Sure thing," I said. Hand on my tie, I stepped into Marty's office, which appeared exactly as I would have imagined it. Repurposed wood. Photos of him on mountain tops and on snowboards. Maps of the globe and graphics depicting their environmental impact. Awards for innovation and humanitarian work.

I thought about what Quentin had said. *In the world of big corporations, there are no good guys, only guys that are good at lying.*

It would be hard for someone like this to lie though.

I placed myself on the far wall, out of Marty's line of sight, but close enough so Serena knew I was there. Her fingers were doing that twisting thing again.

"What can I help you with?" she asked.

Marty perched on the edge of his desk, posture relaxed. Face open. "Like I said, it's a little bit embarrassing. It's regarding one of our lawyers, Catalina Flores. Does that name ring a bell?"

She brightened. "Yeah, for sure. I only met her once though, just outside the building."

"Catalina is a wonderful lawyer, and with a company as large as ours, we always need someone with a brilliant legal mind to make sure we're not breaking any laws," he said. "Funny thing though. Some of Catalina's private files have gone missing from her computer. Very important files. We run a tight ship here, so that's the *embarrassing* part of this. She's not sure what happened to them."

Serena's smile was puzzled. "Um... work files? She and I talked about surfing. I invited her to come with us one morning. That was the extent of it."

Marty mirrored her expression. "So strange. She didn't hand anything to you by accident? You see, we've got new security cameras out front. They'd been put up that morning, as luck would have it. We reviewed the footage to make sure, gosh, that we hadn't had a break-in or something equally as nefarious."

Something about his tone and posture was familiar to me, tapping at a memory or a dream, maybe.

And those hairs on the back of my neck stood straight up again. Serena reached behind her head and tangled her fingers in her bun. I considered the motion.

"Because of those cameras," he said. "We saw her run into you."

"Oh, yeah, you're right," she said. "She crashed into me with quite a bit of power. Almost knocked me off my feet."

"Knocked your bag to the ground, right?" Marty asked. Smooth as butter.

"Um... yeah, if you say so." Her fingers tugged. Twisted. "It was a pretty uneventful meeting."

He was silent, but in a friendly way. As if he was waiting for an admission. "So you didn't end up with anything from our office, then?"

She frowned. "No, not at all. I'm sorry, I wish I could be helpful, but I really have no idea about anything like that."

He rubbed his hands together and shrugged like it was no big deal. "Ah, well. I had to ask. It's the oddest thing. We can't find it anywhere, and Catalina is a wreck over it."

"Can I say hi before I go? I don't know where her office is."

Marty was already hustling us out of his. "You know, she's gone home for the day. I don't know if it's the stress or what, but she said she hasn't been feeling well."

Serena's fingers kept twisting and tangling. But she still patted Marty on the arm before turning around back to the elevators. "No worries. Give her my best, and I hope you guys find what you're looking for."

I followed my wife down the hallway. A woman who was many things—confident, infuriating, brash, courageous.

And, if I remembered her little *tells* correctly, had just lied right to Marty's face.

13

COPE

Serena was silent again on the way home, but this silence had a different pattern to it. Less jumble of nerves and more intense thinking. She'd curled her fingers into her hair so frequently the bun fell apart, golden hair spilling over her shoulders. Every time I looked in the mirror, she was facing the window. I could see the jagged, white scar down her cheek and her teeth, worrying at her bottom lip.

As I pulled into the driveway, I was debating my own next moves and grounding myself in the job at hand. I'd fought with Serena, laughed with her, been in our house, been pressed against her body in an elevator, and witnessed her take a lot of shit she didn't deserve.

My self-control was liable to snap with the slightest provocation. I wanted to crawl into the back seat and let her lay her head in my lap, like I used to when she had hard days. Stroke her hair until she fell asleep.

Instead, I turned around, expecting her to be in motion. She wasn't.

She was watching me.

"Weird day, huh?" I said.

She burst out laughing. "You could say that, yeah." She dropped her head into her hands, where she moaned or growled. I couldn't tell.

"Serena."

When she looked back up, her entire face was flushed. I'd accidentally said her name the way I *used* to. The way a husband says the name of the wife he loves.

"I, uh..." I rubbed the back of my neck. "Listen, that Chase dude was an asshole. The whole way through. And I thought you were incredible."

Her brown eyes widened.

"Your points were clear, your passion was engaging, and everything you said was absolutely true. He shouldn't have dismissed you. Although, ironically enough, him dismissing you proved your points."

She exhaled out of her mouth, long and slow. "Marty and Dave promised me a platform where I could be honest about sexism. They promised a platform *and* informed me they were all in to put some real action behind it as a company. So why did I just sit down with a magazine writer they recommended who was clearly uncomfortable with the subject? And who swore Aerial wanted a puff piece?" She rubbed her forehead with a deep frown. "Dora's been talking to me about productive places to use my anger, and I thought working with Aerial would be like that. *That* didn't feel productive, though. That really pissed me off."

"Marty didn't tell you they planned your first profile to be fluffy?" I asked.

She shook her head. "Two days ago, I met with a marketing team who promised change was what they wanted. Those questions Chase was asking, all the ways he was not listening to me, *that's* not change. That's things staying the same. And if he's not angry about the injustice in our sport, he's not paying attention."

Her throat worked, fingers twisting in her lap again. There was a ragged edge at the tail end of those words that had me fighting the urge to reach for her.

"Do you think Aerial was lying in your meeting about their intentions?" I asked.

Confusion filled her gaze. "I really don't know," she said, sounding distracted. "I hope not. They've always presented themselves with integrity. I'm hoping this was some miscommunication and that this interview with Chase isn't going to cost me the most important sponsorship opportunity of my career."

Before I could respond, she dropped her head back into her hands with a frustrated sigh but didn't speak.

After a few seconds, I said, "You can tell me." I bit back the *sunshine* endearment and added, "If you feel comfortable, that is."

I didn't like this new duality of being the husband she hadn't spoken to in four years *and* her agent.

When she finally lifted her head, her cheeks were pink. "I'm upset because I feel... embarrassed now." She said the word *embarrassed* through gritted teeth. "It happens to me whenever I get angry and push back against someone like that. I get this hot rush of irritation, but as it drains away, there's a voice in my head that whispers, 'You shouldn't have done that.'"

I was silent, letting her process, watching her carefully. I had a suspicion about that tiny voice in her head. It made my chest ache.

"I know it's my parents. All the lies they told me and Caleb. All the ways they told me it was my job to keep men *comfortable* and when they were uncomfortable it was my fault. For not being pleasant or sweet enough."

"Or telling them things they don't want to take responsibility for," I said softly.

She nodded. "Exactly."

My hands flexed against the seat, a response to my own fury. Fury at parents who'd told this woman the only way she could receive love was by being a living doll. Pretty, polite, quiet. They had demanded she fulfill gender roles so strictly that they'd done more than just withhold affection when she broke their rules. Serena and her brother went without food more often than not, locked in their bedrooms and separated from each other. Her first two years of surfing had only happened because she and Caleb invented an after-school program they had to stay late for, which allowed them to sneak out to La Jolla without their parents' knowledge.

"And even though I'm not ashamed of what I said in that interview," she continued. "And even though it's been *years*, I still get this response because of how I was raised, and I hate that it happens."

She was quiet again, and there was a rigid tension in the set of her shoulders and the line of her jaw. When she let her eyes land on mine, the pain there stunned me. This side of Serena was like witnessing a rare phase of the moon. Being vulnerable wasn't her thing, but a long time ago, she'd let me in, dropped her barriers, exposed her fears. Given me her heart.

I'd lost that privilege when we broke up. Seeing it now scrambled my brain and my common sense. I reached forward and held her hand.

"I'm so sorry they did that to you," I said hoarsely. She squeezed back with something like relief, and I felt it. I felt the force of our love, just beneath the surface, as radiant and passionate as ever.

"Thank you," she said on a whisper, then let me go. "And I

appreciated what you told Chase, about your dad, and for defending my experiences."

"I'd do it every single time," I said. "You know that, right?"

"I do."

Her lips were parted, chest rising and falling rapidly. If I didn't know better, Serena was contemplating kissing me. And I knew this woman better than I knew myself.

She *was* contemplating kissing me.

"Should we go in?" She pressed a fluttering hand to her forehead. "I mean, I'll go in. You'll..."

"Falco's shift doesn't start until tonight, so I need to check the house first, and then I'll be posted outside." I opened the door, exiting with a sigh of resignation. I watched Serena walk up the stairs with forceful regret.

There was no reconciliation for us. I held tight to that. We'd once meant the world to each other, so moments like this were going to be as confusing as they were tempting.

Inside, I swept through the lower rooms, checked all the locks, but nothing was amiss. I had my hand on the banister, one foot on the stair, when Serena swished into the living room.

"What's up?" I asked, recognizing the look on her face.

"Here's the thing." She had one hand behind her back. "I'd completely forgotten this, in the shock of having my ex-husband for a bodyguard. But Catalina did give me something."

I closed the distance between us in two steps. Held out my hand. She dropped a USB stick into it with a sticky note that said, *Watch Me :)*.

This time it wasn't just the back of my neck. Awareness shivered across every inch of my skin, heightening my instincts. Marty's strange-but-friendly behavior today hadn't made sense to me. Or maybe that's what made sense about it.

He'd been acting shady as hell.

What had Quentin said this morning? *Call me pessimistic, but I tend to think any billion-dollar company with something to hide is dangerous.*

"Catalina and I really did just talk about surfing, and people send me their tapes all the time to watch. I assumed she was scared to give me a surf video and did it when she picked up my bag."

I held up the stick. "You know, I'm a little rusty, but I thought you were lying to Marty back in his office."

She pursed her lips. "I was in shock after the interview. And confused. And annoyed with Aerial in the moment. It had me questioning them enough to wonder why he was asking me about missing work files. Or why Catalina was suddenly home sick."

I was starting to feel sick too. It was much too soon to really know what was going on, but the moment I relayed this story to Quentin, I could guess the conclusion he would leap to.

It wasn't a safe one.

❦ 14 ❦

SERENA

I pulled on an oversized hoodie and running shorts, then walked back downstairs to find Cope on the couch with his laptop balanced on the coffee table.

I was grateful he hadn't noticed me yet. He'd shed his suit jacket, loosened his tie, rolled up his white shirtsleeves. His shoulders stretched the fabric. His bare forearms flexed with muscle. The sexual desire I still felt for my ex-husband demanded I climb onto his lap. I wasn't skeptical of his reaction. He couldn't hide his body's glorious response while pressed together in that elevator or the fleeting glances filled with want and need. If I did now what I used to do—flirt, tease, *tempt* him into a myriad of sinful pleasures—this body-guard would have me flat on my back before I could say *please.*

My muscles shivered. I was tired, needed to sit on that damn couch before my legs gave out. But my own stubborn self-preservation kept me frozen on the bottom step. It would have been simpler to deny this craving if Cope hadn't spent today proving that four years apart hadn't stripped him of the qualities that made him so easy to fall for: compassion, kindness, unconditional support.

My brother and I stood up for what was right because we grew up in a house where no one stood up for us. We'd learned at a young age that the world was unfair and cruel to a lot of people, but instead of feeling helpless it had given us a direction. A guiding light in the darkness.

Cope was outspoken because of the opposite: two devoted parents who raised him up well, taught him with words and examples. Even now, the protective instinct he'd nurtured since his father's death sprang from an innate understanding of the way people could be hurt.

Having a partner like that—*marrying* someone like that—had been a privilege. This entire day had been an unfair reminder that I'd been very, very lucky once.

"Are you done creepily staring at me from the stairs?" Cope asked, face lit up by the blue of the laptop screen.

I blinked. Realized with a start that I had been staring like a dreamy-eyed fool.

"You don't know what I was doing," I said, lifting my chin.

He peered up at me. "I always know when you're checking me out."

"The last time I did that was four years ago, so you must be confused." I fell backwards onto the couch casually, like it didn't matter, like his nearness didn't matter. The sheer volume of orgasms we'd given each other on this very piece of furniture *didn't matter one bit.*

A smile still played on Cope's lips, but it didn't reach his eyes.

Whatever he thought Catalina had given me was making him nervous. Which, in turn, made me nervous.

"Got anything interesting?" I tucked my feet under me and tried to peek over his arm.

He moved it, tilted the angle of the laptop so I could see

clearly. He held up the USB stick. "I was waiting for you. You ready to watch this?"

"Totally," I lied. The way Aerial had made me feel today—like they were hiding something, like they had lied to me—had set off a chain reaction of wariness and distrust. I wanted them to be *good* though—to be ethical, to have integrity. I wanted this afternoon to be a messy and frustrating misunderstanding, not an indicator of their values.

"My money is still on the odds that this is a tape of her surfing," I said, trying to ease my own nerves.

"Or maybe a really embarrassing stand-up comedy routine she wants your feedback on," he murmured, plugging in the drive. His laptop whirred and blinked as it loaded. "Or, even better, a song she wrote. About you."

I rolled my eyes. "People don't write songs about me."

He grinned, and it soothed the thorny edges of my anxiety. "On the, let's say, *darker* corners of the internet, there are *definitely* amateur songwriters who have uploaded videos of songs they've written asking you to be their best friend *or* brazenly declaring their romantic love."

"And you know this because you hang out in these darker corners?" I asked. "Or do you know this because you're the amateur songwriter in this scenario?"

"Oh, Serena." He shook his head with that charming smile. "I was twenty-two when we met, so you *know* I took out that acoustic guitar I barely knew how to play and wrote cheesy-ass songs about your hair and shit."

I laughed out loud, forgetting myself. Forgetting reality. Merely enjoying the extravagance of this exchange because sitting next to Cope made it too hard to resist.

The moment was short-lived.

"Wait, hold up," he muttered, attention yanked back to the screen. "What the hell is this?"

I practically lunged toward the laptop. A white box

popped up with about ten different files labeled incoherently. A few pictures. Cope clicked on one, and it was a document that listed the names, contact information, pictures, and badge numbers for factory inspectors with the Arizona Safety and Hazards Association.

The next thing was a picture of the current San Diego City Council. Cope squinted at the screen before tapping his thumb on the guy in the middle. "Isn't that David Lattimore?"

"Huh," I said, fingers at my lips. "I didn't know he was a city councilmember."

"Remind me, what does Aerial make and where?"

I sat back on the couch, giving me the perfect vantage point to study Cope's reactions. He hadn't stopped staring at the files. "The Lattimore brothers founded it in the seventies as a direct response to other outdoor adventure companies at the time mass producing goods and clothing without any care given to the impact it had on the environment. If we all shared a common love of the outdoors, then we'd want our gear to do the least damage possible. The center of their mission was climate justice. Reducing their carbon footprint. And producing goods ethically."

He finally twisted around to look at me. "I'm guessing their factories are in the US?"

I bit my lip. "In Arizona, actually."

He nodded like he expected that answer.

"They're well-known for their ethical factory conditions. Living wage, safety, minimizing pollution. A dedication to social responsibility and philanthropy." I flipped up the bottom of my sweatshirt, which I just realized was an Aerial design. The tag on the inside said: *Made in America. Made for the planet.* I showed Cope, and his brows knit together.

He opened the other files, the non-photo ones, and a bunch of legal documents popped up. They were long, hundreds and hundreds of pages, and my eyes glazed over immediately.

"Quentin said they were tied up in private arbitration. Lawsuits not in the public record. Makes for better concealing," he murmured. "I wonder if that's what these are."

"I guess Marty was right, then? That Catalina somehow dropped these work files into my bag by accident?"

I was secretly relieved. Cope, however, was not.

He drummed his fingers on the sides of the laptop, clearly thinking. "Unless Catalina did this on purpose." He ejected the drive and held it tightly in his hand, staring at it. He didn't speak for almost ten seconds, and my simmering worries ratcheted up the longer he was silent.

I ducked my head until I caught his eye. "Spit it out, Cope."

With a sigh, he turned to face me. I backed up a few inches to avoid our legs grazing each other. "Sometimes there are things, bad things, going on at companies, and employees are too scared or have been too threatened to speak up about it. I'm wondering if Catalina passed you information that needs to be exposed. Quentin thought something was up with them from the get-go."

His words sent a chill rippling through me. I pressed my palm to my forehead. "Aerial was dedicated to protecting the environment before it was trendy or popular. Their entire brand is based around ethics."

"I know," he said, still staring at the flash drive. "I'm not saying I *want* to think badly of this company. And we're nowhere close to a complete picture of what's really going on. I am saying that Marty was acting weird as shit when he spoke to us today, right? And an employee attempted to covertly slip you documents that the CEO was trying very hard to convince us he was only a little worried about."

I thought back to our encounter, peeling back the shock

and anger I felt after my argument with Chase and remembering the odd expression on Marty's face. The mismatched tension, the way he was almost *too* casual when he cheerfully informed us that he'd watched me and Catalina on security footage.

I rubbed my arms as goosebumps raced across my skin. "It feels like you're working out a plan."

"I'm thinking I want to show this to Quentin."

"You want to involve more people?" I asked.

His next words were slow. Deliberate. "I think my gut is telling me I'm holding a drive full of bad fucking news. If it's innocent, I'll drive you to Aerial myself so you can return it. But if I'm right, and this company is covering something up, then it's exactly what you said to Chase today. And my best friend happens to specialize in this kind of investigating."

I fell back against the couch cushion, equally wired and exhausted at his suggestion. "We have a responsibility to do the right thing."

"To be clear," he said softly, "I'm hoping my instinct is wrong."

The reality of what we were talking about came crashing down around me. "I just signed a three-year contract with them," I blurted out. "I just became the official embodiment of this company *and* their values. I have to give interviews after I compete tomorrow, talking about how great they are."

Cope's gaze filled with sympathy, muscles primed for action. But he stood up, instead of reaching for me, and I pretended I wasn't disappointed. He began fixing his casual appearance, transforming back into my hired security and security only. Sleeves buttoned, jacket back on, he slid the USB stick into his pocket.

"I will figure this out for you, okay?" His smile was back, and the warmth of it chased the chill away. "It's my job to do so, and I don't want you worrying too much when you've got

Trestles tomorrow." He paused as if considering his next words. "I just... I know us." His tone lowered, infused with intimacy. "On the slightest chance that you were given something important and we found out later that we'd done nothing to stop it—"

I dragged my fingers through my hair. "Talk to Quentin," I said firmly.

He checked his watch then peered out the front window. "I should get out there, check in with my boss. Prep my report for when Falco arrives."

"Right, of course," I said. I walked into the kitchen for a glass of water. Stared at my reflection in the window above the sink. Cope stood behind me, at least six feet away, but it still felt too close. We made accidental, lingering eye contact, and I felt the pull of lust, low in my belly. He eventually cleared his throat, shattering the moment.

"I know this sounds dramatic, but don't mention this to Dora or Caleb, okay? Don't mention it to anyone until I say so."

It didn't sound dramatic at all. If anything, his somber, *I work security let me handle this* vibe amplified my concerns.

It was so not like him. It made me, for the first time, more scared than nervous.

"Okay," I said. "I'll keep it to myself."

A tiny bit of lightness came over his face. "I thought you were going to battle me more on that one. Since I was—what did you say?—'Trying to control your actions and telling you what to do.'"

"For one time only," I said, not fighting the smile tugging at my lips. "And I'm not apologizing for saying that because it's still true."

"I wouldn't expect anything less." He spun on his heels and made it all the way to the door before stopping, turning around with a vexed expression.

"What is it?" I asked.

"Today, in Marty's office, he reminded me of someone, and it's been bugging me." He shoved his hands into his pockets. "I just realized who it was. Gary Duncan."

The spark of warm lightness between us vanished.

"Gary Duncan, the boss you were held hostage with?" I asked. Apparently, the theme of today was *unprepared*. If I wasn't ready for my ex-husband's charm and kindness again, I absolutely wasn't ready to revisit the most horrific forty-eight hours of my life.

And the beginning of the end for Cope and me.

"Yes, that Gary Duncan," he said, staring at the ground. "It was Marty's style of pleasant bullshit. Gary had that same happy humanitarian vibe. His company wasn't as famous as Aerial, but personally he was loved, adored, highly respected. Squeaky clean. But, as we learned after..." He cleared his throat again. "He was up to his eyeballs in all kinds of shady, illegal activity that he hid behind his pristine reputation. Until he couldn't hide anymore. And the bad guys came to collect."

I winced. "I really don't like that comparison."

"Me neither."

I studied his body language. It was rigid, mirroring my own reaction in the car earlier, when I'd talked about my parents. He hadn't hesitated to comfort me, even though it must have violated several specific rules in the bodyguard-client relationship.

"Are you... okay?" I broached. Tentative.

He cocked his head. "About what?"

"Thinking about Gary. I imagine the reminder of being held at gun-point for two days isn't enjoyable."

I was treading carefully. We were blowing on the embers of our worst and hardest disagreement, the turning point from where our relationship had never recovered.

Cope shrugged. "Of course. Why wouldn't I be?"

"Because you went through a nightmare," I said softly.

It was like snapping my fingers. His jaw tightened. His nostrils flared. "I was fine, Serena. And I am fine."

The syllables of my name sounded bitter and unforgiving. Just like our final few months together. At the time, watching my husband hide his fear and pain while simultaneously shutting me out had created a yawning cavern of sadness inside of me. And an urgent desire to *fix* the situation for him, even though he asked me not to. That same urge flared to life now before I could stop it.

"If you ever needed a... a friend... to talk to about those things, I'm here."

Cope shook his head and said, "Thank you, but I don't need to talk about anything."

A buzzing voice in my brain cautioned that revisiting an old, painful argument in this very kitchen wasn't a smart idea.

I ignored it.

"Something is up with your job, you said so yourself. Maybe talking it out or admitting that what happened to you was—"

"I don't want to talk about it," he interrupted. "And don't need to. And are we really going to get into another argument about our chosen careers?"

I felt my cheeks redden. "Actually, *I'm* trying to talk things out. You're the one arguing this time."

His eyes narrowed at me in a standoff we both knew well. "'Round and 'round," he said. "That's how you described us this morning, right? You want to tell me how dangerous my job is and demand that I quit. And I'm only going to remind you that your career is much more dangerous than mine and ask *you* to—"

"Don't," I said sharply.

He nodded with a humorless expression. "Of course, we're

ending our first day working together by rehashing the same fight we had outside the gym."

"Why am I not surprised?" I said, regretting the cynical vibration in my voice. Regretting that Cope and I could only reconnect so much before stumbling back into our worst patterns.

It was infuriating.

He opened the front door and rubbed the back of his neck, irritated. "Listen, I have to go actually do my job now. But I'll talk to Quentin tonight and see what I can find out, okay?"

"Sure, whatever," I said.

He looked like he wanted to say more. *I* wanted to say more. But instead he stepped outside and shut the door behind him. I sagged against the countertop, feeling utterly deflated.

So far, having an ex-husband as a bodyguard had been an irresistibly sexy temptation *and* a mind-fuck of emotional baggage.

Both were distractions I couldn't afford.

Yet both were distractions I couldn't seem to avoid.

15

COPE

Quentin opened his front door and brightened when he saw me.

"Now what a pleasant surprise," he said in his thick Southern accent, which was untouched by his many years in California.

I held up a bag. "I've got bad news for me, good news for you, and a six-pack."

His eyebrow arched. "Beer and good news are always welcome unannounced in my house."

I followed him inside his small apartment. It was essentially a home office more *office* than home. Given his passion and dedication to journalism, it made sense.

He dropped the beer onto the low coffee table in the middle of the living room that opened up into a tiny kitchen. Multiple desks held numerous laptops and screens. Awards for his work hung on the wall. His shelves overflowed with dog-eared paperbacks. Literally—they were jammed on top of each other, taking up any space he had.

I wandered over to the main wall, where white boards, cork boards and calendars hung in perfectly straight rows. It was here that he kept careful track of his stories, sources, and competing deadlines.

I pointed to one covered in pictures, typed notes, and red string connecting coincidences I couldn't see. "How very *All the President's Men* of you."

He cracked open a beer and handed it to me. "I do enjoy a vintage approach to reporting. There's something classic about it. And, I will say, I like to dramatically stand in the center of this room and stare at my theories while muttering to myself."

"Helps, yeah?" I said, raising the beer.

"Yelling out '*By golly, I've got it!*' never gets old." He walked into his kitchen and reached up over the fridge, where I knew he kept his best snacks when working late nights.

Or when his best friend showed up without calling first. Quentin Abernathy was still dressed in what I always called *hipster formal wear*. A long-sleeved, buttoned-up checkered shirt with a thin, blue tie and expensive loafers. He was just a little shorter than me, lean and angular. He was white and had dark eyes, dark brown hair, and a smile I'd once heard described as *artfully impish* by another girl in our freshman year chemistry class. He wore thick, square-rimmed glasses that made him look smart and trendy at the same time.

But I'd known him since he was eighteen years old, and there was no covering up the fact that he was—and always would be—a big old nerd. Over the years, he'd become more *brother* than best friend, and my little sister, Billie, certainly thought so. Given how far from home he lived, Quentin was a regular guest at my mother's dinner table and frequently with us most holidays.

And for two years, Caleb, Serena's brother, had been the third side of our little friendship triangle. Quentin would never say anything, but I knew he missed him something awful.

I did too.

He returned with bowls filled with various snacks before sitting down in his office chair, ankle propped up on his knee. "I need to know about this good news/bad news situation, Copeland."

I tossed an M&M into my mouth, chewed for a second. Then I reached into my pocket and produced the USB stick Catalina Flores had snuck out of Aerial on purpose. I was fucking sure of it.

"Two days ago, Serena was leaving the Aerial offices when one of their in-house lawyers, Catalina Flores, bumped into her out on the sidewalk. Serena dropped her purse, but Catalina picked everything up for her before she could stop her. A day later, Serena discovered this USB stick inside her purse with a note that said *watch me*."

Seeing Quentin realize he was being given a lead was like watching a bloodhound catch a scent in the air. He sat straight up and then leaned forward. "Go on."

"A few hours ago, as we were leaving an interview at Aerial, Marty Lattimore pulled Serena into his office and admitted that Catalina had *lost a few sensitive files* and wondered if Serena knew where they were. They have brand-new security cameras out front, so they saw footage that showed their collision."

"Where is Catalina now?"

I shot him a knowing look. "Suddenly out sick."

He held out his hand, and I dropped the stick into his palm. He spun around and plugged it into his laptop. "I'm guessing you already reviewed this, right?"

"A bunch of legal documents, I think, that I can't fully understand. A picture of the San Diego city council, which includes David Lattimore, Marty's brother. And the badge numbers of the state workplace safety commission in Arizona."

"Where Aerial's factories are," he said, smiling like a kid in a candy shop. "Sweet Christ, what have you given me?"

"I have my theories, but I don't like them," I admitted. It had hurt, seeing Serena so dejected and concerned after feeling like this sponsorship heralded the next great chapter in her career. I didn't want my instincts to be true. Regardless of our multiple arguments today, I still wanted her to be with a company she trusted, a company that wanted to change the world the way that she did.

Quentin's reaction to this story, however, gave me the sinking feeling that I was right.

I let him click around and read, taking fast, scribbled notes on a pad, muttering beneath his breath. When he was done, he spun slowly on his chair, rubbing a hand over his mouth.

"Tell me it's not what I think it is," I said.

"Well, what do you think it is?" he asked. "I'm being serious. I want to know if we came to the same conclusion."

I grimaced. You couldn't work in corporate security for as long as I had and not have *seen* some things. The kind of things that end up as sensationalized news or an award-winning documentary.

"I think Catalina Flores uncovered some of Aerial's nasty secrets. I think she might be a whistleblower."

He tapped his pen on his notepad. "Whaddya know. I reckon I came to the same damn conclusion."

16

COPE

Quentin and I exchanged a look before I sighed and said, "As if this assignment isn't already complicated enough."

"Yes, your ex-wife being given corporate secrets the day before you become her bodyguard is certainly troublesome."

I took another sip of beer with a sardonic shrug. "At least I know the old gut instincts can still be trusted."

He made a sound under his breath. "I happen to think it's our finest tool." He tapped the pen against his laptop screen. "I'm going to need more time with this to put together a picture of what Catalina was trying to tell us. But I'm guessing she grabbed what she could before she could be noticed. Obviously, it's public knowledge that David Lattimore is a city councilmember, so it feels like she included that picture on here for a reason. A clue."

"And the other stuff?" I asked.

"I don't know," he said slowly. "These could be copies of those private lawsuits. And anything involving factory inspectors is a big *oh shit* in my book."

I grabbed more M&M's from the bowl. "Why?"

"Because of what they're supposed to inspect."

"Oh, shit."

"Yeah," he sighed. "It's usually not good."

I sat back in the couch and scrubbed a hand down my face. "Serena has a huge event tomorrow, but luckily I'll be there. Falco's there tonight. I told her not to tell anyone."

"How'd she take that?"

"She agreed."

Quentin seemed surprised. "You must have made her a little nervous then."

"To be honest, I'm more than a little nervous myself." I pointed at his laptop. "This isn't great, period. But on a personal note, she just signed a huge contract with them. Finding out they might be secretly evil when they've always been seen as pioneers..." I shook my head. "That rips a huge hole in her worldview, man. And it's also not good news for her, career-wise."

Quentin was slowly spinning back and forth in his chair. He scrolled through the documents, made a few more notes. Finally, he said, "Why Serena?"

"What do you mean?"

"Say Catalina is our whistleblower. She got the information out, but instead of going to the authorities with it, she purposefully bumped into a pro surfer and dropped it into her purse. What does that get her?"

I rubbed my hands together and pondered his question. "Safety, maybe. We know whistleblowers put themselves in immense personal and professional risk to expose a company's misdeeds. Could be she saw Serena as a convenient tool."

"Hmm," Quentin said. "She's a pro surfer. Pretty well-known. Has money, resources, a platform. And she's not afraid to speak out." He smirked. "I did see that protest she did with Kalei and Prue about the *Men's Workout Journal* article. It was both classic and savage."

I chuckled. "She's not afraid to stir shit up when the cause is good. It's still a risk though. Serena could have never found it or watched it. Or found it, saw it was just a bunch of files and pictures, and tossed it."

"True," Quentin said softly. "It was a risk. Maybe an informed one. Maybe she... I don't know, saw the opportunity and took it while she had the chance."

"Yeah, maybe," I said. "I agree, I'm not clear on it either. Only that she gave information to Serena, on purpose, and Aerial knows that someone copied those private files. Serena has them. Catalina is now out sick."

"And we don't know the gravity of what she gave her," Quentin said.

"Is it too naive to hope that this is all a big misunderstanding and what she gave Serena proves the opposite? That this kombucha-swilling bunch of hippies aren't involved in anything nefarious?"

My best friend gave me a smile that could only be described as artfully impish. "Why yes, it is, Copeland."

I laughed. Placed my beer on the table. "What's next then?"

"I keep the drive and do what I do best. And you keep Serena safe."

"Quent," I said warningly. "Who keeps you safe?"

He circled his finger in the air. "This state-of-the-art security system my overly protective best friend installed for me."

I frowned. "I'm not trying to get into a thing with a security system, but I'm better."

He laughed before handing me another beer. "No, you cannot fight the computer you installed in my house to keep me safe. But I am calling my guy at city police, see what he knows about this company. And I'll get him to check in on

Catalina, make sure she's okay. That should move this process along quickly so you and Serena aren't in this awkward position for more than a week or so." His tone shifted. "I don't need to tell you what happens when a company like Aerial is backed into a corner."

"One that's about to be named an Olympics sponsor," I said grimly. "It's why they hired us in the first place. Heightened security all around given they're about to be under a media microscope."

He started scribbling something down. "Hell, I forgot about that. They've got a lot to lose. However closely you were going to watch Serena, triple it."

"Trust me. That won't be a problem."

He dropped his pen then pinned me with a bemused, shit-eating grin. "Do tell how it's been following your wife around."

"It's been fine."

"Fine, you say?"

"I said what I said." I lifted one shoulder and leaned back against the couch like it was no big deal. Because it wasn't, evidenced by the frustrating fight we'd just had.

"Prickly." Quentin smirked. "I'm guessing it's actually torture, but you'll never say that because you are, and always will be, insufferably stubborn."

My beer paused in front of my mouth. "*Insufferably* stubborn?"

"I said what I said."

I burst out laughing. "That's something Serena has expressed before, speaking of."

"She's always been a smart girl."

Quentin stood up to grab the bowl of chips, patting me on the shoulder before sitting back down. "Tough first day, huh?"

I wasn't sure if it was tough or if I was incredibly stupid.

Four years had passed, but the second we were thrown back together, our magnetic chemistry was still as obvious as the issues we'd never resolved as a couple.

"It's confusing." I rubbed my forehead. "*Very* confusing. Some moments it feels like we never broke up, and we're at our house the way we used to be. As if time never passed and we were never heartbroken. Other times..." I sipped my beer, set it down. "It's a painful reminder of why we didn't work out. It hurts..." I cleared my throat. "Well, I didn't think it would still hurt like this."

My best friend studied me, face pinched with compassion. He'd been my support system after Serena and I had broken up, during that first year when getting out of bed felt like lifting a school bus with only my fingers. He brought me back from the dead with weekly movie nights and by dragging me to every social engagement he could think of. And he, my mother, and my sister had conspired often to make sure I was showering and eating.

"How badly does it still hurt?" he asked.

I jiggled my knee. Studied the ground. "It's taken me a massive amount of effort and self-control to lock the pain away. But I guess I'd convinced myself that pining for her was normal."

"Do you think you have to protect people even when it puts your own mental health and happiness at risk?" he asked. "Because if seeing Serena this much is going to break that giant heart of yours again, maybe you should call Marilyn and tell her the truth."

I grinned. "That will bode well for convincing Marilyn not to fire me. *Sorry I lied to you, but this new client was the love of my life, and I've never been able to keep my head on straight around her.*"

"Huh." He spun lazily in his chair, contemplating me like a story he was about to pitch to an editor. "Maybe I'm talking right out of my ass, but after everything is done with

Serena, you could always move on. Try your hat at something new."

"Like another security firm, you mean?"

"No, siree," he said. "I mean a whole other career."

I resisted the urge to wince. Marilyn thought I was unhappy. Quentin thought I was unhappy.

And Serena? Her concerns about the hazards of my job—and what she called my reckless behavior—had been at the very core of why we broke up.

"I have a calling," I said. "It's my job to protect those around me. I'm like a dog with a bone, I won't let it go."

My father died because he was rescuing a swimmer. He was surfing with friends on a sunny San Diego day when he spotted someone drowning near a well-known riptide area. They all went to help, sliding off their boards and racing toward the arms waving in the air. They hadn't hesitated to do the right thing when a person was in danger.

A couple years after his death, I realized what I needed to do: Be the one who kept my family and friends safe. And I went into a career like security where I was literally paid to protect people.

"Besides," I continued, "being around her might be confusing, but there isn't a chance in hell we'd do something as irresponsible as get back together. We were arguing about the same old shit minutes after seeing each other again. What I do isn't that dangerous, and I'm not going to quit just because she thinks I don't take it seriously enough."

I swallowed roughly. My part in our ending was an uncomfortable truth that I despised confronting. "And I hate being the kind of person who asks an athlete to abandon their career because of what happened to my father. She shouldn't have to quit a dream she was honest about from our first date. But I wanted her to, asked her to more days than not." I grinned at my best friend, trying to ease the tension. "Listen, it's my fault anyway. Falling in love with a professional surfer was my mistake. Just seems like my heart never gets the memo. Or, when it does get it, lights it on fire. We've already talked about getting the divorce proceedings out of the way as soon as this is done."

Quentin's nod was slow and full of understanding. "You've gotta do what's right for you. I trust y'all to figure it out, I really do. But as the person who was there for most of your relationship, I'll just say that you two were the most passionate and impulsive couple I have ever seen. Heck, you got married in Vegas on a whim because you'd had one too many margaritas."

"In my defense, they were stronger than usual."

He smiled, but it was a little sad. "Too much tequila or not, I think it's easy to forget how young you were. How much you'd both overcome in such a short period of time. It never surprised me that a couple with so much love wouldn't handle the threat of loss very well. Yes, you both made mistakes, but it was out of a desire to save one another. That's pretty understandable, don't you think?"

Quentin had been with me through so much.

"Our passion comes with a hardheaded stubbornness, on both sides," I said. "We don't budge. She's not going to stop surfing. And I won't stop living life the way that I do. I've learned that some people can accept loving someone with a job like Serena's. Living with it. I can't."

He sighed with a sheepish smile, then joined me on the couch, handing me the bowl of candy. "Well, I can't say I didn't try. You know I've been Team Get Back Together for years."

I chuckled. "You have not hidden that from me."

He popped a pretzel into his mouth. "But to be clear, the situation sucks."

"It'll be fine," I said firmly. "It's only a little bit of confusion, a little bit of temptation, a few annoying arguments, and possibly stumbling onto a massive corporate cover up. I *told* Marilyn I was bored with my last assignment, and this sure ain't boring."

"You're right about that." He turned on the TV. "You want to watch some of the *Twilight Zone* marathon with me?"

"Fuck yeah," I said.

But for the next few hours, even as I tried to lose myself in TV and good food with Quentin, my confident words tumbled around in my brain like a cruel taunt. I knew I couldn't live with Serena's surfing.

What I wasn't convinced of was my ability to live without her.

The next morning, I was on my porch as the sun rose above the horizon, barefoot and waxing my board. Falco stood off to the side, silent as ever, and I realized it was possible to have a protection agent who really *did* blend into the background.

Not like the giant, broad-shouldered, easy-going man arriving any second now—the one I couldn't stop picking fights with even as I secretly wished he would kiss me.

I sat back on my heels and tuned in to the surf report playing softly from the open front door. *"Good news for everyone competing at the ISC's Big Wave event at Trestles Beach today. Absolutely gorgeous swell already, heights over twenty-five feet just before dawn. I think we're going to see a real bitchin' show."*

Inhaling, I closed my eyes and settled into my body, into my mind. Dora had taught me a visualization years ago that I used before every competition. I imagined the size of each wave, the crystal blue of the water, the crowds on the beach cheering. I pictured the lip, the drop, the curl of the barrel, the cold spray.

I pictured myself winning like I'd promised.

You got lucky at Jaws, and the whole world is going to know it at Trestles.

My fingers flexed against my thighs, but I inhaled again. Exhaled. In the visualization, my arms sliced through the water before I pushed myself up to stand. I felt the board, rough against my feet. The stretch of my arms as they balanced me.

My gut is telling me I'm holding a drive full of bad fucking news.

I opened my eyes, rolled out my neck in irritation, then went back to waxing my board. Even irritated with my ex-husband, I'd still fallen asleep easily, lulled into slumber by the emotionally taxing day.

My dreams, however, woke me often. I couldn't remember what they were about, but the pounding heart, sweaty palms, and dry mouth were signs of anxiety I recognized. I was expected to take pictures and give interviews today for Aerial, but instead of exhilaration I just felt... *conflicted.* Between the flash drive and the infuriating interview with Chase, representing this company didn't feel like a top priority today when, given my contract, it needed to be.

"Ms. Swift?" Falco said. "Mr. McDaniels will be here any second. Is there anything you need before I go?"

I looked up from my board and bit my lip. "I don't think so. Unless you want to tell me any dangers you noticed creeping around my house last night?"

He shook his head. "Quiet as a mouse. No problems. You should be fine for your event."

I didn't really feel fine, but then again, I wasn't sure if Cope had told Falco what was really going on.

"Thank you," I said, standing up and propping my board against the wall. "Will you go home and sleep immediately?"

"Always the plan, ma'am."

Cope's company car turned down my driveway. Instead of acknowledging the butterflies in my stomach, I walked back into the house in search of flip-flops and the bag I'd packed last night. I checked through everything one more time while pretending I wasn't thinking about my ex-husband. Snacks, water, sunscreen, wet suit, life vest, helmet—it was all there, like I'd planned.

The only thing left to do was win.

Bag in hand, I slid on my sandals, stepped out the front door, and froze at the sight of Cope. He stood at the bottom of the stairs, sunglasses off, peering up at me with an expression I couldn't decipher. He wore dark work pants, but his short-sleeved, button-up shirt was linen, and there was already too much bicep on display.

"Good morning, Ms. Swift," he said. The professional edge to his tone subdued those butterflies.

"Hey," I managed.

An awkward tension stretched between us as last night's argument stomped into my brain.

Of course, we're ending our first day working together by rehashing the same fight we had outside the gym.

Cope and I had stubborn streaks so similar that apologizing wasn't something either of us did well. But I was older now, and we couldn't change the fact that we'd been thrown back together even if we didn't like it.

"Listen," I started to say just as he said, "About last night."

We both stopped talking. Cope raked a hand through his hair then leaned against the railing. "Before we pick up where we left off last, can I suggest a truce? Between your competition today and discussing scandalous corporate secrets, it feels like we need to focus."

I pursed my lips. "I didn't hear an apology in there, right?"

"Didn't hear one from you either."

Our stare-down continued, and I already knew this was a lost cause, just like every other circular argument we had in the months before we broke up.

"Given our urgent and bizarre circumstances," I said, "I accept the truce. Maybe we can keep our fights to when you're off the clock."

I despised how disappointed I felt at my own suggestion, knew that I was really craving *intimacy* between the two of us, even if it came in the form of pushing each other's buttons.

It was a craving I couldn't indulge.

His lips twitched, but then he said, "I accept the terms and conditions."

I made the mistake of catching his gaze and the full force of yearning blazing there. I would have offered to shake on our reprieve but couldn't trust my hands not to seek more of him when I needed to seek *less*.

I carried my surfboard under my arm and made my way to Cope's car, giving him a wide berth. He'd installed a rack on top, and it was obvious by the minor dents and scratches it was the same rack we used four years ago. For most of our relationship, we'd driven around in my old pink van, which took us on camping trips and road trips and to competitions up and down the coast.

About a month in, he'd picked me up for dinner in his car, and the surfboard rack had gleamed brand-new. It had been a small gesture, yet his acceptance of who I was in the face of his own loss had meant the world to me.

He had apparently never given it away.

"Thanks for the rack," I said.

"It's really no big deal. I had a few things lying around," he said with a nonchalance that sounded forced.

Pressed onto my tiptoes, I slid my board on top and strapped the front end down while Cope took care of the back.

I couldn't linger on the ease of our movements here or the way the nostalgia thawed our awkwardness. As I began pulling the final strap down, I sensed his nearness just as my hand slipped and dropped the strap. The board shifted fast toward my head. Cope's arms bracketed my shoulders as he caught the board and yanked the strap taut.

I blew out a startled gasp but managed not to fall back against his broad chest. His breath stirred the strands of my hair, and his body heat was sultry on my bare skin.

"Here I am, saving your face from a surfboard again," he said mildly. But I could hear the smile in his voice, and the relief I felt was as confusing as it was annoying.

"I had the situation under control," I said. His palms rested on the car, boxing me in. The tip of his nose passed through my hair *almost* imperceptibly. My body was responding in ways that had lain dormant without him. I didn't dare turn around, didn't dare shatter this different kind of truce, the one born from our wild and passionate attraction.

"You feel ready for today, right?" he asked. The consideration in his voice was almost too much.

"Absolutely," I said. "More than ready. Ready to win."

I studied his hands, splayed on the car in front of me. The size of his palms, the strength in his fingers.

"Did you do all of your pre-competition rituals?"

A rush of arousal had me light-headed. "Not all of them."

I watched his fingers flex against the door, heard the hitch in his breathing, its slight increase. I didn't want to know if he was reliving the memories of our favorite ritual, the one where I'd wake up at dawn and have him bring me to the slowest, tenderest orgasm to soothe my nerves and clear my head. I'd wrap my hands around our headboard as a sleepy-eyed, rough-voiced Cope kissed his way to my pussy and lavished my clit with his tongue. I'd gaze down to see my hips rolling, his head between my legs, those fingers gripping my thighs.

There was no better way to remember that I was born to conquer those waves like a queen.

It was only later, *after* the competition, that I'd drag him back into our bedroom and let the surge of addicting adrenaline seduce us into the filthy, sweaty, hair-pulling sex that was our specialty.

His mouth brushed once through my hair before he whispered, "That's a shame."

And then he stepped away, rounding the car before I could do something stupid and beg him to take me right here, just like this, consequences be damned.

I did climb into the front seat, which was *definitely* not a smart idea. We needed additional space between us, but I was much too concerned with Quentin's thoughts on the flash drive. Cope slid behind the steering wheel slowly, brow lifted. "The protocol is that the client sits in the back so they can ignore me and yell at their assistants on the phone."

"I'm going to guess you don't potentially uncover corporate secrets with all of your clients, right?"

He twisted around in his seat, arm leveraged against my chair as he navigated backwards out of my driveway. "Was it naive of me to assume a respect of the client-agent relationship would be included under the umbrella of this truce?"

I turned toward the window to avoid his face, drifting so close to mine. His mouth curved up slightly—not a full Cope smile, but I still had to hide my own at the sight of it.

"There's a thermos there for you," he said. "If you want it."

My stomach roiled. "I don't do coffee before competitions. Makes me too nervous."

"It's not coffee," he said. "It's hot water with honey and lemon."

"Oh." I opened the top and inhaled the steam. "You remembered." I curled my fingers around the thermos and pressed the heated cup to my chest, soothing some of my jangling energy. "Thank you."

"Anytime."

Cope took the freeway ramp, heading to Trestles Beach, which was forty miles away.

"So what happened last night with Quentin?" I asked. "Did he have any idea of what's actually going on?"

He glanced at me sideways. "I know the kind of headspace you prefer to be in before a competition. Do you want to talk about this now, or will it only be a distraction?"

"Now," I said firmly. "Not knowing is the distraction." My stomach jumped again. "Besides, no matter what happens on the water today, I have to smile and nod and be their ambassador. I need to know what's going on."

His eyes moved to the rearview mirror before he merged one lane over. "Okay. I went to Quentin's last night with the drive and let him examine what was on it. Right away, he—"

My phone beeped three times. I dug around in my bag until I found it.

"This could be about the competition," I said. "Let me check it."

My words trailed off to a whisper as I read the message on the screen. My already-jumpy stomach twisted again, and goosebumps shivered across my skin.

"Serena, what is it?" Cope asked sharply, sensing my fear.

I stared down at the white message box, positive I was dreaming. "It's... it's from a blocked number. The message says *we know you have it*."

I dropped my phone like it was on fire. Cope cursed beneath his breath.

"What's going on?" I asked in a shaky voice. "And why the hell am I getting messages like *that*?"

Based on body language alone, my ex-husband seemed on the verge of some great action—either he wanted to reach for me with tenderness or hunt down who sent that text with violence.

"Can you read it to me again?" The veins in his forearms stood out as he gripped the steering wheel.

I leaned over the console and tapped my screen. "*We know you have it*. Nothing else."

"Goddammit," he said forcefully. "That message just confirmed my worst fears about this."

"Tell me about last night," I demanded.

The distress on Cope's normally cheerful face was freaking me the hell out.

"Quentin has the drive now and is working on figuring out exactly what it holds or what messages those files were meant to tell someone. He's got a law enforcement contact he's reaching out to today to try and find Catalina, make sure she's safe. And to see if there's any more secret dirt on Aerial the general public doesn't know about. He's taking this very seriously, and whatever it is, we will find out, and we will take the proper steps to do the right thing."

I clutched the thermos and waited for him to continue.

"Quentin and I have good reason to believe that Catalina is a whistleblower. That she either purposefully or accidentally stumbled onto something shady or unethical and was brave enough to steal it and get it out into the public. Or, in this case, into the purse of a professional surfer."

I thought about the dark-eyed woman who'd bumped into me. She'd seemed unusually nervous yet picked up my purse so fast I envied her reflexes.

Maybe *meeting* me wasn't what she was nervous about.

"A whistleblower," I repeated cautiously. "Like... like the woman who brought down Enron?"

"Exactly like that," he said.

He flicked on his turn signal and merged easily into the far-right lane. We drove down the exit and onto the road that led to the beach. A long line of cars was parked haphazardly on the side of the street—spectators and fans here for the event. I spotted surfboards and coolers being carried along with lawn chairs and blankets. Cope didn't need directions to pull into the parking lot.

He'd been to this beach many times with his father.

We parked in the back left of the sandy, palm-tree-lined lot in front of a sign that said *Reserved for Competitor Serena Swift*. Once the engine was off, he did a quick scan of our surrounding environment before turning to face me again.

"Revealing a company's misdeeds takes a lot of planning and courage," Cope said. "Whistleblowers have ended up fired, threatened, forced into hiding." He picked up my phone, glared at the message there. "Some have ended up dead. When Jeffrey Wigand went on *60 Minutes* in the nineties to expose the secret that the tobacco company he worked for was knowingly making their cigarettes more addictive, he was fired, publicly discredited, and harassed. He received death threats. The reason Quentin and I are taking this so seriously is because there's precedent to do so."

I could see surfers gathering on the beach, boards flashing in the air like colorful flowers. I needed to get my head back in the game. And then I needed to go represent a company that was maybe nothing but a cleverly constructed lie.

"I can't believe this is happening," I said, still stunned.

"Not every publicly ethical company is ethical behind closed doors," he said. "I don't want to think it either, trust me. But there's enough evidence and enough of a threat now to be on alert."

My heart pounded so hard I could feel the echo in my fingertips. That only happened when I went over the lip of a wave, although this adrenaline wasn't the positive kind. It was the *fight-or-flight* kind.

"Is this..." I swallowed. "Is this why I can't tell anyone?"

"Yes. Do not tell your brother. Do not tell Dora or your friends. If they're focusing on making you feel scared, they will use any option available to them to get you to return the information they believe you stole."

I scrubbed a hand down my face but nodded, a sick sensation in the pit of my stomach. "Okay, I get it," I said. "We need to protect them. Will you tell Falco and your boss?"

He was quiet for a moment. "I don't think so. Yet. For the same reason you shouldn't tell anyone either. We don't know what they're capable of, and I don't want to risk their safety. But..." He rubbed the back of his neck. "But I can't have Falco out there at night thinking everything is fine either. That puts him in danger—puts you in danger too. I'll figure out a way to express my concerns for your safety while shielding him from the other stuff."

I stared out the window at the familiar and happy scenery all around us. How could I be showing up for my first elite competition while all of *this* was happening?

"We will get through this together," Cope said. "I will do everything in my power to keep you safe, Serena."

There was a husky familiarity in that last sentence that had me leaning closer to my ex-husband. Given both our personalities, fighting a common villain together was practically romantic.

"Why give the information to me though?" I asked with a shrug. "I have absolutely nothing to offer this situation in any way."

"I don't think you realize the influence that you have," he said quietly. "I know the awful shit that's said to you out there, but you have more supporters than detractors. You're strong and outspoken; you believe in doing what's right. You're a professional athlete with money and a platform."

Thinking that Catalina had trusted me—a complete stranger—to do the right thing was a weight I didn't think I could carry. Because I didn't believe I had earned it. Although hadn't I worked hard to gain a platform for issues like this one? No matter what we uncovered, Catalina had risked her job and safety to pass along information that revealed this company was committing harm against people or the planet. Or both.

"Well," I said with a humorless laugh. "I have always wanted the ability to speak out on the issues that matter the most."

"And I told Marilyn that my last assignment was boring. Seems like both our wishes are coming true."

Our eyes met and held for a beat too long, betraying the other, much more complicated wishes we had.

"We should get going," I said quickly, putting on my sunglasses and tightening my ponytail. I pushed open the door and stepped out onto sand and asphalt. The rich thunder of the waves just over the dune reminded me of the other scary things I needed to do today.

My water bottle fell through my fingers. Then my bag, scattering food and my wallet. When I stood back up, I knocked my sunglasses off my nose, and they went flying. But Cope was right beside me. He snatched them from the air before they could fall, then opened his palm so I could retrieve them.

He gently touched the sides of my arms, adjusting my position until we were facing each other.

"Shut your eyes," he said softly.

I did, used to following this command of his. His hands slid onto my shoulders. They squeezed, focusing my attention on every point of contact between his fingers and my skin.

"Breathe with me, okay?" There was no patronizing sympathy in his tone. Only empathy. So I did the next part of this pre-competition tradition of ours: reached up and gripped his wrists, creating a neat square of our arms around me. His pulse beat swiftly against my thumbs.

"Okay," I finally said.

"Inhale for four... three... two..." He trailed off on *one*. Together, we held our breath for four counts. "Now, exhale for four... three... two..."

The tips of his thumbs stroked lightly across my collarbone.

"Again," he said.

We inhaled as one. Held our breath. Exhaled as one. Even with my eyes closed, my body was keenly aware of his tempting closeness. The agonizing nearness of his lips. If I pressed up onto my toes, we'd be kissing.

Our inhales and exhales came evenly, tangled together. My wild thoughts lost some of their jagged points. The nerves in my stomach settled. I recalled the years of my training— every wave and wipeout a teacher. I understood the rhythm of those tides, the patterns of each set, all the intricacies of the ocean.

I *knew* her. She knew me.

With one final, beautiful breath, my eyes flew open. I still gripped his wrists. His fingers were gently working on the knots in my neck, right where I always needed a little extra pressure.

"Does this feel good?" His voice was rough, blue eyes darker.

"Very good," I whispered back.

"How do those lungs feel? Any tightness? Anything sore?"

I inhaled sharply through my nose, picturing my lungs expanding like the sunrise over a canyon, bold and bright.

"No pinching," I reported. "No tightness. No coughing."

"Fingers? Toes?"

"All ten accounted for."

"Arms and legs loose?"

He released me with a crooked grin on his face as I shook my body out like a wet dog. I bounced on my toes, felt my heart rate pick up in response to my carefree movement.

"Loose. Strong. Ready."

Gently, *so* gently, he swiped his thumb across the center of my forehead. "And in here?"

"Calm," I said. "Thanks to you."

He stepped back and let me go. "Who's going to win today, Serena?"

His question shocked a happy, relieved smile onto my face. "I am, of course."

Serena's turn was up in twenty minutes.

She stood with a group of women surfers, all of them cheering for Malia Kim who, based on the crowd's reaction, must have been tearing up some massive waves. Serena appeared loose and relaxed with her friends, and I was grateful for it. No matter what was going on in the background with Aerial, I didn't want any of it to affect the concentration she needed to stay safe out there.

I stood right behind her, sweating under the sun, attempting to ignore the sound of the waves shaking the sand beneath my shiny loafers. The air was heavy with music and the smell of sunscreen, thick with fear and euphoria, nerves and elation. Between the crowd's applause and the roars of the jet skis, it was sensory overload.

Yet the only thing I cared about was Serena, the eye of the storm. In between cheers, she studied the water like it spoke a language only she could decipher.

Being back at a surf competition had me battling two different types of nostalgia—the memories of being here with my mom and sister as my dad competed. And the two years I was with Serena, where I tried to make it to as many as I could even though my feelings about them were *complicated*. But if I skipped them, or couldn't get out of an assignment, I spent those hours clenching my fists so hard in apprehension I carved half-moons into my palms.

Off to the left, I noticed two Aerial employees struggling to unfurl a giant banner with the company's logo on it. Press was out in numbers, and the Lattimore brothers had already given a speech when we first arrived. The threat that Serena received on her phone had me suspicious of every person who dared to *look* at my wife as they walked past—but my protective instincts tripled whenever Dave or Marty jogged into view.

I'd already texted Quentin about the threatening message. He had responded with a quick and poetic *Fuck*.

Murmurs of excitement and awe had broken out when Serena stepped onto the beach carrying her board over her head. Dave and Marty had left her alone so far, only waving as she walked past and yelling out, "Good luck today!" I didn't want them in her head any more than I knew they already were. Even now I caught her sneaking glances at them when she thought I wasn't paying attention.

With a few hugs and one last cheer, Serena stepped back from her friends and began tugging on her life vest and braiding her hair back. I shifted my feet in the sand, cleared my throat to get her attention. "Who's going to win today?"

A smile flickered across her face. "I am."

The tiniest gestures, the most minor traditions, had meant so much to her when we were together. I always suspected it was because her childhood was absent a lot of those things. No one was scrawling *have fun at school today!* on the napkins in her lunch box.

"Those waves are probably shitting themselves right now," I said. "They're all like, 'Serena Swift is coming? You guys better watch out.'"

She yanked a thin but sturdy surfer's helmet down over her hair and fastened it under her chin. "Anyone ever tell you that you do a pretty good impression of ocean waves?"

I shrugged, squinted off into the distance. "Face, hair, body, cartoon impressions. I'm the full package."

She laughed, shaking her head. I was tempted to brush away the strand of hair blowing across her face. But then I caught sight of a tall man with blond hair walking over to us.

"Uh, Serena?" I tugged at my too-tight collar. "Is your brother coming today?"

Her eyes widened. "Wait... you see Caleb?"

I nodded at the upstanding member of society wearing a white polo shirt and khaki pants, looking like he'd stepped off a magazine called *Hotties of the Coast Guard*.

He held his arms wide as he got close to us. "I'm surprising you!"

"*Cale*." She punched his arm with excited laughter before he gave her a bear hug. "I'm so happy to see you."

"I'm off duty on a weekend for the first time in months, so I thought I'd see if I could catch your heat," he said. "And is this the bodyguard Aerial gave you?"

Serena bit her lip. "About that..."

Caleb turned, hand outstretched. "Caleb Swift. I'm—" He paused, shoved his sunglasses up into his hair. "*Copeland?*"

I held up my palms. "Before you punch me, I'm only here in a professional capacity as your sister's protection agent. I didn't—"

But my ex-wife's older brother—once, one of my closest friends—didn't rear back and sucker punch me as I'd expected.

He pulled me in for a bear hug too.

"Um," I said, flustered. He let me go and gave his sister a blatantly bemused expression. She dropped to the sand to give her board one last wipe-down.

"You failed to mention that Cope was the bodyguard assigned to you," he said.

"Eh, I've been busy." She waved at the ocean. "Doing things."

"One text," he said dryly. "*Oh hey, big news. Cope is my body-guard.* Ten seconds, max."

If I thought being at a competition again was bad, watching Serena bullshit with her brother was like being forcibly shoved back in time. There were too many painful aspects to our relationship to name, but the splitting up of our found family was one of them. For two years, Serena and her brother were as prevalent at my mother's dinner table as Quentin was. And then Dora. Once my mother discovered how Serena and her brother had escaped their parents, she made it a point to include them in holidays and weekend barbecues. After we broke up, there had been no animosity towards Serena by my family.

It appeared the same was true for Serena, based on Dora and Caleb's reactions.

"I appreciate you not punching my lights out just now," I said.

He grinned. "There's still time, buddy."

"I'll prepare my face."

We were spared an awkward segue by Serena's friend Prue running up to meet us. "Hey, Caleb, hey, Cope," she said, before turning to Serena. "Fun news. I'm towing you—" She paused, turned back to me, jaw dropped open. I gave her a sheepish shrug.

"Little bit of fun news," Serena repeated, "Aerial wanted to put security on me, and as bad luck would have it, it was Cope."

"Holy shit." Prue pointed between the two of us. "Okay, *all of this,* is getting a deep-dive after you surf. But it's your time, babe. They're calling it in a second, and I'm towing you."

Serena hugged her with a grateful smile. "Thank god. And *thank you.*"

Prue squeezed her hand. "You've got this. Look, your cheer squad is over there, waiting for you to kick ass."

I followed her gaze to the group of women holding various *Go Serena* signs. I recognized Prue's wife, Kalei, and a few other surfers that had just been cheering for Malia. Prue wrapped her arm around Serena's shoulders and squeezed.

"I know you're nervous," she said. "But I'm your tow today, and we're gonna crush it."

Serena's beautiful eyes found mine. I winked at her. "Good luck," I said. Caleb gave her a series of high fives until she was laughing.

"Okay, *okay,* I'm ready to do the damn thing."

Prue checked her safety gear one last time, and then my wife was running into the ocean toward the jet ski.

The audience roared in response. An announcer called Serena's name. Each competitor had twenty minutes of total surf time. Their scores were based on the quality of waves they caught, so each heat wound up being a very delicate combination of skill, courage, opportunity, and random chance.

Caleb and I stood shoulder to shoulder, but the moment her feet hit the waves, I glued my focus to the sand.

"Can I ask if Serena's in any real danger here? Or is Aerial just being extra cautious?" Caleb said.

We know you have it.

"She's in no real danger," I said, feeling uneasy with the

lie, even though it was only to keep him safe. "There's someone posted at her house at night, and then I'm with her during the day. It's so calm it's practically boring."

I glanced sideways at Caleb, who was nodding in appreciation. "Glad to hear it. And I hope it's not awkward to say that I'm glad it's you. I trust you."

My eyebrows shot up. "Still?"

"Yeah, *still*. I won't ever speak for my sister, so I'll speak for myself. I know your breakup was complicated, but I also know you do not have a malicious bone in your body. It's not my place, not really, but between you and me..." He slapped me square in the back. "I've really missed you, buddy. I didn't think I'd ever see you again, but I always hoped I would."

"Are you trying to lull me into a false sense of complacency before really punching me in the face?" I asked.

Caleb shrugged. "Only time will tell, I guess."

I laughed, shaking my head. I didn't think about the complications of what we'd learned last night or the very real distraction of my feelings for Serena. I just told my friend the truth.

"I've really missed you too," I said. "*Really* missed you. Quentin has too."

"Well," Caleb said, indicating the ocean. "Maybe after... I don't know. We'll see?"

There was a sincere optimism in his voice that made my chest ache. "I like the sound of that."

The hum of the jet ski tore through the crowd, and I could hear murmuring and movement around us, all the signs of anticipation. I took a step back from Caleb to examine the parking lot, spy on the Lattimore brothers, and scope out anything suspicious. When I turned back, I glued my eyes back to the sand again.

Caleb nudged my arm. "You still do that, huh?"

"What?" I asked casually.

"Watch the sand and not Serena when she surfs?"

I pushed my sunglasses up to look at Caleb, surprised. "You know?"

His expression was filled with empathy. "I noticed you doing it the few times we've watched her compete together."

I winced. "It's a bad habit I can't break."

"Given what happened to your dad," he said. "I'd say it makes sense to me. You don't want to be watching if the worst happens, right?"

He was exactly right. Not once in the two years and hundreds of times I'd been on the beach while Serena was in the water, did I *ever* watch her surf. The crowd's reaction told me when she did well, and even though I didn't watch her, it still made me prouder than anything to hear strangers chant her name. It was only later, when she was safe in my arms again, that I could watch the videos of her taped performances.

Knowing the outcome made it a hell of a lot easier.

It never stopped me from wondering if I was missing something vital though, shielding myself from a crucial element of Serena herself. And she never knew that I watched the sand instead of her. Revealing it felt like a betrayal.

"I don't know how you do it," I admitted. "How you watch her on waves that dangerous and unpredictable."

Caleb grimaced at whatever he was seeing.

"What is it?" I asked.

"She's fine," he said. "She just bailed on a wave at the last second. Either her instincts told her to, or she got nervous, which isn't really like her."

My own instincts told me it was the latter and that it had something to do with the crunchy-granola assholes behind us.

"But to answer your question, I think it all goes back to being there with her from the very beginning, seeing her at twelve on that board like she was born to do it. And even after my training with the Coast Guard, and all the years I've spent in that same ocean, my little sister is *still* more at ease than half of the rescue divers I work with. Not because they're bad. Because she's *that* good. My job asks me to understand tragedy and the ocean's very fickle nature. So I know I can't predict accidents. I can, however, trust that she knows what she's doing out there."

Dora had said something similar back at the pool. All those arguments, when I was terrified something bad would happen to her while surfing, did she feel like I didn't trust her? Because nothing could have been further from the truth. But it certainly would explain her frustrations with me.

The crowd started the early rumblings of a cheer that then dissolved into sounds of disappointment. I didn't even have to ask.

"She bailed again," Caleb said. "I think it might be nerves."

I peered discreetly over my shoulder at Marty Lattimore. He didn't seem fazed by Serena's performance. He was talking excitedly with a group of people, hands on his hips like he was about to lead them on a field expedition.

"I worry... I *worried* about her, constantly," I said.

"Me too," Caleb replied. "I've learned that you can worry about someone while trusting them at the same time. It's not easy, but it's possible."

I peered up from the sand to find Caleb watching me.

"I taught my sister every single thing I learned in my training. And everything she learned, she taught me. We know that water, the sheer power of it, and we respect it. Always."

I nodded and squeezed his shoulder. "I know you do. And I know she does too."

As he turned his attention back to his sister, I risked

another glance behind me. Marty was now studying the water, where Serena was, and he did *not* look friendly.

It was quick—only for a moment and concealed just as fast.

But Marty had stared at Serena like he absolutely hated her.

$\maltese$ 19 $\maltese$

SERENA

Prue was towing me toward the next set, about two minutes out, situated over a deep, cold channel. It was why this part of Trestles Beach could sustain monster waves that frequently measured thirty feet and often higher.

I was sprawled on the back of my board with my fingers wrapped tight around the handle that tethered me to Prue's jet ski. With the waves as heavy and unpredictable as they were, towing out was the safest way to make it past the break without tiring your arms while paddling.

I was going to need every ounce of strength I had. I'd already bailed on the first two waves and by my own count had less than nine minutes remaining on my heat.

We raced through the water, Prue instinctively heading alongside the barrels starting to form. I was so happy she was the one behind that engine right now—trust in this situation was paramount, but so was communication. I knew she'd understand when I wanted to let go and when I wanted to bail. The seconds that existed between making those two choices were precious, and I needed her to act quickly every time.

The wave approaching us was smooth and glassy and curling up fast. Prue gunned it as we hit a patch of bumpy water, and I held on tight to keep from flying off. That smooth wave became a wall of water, and for a fleeting second, I thought I was going to have to fall off my board and dive beneath it.

But Prue hit the curve hard, whipping me behind her, and suddenly I was angled just shy of ninety degrees. My stomach dropped and a cold sweat broke out on my skin. It wasn't that I hadn't paddled right up the face of a wave before. It was that you had to nail the timing *just right* if you didn't want the lip of the wave to catch you and send you tumbling over backwards.

The few times that had happened to me had been some of my most terrifying wipeouts. To free-fall into a churning ocean and *then* have the wave crash down on you and *then* have the force of it whip you up and around like a rag doll wasn't an experience I wanted to relive.

"*Go, go, go,*" I yelled at Prue. I knew not to look behind me and see how high above the water we were. Her ski broke the top of the wave, and I joined her a second after, and then we were rocketing in front of a freshly curling barrel.

If there was a time for me to go, it was now. I caught her head turn slightly, a nonverbal question of *yes?* I was going to miss it if I didn't pull the trigger, but my mind was stuck on an anxious spin cycle.

You got lucky at Jaws, and everyone's gonna know it at Trestles.
This bitch can't surf for shit.
We know you have it.

I forced out an angry breath and went to push up. Prue was clearly waiting for me, holding us in front of the wave while I was indecisive.

"*Go,*" I yelled again, waving my hand so she could see it. She revved up fast so I could use her momentum.

I looked down.

I shouldn't have.

Most surfers, myself included, had a respect for heights, a deep fascination with how high you could go. It wasn't that I didn't feel fear—though that was often speculated about extreme athletes—it was that I understood the difference between healthy apprehension and your gut telling you *don't do it.*

Because we were too high, the angle too steep, and if my board went over that ledge, there was no doubt in my mind I'd be nosediving into the water.

In the mayhem and doubt, I'd let go of the handle. Now I reached so far, I almost fell off my board, balanced on the edge of a thirty-foot wave. I screamed for Prue. Through sheer luck, my fingers closed around the leather and held, but I almost plunged over.

She turned, saw me, and immediately corrected, driving us away from an oncoming set through a spray of harsh white water. When she stopped, she twisted around in her seat.

"Are you okay?" she yelled.

I nodded, gave a thumbs-up. Talking was impossible out here. It was too loud. But I gave her the universal *keep going* hand gesture.

She waited a beat, probably to see if I'd change my mind. But then we were back and racing towards the next set. I wasn't sure how much time I'd lost on that last wave— *goddammit*—and I needed to catch at least one to not be a total embarrassment. The next set seemed decent. The barrels weren't as tall or as clean, but they would have to do.

We dashed up and over the first wave as the second one began forming. She dragged me along the foamy edge and *this* time, I allowed myself to think of Cope.

Cope, laughing with me on our bed. Kissing me beneath the shower spray. Gazing at me in that Vegas wedding chapel as I said, "I do."

"Go, go, go," I yelled, letting go for real this time. The water was already frothy as I pushed up with steady hands and went right over the lip.

There was nothing in the world like going over the edge of a twenty-five-foot wave. The tip of my board slid down a steep side of water, and the sting of the spray slapped my face.

Balanced on light feet, I dropped all the way down the face with the roar of a steam engine in my ears. I could sense the barrel starting to curl over me as the force of the water propelled me twenty, thirty miles an hour. Grinning, my fingers trailed through the water as my heart slammed hard in my chest, and every muscle of my body worked to keep me upright.

To my left, the wave started to break, sending up more spray. All I could see was the dark blue of the barrel and the white foam. My feet wobbled, my board wobbled, but then the wave shot me clean through the end as whitewater crashed alongside me.

San Diego's bright blue sky hurtled into my vision as my velocity eased, and I arced my board away from the rest of the wave. I hailed Prue, already on her way, and dropped cleanly into the ocean. I only submerged for a second—anything longer wasn't safe—but I popped up, wiped the salt from my eyes. She pulled up a few moments later.

"You're a bad bitch, Serena Swift," she yelled with a grin. I whooped, grabbed hold of the handle, and let her haul me all the way to shore. I was out of breath but totally wired, and my body was pumping so much adrenaline through my veins I could have stayed out there for hours. Instead, we coasted up easy onto the sand. A few competition assistants grabbed my board for me, and I threw my arm around Prue's shoulders as she jumped off the ski. I kissed her cheek, and she laughed.

"Did you see it?" I asked, out of breath.

"No, but I'm guessing Kalei did."

A whirl of motion with black hair almost knocked me back into the water.

"*You were amazing,*" Kalei squealed. Then she kissed her wife properly on the lips. "And *you* were queen of the jet skis."

She pressed a cell phone into my still shaking hands. Kalei leaned down and pressed *Play*. I saw a very, very tiny version of myself paddle fast, press up. I went over the wave like it was second nature, looking strong. Powerful. I disappeared into the barrel, and it was shocking seeing such a heavy curtain of water hide me from the world but still protect me in the end.

There was a bright burst of white foam, and then there I was, crouched low and holding the edge of my board. The camera flipped around, revealing Kalei jumping in the air and screaming with a group of our friends.

My hand flew to my mouth, eyes filling with rare tears of relief. And when I scanned the small collection of onlookers waiting for us on the beach, it wasn't my friends or even my brother that I searched for desperately.

Cope stood frozen in his formal bodyguard position. He lifted his sunglasses slowly. A charming smile appeared on his face.

I returned it.

SERENA

An hour later, after Caleb, Prue, and Kalei left, I stood next to Cope and waited for the judges to announce the winner of the women's big wave competition. Despite the threats and secrets and scandal happening in the background of this day, my most pressing concern was whether I won.

The competition judge grabbed for the microphone at the podium and began announcing the first, second, and third place winners. Malia Kim, a mentor of mine, took first place, and two good friends received the others. I jumped up and down with joy, cheering their names and clapping before I realized that my name hadn't also been called.

Turns out, I didn't win.

Not even close.

I came in seventh.

My phone buzzed, and I was instantly cautious. But it was only Dora with a message: *You did a great job, kid, and I'm really proud of you.*

I smiled and pressed the phone over my heart, appreciating her kindness amid the chaos. Once, a few months after she and a lawyer friend helped me with my emancipation, I'd admitted to her that my parents never said they were proud of anything Caleb and I had done. I was barely fifteen and told her it didn't matter to me, that I'd have to learn to be proud of myself if no one else was.

Shortly after, she made it a point to share her pride in anything and everything that I did, no matter how small.

And I learned that it did matter to me.

I turned it on at the gym and watched it with the regulars, her next text read. *They couldn't stop talking about how incredible you were.*

I blinked down at the screen, my racing thoughts finally catching up. That's right. It wasn't only the spectators in the audience who had seen me bail on wave after wave because I was too in my head. It wasn't just supporters either. Men like Kyle and Chase, who doubted my talents and abilities, had also seen it or would read about it tomorrow. The people who'd written nasty YouTube comments, the famous surfers who'd declared me reckless and undeserving. Even Aerial had proclaimed me *the surfer to watch* and thrown a giant spotlight on my face for all to see.

And I had lost.

I had certainly held my own during my first elite event, surfing alongside some of the best women big wave surfers in the world, people I admired, who had mentored me on my journey. Seventh place should have felt like a badge of honor.

Instead, I only felt a surge of failure, a spike of embarrassment, and then, finally, anger.

I dropped my phone back into my bag as a dull fury coursed through me. Although this time I was mad at *myself.* Mad at my own distraction and self-doubt out there. Mad that I hadn't trusted my own skill, that I'd let the opinions of others dictate my success.

Cope's arm brushed against mine. He'd stood next to me

—silent and still—during the whole ceremony. Now, he leaned down and whispered, "Would you like me to punch the ocean in the face for you, Ms. Swift?"

It startled a grateful laugh out of me. "Thank you, but the ocean wasn't the problem this time. It was me."

He cleared his throat, drawing my attention to his pensive expression. "I know it isn't scientifically accurate, but my dad used to say that some days the ocean just hated your fucking guts."

"He used to say that?" I asked, delighted. Cope was always deliberate about which memories he shared of his father. Each reveal was meaningful.

"Oh, yeah. It would make me and Billie laugh and laugh to hear him come home and say, 'Well, I don't know what I did to piss the ocean off, but she gave me the worst waves and pushed me right off my board.'" He very gently nudged my shoulder with his. "Sounds like you must have flirted with the ocean's boyfriend or something. She gave you *all* the worst waves."

My ire cooled down a little, and my shoulders relaxed. "In my defense, her boyfriend is very cute."

"Don't let *her* hear you say that," he said with a wink.

Marty and Dave appeared in my line of sight so abruptly I startled back an inch. Only Cope's steady hand kept me from falling.

"Serena," Dave said. "Nicely done out there. Just a beautiful performance."

I opened my mouth to answer, but nothing came out. Their posture was relaxed and happy, which only upped the weirdness of the moment. The cold truth of what Cope told me earlier and the threat of that text message tied my stomach into hard knots.

Not every publicly ethical company is ethical behind closed doors.

"Thank you. I appreciate that," I managed.

Marty touched my elbow, and I felt—rather than saw—Cope's hackles go up. "And it's really okay that you didn't win. We're investing in you as a person, a champion for change. Medals will come and go."

I swallowed thickly. That was a nice thing to say. But I no longer believed these brothers were nice.

"That's very true," I said. I took another step backward until Cope's palm steadied me again.

Dave rubbed his hands together. "Exciting news. While you were surfing, officials called The Wedge for two days from now."

My jaw dropped. "In two *days*?"

He nodded. "They say the perfect waves will be firing in forty-eight hours. And we know Aerial's newest ambassador is going to crush it."

The waves at The Wedge were famous for their peaked shape, formed by the rock jetty that caused huge sets of water to converge into steep, sharply pointed pinnacles.

They were gorgeous. They were highly erratic. And they created a powerful backwash that could suck a person back into the break if they didn't swim their way free or sink below the surge.

The timing sucked though. My body usually needed more than just a day of rest. But we were surfers, beholden to the weather and forever bound to our god: the surf report.

"I'll certainly try," I said. "And you two will be there as well?"

"We wouldn't miss it," Marty said. "Plus we'd like to do a more formal press conference about the Barcelona Olympics at The Wedge, have you there doing more interviews."

"*Speaking of,*" Dave continued. "Before you go greet those adoring fans, let's get you in front of the local Channel Six news for a quick taped interview. You good? You feel ready? Do you need anything? Water?"

Marty and Dave peppered me with questions as Cope and I, dazed, followed them to a reporter and camera man standing beneath the Aerial company banner.

"It's okay, I'm fine," I said slowly, even as my thoughts were a jumbled mess of confusion and resentment. Was I about to represent a company that *lied?* And what did it mean that I was their new spokeswoman?

But there wasn't a second to dig my heels in or hesitate. The Lattimore brothers shoved me in front of a microphone before I'd even caught my breath.

The reporter was a younger woman with light tan skin and short, curly black hair. "Serena Swift? I'm Rosa Hernández with Channel Six news. This is a taped interview we'll be doing with Dave and Marty, so if you mess up don't worry. We'll be editing this for time either way."

I tucked a strand of hair back into my high ponytail and hoped that I appeared somewhat presentable. "It's nice to meet you. I'll try not to mess up too badly."

She pursed her lips but didn't respond, touching her earpiece. She nodded at whoever was speaking to her, and then her face lit up with an easy-going smile. "We're here today with hometown heroes David and Marty Lattimore, the founders of Aerial, and their new ambassador, pro surfer Serena Swift." The mic flew right back to me. "Serena, you did *not* win, even though you were favored to by a lot of people here today. How does that feel?"

My eyebrow arched of its own accord before I reigned in my original response. "I wanted to win, of course, especially since Aerial is doing so much for my career. But I was up against some incredible athletes today, so it was really an honor just to compete alongside them."

"And what did it mean to you, being on those giant waves today?" she asked.

I smiled. "It means everything to see the ISC recognize

that women deserve to be surfing the biggest waves, that we're as talented as men, if not better. For much too long, we've been forced into the shadows, ignored by the—"

Dave clapped his hands together sharply, and I stopped talking, all of us turning at the sound.

"You know," he said. "We chose Serena because of her passion and her spirit, and that was evident on the water today. It's not always about winning; it's about what you, as a person, stand up for. What change do you want to see, and how will you bring it about?"

My eyes narrowed for a second. "I couldn't agree more. Raising awareness of gender inequality is the *most*—"

"Serena, do you want to go sign some autographs?" Marty asked. "Oh, and so sorry, Rosa, but you can edit this out, correct?"

"Of course," she said. "We've probably got enough sound bites from Serena. We can move on to your portion of the interview if you'd like."

"We'd love it," Dave chimed in. "Does that work for you, Serena? Sorry again for the change-up. I'm just noticing that the crowd is getting a bit restless, waiting for you."

The brothers faced me with matching folksy smiles of appreciation as if they hadn't interrupted me, twice, while I was trying to express myself. They were amenable and soft-spoken, making it hard to pinpoint the bullshit wrapped in sincerity.

"Are you sure?" I asked, with my own folksy smile. "I've got plenty to say on a lot of issues, as you're well aware."

"We're sure," Dave said with a subtle edge in his tone and a flash of irritation in his eyes.

We know you have it.

My stomach roiled again. "Sounds like a plan. I'll be over there signing autographs. Rosa, it was lovely to meet you."

The moment I turned and left them, heading towards the

small crowd of fans, Cope dipped his mouth to my ear. "Seems like both brothers are assholes, right?"

I cast him a sideways *you could say that again* look but we were swept into a swarm of people a second later without time to debrief. I was actually grateful for Cope's security presence. He was a natural at handling the crowd respectfully while making sure I was able to greet every person. I autographed surfboards and hats and took cute selfies with fans.

And the back of my neck prickled with unease the entire time.

Just as I was wrapping up, I felt a tug on the bottom of my shirt. A tiny girl surfer stood with her parents, staring up at me with sand still in her dark brown hair.

I grinned and sank to my heels to put us on eye level. "Hey there."

"Are you Serena Swift?" she asked.

"I sure am," I said, holding out my hand. She shook it with a giant *I can't believe this is happening* smile. "What's your name?"

"Luisa," she said proudly. "I'm a surfer. I'm in surf school right now."

"Right on." I gave her a high five. "You're starting way earlier than I did. That means, by the time you're *my* age, your technique will be even better."

"You think so?"

I squinted up at Cope. "What do you think?"

He dropped down, mimicked my pose with his elbows propped on his knees. "Miss Serena knows everything there is to know about surfing. So if she says you're going to be better than her, she means it."

I cocked a thumb at his face. "He's right."

"I'm already better than the boys," she boasted, then peered at Cope and said, "Sorry."

I hid a smile. "And don't you forget it."

"And I *suck* at surfing," he said. "So I already know you're better than me."

"He's really bad."

"She laughs at me every time I try to pick up her surfboard," he added.

"Is he your boyfriend?" Luisa's tone made it clear she would find having a boyfriend exasperating.

"He's my bodyguard," I said quickly. "He keeps me safe from mean people."

"Oh, okay," she said, sounding wise beyond her years.

"I surf down at La Jolla most mornings." I looked up at her mom and dad. "If she ever wants to join us, please bring her along. Just message me on Instagram?"

"*Thank you*," mouthed her dad.

"It's no problem, really," I said, turning my focus back to her. "You're going to be a force to be reckoned with, Luisa."

"I'll try my best," she said, extremely seriously.

As soon as we said goodbye, and finally made it to the parking lot, I was dead on my feet. I couldn't see Dave or Marty anymore, but I was too exhausted to be concerned or afraid.

"Can we go?" I said to Cope on a giant yawn.

"Absolutely."

The assistants had already secured the board to the top of Cope's car, so I threw my bag in the back and leaned against the side door for support, rubbing my eyes. Yawned again.

I blinked, and Kyle was suddenly standing there. Technically he was ambling across the lot in his board shorts with a towel over one shoulder. But when he spotted me, his arrogant smirk made my skin crawl.

"Whatever you want, Kyle. I'm already over it." I sighed. "Can you go?"

"Hey, Swifty," he drawled. "Sure was fun watching you

choke out there today. Didn't know they'd turned the women's heat into amateur hour."

I flipped him the double bird. "My two middle fingers should sum up my thoughts on that."

His smirk turned mean. "I told you people would know the truth. You got lucky at Jaws and sure as shit aren't ready for the ISC level." He shrugged. "I mean, we all just saw it, right?"

He took a step closer into my personal space.

Cope appeared from behind with a smirk. His hand hit Kyle's chest as he pinned him easily to the car door. Kyle's eyes went wide as he took in Cope's much taller, much bulkier form. "Kyle, is it?"

"Who the hell are you?" he asked in a small voice.

"I'm Ms. Swift's personal security, and I *believe*, if I'm reading her gestures correctly, she gave you the universal one to *fuck off*. And yet here you are, not fucking off. Do you see why I might be upset?"

Kyle squirmed beneath Cope's hand. "I can walk wherever I want, bro."

Cope appeared to ponder this for a second. "Yeah, that's not true, actually. Because as long as I'm around, you can't walk near Ms. Swift. Especially if she's already politely asked you to leave her alone." He lowered his face to Kyle's. "And if you bother her again, I will take great pleasure in feeding your face to a pelican. That hungry looking bastard over there in particular." He released him with a smile. "Now fuck off."

Kyle shuffled away, releasing a string of expletives directed at us both, but it gave me great, *great* pleasure to have witnessed that exchange.

"Bye, bro!" Cope called after him.

He opened the door, and I climbed into the passenger seat with a grateful and exhausted *"Thank you."*

I bunched up my sweatshirt against the window, slipped

off my sandals, and curled into the best sleeping position I could manage. Cope had witnessed this transformation hundreds of times before, so as he climbed inside, he gave me an understanding nod.

"You need anything?" he asked softly. "You feel okay, right? Nothing hurts?"

"I want my bed and to eat a million cheeseburgers," I said, yawning again. His answering grin awakened the butterflies in my stomach.

"As you wish," he said. I let my eyelids close, then heard him whisper, "Creepy son of a bitch."

I sat straight up. "What is it?"

Marty was waving at us from directly in front of the car.

"Oh, fuck," I said, sinking back against the seat and rubbing my face. Cope rolled down his window and gestured Marty over.

"Did you need to talk to Serena, sir? I was just driving her home."

It was easy to read the lines of my ex-husband's body language. Tight jaw, rigid spine, fingers clutching the wheel.

"Hi there." Marty waved at me.

I waved back, weakly. "Is everything okay? I finished signing autographs and figured it was fine to head out."

"Oh, of course," he said, friendly as ever. "I just wanted to ask if you wouldn't mind swinging by the offices tomorrow morning? We've got some mock-ups of the *Heavy* article to review with you, and I'd love to get your opinion on a few things."

I shrugged. "Sure, that should be fine."

"Great, great, great." He patted the door, looked between the two of us. The hairs on the back of my neck rose up again. "I hate to ask you guys this, honestly it's *so* embarrassing, but you really haven't come upon any work files of ours, have you? Not in your bag or your car or somewhere in your house?"

I didn't like the look in his eyes when he said *your house.*

"No, sir," Cope said evenly. "Falco and I have been with Ms. Swift every day, and we've seen nothing come up."

"Drat," Marty said. "Well, okay then. We're trying to turn over every stone, so I'm sorry for asking you twice."

He was already turning away when I leaned across the console. "Is Catalina feeling better?"

He paused mid-step. "You know, she's still sick. Has a nasty bug, it seems." Marty waved again as he started back to the beach. "Hopefully, it's not going around."

Cope rolled up the window, and we both watched silently until Marty disappeared from view.

❧ 21 ❧

COPE

I stood outside Serena's house on high alert.

When we finally arrived home, I'd shaken a very cute sleeping Serena awake. Bleary-eyed, she watched me silently as I checked and double-checked every lock, window, door, and shadowy corner. Then I checked it again. I knew as soon as I left she was going to soak in a hot bath then nap—it was what her body required of her after every event. It was like watching a machine finally shut down to rest.

I tried *not* to think about the third thing on that list of what she needed—it came after her nap and before she gorged herself on food.

Serena shoved me back onto the bed, sending the pillows flying to the ground. "You're not too tired?" I asked, then immediately lost the ability to speak. She reached down for the hem of the short dress she'd slept in and lifted it over her head. She was gloriously naked, tan and freckled, and she crawled up my body like a wet dream come true.

She was never too tired, and I learned to stop asking and start enjoying what would inevitably be some of the hottest sex of my life. The combination of our love and lust, plus her reaction to adrenaline and danger, *always* left us slick with sweat and covered in bite marks and scratches.

A car rolled down the street above her driveway. This was the third one in the past hour, but it was that time of night, and Serena said her neighborhood had quite a bit of traffic.

I still recorded it though. I scoured Falco's logs from his night shifts and came up empty—no footsteps or flashlights or strange sounds. That should have been relieving, but ever since Serena had placed that drive in my hand, my instincts had been shouting different versions of *this is wrong*.

And that was before she'd received her first threatening message.

When Quentin called a few minutes later, I picked up on the first ring. "Howdy."

"How'd it go today with Serena?" he asked, fingers clicking away on a keyboard in the background. "Everything work out?"

I stepped out into the front yard, where I had a better view of the whole house and its various entrances. "Not really. Serena received that message early this morning. Our buddy Marty found us in the car as we were leaving and asked if she'd come to his office tomorrow for a meeting. Before he left, he asked if we'd *stumbled upon* the missing files he'd mentioned. And told us Catalina was still out sick."

"Ah," Quentin said. "My guess is that Marty suspects the information has gone missing on purpose but has no clue where it ended up."

"And they'll try various threatening tactics to see what shakes loose," I added. "Serena probably isn't even the only person they suspect."

"You're gonna stay with her during that meeting, right?"

"I'm not leaving her alone with that creepy fuck." I glanced over my shoulder at the trees that bordered the property. "He and his brother remind me of Gary Duncan."

There was a pause on the other end. "I'm sorry, *who?*"

I repeated Gary's name and waited.

"Hell, Cope," he drawled. "That ain't good."

"It's their endless friendly energy paired with Aerial's uncorrupted reputation. They're like happy drones. I can't put my finger on it, but it *feels* like they're hiding something behind their cheerful mission statement. Before the incident, I studied Gary for hours every day, for six straight months, *searching* for signs that he was a real human being and not just a nice teddy bear in a fancy suit. Cracks in the veneer or an imperfection. He never snapped; he never raised his voice. He was respectful and kind."

"And he was actively in business with this city's most dangerous criminals," Quentin added.

"Yeah, and not by mistake. This wasn't a story of a nice man getting in over his head. Gary was a criminal mastermind." I rubbed the back of my neck, still uneasy. "Is it too much of a leap to say I think the Lattimore brothers might be similar?"

I watched the lights in Serena's windows flicker on behind her curtains, from upstairs to downstairs. She was probably waking from her nap. I checked my watch—I was off duty in an hour.

"Not at all, especially after you hear what I've found out so far," he said. "Those pictures and names all belong to quality control inspectors in Arizona, tasked with monitoring factories in the state and ensuring they're adhering to strict safety guidelines and working conditions. Aerial's well known for making their products in the US using fair trade practices and paying higher wages. In fact, that allows them to up-charge the customer to cover the cost of doing things ethically."

I rubbed the back of my neck again. Spun around once in the driveway but still didn't see anything. Or anyone. "That's a very intriguing angle. Maybe they're hiding something at those factories."

"My thoughts exactly. I've got a few reporter buddies in Phoenix, so my first step is to get one of these fine folks pictured on this drive to give me some anonymous information."

"You think that'll work?" I asked.

"I think I've gotta try," he said. "And I'm talking with Joey tomorrow. My law enforcement contact. I want to see what he can get me on David Lattimore, the city councilmembers, and any dirt on company fraud in the city. He's already started the search for Catalina but hasn't found her yet."

I slipped my hand into my pocket, nodding along. "Can you come over tomorrow night to Serena's place? It'll have to be after Falco's shift starts, so I'll need to sneak back into the house before he catches me. But if things start moving fast, I want us all on the same page."

"Of course," he said. "Send me anything else you find out. And be careful at that meeting tomorrow."

"They can't know we have it," I said firmly.

"Good thing you're the best bodyguard the world has ever seen."

"Just need my boss to see that," I said with a grin. "Call me if you get freaked. Check that your doors are locked three times."

"Already on it, my friend."

The front door opened, and golden light spilled from the kitchen. Serena stood in the doorway, hair wild and loose, wearing a Sublime band tee-shirt she'd had since high school and a pair of running shorts. She looked content and wide awake. I could hear reggae music coming from the speakers in the living room.

"Do you want one?" She held out a Pacifico. "I can see you

pacing back and forth from inside. At least come in where you can be worried and have a beer at the same time."

I hesitated. "I'm still on the clock."

"What if I promise not to tell on you?"

I walked to the front door already knowing that being around Serena turned me into a damned fool. But there was no denying in this moment that I wanted it—wanted the warm lights of *our* house, wanted to drink a beer at *our* kitchen table, laughing with the woman I wanted most of all.

I took the beer she offered and brought it to my lips. "If you do tell on me, I'll get in trouble. Just keep that in mind."

I slipped past her and tugged open the first few buttons of my shirt.

"I'm pretty sure you've always *been* trouble," she said. Grabbing her own beer, she hauled herself onto the island, bare legs dangling. She held my gaze as she drank, her dark eyes bright with mischief. I recognized her reaching for comfort here—it had been an exhausting, scary, and confusing day, and with the music and the alcohol, it felt like a stress relieving reset.

But this wasn't any reset after a hard day. *This* moment had the markings and texture of our married life, so similar my head swam with déjà vu. She must have felt it too, setting her drink down as our eyes stayed leashed together. Years of unfulfilled yearning hung heavy in the air between us.

The knock at the door startled us both. I held my hand out and a finger to my lips.

"Cope, don't worry, it's—"

I cracked the door open half an inch. "Oh."

"—just our food," she finished. Sliding off the island, she stepped in front of me, tipped the delivery guy, and returned with a white bag smelling like heaven itself. With a sly grin, she pulled a Styrofoam container out and handed it over.

"For me?"

"Yeah, for you," she said, laughing a little. "It's to say thank you. For everything that you did for me today. You helped me focus. You threatened to punch the ocean in the face when I lost. And then I got to see you tell Kyle, who I *fucking hate*, that you planned on feeding his face to a pelican."

I tried not to laugh but couldn't stop myself. "It was certainly one of my more *inspired* threats."

I flipped open the Styrofoam and saw my favorite burger from my favorite restaurant. "Serena. You didn't."

"Oh, I did."

She was back up on the island, legs crossed, eating French fries. I wanted to kiss her for a million years.

"So I'll just..." I hitched my thumb at the front door.

"Um, actually." She put her food down, licked ketchup from her fingers. "Do you want to eat in here? With me? You can worry and drink beer at the same time, like I promised."

"I assumed you were only being nice."

She extended her leg, hooked her foot under the bar stool and pushed it out a few inches. "Have a seat."

There'd been a moment, just like this, right before I kissed her for the very first time. When a decision had presented itself. When I could have avoided all of this *heartbreak* if we'd never dated in the first place.

I sat down carefully, on the bar stool we'd picked out together, at an island in a kitchen we danced in, laughed in, fucked in. Setting my food down, I peered up at my wife sitting above me, wearing a pretty smile so hopeful all other choices were abandoned.

And just like that day, it wasn't my brain or any type of rational thought that decided our destiny. It was the messy organ in my chest, clamoring to be heard, that said: *Do it.*

22

COPE

Serena ate her burger in about three bites flat, then licked her lips, satisfied, like a lioness after the hunt. She surveyed my food.

"Serena."

"Mhmm?"

I cut about a quarter off my cheeseburger and handed it to her. "You do this every time."

"I surfed a giant wave today," she said with a cheeky look. "All you did was stand still."

I leaned one arm over the back of the chair. "Have you ever tried to exude *menacing* while staying completely silent? It's all in the micro expressions."

"And what's that?"

"The muscles in my face that subtly say *I will fuck you up with my fists and witty rejoinders.*"

She narrowed her eyes and cocked her head. "Are you doing it now?"

"Maybe."

I made a series of small facial gestures. She clutched her chest and gasped. "That really was menacing."

I shrugged and took advantage of her distraction to swipe her beer. Took a sip from it. "I don't like to use the word *expert* lightly, but I think my unique set of skills speak for themselves."

She snatched her drink back. "I believe you stealing my beer would qualify as being overly familiar, Copeland."

"I believe you eating your agent's food also qualifies as being overly familiar," I said, pointing at her as she was mid-bite. "And you've been *real* fucking chatty."

"I sat in the passenger seat too," she said smugly.

"So you *do* want to get me in trouble, don't you?"

"That's always been the plan."

Chuckling, I ate a French fry and smiled up at her. Her voraciousness had been one of the things I admired about her the most. She had a greed for *living*, for experiences, for taking what she wanted without judgment. She indulged her desires—whether it was eating one and a half cheeseburgers or dragging me on a spontaneous road trip.

I regretted not telling her that more when we were together. Losing my father had elicited dual reactions in me: a need to keep everyone I loved under lock and key so nothing bad would ever happen to them as well as an eagerness to consume all the good parts of life that people often took for granted. Both existed within me. One just had a stronger hold.

My mother had words of gentle wisdom after we broke up: *We can't protect the ones we love from this world the way we want to. Tragic accidents will happen regardless of what we do. Losing your father was the worst, the worst, thing that ever happened to me. But not fully living, not allowing those around you to do the same, isn't the solution. I've certainly wanted to lock you and Billie in this house and keep you within my sight. Believe me, the impulse doesn't disappear. It's how you learn to live with it.*

The problem was I wasn't sure if I could do that.

Serena was still laughing and eating my food when her phone beeped with a message. She checked it, and I hoped with everything I had that it was something normal and not a creepy threat.

"It's Caleb," she said. "Giving me shit about you, of course."

I swallowed a sigh of relief. We were being provided a respite from the fear and complications of the world outside this house, and I didn't have the willpower to run from it.

"I really did expect him to punch me in the nose," I said. "For a couple of different reasons."

She tapped her fingers on the glass of her beer. "Yeah, well, Caleb doesn't hate you. He never, ever did. He's always been very respectful of my decisions." Her throat worked as she stared at me. "Not that he didn't, you know, see some things after we broke up. He definitely had to come over here and remind me to shower and eat. I had an all-ice-cream diet for weeks until one day I puked while doing squats at the gym and Dora made me go to the grocery store and buy vegetables."

Knowing Serena had suffered the same way I had was as wretchedly painful as it was affirming.

"That was very nice of your brother to spare my face," I said. "He doesn't really hate anyone though, right?"

"No," she said softly. "He doesn't. Not even our parents. For him, it's more of an erasure of their existence. The night he got me out of there, I'll never forget the way he looked. He was only eighteen years old, but he seemed so wise and mature. Being away at college helped him to see their emotional abuse more clearly. All the mind games and manipulation. That night, he turned to me as he backed out of the driveway and said, 'We don't need them anymore. We've got each other.'"

In the two years we were together, I had never met Serena's parents and understood that I never would. She'd made it clear from the beginning that her family was structured differently, and I admired her ability to find love when it hadn't been given by her parents.

"I've missed your brother," I said, hedging a bit. "And my family has really missed having you around."

"Really?" she asked, sounding surprised. "They don't, um…"

"Never," I said firmly. "My mom and Billie were more angry with me after we broke up. And Quentin has been casually requesting that we get back together for four years now."

Her smile was shy. Cheeks a little pink. "That's good to know."

She leaned back on her palms, looking satisfied. She uncrossed her legs, turning until they dangled a mere two inches from me. All that smooth, toned skin, those muscled thighs, the freckles I'd kissed and kissed. I couldn't stop the train of my—now horny—thoughts.

Because Serena had taken a bath, taken a nap, and obliterated a meal. That left one last thing she always needed, and *goddamn* I was weak enough in this moment to eagerly obey if she demanded it of me. It would be no sacrifice on my part.

"Do you know what I think about when I drink Pacifico?" she asked.

I went still. "What?"

"Cordelia's."

Electric heat lit up my nerve endings. Serena was testing the waters, dipping a toe in.

"You mean that dive bar in Las Vegas?" I asked. "Hot damn, I haven't thought about that place in forever."

That was such a fucking lie.

From the moment I opened that file to find Serena's beautiful face staring back at me, the sexy, messy, spontaneous events that led to our quickie Vegas wedding had been playing on a constant loop in my head.

"Me neither." She took another long sip, gaze pinned to mine. "I still maintain that if we'd never switched to margaritas that night, we never would have gone through with it."

"Huh," I said. "That's funny because it was your idea to order them."

Her jaw dropped. "You take that back."

"What?" I laughed. "It *was*. I was the one who wanted to stop after three beers. You decided to then tack on three cocktails each."

"That is such bullshit, and you know it." Her attempt at a straight face was failing.

"Is it though? I believe I'd said something along the lines of, 'It sure is time for us to be responsible, sober people and head back to the hotel for some quiet, polite sex and an early bedtime.'"

"Name a time when you wanted polite sex." She crossed her arms, crossed her long, delicious legs.

I opened my mouth to argue. Snapped it shut. "I might be embellishing."

Her eyes were flirtatious. "If we're taking this time to air out our grievances—"

"Are we doing that? I thought I was only here to eat a sandwich."

"—then you have to finally admit that you had an ulterior motive when you bought those plane tickets for us that weekend."

I considered maintaining the line I'd held from the beginning. Our Vegas weekend was a spur-of-the-moment luxury because we were twenty-four and stupid in love and plane tickets had been cheap. There was a hell of a lot of *truth* in that statement. But it wasn't until that night, that moment, drinking tequila under fake palm trees wound with

Christmas lights, that I fully understood those ulterior motives myself.

"What if we just did it?" I said, brushing my lips against Serena's. She tasted like strawberries and salt. "What if we got married at the Elvis chapel next door?"

"Tell me why you want to." she'd said, breathless.

I trapped her legs between mine on the stool and tangled my fingers in her long hair. I dragged my mouth up to her ear. "I want you to be my wife. I want you for my forever. I want to be yours. I want you to be mine, *Serena."*

I took so long to answer that she started to laugh behind her hands.

"Okay," I said. "I guess we're doing this then?"

"Admit it. You know you want to."

For some reason, this point in time didn't feel like it would ever come again—to get closure over beers and cheeseburgers. We only had more competitions and a corporate scandal in our future.

But right now?

I put my drink down and didn't break eye contact. "It will not surprise you that I had decided you were the one for me after our second date. It didn't matter *where* we got married or when. I know now that I pushed for us to go to Vegas because I couldn't stop thinking about being your husband."

She sat stunned. Silent. "Our second date?"

"I'm telling the truth."

She chewed on her lip, studied me closely, like she couldn't anticipate what I was going to do next.

"Can I ask you a question now?"

"Of course," she said.

"That wedding with our Elvis impersonator wasn't real," I said. "It was all for show. We had no license, and it wasn't legally binding. It's the kind of ceremony they put on for a tipsy couple wanting to be spontaneous. It was impulsive and daring. And sexy." I didn't hide the lust in my eyes, didn't suppress our honeymoon night memories. "When we got home, it could have stayed a fun and silly memory. But you proposed we file for a marriage license that weekend to *make* it real. Why? I was the one who pushed us to do it that night. On the flight home, I assumed you wouldn't want it to be official."

She looked down at the island, tucking a strand of hair behind her ear. "I couldn't stop thinking about being your wife. Didn't want it to be a sexy weekend fairy tale. I wanted all of you."

The air between us was charged with a crackling tension. I could only hear the blood rushing in my ears, my heart a heavy *thud* against my chest. I stood up from the stool to place our plates in the sink. I gripped the countertop as I breathed in and out, a pitiful attempt at slowing my pulse. I caught my reflection in the window. Caught Serena, staring at me. She was as beautiful as the day I met her. As beautiful as the day I married her.

"Cope."

The raw emotion as she said my name had me dropping my head forward with a sigh. I remembered this—the sounds and sensations of what came after every truce between us near the end. On the clock or not, it didn't matter. Our problems would find us, would crowd into every intimate moment when we let our love and lust run unchecked.

"Serena, don't," I begged wearily. I didn't want to unpack the hurts and miscommunications that led to our breakup. I wanted warm kitchen light and cold beers in Vegas. I turned around reluctantly and crossed my arms over my chest. She slid off the island and mirrored my pose.

"I can't..." She paused, stared briefly at the ground. "As comforting as reminiscing about our happiest memories is, it's *impossible* for me to ignore what happened a month after we got home from Vegas. Right? Like are you really going to be my bodyguard for the next couple weeks as we never address what *actually* ended our relationship?"

I took a step closer to her. There was more soft frustration in those words than finger-pointing, and some part of me recognized she was trying to talk and not fight. But my still-broken heart overpowered my ability to acknowledge her intent.

"You invited me into *our* kitchen where you brought up all those happy memories," I said accusingly.

Hurt sparked in her eyes, but anger flared a second later. I hated how easy it was to trick us into arguing, but the conversations that lay beyond them were still too terrifying for me.

"You mean I invited you into *my* kitchen?" she shot back.

"Our kitchen, Serena. At least it was until you left me to go tour in Australia three months after our fucking wedding."

"We needed a break," she whispered fiercely.

I took another big step towards her, lured by an irritating lust. To show her what I'd been aching to do since she stepped into that room two days ago. To demonstrate the filthy fantasies I couldn't shake, the ones where I finally indulged in giving us both the sweaty, heart-pounding sex we craved.

"Right," I said. "And in your mind, a break meant leaving your husband to fly halfway across the world and then not call or contact him for ninety days. We didn't *talk*."

Her dark eyes narrowed at me. "We weren't talking before I left, so I'm not sure why that surprised you. And communication works both ways. You didn't call me either, even though I spent more nights than I care to admit waiting by the phone for you."

That direct hit was intended for me, and it brought up so much confusing guilt I almost walked away. But I was also—

somehow—directly in her space without realizing it, and my feet refused to move.

"Then why didn't you *call?*" I demanded.

"Why did you *leave?*"

We were less than six inches apart now. Her heavier breathing matched my own.

"How come," she said, voice tight. "I came back to our house after my tour to find my husband had abandoned me and didn't even leave a note?"

"I left you six months of rent."

Her eyebrows shot up. We were one inch apart now and racing toward a dangerous temptation, the kind of impulsive act the two of us embraced when we were young and stupid. "Sorry, I didn't realize that was an official way to dump someone."

I closed the remaining distance. "I wasn't going to wait around for you to officially break my heart after three months of silence."

The truth tore from my throat—instead of sounding mad or arrogant, the words were saturated with my unresolved pain and unending *want.* It flipped the switch, let years of lust burn hotter than this argument, and what happened next was inevitable from the second I'd been handed that folder.

We reached for each other at the same exact time.

Serena grabbed my shirt and yanked as I scooped her back onto that island.

And I kissed my wife for the first time in four years.

This wasn't our first kiss. There was no tentative tasting, no learning the shape of each other. I claimed her mouth with a barely suppressed growl as she wrapped her legs around my waist. She gripped my face, and I dove my fingers into hair I never thought I'd touch again. The feel of it, the smell of her, had me deepening a kiss that was already frenzied. *Mangoes, saltwater, sunny afternoons on the beach.* She smelled like home and tasted like my favorite memories.

She opened wider for me, tongue against mine. We didn't come up for air, only bruised our lips as we pressed every inch of our bodies together. I bent her all the way back until her shoulders hit the island and her knees rose higher on my waist. This wasn't a tender moment of reuniting lovers. This was a wild sexual frustration that demanded we submit. This was every unfinished disagreement, every dream and fantasy, every stolen glance and connection we couldn't deny.

My hands smoothed down her bare thighs, and the tips of my fingers dipped beneath the edges of her shorts. I let out a strangled groan of pure gratitude. I didn't think I'd ever touch Serena again, yet here I was, in our house, with the woman I'd married writhing beneath me.

She tilted her head back, exposing her throat, and I took advantage of the new access she granted. I dragged my mouth up the side with hard kisses more bite than caress.

"I'm not going to forget we didn't finish arguing just because we're doing this," she panted, digging her nails into my back.

"As if I'd let you forget," I grunted against her skin.

"Good," she moaned.

"*Great*," I snarled, licking her neck. She gasped and yanked me back to her mouth, and I very, very dimly registered what I thought were tires on gravel outside.

That would be my partner, arriving for his security shift.

Passion chased reality away though, and Serena tasted too delicious to stop, felt too perfect beneath my hands, was too pliable and ready.

"I know what you want right now." I cupped my hand over her breast, and we both shuddered and groaned. *So perfect.* "Let me give it to you."

"How would you know what I want?" she asked, but it was more flirtatious than an actual taunt.

I pinched her chin to keep her still as our eyes locked together. "Because I'm your *husband*. I remember what my wife craved after a day like today—to be pinned down on our bed and ridden hard. To come on my cock until you can't take it anymore."

She released a sigh that pierced my chest. "Yes," she whispered, hands flying to my belt. "*Please*."

A car door slammed. Falco's door. I *still* didn't stop kissing her, drinking in her need, stroking my tongue against hers as she started working my belt open. We were putting it all on the line—her safety, my job. But we just needed ten minutes. If we only had *ten fucking minutes*—

Knuckles wrapped against the door.

"*Goddammit*," I swore against her mouth. I pulled back reluctantly and knew we wore matching expressions of dazed lust—flushed cheeks, eyes wide, lips swollen.

Another knock at the door.

"Ms. Swift? Cope?" Falco said with a hint of alarm in his voice this time.

Serena slid off the island and began putting her clothing and snarled hair in order. I scrubbed a hand down my face, as horny and irritated as I'd ever been.

"I'll go upstairs, pretend I was doing one last check of the windows," I whispered. "Okay?"

She nodded. "Got it."

We were hurtling back into the reality I desperately wanted a break from: heartbroken husband and wife forced together as bodyguard and client suddenly amid a dangerous scandal.

So before she could turn away from me, I held the back of her hair and pressed a long kiss to her forehead, lingering for seconds we didn't have.

I tore myself away before I sacrificed everything for one more minute of Serena back in my arms. Walking to the staircase, I was grateful she'd closed all the curtains, hiding us from view, before I'd gone ahead and obliterated every protocol in the damn book. I took the stairs two at a time and heard Serena at the front door.

I waited on the landing with shaking muscles. We'd been interrupted before we could finish arguing *or* fucking, and the incompletion had me wired and antsy.

"Falco?" Serena said like she was surprised. "I'm so sorry. I had my headphones in while doing the dishes and didn't hear you."

"It's no problem, ma'am," he said. "I was just worried."

I glanced in the mirror by the bedroom—rehooked the buttons of my shirt and made sure my erection wasn't immediately obvious. Then I strolled back down the steps.

"Hey," I said. "I was upstairs doing a quick check of the windows before my shift ended."

If Falco noticed the kitchen's slight disarray or Serena's wrinkled shirt, he didn't mention it. "Everything's okay?"

"Can we check in outside?" I asked. I gave Serena a nod and said, "Have a good evening, Ms. Swift."

I turned on my heel before she could reply, too worried we'd betray what happened between us. Falco joined me on the porch, closing the door behind him. I still felt the need to protect him from the possibility of Aerial's dangerous reach, so I wanted him on high-alert even if he didn't know the full story yet.

"I made a note in my reports today for you," I said softly. "But at the competition, I got a real bad vibe from a few of the fans. Creepy vibes."

His brow furrowed. "Did they speak to Serena?"

I shook my head. "No, but they stared at her in a way that made me really concerned. Were hanging around the parking lot when we left too. I didn't catch a tail but didn't want you unprepared for something weird happening tonight. Stay sharp, okay? Call if you need backup or feel like something's off."

"Will do," he said.

I clapped him on the arm before I left. I didn't turn around. I didn't try and catch one more glimpse of Serena, didn't risk one more opportunity to run back into a home once filled with our love and now only filled with tense complications.

The moment I slid into my car, I pressed my hand over the left side of my chest, curling around the ache there.

I'd been lying to myself since day one.

There was no way I could take this job and protect my heart at the same time.

At 7:31 the next morning, I pulled open my front door and wasn't surprised at all to find my ex-husband leaning against a tree in his running clothes. His expression was part-smirk, part-annoyed.

I knew the feeling. I'd woken up with an anger as powerful as my sexual frustration, and the man in front of me was almost entirely responsible.

"Good morning, Ms. Swift," he said, voice still gravelly. It was as rough as the words he'd growled at me last night: *I remember what my wife craved after a day like today—to be pinned down on our bed and ridden hard.*

I'd been tortured by erotic dreams all night—dreams where we hadn't been interrupted, where Cope had fucked me on that counter with his palm pressed to my mouth as I came over and over. What made it worse was that it wasn't just a fantasy.

He *had* fucked me like that before.

"Good morning, Mr. McDaniels," I said petulantly.

I didn't miss his hungry eyes scanning my body. I only

wore a pink sports bra and tiny bike shorts, and *maybe* that had been to aggravate my very aggravating bodyguard.

"Let me guess," he said. "We're not even going to *try* and maintain the truce we set yesterday about arguing while I'm on the job, correct?"

I shut the front door behind me. Yesterday's argument—we were three-for-three, now—had stirred up more hurtful memories than I wanted to admit. And since the activities I usually did to burn off this spiky sensation weren't available—sex with Cope or surfing—I opted for a hard, sweaty run instead.

"I'm pissed about a lot of things right now, and *yeah* you're one of them," I said, taking off at practically a dead sprint. I didn't worry that he'd catch up with me immediately. He did and pulled his shirt off at the same time, tossing it back towards the front porch.

"What are you doing?" I asked, trying not to stare.

He shrugged and said, "I heard it's gonna be a hot one."

I managed to barely tear my attention away from his broad, muscular chest before I tripped over something. Last night's romantic intimacy—before we fought and angrily made out—had lured me back to a past before we'd crashed against differences too complex to mend. I'd made one tiny attempt, had tried to broach our awful breakup and its many unanswered questions, and it still spiraled into snarky bickering.

I ignored his comment and turned down the road toward the nearby cul-de-sac. We were already panting, arms swinging and feet pounding on the sidewalk.

"I can guess," he started to say. "Why you're pissed at me. But who else is on your shit list this morning?"

"Aerial," I said harshly. "Besides the fact that having them stop me from talking about gender inequality in the middle of a TV interview was infuriating, I'm actually more concerned about what's on that drive Catalina gave us and if she's safe."

I caught the clench in his jaw. We'd been too busy flirting to process our interactions with the Lattimore brothers yesterday—or my very real fears about Catalina's security.

"Quentin is speaking with his law enforcement contact today, and he's entrusting him with trying to find Catalina. That's the priority. He also did some digging into those badge numbers. Turns out they're quality control inspectors that look into factories like the ones Aerial uses to produce their clothing and gear." Cope ran a hand through his hair and huffed out a breath. "His first suspicion is that something bad is being concealed by the inspectors."

I turned to him. "Like they're not safe or something?"

"Yes. Unfortunately."

Fury raced up my spine. "So maybe this company that espouses all of these *we're changing the world* ideas is actually a giant fraud?"

"We don't know the full picture yet," he said. "But they're lying about *something*, and whatever it is that Catalina gave us is enough of a bombshell they're starting to threaten people to get it back."

My throat tightened. "I hate feeling like I was tricked about more than just their ethics. Maybe Quentin was right. Maybe Aerial isn't ethical behind closed doors. And maybe they only want women to be bikini models rather than athletes after all. They promised advocacy on gender inequality; they promised taking a stand. So far, it's been a lot of words without direct action backing them up."

We were quiet for a moment before I said, "I wanted them to be better."

"Me too."

"They *should* be better."

"Yes, they should," Cope said. "And if they can't be better, then we need to do what we can to hold them accountable. Quentin said he can come over tonight after he's talked to his sources to fill us in on what he's learned. I just need to sneak around Falco so he doesn't see us meeting. But Quent is hopeful that, between the authorities and his editor, concrete action will be taken soon."

My anger toward Aerial didn't abate—there was too much to be angry *about* even with a partial understanding. The thought that this feeling could be directed toward an action, however, changed my perception of it.

Just like Dora had said.

The question always is: Will you let the anger eat you alive? Or will you use it to accomplish something useful?

We hit the end of the cul-de-sac and rounded the turn to head back to the house, both of us breathing hard now. It *was* hot, and I could see the sun glinting off the light sheen of sweat on Cope's shoulders. Everything that happened between us last night came screaming back into my head, from the heartbreak scrawled across Cope's face to the desperate way we'd kissed each other.

Every interaction between us—blistering remark or tender caress—only illuminated the complex intersection of fear and risk, of love and loss, our relationship was trapped in. It was a familiar—and fucking *frustrating*—pattern.

"If shit actually goes down with Aerial, you might not even be my bodyguard for much longer," I finally said in a voice as shaky as my legs.

His jaw clamped tight again. "Regardless of what happens with the whistleblower case, I was only going to be with you until the event at Huntington Beach. If the waves are firing so great that they're calling The Wedge for tomorrow, I could be out of your hair sooner than you think."

"Wonderful," I said, already steeling myself. "I need less distractions in my life anyway. You swore that, if we were civil to each other, everything would be fine, and *none* of that has happened."

Cope made an exasperated sound in the back of his throat. "I'm sorry. Am I a distraction to you now?"

I tossed him a glare then kept running.

His chuckle was humorless. "I wasn't aware anything distracting had happened between us."

"You know last night was a distraction for a hundred different reasons, the least of which was kissing each other," I panted. "Again."

"Didn't you invite me in for dinner and reminiscing about our wedding?" he shot back.

"I was being *nice*," I said through gritted teeth.

"What we did on that island wasn't nice," he said on a low growl. An intense desire for him coiled low in my belly. "And I'll remind you that you're not the only one with a job and a career on the line here. One word of this to my boss, and I'd be fired immediately."

We were at the top of the driveway. Everything burned, every muscle and nerve ending.

"Then why..." I panted, annoyed. "Did you *take* this assignment? One word to your boss, and she would have given you a pass on having to work with your distracting ex-wife every day."

"Oh, yeah?" he said. "You could have reported it to my boss too. Would have gotten a pass on having to work with your distracting husband every day."

"*Ex*-husband."

We hit the porch at the same time, and Cope was hot on my heels, slamming the door behind us as we walked into the kitchen. I had my hands on my knees, trying to catch my breath. Drops of sweat ran down Cope's stomach, and his chest was heaving.

Neither one of us had a smart-ass response to the glaring

truth of our current situation. My ulterior motive was as sneaky as Cope's had been when he'd suggested we have a spontaneous Vegas weekend. I believed him when he said he didn't realize it until we were stumbling to the chapel.

Because I didn't realize how happy, how *relieved*, I would feel when I discovered Cope was my new bodyguard. Wasn't there a part of me that had wished it would be him?

Now he stood in front of me with his hands on his head and blue eyes pinned to mine. "*Jesus*, Serena, before our fight I thought we were getting somewhere for once."

The longing in his voice stopped me in my tracks. All of the frenetic anger was transforming into a different kind of anguish, of wanting each other but not having, of running from our complexities instead of confronting them.

"If we want to *get* somewhere," I said. "Then we can't just talk about our happiest memories and sidestep the real reasons that broke us up. And I don't mean pointless bickering either." I gathered the kind of courage I usually relied on to tip over the lip of a wave. "I thought we needed a break because you were taken hostage at your job a month after our wedding, and everything changed for us after that."

His eyes immediately shot to the ground.

"Cope, please."

After a few excruciating seconds, he looked up at me reluctantly.

"You wouldn't let me worry about you. You wouldn't let me talk about it. *You* wouldn't talk about it. You shut me out, like you always do when you don't want to confront anything hard or sad. You don't get to be the only one that worries in a relationship. You can't express your fears about my safety all the time and then not let me do the same. That's why I thought, when I signed up for that tour in Australia, we could use it for a break. To clear our heads. I just needed a little space to think."

He propped his hands on his hips. "It was one incident," he said. "*One* time. And yeah, it was fucked up and dangerous, but you actively seek out a sport that kills people, and you're never going to quit. And I hate asking you to quit." He cleared his throat, cheeks pink. "You can't be the only one that gets to work a dangerous job. You can't make *me* worry all the time while you rest easy at night."

Tears filled my eyes, which rarely happened. "That's why you left me then?"

Pain rippled across his face. "And is that why you left?"

"I thought I was doing the right thing for our marriage," I said, my voice a rough scrape of emotion. "I thought I was saving it, not ending it."

Cope never told me that he hated asking me to stop surfing—but what started as something he'd bring up infrequently became a persistent request, especially after the incident. But, then again, I was so terrified after he'd been taken hostage, I kept turning that same request right back around on him.

Still—that small reveal felt purposeful enough to shove me toward something truly scary.

"Well," I said. "If this is the last time we get to talk about *us*, then you should know that marrying you was the best day of my life." Holding his gaze right now was terrifying, but risking it all felt necessary. "And... and I miss you every day."

Cope went utterly still. "What did you say?"

I closed my eyes, feeling stripped bare. "I miss you every day. I dream about you and fantasize about you. I think about you constantly, and I've *never* been able to stop. Do you... do you ever miss me too?"

His response was to walk towards me until I was backed against the wall. His hands landed on either side of my head, and he was breathing hard like we were running again. I understood this exertion—the energy it took to deny what you crave, to resist the very thing that tempts you.

Cope's fingers slid tenderly into my hair, and then he kissed me with four long years' worth of missing one another. This kiss was ache and anguish, regret and reverence. His mouth slanted over mine with a precise passion that sent me pressing onto my toes and seeking more.

I opened for him, tongues stroking together, my arms wrapping around his neck. His bare chest was warm against my skin. And he tasted like all the best things of our past— like hot coffee and sunrises, lazy weekends in bed, strawberry margaritas minutes before saying *I do*.

"Miss you?" he whispered against my lips. "*Miss you?* I *ache* for you, Serena. Every hour of the day. I've tried to convince myself I moved on, but it's never, ever been true. Not in the least."

Cope grabbed my hand and pressed it over his own heart. "I'm pining for you, sunshine."

SERENA

I'm pining for you, sunshine.

My world exploded, filling with vibrant sparks of color and a dizzying hope. I held Cope's hand over my own heart and pressed our foreheads together.

"I'm glad I'm not the only one," I whispered back. We stayed like that, acknowledging the full weight of our admissions. His knuckles stroked up my throat, catching under my chin and lifting it so our eyes met.

"Not much has changed since last night, except that having sex with each other is now an even worse idea."

He was right. Last night's kiss felt like two ex-lovers seeking sexual comfort. The consequences were easier to untangle after a slip-up like that.

Now we were kissing after creeping closer to forgiveness and understanding, which had far greater consequences. There would be no easy untangling, only more heartbreak.

"I'm willing to risk it if you are," I said. I trailed my fingers down his chest, nails scratching along ridged, flexing muscles.

"You have always been my most beautiful risk," he said.

He captured my mouth again, taking what he wanted, devouring me as desire flooded my body. He lifted me against the wall, and I wrapped my legs around his waist. Cope kissed along my neck while I ran my hands through his hair.

His hips kept me pinned as his long fingers gripped my thighs, spreading them open. I was only wearing thin bike shorts, so of course I could feel every delicious inch of his hard erection. Lips brushing mine, he dragged his cock deliberately across my sex. My toes curled against his back as he moved his hips sinuously between my legs, each time putting more and more pressure against my clit. I clutched at his hair and gasped.

"Oh *god*, don't you dare stop." I sighed.

"Never," he said. "I've been fantasizing about watching you come while fucking my own hand for four years now." He ground harder, deeper, held me pinned to that wall, and dry-fucked me like we wore no clothing at all. A drop of sweat rolled down the column of his throat. I caught it with my tongue, licked his salty skin as he released a strangled moan. He scraped his teeth across my lower lip. Our kiss turned greedy. Sloppy. With every thrust, the pictures on the wall rattled and shook, and my cries grew louder.

"I'm close already," I moaned. "Yes... just... *Cope, faster please.*"

He moved with a furious finesse. "Tell me what you think about when you touch yourself."

I arched into his touch, his fingers holding me tight. It had been so long—four years exactly—since I'd felt this way.

"The cabin in Tahoe," I managed to say. "You took me on that soft rug in front of the fireplace so many times I couldn't walk the next day."

He grunted against my ear, breath short and harsh. His shoulders and biceps flexed from exertion. "I think about that weekend all the time, sunshine."

We'd gone for our one-year anniversary, twenty-three years old and *insatiable* for each other. I'd woken the next morning with rug burn and bruises, every muscle tender, every strand of hair twisted into knots.

His mouth teased the shell of my ear, nuzzled through my hair tenderly even as what he did to my clit was filthy. "I laid flat on my back that night, and you rode my face until you couldn't take it anymore."

Pleasure spiked through me. "Yes... *yes*... I loved using your tongue like that."

"It's still there for you to use," he said. "I had to jerk off last night, thinking of you."

I was so close. So fucking close and picturing Cope's fist working up and down, forearm flexing, head back. "Tell... tell me."

He stared at me as I started to unravel and unwind. "I thought about sitting on that damn stool with your pussy bare and glistening for me. I thought about eating you out right on that island, enjoying you like a fine meal while you screamed my name."

His fantasy came true.

I came so hard I could only flail against his body, clutching his hair. I was airborne again while still experiencing aftershocks. Clinging to Cope, he walked us right into the living room and onto the couch. He laid me down gently, then tore off my bike shorts with eager hunger on his face. A second later, he lowered his body on top of mine.

We went still, although our muscles shuddered, and my internal walls still quivered with pleasure. This was real, not some delicious fever dream. He pressed our foreheads together and lifted my right leg up and over his waist. I couldn't stop touching him—his stomach, his arms, his shoulders, his face.

"I missed you so much. I missed *this* so much," I said.

Cope kissed me—hard, brutal—and I arched my body against his, ready for more. He shoved his shorts down to stroke his cock. It was as beautiful as I remembered—thick, long, veined, perfect.

"Please," I whimpered. "*Please.* You know how I need it."

Cope was shaking from restraint. He slid my underwear to the side, and the head of his cock brushed at my entrance. "Bare, Serena?"

I nodded. Kissed him. "I'm still clean and safe. Are you?"

He nodded with his eyes closed. When they opened, the vulnerability there was the man I fell in love with—the man who used humor to protect himself, who would do anything for the ones he loved. The man who would gladly move mountains to keep me safe.

"Are you sure?" he asked. "You have to tell me you're sure or... or we have to stop. I won't survive it if this isn't real."

I stroked his forehead. "That day you came to me and said you found cheap tickets to Vegas, well... I'd been looking at those same tickets too. Because I didn't know what to do with the fact that I wanted to marry you, desperately. I sort of hoped, if we were there, we'd get swept up into the moment and do it."

I had never, ever admitted that—I'd barely admitted it to myself.

Cope's eyes searched mine, and then we were kissing, kissing like there was no limit to our time together. And then I felt his cock, and then his hips shifted, and then, after four long years, Cope was inside me again. My body stretched to accommodate every single inch of his huge length. My nerve endings sang with pleasure and the sweet, heady feeling of being filled by the man I craved the most. We shared a grateful moan as he held himself still, allowing me to adjust, allowing both of us to acknowledge the full euphoria of a sensation I thought I'd never experience again.

"You have no idea…" He moved out of me, then drove back in with a sigh. "You feel fucking incredible."

I reached down and grabbed his ass, pulling him tight against my body. "I believe I was promised to be pinned down and ridden hard."

"Good," he groaned. "Because there's nothing I want more than to feel you come on my cock."

He didn't need any more convincing to give me what I desired. His thrusts were steady and deep and fast—fast like a couple who hadn't fucked in years, like a couple who had never stopped wanting each other. Fast like two people clinging to each other on a couch, bodies moving as one, the sun filtering in through the window on their slick skin.

There was no more talking.

Our lips stayed together, and Cope fucked me hard and dirty—the couch scraped across the floor, the house filled with our sounds of pleasure. Every fraught groan of his, every frayed breath, every frenzied kiss had me eager to climax again. My nails dug into his muscles, urging him on. He growled my name against my throat and closed his teeth around the skin, nipping me, marking me, taking me so deeply I'd lost hold of my rational thoughts. He reached behind and grabbed my hands, held them down onto the couch and circled his hips.

"How do you…" I bit my lip. "How do you *do* that?" I studied the joining of our bodies, memorized this moment, that feeling, of being wholly connected with my husband again.

"Do what?" The smug bastard still managed an arrogant twist of his lips when I'd been reduced to just biological urges. He did it again, stroking his cock deep, using it to work the angle I needed to get off.

"How do you know what I want?" He was pressing hot kisses to my cheek and along my jaw.

"You taught me how to fuck you, Serena," he rasped. "You taught me how to give you the pleasure you deserve." He dropped his hips and ground against my clit. My back arched right off the cushion. "Do you think I could forget how amazing this feels?"

He hitched my leg higher and increased the pressure of his lower body onto my clit. He was so *fucking* deep, and the orgasm waiting for me felt even more powerful than the first one.

"Come with me, please," I whispered.

He let go of my wrists, wrapping his hand around the arm of the couch for leverage, driving between my legs with purpose. His other hand cupped my face so we could watch each other release.

Seeing Cope orgasm had always been the hottest part for me—all that good humor and confidence unraveling at the seams, leaving him nothing but a man bound to his baser needs.

"Serena," he grunted. "Fuck, I can't... it's too good."

"*Yes*," I panted, staring at him with anticipation. I was already starting to clench around his cock, and he was fucking me relentlessly. "Come with me, *please*. I need to see you." I wrapped my arms around his neck and held on tight, let him ravage me on this couch the way he yearned to. His breathing was harsh, voice hoarse, my name falling from his lips over and over. My orgasm struck out of nowhere, an absolute detonation of sheer ecstasy, and as my body lit up with joy, my husband came with a shout and a curse.

He buried his face in the crook of my neck, kissing my cheek as he caught his breath. I was comprised of nothing but aftershocks and a bone-deep satisfaction. I nuzzled the hair at his temple and trailed my fingers up and down his spine, relearning the patterns of his body. It took a whole minute, maybe more, before our breathing slowed to normal.

"Do you remember the first time we had sex?" he asked. His voice was scratchy, muffled against my skin.

I smiled at the memory. "Of course. We had sex on that old couch of yours, in that apartment in Ocean Beach. You had invited me over to watch a movie, and it was so obvious what your plans were."

"Is it because I never actually turned on the movie?" He was kissing between my breasts and lightly along my stomach.

"And because I got there, took off my jacket, and we were hardcore making out not one second later."

He nuzzled his nose against my ribcage. My thumb caressed the hair at his temple. "You rocked my world that night."

I laughed. "Shut up."

"Oh, you did. I saw Quentin the next morning and still had my sex hair and the string of hickeys you'd left on my neck—"

"*Oh my god, I didn't*—"

"— and he took one look at me and said, 'So when's the wedding?'"

"Well, he was only off by about two years."

Cope propped himself up on his elbow, face dreamy and contemplative. He swept the hair back from my forehead and kissed me there, kissed the tip of my nose, kissed my mouth. We gazed at each other for a long time until his pining was as tangible as the birdsong outside the window.

There exists a split-second in surfing when you decide to ride or bail, to fly free or pull back. Both choices have consequences, both are equally important. I could see my other choice here: to bail yet again. To pull back, to claim that our differences couldn't be overcome and to revert to the way my life had been only a week ago, a life where I was safe from future pain but heartbroken just the same.

Our fight last night about our breakup had lingered

because the regret and guilt I carried still weighed heavy on my mind. I wasn't ready to apologize for all our other stuff yet—there were too many complicated layers we *both* needed to sift through, too much to own, too many patterns to analyze.

But I was twenty-four when we broke up, young and even more hard-headed. Whenever I thought back to how I'd handled everything, I flushed red with shame. I'd spent three whole months in Australia lonely and anxious and pretty damn sure I'd made a *huge* mistake.

I was just too stubborn to admit it.

"Cope," I said, touching his face, "I'm so sorry for how things ended between us. I'm sorry for not reaching out, for leaving you here after what you'd gone through, for not making it clear what I wanted. I'm sorry about all of it."

He blinked, eyebrows knit together, like he hadn't expected a word I'd said. "You don't have to apologize right now."

"I need to. I don't want to..." I shook my head. "We can't ignore it any longer."

He tucked a curl behind my ear. "I'm the one who's sorry, Serena. I should have stayed. I should have waited for you. I was an immature dick who let the woman of his dreams walk out the door. I didn't even try. I was *furious* with myself, for months. Kept driving by the house at night, and would see your van and the lights on, and it felt like a life that wasn't mine anymore."

"Oh, Cope, I was just so angry and stubborn. And I never should have forced your hand," I said, needing to own this part fully. It was the only way forward for us.

His mouth curved into a sheepish smile. "Yeah, well, I left without saying goodbye like some grade-A *douche bag*. Who does that?"

"People like *us*," I said, returning his smile. "Two young

people wildly in love, stubborn as hell, and much too impulsive for their own good."

"I still think about it a lot. And regret it, though," he said.

"I do too," I admitted, and there was a loosening of the remorse I carried in my chest. A loosening and a deeper understanding.

His head dipped for a sweet, lingering kiss. The kind of kiss romantic dreams are made of. "So when are we going to address that *you* had a Vegas plan with an ulterior motive too?"

I burst out laughing. "If you're going to be smug about it, then I wish I never told you."

He laughed with me, held me close. "In what universe did you think I wasn't going to be smug about this?"

"I guess in the same universe where you innocently requested polite sex."

His cocky grin had my toes curling. Again. "I have always been a gentleman around you, Serena Swift."

"That has *never* been true," I said, shocked. "You are such a freaking liar."

In the real world, my bodyguard was going to have to drive me to Aerial's headquarters soon, where we'd once again confront a company's lies while trying to uncover the extent of their misdeeds.

But trapped within the golden sunlight of our living room, there was a privilege to this slice of time, the two of us kissing as if we'd never been apart at all. And I could only hope, with every fiber of my being, that the risk we were taking together wouldn't break our hearts all over again.

✥   *25*   ✥

COPE

An hour later, and I was walking Serena through the parking lot of Aerial, staying three feet behind her, per protocol, and completely silent in my black-suit-and-sunglasses combo. I was oddly grateful for the role of agent here—it kept me from doing what I wanted to do, which was run through the streets of San Diego yelling, "Serena and I had sex!"

Technically, I'd been tempted to do that the *first* time we had sex on that old couch in my apartment. But Quentin had talked me out of it.

She turned around, just outside the lobby doors, smiling at me as brightly as the summer sun shining above us. She wore a long, dark-purple skirt and a white tank top, her hair loose over her shoulders. I knew that expression on her face—relaxed, satisfied, happy.

This was the way Serena looked after she caught a perfect wave or while watching the sunrise every morning. This was the way she looked waking me up in my sleeping bag on camping trips. *Stay there*, she'd say, *I'll make you campfire coffee.*

"Cope?" she was saying, but it was hazy. Muffled. "Cope? Your phone is ringing?"

I blinked and shook my head. We had sex one time, and I was already distracted—not great for a man whose *sole job* was to *not* be distracted.

Although who the hell was I kidding? She'd been nothing but a persistent, frustrating, beautiful distraction this entire time.

I checked the screen. *Marilyn Banks*. Dread filled my stomach. Holding up a finger, I said, "I need to take this. Wait in the lobby but where I can see you, okay?"

She smirked at the directive but complied. Beneath that newly calm exterior, I did catch her twisting her fingers in her lap a few times on the car ride over. Our sex euphoria was, unfortunately, fading away and being replaced with whatever the *fuck* was going on in this exact building.

"Good morning, Marilyn," I said. "Is everything okay?"

"Of course," she replied. "I was just calling to check in. I spoke with Falco last night, and he confirmed your daily reports that things have been pretty simple with Ms. Swift."

I miss you every day. I think about you constantly. I've never been able to stop.

"Simple is the perfect way to describe it," I hedged.

I caught the sound of papers rustling. "Although he did mention that you asked him to keep an eye out for a few fans that gave you a bad feeling? Anything I should be made aware of?"

I wasn't sure what I felt worse about: withholding my former relationship with Serena or not divulging that my client was involved in a whistleblower scandal. "Not really, no," I said. "Just one of those gut feelings, but she has a competition tomorrow, and if I see them again, I'll make note of it and coordinate further."

"Excellent, and please do," she said. "Falco also reported

that there doesn't seem to be any of your recent issues working for Ms. Swift. He said you seem eager to work and focused."

I've been fantasizing about watching you come while fucking my own hand for four years now.

"That's good to hear," I said.

"She even reported to Falco she was pleased with your work thus far."

A strangled sound came out of my mouth. I stared up at the sky. "Uh-huh."

Serena, coming against that wall as I ground our bodies together, her skin hot against my mouth, our bodies slick with sweat, the throaty way she moaned my name over and over and over—

"This news is promising," Marilyn said, interrupting my horny memories.

"Told ya I was the best," I joked.

She hummed and then said, "You'll notice I did not imply, in any way, that you were off the hook or no longer under my scrutiny."

I cleared my throat. "Yes, ma'am, I understand. I really do appreciate this second chance."

Even as I said those words, they sounded oddly hollow to my ears. Probably because every person in my life right now believed I was unhappy. I felt it though, a quick squiggle of doubt when I tried to picture doing this job after my Serena assignment was up. When I went back to protecting multi-millionaires who only cared about themselves and not the way their actions affected others.

It was The Serena Effect, being around her passion again, her sense of justice and purpose in doing the right thing. I'd been raised to do just that, and when we were dating, it was early enough in my career to trust that I was.

"Stay sharp," Marilyn added. "And call if anything concerning comes up."

"I will, and thank you," I said before hanging up with my stomach in knots. I trusted Quentin's expertise around this more than the need to follow procedures, but even though I was only doing it to keep her safe, something told me Marilyn wouldn't feel the same way once she found out.

Serena looked at me from where she stood in the lobby, dark eyes connecting with mine. It was like taking a goddamn arrow to the heart. But then she checked her phone and went totally pale at whatever she saw there.

I was through those glass doors and by her side immediately.

"Cope," she whispered, unsettled.

"Why don't we wait on the couches over there," I said, aware of people watching us. The receptionist waved and mouthed, "One more minute." Serena smiled back weakly before following me. She sank onto the cushions, spine straight, and discreetly passed her phone over.

The message was from a blocked number again. *We know you have the information. Give it back, or things are about to get a lot worse for you.*

Fury churned in my gut. I took a screenshot and sent it to Quentin.

They're ratcheting up the threats, he replied. *Will bring more news and intel tonight at Serena's house.*

I slid the phone back and showed her Quentin's response. She nodded, swallowing hard, before fixing her expression. She reached for the *San Diego Times* open on the glass table and angled it on her lap so I could read the article catching her attention. The headline was about Aerial sponsoring next year's Olympics in Barcelona.

Their investment in the world's most famous sporting event marks a new tone, one that emphasizes sustainability and environmentalism over profit. Advocates for climate justice have praised the move as the right step forward.

I scanned the rest of the article quickly and stopped at the space below the fold, where there was a sizable picture of Serena standing in her wet suit with her surfboard at the *Jaws* competition.

She shifted on the couch and passed the article to me.

The company recently announced the newest ambassador of its eco-conscious brand: the sometimes controversial Serena Swift, who caught Aerial's attention after dominating what was measured to be a fifty-foot wave at the popular Jaws pro surfing event.

That churning fury faded to a tiring disappointment in this description of her. There was no way to say anything or do anything in front of all these people, so I took out my own phone and sent her a covert text message: *For the record, I thought your post about the Men's Workout Journal list was hilarious, not controversial.*

Her lips curved into a smile. She responded: *I was very proud of it.*

There was a beat, and then she said: *Talking about the things people want to ignore is always controversial.*

Marty strolled into the lobby, whistling, and the back of my neck prickled with danger.

"Good morning," he said. "You two seem relaxed and happy. Serena, you're practically glowing."

"I had a great night's sleep," she replied.

He reached for the newspaper and snatched it from her fingers. "Did you read our big article in the paper? It's only up from here."

Her smile was fixed in a way only I'd recognize. "I'm looking forward to representing a company with such a strong moral code."

I studied my shoes to hide my smirk.

"And Mr. McDaniels, we're happy to have Banks Security support us these next couple weeks," he continued, giving me a jaunty little pat on the arm that made me want to break his fingers. "Serena's profile is only going to explode from here, and we want to make sure you're on high alert at the next couple events. Lots of fans, lots of admirers, and we know how those crowds can get a little overwhelming when you're preparing to compete."

"Happy to do it, sir," I said. "I shall remain dedicated and focused on whatever tasks Ms. Swift might need from me."

"*Wonderful*," he said. "Dedicated and focused. What a guy, huh?"

Her eyes flashed with secret humor. "Mr. McDaniels has shown himself to be quite skilled in many different areas."

You taught me how to give you the pleasure you deserve. You think I could forget how amazing this feels?

"So glad to hear it," he said. We followed him back down the long hallway with framed pictures of athletes in motion. My wife sensually swished her hips in front of me like a tease, making me want to break a lot of rules by catching her at the waist and dragging her into one of these empty offices. See what kind of sexy fun we could get up to in a building filled with flat surfaces.

There was no preparing for the way it felt to openly desire Serena—and be desired by her in return. Her beautiful honesty this morning had pressed open the memories of our relationship I didn't like to analyze because avoiding my own guilt and regret was easier than accepting it. I didn't think I'd ever hear Serena say, 'I miss you every day, and I've never been able to stop,' didn't think I had a partner in this mutual pining I'd carried for four years. Sex between us had always been intimate—but expressing our apologies and secret longings had only deepened it.

Marty welcomed us into the room where Serena had been interviewed by Chase just two days ago. "Thank you again for coming down today. I'm sure you're exhausted from competing."

"I'm fine," she said. Her enthusiasm had dimmed as soon as we stepped through the doors. He didn't seem to pick up on it, pouring her coffee and giving her a seat at the very end. The long table was full of Aerial employees—the marketing team, I guessed. They shared Marty's affable, outdoorsy exterior and were busy examining large sheets of paper arranged in the middle.

I placed myself in the corner, desperate to know what Quentin had found out and trying to decipher whatever game these brothers were playing. The messages were escalating in tone. And the look on Marty's face yesterday—when he stared at Serena like she was his mortal enemy—didn't match up with the friendly vibe permeating this room.

One guy leaned over in his seat toward Serena. "Tough set out there at Trestles, huh?" he asked.

She lifted a shoulder. "Sometimes it's just not your day."

"Fucking sucks," he said. "We all pegged you for the top spot."

"And we're perfectly okay with it," Marty cut in. "Our brand sponsors don't have to do anything for Aerial except be themselves. Besides, The Wedge is firing tomorrow, and I've got a good feeling about her chances. What do you think, Serena?"

"I'm prepared to win," she answered smoothly.

I squeezed my left wrist tighter. For an extreme athlete like Serena, giant, unpredictable waves known for sucking surfers into whirlpools *would* be exciting. I had memories of my dad saying the same thing, getting up at 4:00 in the morning to surf The Wedge when the reports were favorable. He always returned, shaking his wet hair out like a dog and grinning from ear to ear.

"Those waves today were priceless!" he'd say. Beneath the grief over his death was the reminder that this sport had meant *joy*

to him. That grin on his face was the same one Serena wore walking out of the ocean, wild-eyed and elated.

Her joy was priceless too.

If Serena and I were attempting to move past our old hurts, then I was going to have to work on that whole worry *and* trust thing Caleb talked about.

"I am *loving* your enthusiasm today," Marty said, clapping his hands together. "Now let's get a peek at the mock-up of this article. We've worked with *Heavy* for every ambassador debut we've done, and we trust them to find the right angle, of who you are and what you represent in our industry."

Serena seemed briefly nervous. "Did Chase say anything about the interview?"

"Nope," he said. "Only that you'll be meeting next week so he can get a few final thoughts." He waved her over to the table. I couldn't see what she was looking at, but I could absolutely see her reaction to it.

Her lips curled and her cheeks went red. She swallowed a few times before saying, "What is this?"

"Your article," he said, sounding pleased. "I mean, we need your *actual* words and responses in here, but they were able to block a few items about you, and we'll be photographing you wearing some of our newest line of bathing suits."

"Bikinis?" she asked.

"Of course, why not? They're made in America, sustainably produced, with recycled polyester. A real first for the industry, which is why it should be worn by a trailblazer like you." He tilted his head as if just now realizing her very obvious discomfort. "What's wrong? You don't look happy. Is it the coffee? It's fair trade, you know."

"It's not the coffee," she said slowly. She leaned on her hands across the table and tapped a large box of text. "*We sat down with the hottest woman in surfing to talk about her favorite smoothie recipes, the mascara she can't live without and how she gets that six-pack.* Is that definitely going into the article?"

Marty hesitated. "Well, to be honest, yes."

I fought to keep my face passive while wondering what it would feel like to kick Marty square in the nuts just for fun.

"It sounds like you've already decided what my *angle* is going to be, then? Bikinis and smoothies?" She stood up and crossed her arms over her chest. "I'm a professional athlete. I can hold my breath for four minutes under the water and can out-bench-press every person in here. *This* says I'm nothing but a sex symbol, and I expressed to Aerial from the very beginning that I wanted this company to actively *combat* diminishing women in the sport."

Marty set his own coffee down and gave Serena a sympathetic smile. "I hear you, and I'm listening. Let me be perfectly clear. This first article about you? We want it to be fun, personal, and positive. And yes, we even want it to be..." He dropped his voice like he was embarrassed. "A little bit *sexy*. We might be on the forefront of climate justice, but sex still sells, and we need to sell. Your role, in fact, is to help us sell." He shrugged casually, even though he wasn't the one being paraded around practically naked in a magazine. "We get a few of the *sexy* ones out of the way, right off the bat, and then you can start tackling some of that heavy stuff."

Serena arched her brow and didn't back down. "You literally just said you wanted your ambassadors to *be themselves*. Nothing about the angle of this article feels like me. I can be a positive role model in this industry *and* draw attention to how we can do better. It's not either-or."

He was nodding along in a parody of listening. Every interaction with one of the Lattimore brothers peeled back a layer of whatever fake personality they had constructed. Because as I studied the body language of the marketing team, they were annoyed and offended by what Serena was saying—the exact opposite of what they'd promised her.

Maybe they were all liars.

"At Aerial," he said, tone patronizing. "It's very important that our ambassadors have a positive influence and attitude."

Irritation was scrawled on her face. "I really want athletes that look like me to be taken seriously and given the respect they deserve. I'm pretty sure I can handle doing both of those things at the same time." She shook her head. "I don't approve of this article or the angle. I just don't. Your last few ambassadors were giving interviews on harmful micro-plastics and low-waste lifestyles immediately. The only difference is that they were men."

There was an undercurrent of *you'll do what we say and shut up about it* running through this conversation, and it had me on edge.

For the forty-eight hours I had a gun trained on my face as a hostage, I'd watched Gary Duncan transform from his nice guy exterior to a man driven by pure greed and the belief that he could do whatever the hell he wanted.

I never forgot that, never forgot how he'd betrayed my trust as the person sent to protect him twelve hours a day. Those same vibes, that same instinct, were starting to go haywire now. Serena's eyes darted to mine as if picking up on my concern.

Marty moved to her side and lightly patted her shoulder. She stiffened next to him. My vision started to go red at the edges.

"This is a long partnership. One that I'm truly looking forward to. Sometimes, during this partnership, we're going to disagree on our shared vision or goals. That's okay with me, it's part of the process. Now, the *icky* part of this is that contractually you owe us this article. And while we appreciate your feedback, and we'll take it into consideration, I wasn't asking for your permission or approval."

"Excuse me?" she asked.

"We're going to move ahead regardless. This was more of a courtesy than anything else," he said. "We thought you'd be excited to see such a huge piece of publicity."

I wondered if Serena caught the impatience in his compassionate tone. I sure did.

She kept her posture straight and stared right back at Marty. "I won't pretend that *this*—" She pointed at the mock-up. "—is okay with me. I'll fulfill my contractual obligation, but I'm not going to stay quiet about the things I care about."

Her voice was hoarse with emotion—but I didn't miss the fear in her eyes. She'd made this company unhappy, and they were about to be even more unhappy after Quentin broke whatever story this shit-show was actually about. Her fingers twisted together, but she held her head high with confidence.

"And we would *never* ask you to stay quiet," Marty said. He held his arm outstretched to the door, clearly indicating that this weird-ass meeting was over. "Just remember—*positive*. We're happy, you're happy, and together we're going to make big changes. *Big* changes."

"Sure, but I still have—"

"Mr. McDaniels?" he said, speaking directly over her. "Thank you again for your great work. Looking forward to seeing you both at The Wedge tomorrow for our press conference. It should be a beautiful day for Aerial *and* for you, Serena."

He shook her hand, and mine, with rapid-fire movements, ending the conversation and gently shutting the door in our faces before either one of us could blink.

"What the fuck," Serena said.

I hid my nervous laughter with a cough into my fist. Then I placed my palm low on her back and guided her two offices down into a room I'd clocked as dark and empty when we passed it earlier. I hustled her inside and shut the door behind us.

"Still what the fuck?" she repeated.

"I have an idea," I whispered, tugging her close to me. "And I'll preface it by saying that this idea is a) *absolutely* not in the bodyguard handbook and b) *highly unethical* or, some might say, *actually illegal*."

Her lips were twitching. "Go on."

"I hate that Marty dude."

"Couldn't agree more."

"What if we broke into his office to search for incriminating information or clues?"

She chewed on her lip, considering it. "This has *get spontaneously married in Vegas* vibes written all over it."

I flashed her my cockiest grin. "And look how great that turned out."

26

COPE

As soon as the elevator doors closed, Serena reached into her bag and handed me something slender and metallic.

A bobby pin.

"Reading my mind, sunshine?"

"It's all those spy movies you used to make us watch," she said with a sly grin. "I picked up on some things."

I took it from her fingers and worked it open, slipping it inside my shirt cuff. Then I dipped my mouth to her ear. "But you never could focus on the movie, could you?"

She twirled a strand of hair around one finger. "And you were so easy to distract, weren't you?"

The elevator doors opened.

"After you, Ms. Swift," I said. Her brown eyes sparkled when they met mine, and I couldn't deny the simple satisfaction of flirting with my wife again.

I followed behind her as she walked toward the office where Marty had first asked us about the missing information. Serena had prepared a flimsy excuse for why we were up there—got lost looking for the bathroom—but Aerial employees didn't appear suspicious. They bustled about, heading to meetings, and greeted her enthusiastically when she made eye contact.

We turned the corner, and I saw Marty's office door, closed and presumably locked. I would need to move *extremely* fast to pick this lock before a random staff member walked down this hallway. A group passed us by, gawking at Serena in a *can I have your autograph* way, and she stopped abruptly to address them.

I stood by her for all of ten seconds before I realized she was giving me a diversion. As she chatted brightly, she pulled their focus, down the other end of the hallway, closer to the elevators. I backed away from them slowly with my phone to my ear in case I needed to pretend to be on an urgent call. Glancing both ways, heart beating a ridiculous tattoo, I leaned against the wall right next to Marty's door while blathering into my phone.

"Uh huh... wait, what?... no, that can't be..."

I slid the pin out, into Marty's door, twisting the way I'd been taught. And, *thank the gods of corporate scandal*, it clicked open like a dream, and I stepped inside.

I pressed my back to the wall and let my eyes adjust to the dim light. There were no overhead lights on, only what was filtering in from the windows, and right away I could see how clean and sanitized this space was. In the right-hand corner was a small white table with four blue chairs. There was a low, gray couch and a table with a coffee pot and succulents. His desk had multiple monitors, a few filing cabinets, and what I assumed was a coat closet.

I scanned the room quickly for security cameras or any kind of motion sensors. My clients often had state of the art equipment in their offices, most barely visible, but I'd spent a lot of hours just standing around. I was basically an expert in spotting tiny, inconspicuous cameras. I didn't find a single one but knew there was still a risk we'd show up on a video loop somewhere—Marty had told us himself that Serena had been spotted talking to Catalina by their external cameras. We could have been filmed in the elevator, filmed in that hallway...

The voice in my head that often sounded like Quentin said, *this wasn't your best idea, my friend.*

I heard a soft, frantic knocking. I pulled the door open a few inches, and Serena slipped inside, blowing the hair from her face with a jittery smile.

"You broke in," she whispered.

"As you mentioned, I'm quite skilled in many different areas," I whispered back. "Also, my dad taught me how to do this."

"He did?" she asked.

"Part of his anti-establishment teenage years," I said with a wink. "And I'd say we have five, ten minutes max, before Marty finishes that meeting and comes back here."

"What should I look out for?" she asked, already moving toward the desk. I followed her, every sense buzzing and alert.

"Anything legal or about their factories in Arizona or the city council. Definitely anything with Catalina's name on it. Don't disturb stuff you can't put back exactly the way you found it."

She took the desk, and I went for the filing cabinets. Two of them, big and sturdy, and every damn drawer locked. I expected nothing less of the CEO and, unfortunately, couldn't bobby pin my way into those suckers.

I peeked through the small wire recycling bin but saw only receipts from the local food co-op down the street. His monthly planner was open on the very end of his desk—neat, orderly, filled with legible blue writing. Serena was sifting quickly through files, office supplies, random books. I pulled open the nearby door. It was indeed a coat closet, dark and not very deep. I turned on the flashlight on my phone, pushed past his multi-colored assortment of wind breakers. Nothing behind them. Nothing beneath them. Serena made a sound of frustration.

"It's just meeting notes, schedules for his yoga classes and vegan lasagna recipes. If we could get onto his computer, I'm sure we'd find something. But that feels *really* illegal, right?"

I glanced at the clock on the wall with a growing sense of dread. "This was, I'm now realizing, a pretty stupid idea."

The sound of footsteps echoed down the hallway, followed by raised voices. *Marty's fucking voice.*

Serena's eyes widened like a deer in the headlights.

"Okay," I whispered, yanking her against me. "This was a *really* stupid idea."

I did the first thing I could think of—step us backwards into the coat closet, shut the door as quietly as possible, and pray that Marty wasn't coming to his office to get a wind-breaker.

She squeaked in surprise as I held her tight against my body.

"Shhh," I whispered, covering her mouth with my hand. Her fingers clutched my wrist, and I swore I could hear her heartbeat. Or maybe that was just mine. A thin strip of light between the door and the floor illuminated our feet. We could hear Marty's voice, but it was still muffled.

"I will not let anything happen to you, sunshine," I whispered at her ear. She nodded, clutched me harder. We both needed to slow our breathing down or we'd give ourselves away with our loud, nervous panting. I inhaled slowly, like we did before her events. Exhaled. A beat passed, and then she did it with me.

"So I'll let Chase at *Heavy* know that we're good to go, and then I'll get final approval from Dave," Marty was saying as he stepped into his office. The person with him mumbled a response. It sounded like Marty was opening up those damn filing cabinets.

In the intervening seconds, I wracked my brain for a reason why Serena and I were in his coat closet, in case we were found, and only came up with a very feeble, *we needed to make-out right this very second, and your coat closet was our best option?*

Falco was going to kill me.

Marilyn was going to kill me.

Quentin was going to laugh and probably put me in one of his articles.

"She's going to be fine, right?" the other person said. "Because it's, like, day three, and she's already been a problem."

Cautiously, so cautiously, I held Serena more tightly and let my lips drop to her hair. I could feel the tension shaking her muscles.

"Who, Serena?" Marty asked. He sounded no less pleasant in this private setting than he did in that meeting. "She's going to be great. She's *exactly* what Dave and I wanted even though the Board wasn't so happy. I obviously don't want it to come to this, but she's had sponsors before. She knows if she doesn't follow through on what we ask her to do she'll be in breach of contract and won't get paid." Desk sounds— drawers opening, pens rattling. "Money is a wonderful moti- vator regardless of who you are."

I brushed my lips across her temple.

"She's not easy," the other guy said.

"Easy is boring and doesn't sell," Marty replied. His foot- steps roamed across the office, pausing directly in front of the closet door. I pressed my hand harder against her mouth, and I think we both stopped breathing. "We knew her reputation before hiring her. In fact, it's why we sought her out. She's the most beautiful woman in surfing, and even better, she's a real firebrand at that. Controversy sells, even if she's—" He dropped his voice. "—a pain in the ass. But a gorgeous woman who sparks controversy sparks *business*."

He was hovering by the door, and I was now essentially hovering out of my goddamn body with anxiety.

"In the end, we can still control her. She needs us, not the other way around." He moved across the room, away from the door. Serena and I deflated like balloons, although the energy radiating from her was fiery. A crash of what sounded like glass cups fell to the ground, and we both jumped a foot in the air. One of the coat hangers swung out hard, and I reached up and caught it right before it hit the door.

"Are you okay?" the other guy asked with real concern in his voice. "I can clean that up."

"I've got it, *thanks*," he snapped.

An awkward silence followed between the two men.

"I'm fine," Marty finally said. "I've just got a lot on my plate right now." He smoothed his voice over, but we'd both gone rigid at his change in tone.

Marty Lattimore was stressed out. And I had a feeling it had to do with that little USB drive currently in my best friend's possession.

"Let's go," he said. "I'll clean this up later. We're running late for our next meeting."

The office door shut behind them. We waited a few seconds, but then Serena was shoving the door open and stepping back into the dim light. I checked we hadn't disrupted the jackets too much before raking my hand through my hair.

"Holy *shit*, that sucked," I said, breathing out a massive sigh of relief. "We need to go. Like now."

Serena twisted around and stared at the pile of broken

cups—the cause of Marty losing his temper. "He's nervous about something."

"Yeah," I said. "He's nervous about what we're keeping from him. And I'd really rather go discuss that with Quentin and get out of here before they spot us."

Determined, Serena grabbed his planner from the desk and shoved it into her bag. When I gawked at her, surprised, she tossed her hair with a defiant look.

"We're taking them down," she said. "And I don't care what we have to do to make it happen."

I wrapped my arm around her waist, pulled her against my body, and kissed her. "That was some impressive cloak-and-dagger work."

She snorted. "I almost fainted in the closet when Marty got too close."

I lifted a shoulder. "Baby steps, sunshine. There's no one else in the world I'd want to expose a company's heinous secrets with than you."

She brushed her lips against mine with a smile. "You're such a romantic."

We walked back through the parking lot at Aerial as casually as possible. The stolen planner in my bag felt like a neon pink arrow pointing directly at our heads. But I kept my shoulders back, smiling politely at the employees and hyper-aware of any man who bore a resemblance to a Lattimore brother.

"So now we're going to get in the car," Cope said softly. "And drive away, and if anyone stops us, I'm sure I'll come up with an ingenious lie right on the spot."

"You don't have one already prepared?" I whispered. A bead of sweat slid down my spine.

Cope unlocked my door and opened it. "Believe it or not, that was my first time breaking into an office and stealing private property." His lips quirked. "Sorry, *I* didn't steal it. You did, sunshine."

I slid inside and narrowed my eyes at my smirking, much-too-handsome ex-husband. "Only after you convinced me to commit an act you described up front as *highly unethical*."

He shrugged. "Semantics."

But I didn't miss the lines around his mouth or the tight

clench of his jaw as he crossed over to the driver's side just as I was sure he noticed my jittery voice. A powerful combination of adrenaline and fear coursed through my bloodstream, mimicking my body's reaction when I stared down the drop of a wave while balanced on a board.

No rush of liberating, addicting speed followed though.

Instead, as Cope started the car and glanced in the rearview mirror, the sheer weight of our responsibility was fully realized.

"I meant what I said back there." I turned towards him in my seat. "I want them to pay for whatever harm they're committing and lying to the public about."

"I'm with you on this, no matter what," he said. "I'm also really sorry you had to hear them talk about you like that."

I shivered at the memory of having a front row seat to two men casually bragging about manipulating me—discussing me like a problem to be managed and not a human being.

We can still control her.

"I'm not sorry." I took out Marty's planner and flipped through pages of banal weeks with things like *pick up more oat milk* written down. "At least I understand their ulterior motives in hiring me. Why they seemed so excited to work with me while also being quick to shut me up. Women athletes have been treated like this since the dawn of time. Many *much* worse than I've experienced. Besides, you know my parents used to say a lot worse to me, so I'm used to it."

"It's atrocious, and there's no excuse," Cope said firmly.

My skin warmed with his support. "I agree."

He nodded, then turned an intense gaze back to the rearview mirror. "Anything in there to note?"

I shook my head. "Meetings, a few phone numbers. Notes for his assistants." Something fell out from a side pocket.

"There's a business card here. Name is Sylvester Boggs with information on his law firm in downtown."

"Boggs?"

"Yeah, do you know him?" I asked.

Cope frowned. "I don't think so, but it's ringing a tiny bell." He merged into the right-hand lane, looked in the mirror again.

"Is everything okay?"

His brow arched. "I think we're being followed right now. Since we left the parking lot. Black SUV, tinted windshield, a few cars back. I just merged with no close exits, and our friends are... *yep*, right behind us again."

"Shit."

"My thoughts exactly," he said, clearly distracted. "What are your plans today?"

I scrolled through my phone. "I need you to drive me to a massage in an hour with the therapist who helps me after competitions. Then straight home to rest and stretch and eat my weight in carbs. Dora's coming over late, before dinner, to review some of my tapes."

"Okay." He swallowed hard. Merged again. "Aerial isn't stupid—they can clearly find your home address, but Falco hasn't reported seeing anyone on the property at night, and this is the first time I'm catching a tail. They could have confronted us in the parking lot but didn't. Which makes me think they're trying to intimidate, same as the text messages. A common tactic used on whistleblowers, basically scaring them into silence instead of exposing their nasty secrets."

I stared at my side mirror, where I could just make out the tires of the SUV behind us. "They've got a lot at stake right now."

"Indeed, they do."

He pulled down the closest exit, narrowly avoiding missing it, and the SUV roared past us. He let out an even breath before coming to a stop at the red light at the foot of the exit. "I just pulled the easiest trick in the advanced driving book and lost them so..." He shrugged. "I don't think we're working with stone-cold mercenaries. Probably a couple of local guys who don't mind dipping their toes into nefarious business if it pays well."

My heart hammered against my chest. "I still would rather not be followed by *anyone*."

He grinned, driving through the now green light. "It's one hell of an inconvenience, that's for sure."

I studied his reaction—that smile of his had absolutely charmed me when we first met. It was also his most common defense mechanism when he felt scared or stressed but didn't want anyone to know.

When he was finally, *finally* rescued from the hostage situation, I'd run through the halls of that hospital like a track and field star, skidding to a stop in the doorway to his room, where he sat with his mom and Billie. He was hungry, dehydrated, and sore, with lacerations on his wrists, but the doctors had otherwise declared him fine.

"Miss me?" he said with that same quicksilver smile. There were shadows under his eyes and a hollowness in his cheeks, and he seemed shocked at my distraught reaction.

"I thought..." I gasped. "We thought... Cope, we thought they were going to kill you." Those words scraped up my throat, leaving pain in their wake. He only shook his head and opened his arms to me. "They can't take me out that easy, sunshine."

I could count the number of times I let myself cry in front of other people. That day was one of them—huge, grateful sobs as Cope stroked my hair soothingly, as if our roles were reversed. As if I'd been the one to survive an incredible trauma, and he was taking care of me.

"Can I ask you a question?"

"Of course," he said.

"How are you so calm right now?" I asked. "We just broke into a man's office, and we're being tailed by guys trying to scare us."

He reached over and threaded our fingers together. My body instantly relaxed.

"It's a lot of training," he said gently. "It's years of learning how to handle a car and oncoming threats at the same time. Years of learning how to stay focused and loose so your client doesn't get scared."

He brought my hand to his mouth and kissed me there—it was such a tender gesture I was momentarily speechless. "It doesn't..." He cleared his throat. "It doesn't mean I'm also not scared. Especially since you're not just any client. Joking around helps me not get swept up in the fear. Because the thought of two random dudes being paid to intimidate *you*, to scare *you*, to make you feel like you don't deserve to speak the truth, is a mental pathway I can't walk down. I can't trust myself to stay in control when it comes to someone hurting you."

We stopped at another red light. I reached for his tie, dragged him across the console, and kissed him. He kept our mouths close. "I listened to what you said," he whispered.

"Thank you." I kissed him one more time before reluctantly releasing him.

"How do you prepare to hold your breath for four minutes?" he asked, turning down a palm-tree-lined side street. "It scares the shit out of me even if I'm just watching you."

I hesitated, pleasantly surprised at his question. In the past, talking about my training was either too hard or led to an argument.

"Tons and tons and tons of practice," I said. "Understanding the way my lungs work, what risks to be aware of, and how to prioritize my safety above all else. Safety is all I think about."

His eyes flashed to mine, like *he* was pleasantly surprised by my response.

"I listened to what you said, Cope," I whispered. "I am listening."

I never, ever doubted his desire to see me on those waves, achieving my dreams. I just recognized the painful contradiction that desire created for him—to be in love with a person who competed in the exact sport that killed his father.

It was the complex knot in the center of our issues, one that required delicacy and empathy. I realized now how often I must have gingerly side-stepped discussing these details with him, not wanting to add to his grief.

"You were so powerful and graceful the day you did your apnea training in front of me," he continued. "I thought you were an inspiration."

"You mean when I come up sputtering water everywhere out of my mouth?" I said lightly.

"You make it look beautiful," he said. "My dad did that sort of training when we were growing up. Billie and I thought he was like a wizard. Totally magical. Just like you."

"You think I'm magic?"

He kissed my palm again. "I've always known you were magic."

It was such an inconvenient time for my ex-husband to reclaim my heart.

28

SERENA

Dora placed the tablet on my knees and pressed play. I watched a tiny version of myself zip through quick, heavy barrels of water on my board. "See how they tend to angle up here and here," she said, tracking the movement with her finger. "That's what you need to watch tomorrow, kid. If the water shifts like that, it's the undertow."

I nodded, chewing the tip of my thumb. I played the video again, needing to remember my techniques and memorize the many hidden perils of The Wedge.

I tapped the screen. "Can't forget this move." In the video, I arced my board up the wave, shot off the water and spun around in the air. A trick called the *aerial*. It seemed especially fitting.

"If you pull that off during a competition, I'll buy you a whole cake," she said.

"Wait, seriously?"

She shrugged, leaning back against the banister. "Sure, why the hell not."

"One aerial it is, then."

It was a gorgeous San Diego night—warm, with a soft breeze rustling the palm trees over our heads. We were sitting on the steps of my front porch while I took down notes. Dora had arrived a few hours ago with a cheese pizza and bags of ice. Regardless of the growing dangers of the whistle-blower situation, I would be facing waves tomorrow as erratic as they were enormous. They were also rare in their proximity to the shoreline. While jet skis would be there in case of rescue, I would be paddling out, putting additional strain on my already overworked muscles.

Surfing tomorrow, unprepared, wasn't an option.

"Here," she said, handing me another bag of ice. "Right on your elbows now."

I complied but rolled my eyes like a teenager. "My elbows aren't sore."

"*Yet*. But you'll wake up tomorrow in serious pain if you don't." She chewed on a bite of cold pizza. Breaking the crust in half, she passed part of it to me. She knew I needed to feed my muscles and maintain my energy.

She also knew that food had been one of the many tools my parents used to manipulate Caleb and me. If our behavior disappointed them, we found ourselves without a meal that day. Sometimes two.

When Caleb and I left, we were eighteen and fourteen, so we could barely afford a run-down, one-bedroom apartment near his campus. He took the couch, I took the bed, and we finished high school and college respectively by fending for ourselves. He'd gotten a job, and I was already making some money from surf competitions, but we were young, and finances were lean.

Our parents had been wealthy and image-obsessed, which helped us stay away from them more easily—and later helped keep the emancipation process simple. They had a reputation to maintain after all and certainly didn't want to be unmasked as the abusers they really were.

After about a year, they gave up trying to lure us back. My brother and I didn't miss them.

Dora had led the legal process to emancipate me, gotten me my agent, and started me on the training I needed to surf the biggest waves. She made sure we were fed, surprising us with meals when she happened to be "in the area" or inviting us to dinners at her house with her surfer friends where she'd load us up with enough leftovers to last a week.

She never questioned our tough decisions or unconventional life. She'd had to carve her own path too.

She brushed crumbs from her hands and straightened her legs out next to mine. I felt her studying me closely as I munched on bread and watched videos of dangerous waves.

"How's that brain of yours?" she asked. "I don't want you all fucked up out there, angry about that Aerial meeting you told me about earlier. They're not worth you getting hurt if you're distracted."

"I feel ready to win," I said. "I promise. Eyes on the prize, and safety above all else."

"You're sure? Cause, uh, you kinda got a lot going on right now."

I swallowed a nervous laugh. She had no idea. "I feel calm, even after that meeting where my entire value as a professional athlete was reduced down to *sex symbol*. When will they learn we're not surfing for men's entertainment *or* approval?"

Earlier over pizza I had shared every detail of Aerial's article, and together we'd stewed in our collective outrage.

"For some of them? Never," Dora said. "*You just sit on that board and look pretty.* That's what we used to get all the time, as if being on the water was nothing but a fun lark for women. We were toys to flirt with and objects to surf around, but at no point were we considered real competitors." Her mouth curved into a half grin. "Until, of course, I did start competing and beat 'em all."

"They never knew what hit them," I said, laughing.

"No, they didn't." She nodded at me. "And until then, we keep shouting about it. We don't need their permission to fix things."

"True," I said slowly. Her sentence had sent another shimmer of inspiration through me.

Dora cocked her head and nudged me with her foot. "That being said, I don't want you spittin' fire over those clowns tomorrow and getting hurt because they're ruining your focus."

I smiled at her concern. "Believe it or not, I am extremely focused."

Her advice to me all these years had been spot on—I needed to find a place to direct my anger. Knowing now that we were going after Aerial had sharpened my wild and fiery thoughts into a precise blade, a weapon I could wield and not a burden I was controlled by.

"What changed?" she asked.

I searched for Cope's familiar form, guarding us from the edge of the tree line. He turned around as if sensing my attention on him.

I've always known you were magic.

It hadn't taken much for the undeniable pull between us to grow strong as a riptide again, sending us crashing toward what I hoped was understanding and not misery. There was something much too addicting about Cope's vulnerability and trust in the car today, the tender way he kissed my hand and listened to me.

We had never wanted for the exciting parts of being in love: passion, fun, laughter, joy. It was our pain and grief, our loss and scars, that had been the stumbling blocks.

"Everything has changed," I whispered dreamily. I cleared

my throat. "Let's just say, I'm feeling more like myself than I have in a long time."

Dora stared back and forth between me and Cope. "Say no more, kid."

We sat in companionable silence for a few minutes, listening to the birds and the breeze. I ran my thumb over my bottom lip, thinking, caught up in those sparkling realizations I kept having.

"Did you ever wish that the entire surfing industry wasn't dependent on athletes getting corporate sponsors so they can afford to train and compete?"

"Oh, all the damn time," she said. "Talk about a barrier. And it keeps out a lot of folks that don't look like, well—" She nodded at Cope's broad back. "—that don't look like him. You can't compete without funding, but you can't get funding if you don't compete. And women who get sponsors are still paid less than men."

"Even though we're equally risking our lives," I said. Then I winced, stomach churning. "And Marty made it clear today that I'd secured this sponsorship because I was the, quote, 'hottest woman in surfing.' It's despicable and really unfair, but *pretty* athletes always have an easier go of it."

Dora made a sound of agreement. "Hard as that is to sit with, you've had a lot of money thrown your way because of it."

The back of my neck got hot. It *was* hard to sit with a system that discriminated against me *and* benefited me. But I knew what Dora would say in response to my discomfort: *What the hell are you going to do about it?*

"You're right. I have, and it's still wrong. It's a bad system," I said firmly. "Maybe I'm starting to wonder if there's another way. A way to fix some of these flaws."

She nodded, standing up and stretching her back. "There's always another way."

She walked inside with our plates and the tablet. And I slotted this conversation into the part of my brain that had been marinating on a half-baked wisp of an idea that wouldn't leave me alone.

The sound of tires on gravel caught my attention, but it was only Quentin pulling down my driveway in his old busted-up Jeep. He and Cope shared a quick conversation through the side window before he parked and got out, swinging his leather messenger bag across his chest.

Nostalgia squeezed at my heart as he walked up to the house, armed with takeout I recognized and a roguish grin. When we were together, Cope, Caleb, and Quentin had been inseparable. We'd spent far too many nights sitting around beach bonfires with beers in our hands and music on in the background.

He straightened his glasses and smiled up at me. "I don't see you for four years, and you immediately go and get your-self into trouble."

"As Cope would say, I'm just naturally a pain in the ass," I said.

He laughed and then scooped me up for a hug.

"I've missed you, Quent," I said.

He released me but squeezed my shoulder. "And I you, Serena Swift. But let me be perfectly clear, as the person who's had to be around your husband for four long years now, that man has missed you *more*."

I brushed the hair from my face to hide my blush. Dora walked out a minute later, saw Quentin, and clapped her hands together in excitement. As she hugged him, laughing, Cope appeared behind them.

He caught my eye over Quentin's shoulder, and the raw emotion there stilled me. This was how I'd felt seeing him with my brother again, the bizarre sense of our lives snapping back into place. It was jarring—but not in a bad way.

"Quentin Abernathy, you seem smarter than ever," Dora said. "I read every one of your articles each week, so you know."

"What can I say?" He shrugged. "I'm damn good at investigatin'. And you don't look to have aged a bit, Miss Dora."

"I haven't," she said. "I refuse to."

"Good," Quentin said seriously. "Don't do it. Should I swing by your gym soon and get my ass readily handed to me in one of your workout classes?"

"I don't know. Will you bring by some of your mother's chocolate meringue tarts?" she asked.

"You drive a hard bargain." He sighed. "That also means I need to *bake,* although I do enjoy cooking late at night while on deadline."

She clapped him on the shoulder as she walked past. "Seems like you solved your own problem there as usual. I'll see you in class."

When she reached me, she held up her hands, like always. I gave her two high fives and then a swaying hug.

"I'm still prouder of you more than anything," she whispered. "And you better be getting back together with that man in a suit who's been staring at you like you're his favorite dessert this whole time."

"*Dora,*" I whispered back, before dissolving into a fit of laughter. "Thank you for the pizza and the advice and the shared outrage."

"Don't forget to *ice.*"

I crossed my heart. "I won't."

Cope escorted Dora to her car, and I couldn't hear what she said to him, but it involved some intense shadow boxing. Meanwhile, Quentin cleared his throat and lifted the white bag. "Carnitas tacos for the big wave surfer."

I snatched it and walked inside with him, opening the bag to inhale the scent of marinated pork and spices. "Don't tell Caleb, but I think I officially like you better than him now."

"I'll take it to my grave," he said, dropping the six-pack he brought in the fridge but not before opening a beer on the bottle opener I still kept under the counter. He glanced at his phone. "Your other guard is arriving right about now, right?"

"And we need to go distract him so that Cope can sneak back in here," I said, pulling the blinds and curtains closed on the first floor so Falco wouldn't see his partner enjoying a casual taco dinner with their client.

"I'm ready," he said. Bringing his beer, he left the messenger bag on the bar stool and followed me out to where Falco was now standing with Cope. They wore matching somber expressions that immediately gave me goosebumps.

"Do you know what they're talking about?" Quentin asked.

"No, but Cope looking that serious is creeping me out."

"Me too," he said. As we got closer, Cope waved at us as he slid his sunglasses into his suit pocket. "Have a nice evening, Ms. Swift. I'll see you in the morning for the competition."

Quentin and I smiled politely in response as Cope got in his car and drove back up the driveway—although I knew the plan was for him to park farther down the street, walk down through the woods that ran adjacent to the property, and sneak in the back.

Falco gave us a short nod before walking toward the front. "Hello, Ms. Swift. Do you have company for the whole evening?"

We both went fire-engine red in the face, but Quentin recovered faster. "I'm just a friend of Serena's from years back. I brought her some good luck tacos before her big event tomorrow."

Falco frowned as he listened but then shrugged. "Okay."

"For the record, we're not together. Like that. In any way," Quentin drawled, ever the gentleman. "Ever."

"I think he gets it," I said, trying not to laugh. "Quentin is a reporter for the *San Diego Times*. Do you read the paper, Mr. Falco?"

He was tightening his tie and smoothing it into place. "No."

Quentin rocked back on his heels. "Do you read any paper, sir?"

"No."

I touched my ear and discreetly peeked around Falco's massive form to see a blur of hushed movement in the trees I hoped was Cope. He was supposed to slip behind the back of the house with a key to the patio door.

"Mr. McDaniels finished the check of the locks and entrances before I arrived," Falco said. "Unless you need me, I'll be right outside until morning."

"Can I get you food? Tacos?" I asked.

"Just here to do my job, ma'am," he said. "I don't need anything."

"Well, thank you then," I said. "And have a good night.

I tugged Quentin back to the house, pushing open the front door and ushering him inside. Cope was sitting at the island—jacket off, tie off, sleeves rolled up—arranging our food and only slightly out of breath.

"Copeland," Quentin said, stealing a chip and dipping it into salsa. "Well done sneaking in like a teenager who broke curfew."

"I might have some experience in that area," he said, winking at me. "If Falco comes in and finds me here, I don't have a good excuse and will probably just run away into the night."

"Innovative," Quentin said. "I like it."

As he busied himself with his laptop, I pulled up a stool

next to Cope, mesmerized by the one inch of bare chest exposed by his unbuttoned collar. This was our first time being near each other in hours. With Quentin otherwise occupied, Cope tucked a strand of hair behind my ear, his finger lingering on my sensitive skin.

I shivered. I remembered what those hands of his could do.

"What were you talking to Falco about?" I finally asked.

His attention darted to Quentin's laptop screen. "I told him we'd been followed this morning, so he was extra alert tonight."

"That was smart," Quentin said. "This can't be kept a secret much longer, and you two are going to need protection."

My phone vibrated where it lay on the table.

"May I?" Quentin asked.

I nodded. "It's probably Kalei or my brother."

Quentin read whatever was on the screen, swore, and then handed it over. I snatched it from him, heart sinking.

We shouldn't have to ask you three times, Serena. Give us what you have.

"Fuck me," Cope whispered.

Quentin was already typing away on his laptop. "Now's as good a time as any to talk about what's on that drive Catalina gave us." He waved us over. "Because I've spent the past few days digging as deep as I could, and I'm sad to say I only have bad news."

"How bad?" Cope asked.

"Our friends at Aerial? They've been lying this whole damn time."

❦ 29 ❦

COPE

If the situation was different, I would have been overjoyed to sit around our old kitchen table with my wife and best friend again, drinking beer and eating tacos. But the energy was heavy with tension, and the closed blinds and curtains only added to the somber mood.

I looked sideways at Serena, who sat with her leg pressed to mine. I dropped my hand onto the top of her thigh and gripped her knee, marveling at the play of soft skin and hard muscle beneath my fingers. A touch like this—the barest intimacy—now felt weighted with emotional meaning. It had been denied to me for such a long time.

She laced her fingers through mine with a shy smile.

Quentin spun in his chair before taking a sip of beer. "I'll start by mentioning that the original USB stick that Catalina gave to you is in a safe deposit box I opened up for situations like this. I've also got copies on this laptop. You two save it anywhere?"

"No, sir," I said.

"Good," he replied. "The fewer people involved, the better before we break the story. If they're sending nasty messages and starting to follow you, we need to move fast. They're not going to play nice much longer."

"This has been nice?" Serena asked.

I shifted next to her. "Unfortunately, yes. I still think they have several employees pegged as the whistleblower and don't know who has what. They're trying to flush out the weak link with scare tactics that can't be directly traced back to them."

Quentin pressed his lips together. "Legally, they need to appear wholly innocent of these threats, which is why the blocked number, the SUV tail, even Marty's *aw shucks, we lost some files, can you believe it* act is on purpose. They can rely on their pristine reputation to cover their tracks. And rely on their friendly charm to get you to give it back. As if *all of this* was just a big misunderstanding."

She spun her bottle on the table. "They are excellent manipulators."

"Well—" He sighed. "—that's in line with what I'm learning about our favorite brothers. I met with my guy from San Diego PD, Joey Decarlo, and asked him to check in on Catalina once he figured out where she lived. I tried to weasel that information out of the receptionist at Aerial, but unfortunately she's quite dedicated to employee privacy. According to her, Catalina is still out sick and has been since that night she met Serena. I've called and contacted every phone number and email listed for her on their website. I even tracked down what I think are her social media pages, but no response."

"Am I right to be worried for her?" Serena asked.

He cut his gaze to mine then back to her. "I think so, yes. At the very least, she is scared to come to work, which is already worrisome if they've been threatening her. Passing that information to you put a big target on her back."

I stretched my arm across the back of Serena's chair. "The best-case scenario is that Catalina is hiding on purpose. She could be staying with friends or relatives even. She seems smart and strategic. Even if the decision to give the information to you was spur of the moment, let's hope she had a safety plan in place."

She blew out a shaky breath. "Let's hope. And thanks for checking in on her, Quentin."

"It's no problem, and Joey is good people. I didn't tell him much but got across that her life could be in danger."

Goosebumps broke out along Serena's legs, so I rubbed my hand up and down her skin, warming her up.

"What else did Joey have to say?" I asked.

He munched on a tortilla chip, pushing the basket toward me with his index finger. "That's the thing. I met with Joey for breakfast this morning, asked him what he knew about David Lattimore and the city council. Told me he's best buds with Foster Hemmings."

"The man he's posing with in that picture?" Serena asked.

"The very one. He's been on the city council for years, a real San Diego institution. And when I say *institution*, I mean sack of smelly shit."

I unfolded my arm and leaned across the table. "Councilman Hemmings? The real estate broker?"

"Yeah, why?" he said. "You know him?"

"I don't, not personally," I said. "But my last client, Mr. Arnold Sheffield, was *also* a sack of smelly shit." I pointed at the photo on the laptop. "I didn't recognize him out of his golfing gear, but once a month Arnold and Foster golfed together at the La Jolla Country Club. They're real pals; they go way back."

Quentin whistled low under his breath. "That tracks. David Lattimore is a member of the La Jolla Country Club, and they're often seen together. It's the most expensive club in the city. Elite and exclusive, although they certainly don't mind that Foster Hemmings is a well-known skeeze-ball. He's been accused of taking bribes for city services, for bankrolling his own projects using tax-payer dollars. For harassment, abuse."

"Sounds like a real class act," Serena said with an eye roll. "But what is David Lattimore doing cozied up to *him*?"

"I don't fully know yet," he said. "But the connection isn't great. That man is known for paying to hide secrets, breaking the law, and using his money to do whatever the hell he wants." He fished his phone out and scrolled through it. "Worse is the voicemail I received right before driving over here."

He pressed play and dropped it in the middle of the table.

"Quentin, it's Decarlo. Listen, I don't really know what's going on with you and Aerial, but I ran your question up the flagpole, tried to get any dirt on their business dealings, and was told from up high to basically shut the hell up and stop askin' about it. I wish I had more, and I'll find Ms. Flores for you, but my guess is powerful people are protecting this company. Sorry."

Serena's eyes went wide. "What the fuck?"

I shook my head, confused. "But Aerial has been around for over forty years without a mark on their reputation. If they've been lying or bribing or whatever, it can't have been for the whole time, can it?"

He spun his phone on the table. "I don't think so, no. I've spent most of my career investigating fraud and corporate scandals. Forty years is a long time to hide your sins. Not impossible, but unlikely."

She leaned her elbows on the table. "What are these sins they're so keen to hide?"

He straightened his glasses before answering. "I have a few messages out to a potential source. One of the factory inspectors in those pictures is willing to go on the record about what they were asked to do and by whom. And how it relates to those lawsuits Catalina copied over for us."

"The ones in private arbitration?" I asked.

"Exactly," he said. "From what I can tell, this inspector wants to comment on what he has been bribed to do for the past five years at least. That is to look the other way and sign off on reports that verify working conditions and environmental processes in those factories."

"*What?*" Serena and I said in unison.

Quentin pointed at the files on his laptop, clicking them open. "These are wrongful death lawsuits. Personal injury lawsuits. Employees claiming unsafe and hazardous working conditions made worse by the fact that they're breathing in harsh fumes and exposed to chemicals known to cause disease."

He opened Marty's planner, the one Serena had taken, which he'd picked up from me while she had her massage appointment. He held up the business card for Sylvester Boggs. "There's no record of Aerial hiring Mr. Boggs, but I am *very* familiar with this scumbag."

"So was Cope, when I said his name," Serena said.

He nodded at me. "I can guess why you are, my friend. Sylvester Boggs has a long track record of protecting wealthy companies in wrongful death or injury lawsuits. His name would pop up all the time when I worked the crime beat a few years ago."

Clarity dawned on me. I rubbed my forehead, remembering. "Not Sheffield, but the client I had before him. The guy worked in food supply and hired Boggs when workers at his meat packing factories complained of horrific working conditions."

Serena studied me. "Are *all* of your clients basically Bond villains?"

That uneasiness I'd been feeling lately multiplied. We were sitting here discussing horrible crimes committed against human beings and the environment, so I was amped up, ready to take these assholes down.

And realizing that, yeah, after Serena's assignment, I'd be placed with another Bond villain again. And again, and again.

At what point was I part of the same problem?

"It would appear so," I said grimly. "At the very least, they're all rubbing elbows with these slimy bottom-feeders. It isn't a good look, for them or for me."

She squeezed my hand beneath the table.

"When you said Aerial was lying, you really meant it?" she asked Quentin.

"Yes, ma'am."

Her fury was evident by the fire in her eyes. "But Aerial has always claimed the opposite in how their clothing and gear is manufactured. It's their entire *brand*."

"That's why these are private lawsuits," he said. "That's why they bribe the factory inspectors. It's still cheaper to do that than to pay your employees a fair wage using recycled materials better for the earth but much, much more expensive." He clasped his hands together on the table. "This is just my initial research, and my source will go far in painting a clearer image of how deep this goes. But what it looks like is that the workers in their factories have gotten sick, injured, and died so Aerial could make more money." He touched Serena's hand. "I'm so sorry."

It was hard to fully describe the anger, disappointment and shock etched in her face. And every truth Quentin revealed only added to the sick twisting feeling in my own stomach.

"So what's our plan then?" she asked.

"In an ideal world? I'd write the story with sources and as much information as I could gather. Work with Catalina and ensure she's protected before we move forward with the article. This would be..." He paused. "This would be huge news, y'all. Certainly not the first big company to mistreat its employees and falsify their claims, but it's a beloved one with devoted fans."

A hefty pause stretched between the three of us. Serena stared down at the table, and I stared at her. I knew enough about these cases to know what Quentin was going to tell her next, and it was the part I hated the most.

"Serena."

She glanced up at his tone. "What is it?"

"You've been my friend for a long time. But I won't bullshit you about this, and I'll share the same with Catalina. The media is not kind to whistleblowers, especially if they're women. Catalina is going to take the brunt of it, but you're a professional athlete with a well-known name. It's gonna stick to you, darlin'. They will try and discredit you. Plus, you're the face of their company. I'm sure you'll find a way to get out of that contract, but it will be impossible for you to hide from this." He leaned over, held her gaze. "I couldn't have you saying *yes* without me being abundantly clear."

Hearing Quentin say it out loud was worse than my late-night anxieties. If anyone could withstand a situation like this, it was Serena, and I knew she'd make sure Catalina was protected and supported. I just couldn't stomach the thought of what the public might do to her.

"Yes," she said in a clear voice.

"Yes, as in, you're ready to move forward?"

A smile like I'd never seen spread across her face. "Yeah, I'm fucking ready. Besides, I've already got a *controversial reputation*, according to Marty, so I might as well lean into it."

I reached over and touched her hand. "It's the right thing to do. And I knew you'd say yes. It's also very brave."

She shook her head. "Staring at a wall of water you have to paddle up is brave. This is *right*. Aerial hurts human beings *and* the environment for profit and lies to the public while doing it. I don't see another option here, do you?"

"No," I said firmly. "I do not see another option."

Her fingers tightened in mine. "They can come for me all they want. I'll be too busy winning competitions."

Quentin chuckled while nodding his head. "We'll be with you every step of the way, I promise."

Beneath the table, I kept holding her tight. I don't know what she saw in my face when she looked at me, but it put heat in her cheeks.

I knew what I was thinking, though.

Quentin cleared his throat awkwardly, cutting through our charged moment. "I'm going to talk to my editor, my sources, and keep pulling this story together. And Joey is searching for Catalina. And *you*, Serena, probably need to get some rest before tomorrow, right?"

"Rest, yep," she said, chewing on her lip. "I'll be getting a lot of rest, thank you. Will you call me as soon as you have word on Catalina? Or any other developments?"

"You can count on it," he said, packing his things into his messenger bag. When he stood up, she pulled him in for a long hug—he raised his eyebrows at me from over her shoulder. I wasn't positive but thought he was saying something like, 'Are you two back together or what?'

"Thank you," she said. "So much."

"Please, you know investigating corporate malfeasance is my idea of a good time."

She pulled back and pinned him with a look. "It's important, and I know you'll do an amazing job."

"I will try my best," he said. As Serena was putting food and drinks away and clearing up the kitchen, I walked my best friend to the door. I couldn't walk him to his car, or Falco would see me, but it also meant that Serena was privy to our entire conversation. I took great pleasure in shrugging nonchalantly while he stood there trying to nonverbally ask for an update. When her back was turned to the sink, water running, I mouthed, "Things are good." Then I gave him a dorky thumbs-up.

If we had privacy, I would have told him that we'd had the most incredible reunion sex the world has ever seen. And then opened up to each other about some of our most intense areas of mistrust.

It was far more than *good*.

Sighing in defeat, he opened the front door a half inch. "As always, it's been a pleasure, Copeland."

"And you as well, my friend." Dropping my voice, I asked, "And you feel safe at your apartment, correct? You'll make sure you aren't followed?"

"I'll drive in meandering circles for a bit just in case, but I really do feel fine," he said. "My gut says this is going to get a lot more intense before it gets better, so I'm happy y'all have each other."

I squeezed his shoulder and clapped him on his back before he left. "Text when you get home. I'm only a phone call away."

I heard him whistling as he walked to his car. I checked and double-checked every point of entry on that first floor, peeked out through the curtain, and was comforted by seeing Falco, standing in the dark.

Serena was already on the second floor, where our bed was. Heart in my throat, holding my breath, I slowly climbed the stairs and found Serena leaning against the closed bedroom door. She'd changed into a large, faded black tee-shirt that fell just past the curve of her ass, the front faded with a logo I hardly remembered anymore.

She was wearing one of my shirts. A favorite one. I'd left it for her on the horrible day that I packed up my things and drove away.

"Are you wearing my shirt?" I asked.

Only a few feet separated us.

She fingered the fabric. "I wear it when I miss you."

"How often is that, sunshine?"

"Every night."

My hand tightened on the banister, preventing me from doing what I craved. "Are you comfortable with what we talked about? With Quentin?"

She nodded. "I'm furious."

I didn't think it possible to pack so much jagged pain into two little words.

"I'm so furious it feels like it might tear me apart," she said. "But I'm ready to fight for what I believe in. I'm ready to fight for what's right. Are you, Cope?"

My mind filled with images I'd locked away for my own self-preservation: Serena dancing around a bonfire on the beach, laughing beneath the stars. Serena blowing me a cheeky kiss in her thrift-store wedding dress as she walked down the aisle. Serena licking her fingers happily while cooking bacon in a camp skillet.

I took a step closer to her.

"Yes," I said. "Of course. I'm ready to fight for everything. Even if it's hard."

"That kind of fight is always worth it."

I took another step.

"Even if it's scary?" I asked.

One more step. I could count the freckles on her face, see the scar on her cheek.

"Especially if it's scary," she whispered, head tilting back to hold my gaze. I closed my hand around her hand, holding the doorknob, the only thing keeping me from our marriage bed.

"Will you stay with me tonight?" she asked.

"As your bodyguard?"

"No," she said. "Will you stay as my husband?"

Intoxicating possession flooded my veins. The absence of that word—*ex*—didn't escape my notice. My mouth dipped to hers, grazing our lips together. I dragged my fingers up her thigh, lifting the fabric of the shirt when I reached the juncture between her legs. Her mouth opened on a gasp.

"Do you want me in our bed?" I asked.

She clutched my shirt, pulling me closer. "*Please.*"

I palmed her sex and enjoyed her throaty moan. I slipped one, then two fingers inside her underwear, sliding through her hot, wet folds. I found her clit, circled with the barest amount of pressure. "Do you remember how fast you came for me in that elevator after our wedding?"

"Yes, *yes*," she sighed. I nudged my nose against hers, teasing, not letting our lips connect. I increased the pressure of my fingers, still keeping it light.

"And why was that?" Her head tipped back, and I kissed down her throat, working her clit in ever-increasing pressure. Her hips were starting to punch forward, seeking more friction.

"I don't recall."

I bit her neck. "Don't lie to me."

She laughed, but it ended on another moan as my hand moved faster. "Oh, *fuck*."

"That's not an answer, Serena." I let go of the doorknob and turned her face to mine. I pressed my thumb into her lip, and her tongue darted out, licking. "Be a good girl and tell me what I want to hear."

Her eyes flashed with pleasure. I remembered everything about this woman, including her dirty little secret. There was no faster switch to turn her on than by giving her an order.

"It's so good," she panted. One hand gripped my shirt, the other wrapped around my wrist, trapped between her legs. She was starting to grind against my fingers, like she had that night, and the sight was so hot my control almost snapped. "It's so good, so good, *please don't stop.*"

"Why did you get off so fast that night?" I asked. Her beautiful face was flushed, sweat beading on her brow.

"Because you're so... *fuck*, your hands are perfect." Her head fell back, and she almost yanked my shirt off. "Because you always make me come. *Always.*"

My hand landed next to her face so I could lean in, angle my motions just right while watching my wife climax on my fingers. She started to chant my name, and I kissed her, unable to resist her plump lips any longer. She opened for me, deepened our kiss, hands sliding into my hair and pulling. We tasted each other, tongues stroking, lips bruising. I felt each whimper, her breath like a caress, her ecstasy evident in the way her mouth moved against mine.

"Oh god, oh god," she cried. "Cope, *Cope.*"

I twisted my hand, gave her the *exact* pressure I knew she needed.

"Come for your husband now," I whispered, the tenderest command I could manage. Serena flew apart around my fingers, and I caught her beneath the knees to keep her standing. I held her to my chest as she caught her breath, feeling like I was back on that elevator again—so desperately in love my heart couldn't contain it.

She tipped her head back with her lips parted, dark eyes searching mine.

The door clicked open.

"I want you to fuck me on our bed," she said.

30

SERENA

I could barely stand after the orgasm Cope had given me against the door. But that didn't stop me from dragging him inside. He stepped into our bedroom, rubbing a hand across his mouth and eying me like a starving man. He kicked the door closed behind him and began unbuttoning his shirt, revealing the smooth planes of his chest, covered in dark hair.

"Serena."

His rough voice snapped me to attention. "Cope?"

"Take your fucking clothes off."

I tore off his shirt and threw it across the room. Hooked my fingers into my underwear and eased them down my legs. I finally stood naked in front of my husband for the first time in four years, but I was much too distracted by his body. His white shirt, sliding off those broad muscles, revealing abs I'd been obsessed with. Still staring at me, he worked off his belt. Tossed it.

"You are a dream come true," he said hoarsely.

I was stunned speechless. He kicked off his briefs and wrapped a fist around his thick cock. He stared at me, as vulnerable as he was arrogant, as his arm flexed with motion.

I gave in to my nightly fantasies. Pushed him hard against the door and fell to my knees. I gazed up at him like he was the burly, bearded god I worshiped.

The man staring down at me was one who'd ceded all control to his darkest passions. He speared his fingers through my hair and swiped his thumb across my mouth.

"I want this," he growled.

"Then you should have it," I said, running my tongue from the root of his cock to the tip. His fist hit the door, and his relieved groan reverberated through the room. I opened my mouth wider, taking him deep as I dug my nails into his firm ass.

"*Serena*," he moaned. "I've missed this so much."

I hummed around his slick skin and slid him to the back of my throat, let his strong fingers in my hair dictate my rhythm and pressure. He flexed his hips and fucked my mouth thoroughly. I kept my eyes lifted to his and watched Cope lose his mind. One hand gripped my head while the other drifted to my breasts, cupping them roughly, pinching my nipples, making me moan around his cock. My head bobbed up and down, urged on by his hand and the sounds he made. Those abs of his flexed and tightened as his jaw dropped and his head fell back, exposing his throat. His breath came harsh as he yanked on my hair.

"Your mouth is perfect," he grunted. "Everything about you is perfect."

I swirled and fluttered my tongue around the tip in response. He looked down at me almost angrily, fire in his eyes, and I took him as deep as I could, relaxing my throat. Holding him captive there. His thick thighs started shaking. He loved this battle for control we always had, falling apart in my mouth the same way I fell apart beneath his tongue.

The night we'd gotten married, before he'd licked champagne from my fevered skin, I'd shoved Cope against the hotel wall and sucked him off in the hottest, sloppiest blow job I'd ever given in my life. It was an act of pure joy, and he didn't seem to mind as his come spilled from my lips and dripped down my body.

On that night, I had watched him just like this, enthralled. I witnessed him lose all sense of decorum or control. I felt so connected in that moment, the way I did now—it was the ultimate intimacy.

I slid my lips up and down in a faster rhythm. He twisted the strands of my hair, and I groaned, wrapping my hand around the base of his cock.

"Nothing should feel this good," he said with a groan. "This, you, that hot fucking mouth of yours. It should be forbidden. It should be *illegal*." His thumb stroked tenderly across my cheek. "You make a man want to risk it all, you know that?"

I sat back on my heels, letting his cock slip from my mouth with a *pop*. With his hands gripping my face, I stared up at Cope from on my knees and understood that we shared the same power. "You make me want to risk everything too."

With a growl of frustration, he hauled me to my feet then lifted me, wrapping my legs around his hips. We couldn't stop kissing, hands roaming everywhere—pulling, scratching, remembering. I clung to him tightly as he lowered us onto the bed, wasting no time in dropping his head to my breasts. They were small against his large, strong hands, cupping and worshiping me there. His tongue circled my nipple, lapping it lightly while he pinched the other. My core tightened reflexively, already seeking friction, pressure, to be filled.

"I've missed every inch of you," he groaned against my skin. "I dream of you every night. Of this body, of the sounds you make for me, of the taste of your cunt on my tongue."

My back arched off the bed, and my fingers gripped his hair. He pressed open-mouthed kisses—with teeth—across my ribcage, my stomach, the curve of my thighs. He was feasting on my body with a look of pure astonishment, like I might disappear if he let me out of his sight.

I writhed beneath his skilled mouth, shivering with sensation. His palm smoothed down my thigh, circled my hip, then squeezed my ass. He began kissing me again as his fingers teased along the seam there, sliding along my back entrance.

"Oh, *yes*," I hissed, digging my nails into his shoulders. He was my husband, after all—he knew every single secret my body held.

With a low, rumbling groan, he applied the sweetest pressure to the ring of muscle there, not entering me but stroking out sensation. Lazily. Decadently. He licked a path across my collarbone, between my breasts, sucking my nipples between his lips as he worked magic with those fingers.

It was the most tortuous foreplay, a sustained note of luxurious pleasure. I was suspended in ecstasy, and Cope was enjoying every single inch of my body, remembering my desires.

He dropped to his knees on the floor and pulled me gently to the end of the bed. I propped up on my elbows to enjoy the view of his trunk-sized shoulders, bare and ripped. His messy hair and beard and that arrogant grin stealing my breath. He slid his palms down my inner thighs before spreading them, dropping them on either side of his face. He sucked two fingers into his mouth, and then slid both inside of me.

I stretched my arms over my head, feeling indulgent. Then reached down to let my fingers tangle in his hair, tugging lightly when his tongue landed on my clit. With slow, steady movement, Cope fucked me with his fingers and fluttered his tongue across my skin.

Outside of this room was the distant sound of crashing waves, an endless cycle, the background music of my entire life. They couldn't match the sounds I made now, as he brought me close again, leading me to the edge of ecstasy. One hand clutched the mattress, the other his hair. I was writhing, rolling my hips, as his tongue danced across my clit with precision.

His fingers moved quickly—in and out—a constant tease as I rose and rose. A bead of sweat slid between my breasts, my breathing was rapid and shallow. I opened my eyes to look at Cope, startled to find him staring at me with raw intensity. He growled my name but didn't stop licking my pussy, didn't stop flexing those fingers in the most delicious way. I held that gaze, refusing to back down as I felt my orgasm beckon.

"I need you," I gasped. "All of you, *please*."

That snarl was back. It had goosebumps igniting along my skin. I backed up on the bed as he prowled toward me, crawling until his hands were planted on either side of my head. He gave a slow, easy grind of his cock against my clit, and my eyes fluttered closed. Then I was flipped onto my stomach. His tongue licked up the length of my spine. When he reached the back of my neck, he buried his face in my hair with a shuddering inhale.

"Serena," he sighed. "*Serena,* you have all of me."

He notched the head of his cock at my entrance and flexed forward, careful of the tight angle. But he knew, *he knew*, it was my very favorite. Because of what happened next —every inch of his body pressing to mine, keeping me close, keeping me safe. In this position I felt cherished and debauched and protected and so totally *his*.

It was everything I ever wanted but was afraid to ask for, pinned down and ridden hard but liberated with euphoria. He fully seated himself with a raspy moan and entwined his fingers with mine.

My husband started to move between my legs, a heady, addicting drag of his hard cock against my inner walls. I shuddered and cried out, which had Cope humming against my ear.

"You remembered," I sighed, cheek pressed to the bed. His heavy body curled over mine, mouth grazing my temple, my neck.

"Of course," he said on a groan. "This is all of me, sunshine." He pulled back then thrust—harder this time. My fingers squeezed tight to his. "So make me work for it. Make me work for the privilege of fucking you."

He rocked in and out in a maddening rhythm. "You want my dedication and focus?" This time, his reentry was an agonizing, inch-by-inch claiming that made me scream in frustration against the bedsheets. He bit down on my ear and whispered, "Then you got it."

31

COPE

ime ceased to exist, as did reality and consequences.

The moment she opened the door to our bedroom, my heart was *all* the way in. With my body pressed to hers, I recognized that we'd reached a new threshold, one we couldn't come back from now that we'd crossed it.

This reunion was different from the sex we'd had this morning. It wasn't a hot hook-up between two ex-lovers. It wasn't closure, it wasn't an ending, and it wasn't a fun, sexy mistake either.

If we hadn't pursued anything further, I would have told myself that exact stream of lies.

It was just for fun. We were under a lot of stress. Mistakes happen.

Our bodies moving together on this bed, our frenzied release, the sweat on our skin—this was purposeful. I was her husband, she was my *wife*, and we had every right to want each other like this.

This wasn't closure. It was a *turning* point.

I pushed up onto my hands then sat back on my heels,

bringing Serena's hips with me. I took a moment to enjoy the gorgeous curve of her spine, the span of her waist, the freckles, the scars, the tan lines. I smoothed the unruly curls from her face—she was blissed out and biting her bottom lip. She was a fucking *vision*. My self-control had snapped the second she dropped to her knees in front of me, and it had only gotten worse as she took my cock between those pretty lips and had me seeing stars.

Having my tongue between her thighs again had been an actual exercise in self-restraint. The urge to fuck my own fist while I licked her clit was overwhelming. A man could only take so much, and Serena was an expert in finding every single button I loved and *pushing* them.

"Cope," she begged, "I need *more*."

As if I could deny this woman anything.

I moved to my knees, steadying myself, fucking her in the same slow, deliberate rhythm. Then I drove hard. Harder. She fell forward with a gasp and twisted her fingers in the bedsheets.

I grabbed a mass of her curls and waited for her plaintive "*yes*" before gently tugging her head back. She had a competition tomorrow, after all, and I was always aware of the impact our sex could have on muscles that needed to be flexible.

"Perfect," she sighed. I pulled just a little bit harder, caught her husky moan, and gripped her hip with my other hand. I doubled my speed, driving my cock between her legs in long, deep strokes. She was so wet. She was so familiar. I held her hair and drilled harder, my hips pumping against the curve of her ass, those husky moans of hers transformed into full-blown sobs of pleasure.

My head tipped back on the ecstasy of it all, the intensity infiltrating every nerve ending, every inch of my body, fracturing my focus.

"I'm so close," she said, thrusting back against me, taking

me even deeper. My world narrowed down to my fist in her hair, the curve of her back, her pussy gripping me with every thrust. "So close, so close, *Cope*."

I licked the pad of my index finger then slipped it between her legs, catching her clit as I kept up the demanding rhythm. Her fingers tore at the sheets. Her mouth opened in a cry. She was wet, ready, clenching around me. I watched, astonished, as she came and came, shuddering, smiling, chanting my name.

I gave in to my body's plea for release. My climax was strong enough to steal my vision and seize my lungs. I groaned Serena's name on my final, ragged strokes. Pushed the hair from her face and saw her smiling dreamily. Then laughing.

I pulled out gently and kissed the small of her back—she tasted like salt and sex. I crawled onto my side, still breathing like I'd just gone for a hard run. She was on her stomach, big brown eyes watching me.

"Are you okay?"

She grinned. Laughed again. Kissed me, a little sloppily. I joined her, pulling her flush against the front of my body, our faces only a few inches apart. "Do you find my dedication and focus amusing?"

"That was the best sex I ever had in my life."

I kissed her forehead. "Oh, yeah? Better than our honeymoon night? I did drink champagne *off* of you. I would hate to think my performance in that hotel room was *sub-par*."

"I didn't think it could get any better." Her voice was raspy. "But then it did."

I smoothed my palm down the slope of her spine and back up again. She sighed, relaxed, and looped her leg over my waist. I took a moment to accept where we were—in our house, in our bed. The sheets and pillows were the same, the rug was the same, even the curtains.

It was Serena and I that were different now.

"Was that what you needed tonight?" I asked.

"I wanted you," she said. "Sex was a bonus. But I wanted you here, with me. Like this."

Emotion gripped my throat and I had to swallow a few times to regain control. "I wanted to be here with you too."

She blinked heavily and yawned.

"You should sleep," I said. "We have to get up in, *holy shit*, six hours."

"Not yet." Her fingers traced my lips, down my chin. "Can I talk to you about something? About us?"

"Of course," I said.

Nerves fluttered in my chest. Less than twenty-four hours separated us from that first kiss in the kitchen until now. And I was already in too deep.

"When I was growing up, my parents tried to control my emotions pretty severely," she said, voice soft and lyrical on this vital night. "If I got *worked up* or was unladylike, they would shut me down. And they would shut down too. They thought avoiding it and forbidding it helped me get my unseemly emotions under control."

Her fingers traced along my jaw, to my ear. "It made me feel very alone. I was lucky I had Caleb. Anytime we were together, he let me rage, or cry about something sad, or be frustrated or pissy or *inconvenient* with my intense feelings." She held my gaze but looked worried. "When I think back to those months after your hostage incident, I think I reacted so negatively because I felt like a little girl again. Helpless and angry."

Serena had wanted to talk about what happened to me constantly and my resistance to that had scared her. She didn't sleep, was plagued with night terrors, watched me every day like she suspected I might have a break down.

I, on the other hand, wanted to go back to normal immediately with funny jokes and silly work anecdotes. Because I'd survived, hadn't I? Rehashing those two days seemed pointless to me. More importantly, *I* was supposed to be protecting her, not the other way around. She was the one with the death-defying career.

But the combination of the late hour and phenomenal sex was tapping at the locked box in my brain marked *terrifying shit I never want to think about again.*

I kept up the motion of my hand, smoothing up and down her back. "Did I make you feel alone during those months?"

She hesitated, going rigid. We were walking across a bridge that was simultaneously being built right in front of our feet. Every reveal, every vulnerability, felt like placing the next board down without knowing if it would stick.

"I did feel alone," she said. "But I'm not telling you this for sympathy. I'm trying to explain why I felt like I was falling apart, that *we* were falling apart during that time. I didn't feel like I could express myself, so the only thing I ended up doing was begging you to quit your job."

I sighed. "And all I did was beg you to quit your job." I paused. "And your dream."

"Hindsight?" she said. "I don't think either of those requests were productive."

I chuckled and kissed her fingers. "Wait. Arguing about the same thing over and over is *bad* in a relationship?"

"So I've heard." She brushed the hair from my forehead. "I should have given you more time. As much as you needed. I can't begin to imagine what you went through."

A memory forced its way in—the dull, distracting ache in my shoulders from having my hands tied behind my back. The hollow hunger. The way my tongue stuck to the roof of my mouth.

The gunman giving me a darkly sympathetic look, like I'd

pulled the fucking short straw that day. *If your boss doesn't give me what I want, this isn't ending well for any of you.*

"I've held on to my anger at how things ended between us because it was easier to exist with those feelings than to acknowledge the part I played. Easier to acknowledge that I still—"

Serena trailed off, but my heart surged in my chest at what I thought, what I *hoped*, she was trying to say.

Did she feel it too? The inevitability of our once-in-a-lifetime love?

"What I'm trying to say—" Her voice shook. "—is I'm sorry for forcing you to heal within my timeline and my parameters. It was unfair and immature of me."

I slid my palm against her cheek. "I'm sorry I made you feel so alone. That I locked you out, made you feel like you had to censor yourself. You were in so much obvious pain, and I brushed you off and refused to listen every time." I tucked a strand of hair behind her ear. "I hated when you did that to *me* because I couldn't protect you if I didn't know what was hurting you. It used to make me feel helpless. Inadequate."

She nodded. "This is resonating with me."

"Yeah?"

"The situation with Aerial scares me. The threats, being followed. Everything Quentin said tonight about what they could do to try and keep their reputation clean. I don't want them to hurt people anymore and lie about it to make more money. I also don't want them to hurt anyone I love."

"You're scared?" I repeated.

"I am, yeah."

She was handing me another part of the bridge.

"I'm scared about you surfing The Wedge tomorrow," I said. Tentatively. "Not because you can't do it. I know that you can. But my dad both loved those waves and told us all the time how dangerous they could be."

I searched for signs on her face of our many past disagreements. But she kissed me instead, lingering for a while.

"I'm ready for tomorrow," she said. "But I'd be lying if I didn't say I'm always a little more afraid at The Wedge. They're smaller than the bombs at Nazaré and Jaws, but they come in so fast, and the undertow is really strong."

I brushed my lips against her forehead, grateful for her honesty. Maybe never seeing her admit fear only over-activated my own, as if she wasn't taking it seriously.

That realization sat heavy in my mind because Serena *and* Marilyn had described me as *reckless* lately.

"How about I tell you if I'm scared?" I said. "And you do the same thing?"

Her smile was brilliant, even in the dark. "I'd like that."

I pulled her close to my chest, wrapping my arms around her as her breathing slowed and her body fully relaxed against mine. A bone-deep exhaustion tried to claim me, but I resisted it for as long as I could. I was with Serena, in our bed, falling asleep with our limbs entwined like we had every single night for two years.

This second chance of ours couldn't be coincidence. And we couldn't mess it up this time.

The hard, beautiful truth was the last thing I thought of before finally drifting off to sleep.

We were each other's destinies.

How could I let her go again?

32

SERENA

It was an hour before dawn.

The entire house was still and hushed in the dark purple twilight. I clicked on the salt lamp on the dresser, bathing the bedroom in a pink light. Then I perched on the bed and watched Cope sleep.

He'd held me close all through the night, the sound of his heartbeat a steady metronome that lulled me into an undisturbed slumber. Between the mind-blowing sex, our conversation, and the plan we'd made for Aerial, I woke up clear-eyed and eager for today.

I told the truth last night—I *was* afraid of the danger that faced us going toe-to-toe against a billion-dollar company. It was a fear paired with responsibility though, which made it easier to sit with. That type of fear, I was discovering, was its own kind of focus because it held the possibility of justice and a happy ending.

My body was already buzzing with preparedness, toes curling against the carpet, my mind replaying my training videos from yesterday.

I reached forward to brush the hair from Cope's forehead.

Sleeping next to him was like sleeping with a tender-hearted teddy bear who always won in a fight. He was all thick, strong thighs and ridged muscle and chest hair I loved to yank on.

And he was so cheerfully casual about his skills I often forgot the way he could control his body, those tactical punches and kicks revealing the hand-to-hand combat expert hidden beneath his lopsided grin.

"I can feel you doing that creepy staring thing again," he whispered, lips quirked but eyes closed.

"As if you never watched me when I slept," I whispered back.

He opened his eyes and rubbed them with a massive yawn. "*Wow*. Called out before the sun comes up, damn." He blinked rapidly. "Wait, is that just a plate of bacon?"

"And a cup of strong coffee."

He sat up like I'd informed him he'd won the lottery. "Did you get up early on the day of your competition to... *make me a plate of bacon?*"

I smirked. "A small token of my gratitude for fucking me into oblivion last night."

Cope fisted a hand into my shirt and pulled me forward until our lips danced barely an inch apart. "Are you a dream?"

"I'm all real."

He crashed his lips to mine in a *very* dirty kiss. I laughed against his mouth, threaded my fingers into his hair, and gave in to him. Two seconds later, and I'd dropped the plate onto the bed and let him scoop me against his chest and kiss me even harder. Both hands gripped my face, holding me still, as he ravaged my mouth the way he'd ravaged me last night. We parted, and I inhaled a shaky breath.

"I just..." He pressed our foreheads together. "I fucking love bacon so much, Serena."

I burst out laughing and shoved at his chest. "I *know*. That's why I cooked it for you, you dick."

He took the plate and winked at me. I turned on the surf report, volume low, then passed him a mug of coffee. We had half an hour to waste before the day officially began—a whirlwind of packing, waxing, stretching. And at the competition, he'd be my bodyguard, not my sleepy, sexy husband. So as he munched happily to the sounds of swell measurements, I climbed back onto the bed and settled myself between his spread legs.

Turning my head, I caught his shocked and then emotional expression. He placed the plate down and laid his hands between my shoulder blades, a wisp of a caress.

"Can you braid my hair?" I asked.

"Are you sure?"

I bit my lip. Nodded.

The expression on his face was the same one he'd given me when I stepped out of the thrift store dressing room in the short white dress I'd been lucky to find. It was total astonishment. I turned back around, overwhelmed, but then smiled when I felt the gentle tug at my scalp, the mess of my curls being gathered back between his careful fingers.

Cope was braiding my hair.

I couldn't remember how we'd started this tradition except that it seemed to always make him happy, doing this simple thing for me in the morning. And I struggled to admit that kind gestures like this filled a hole in my heart borne from my parents' total disregard for their children's well-being. Self-soothing was a behavior I became very good at it.

I focused on the tug and release of my hair being woven into a braid. His fingers stroked against my scalp, pausing to scratch. This was intimacy cranked up to eleven. Combined with last night's passion, we'd flung ourselves into the most treacherous territory.

But despite my promises from last night, I didn't do what

I should have done. I didn't say, 'I'm still in love with you, Cope, but I'm terrified we'll hurt each other again.'

"Fair warning," he said, "I haven't done this in a while. I'm probably going to make your hair look terrible."

"A risk I'm willing to take," I replied.

He scraped another clump of curls back. "You know who I dreamed about last night?"

"Who?"

He kissed my cheek. "Frankie and Loretta."

I smiled, surprised. "The Elvis Presley sisters?"

"Are there any others worth mentioning?"

The Vegas wedding chapel we'd stumbled into across from the dive bar was called Blue Suede Shoes and promised *the best Elvis experience on The Strip!* It was small inside, walls painted white with famous Route 66-style neon signs hung everywhere. *Route 66 Drive-In Theater. Blue Swallow Motel. Dell Rhea's Chicken Basket.*

The actual chapel was covered in neon hearts and fake palm trees, and the woman who married us—Frankie—was an Elvis Presley impersonator. Her sister, Loretta, ran the business side of things. Although she stood next to us and bawled her eyes out during the ten-minute ceremony like she was a close family friend and not a literal stranger.

"Loretta cried harder than any person I've honestly ever met," he said. "You ever think about the couple getting married before us?"

"Oh, you mean 5:30?"

When we'd wandered in, Loretta had taken one look at us —giggling, hands clasped, smelling of tequila—and said, "We've got a 6:30 slot in an hour if you want it? Only caveat is we don't do the licenses here, so our ceremony is known as a 'staged' wedding. We also call it a 'not real' wedding or 'completely fake.'"

That sent me into peals of laughter, but Cope was just sober enough to agree and sign the paperwork.

"Yeah, those two," he said. "That super unhappy and serious couple waiting in the lobby. I think about them all the time."

"They seemed *mad* at each other," I said. "Loretta kept saying, 'Chin up you two, it's only for forever.'"

He laughed against my hair. "Oh my god, I'll never forget those sisters for as long as I live. Frankie coming out, dressed as Elvis, strumming that out-of-tune guitar."

My shoulders started shaking. "Did you think you would ever see me get escorted down the aisle by a lady Elvis?"

"And they say dreams don't come true."

I dropped my head into my hands, unable to stop laughing. After a second, Cope tugged on my now-finished braid, tilting my head back. He kissed the top of my hair. "At least the thrift store was fun."

"We almost had *sex* in the dressing room."

"I was really excited to have our first dance to 'All Shook Up.'"

He looped his arm around my front and pulled me back against his chest. "It was the kind of fake, not real, staged wedding I always wanted."

"Even though everyone was mad at us for doing it spur of the moment and not inviting them?" I asked.

That had been part of the appeal for us—the whole night and into the next morning was one illicit, sexy secret that only Cope and I shared. It felt wrong in a delicious way, something slightly taboo and scandalous.

It was only when we arrived home and I suggested we make it official that we told our friends and family we were married.

"My mother has still not forgiven me," he said. "Billie wouldn't talk to me for a week."

"Dora shrugged and said, 'figures,' and then handed me another weight," I said, shaking my head. "Though part of me thinks if she'd been there, she would have cried harder than Loretta."

"It would be Niagara Falls," he said. "Hands down. Or maybe tied with Caleb."

I chewed on my lip. "I did feel awful about that afterward. He should have been there. If we..."

I stopped, embarrassed. 'If we did it again' was what I was *about* to say, but we couldn't open that can of worms when I needed to be getting ready to surf in a few minutes.

Cope, thank god, took pity on me. "Quentin said something like, 'Aw, dammit to hell, Cope, I already wrote my best man speech.'"

I smiled at his impression, but the tail end of this conversation was making me sad. "I guess, looking back on it, I wish everyone had been there. That we'd made a less impulsive choice, as memorable as that night was."

"I wish we'd done a lot of things differently." His jaw clenched as he stared at me for such a long time I got flustered.

"Are you okay?" I asked.

He shifted us around until I faced him on the bed. His knee was propped up next to him, right elbow balanced on it.

"I've never watched you surf before," he said, uncharacteristically nervous. "I've watched your videos, hundreds of times. But I can't in the moment. I *haven't* in the moment. I stare at the sand the whole time and listen to the sounds the crowd makes to discern if you're doing well or not." His mouth tipped up. "Spoiler, you're always doing well."

"You watch the sand?" I asked. There was no way I could have known—I was always too far out, and every time I walked out of the water he was always standing there with a grateful smile.

"I don't want to..." He cleared his throat, flushing a little. "I spend the whole time worried about you. Like I'm going to watch something horrible happen to you out there. On our third date, when I met you at your surf spot in La Jolla, I spent that morning trying to drag my eyes up from the beach to where you were." He rubbed the back of his neck. "It's because I think about my dad. But not telling you always felt wrong to me. Like I wasn't celebrating what made you who you are."

When I was younger, this type of admission from Cope would have elicited a frustrating blend of reactions—empathy, of course. And tenderness. But also a spiky defensiveness that reared its ugly head any time I felt he was trying to get me to quit surfing.

I assessed him now—the sincerity in his voice, his earnest expression. This wasn't the old Cope, and I wasn't the old me either, much as we'd fallen back into those bad patterns in the very beginning.

"I'm not upset about that at all," I said, reaching for his hand. I laced our fingers together. "And you don't have to feel badly about it either. When I'm riding a wave, my senses shrink down to only what's most vital. Every drop of water, every sound, the smell of the air, the shifting of my feet on the board. I'm utterly unaware of anything else. I've never thought about what it would be like to *watch* me because I'm so focused on just doing it." I held his gaze, dug a little deeper than I usually felt comfortable doing. "When you were gone, those two days, and we were stuck in your house watching the ticker tape and the news updating us, I really thought I was going to lose my mind. If that's how watching me would make you feel, don't do it."

He cupped my cheek, thumb stroking across my skin. "But maybe I can today? I want to this time."

"Well, now I just got nervous," I said, smiling. I pressed a hand to my stomach. "What if I suck and you're watching?"

"I believe scientists have proven it's mathematically impossible for you, Serena Swift, to suck."

He smiled with me, giving me a nod of appreciation.

I slowly untangled us, much as I wanted to keep pulling back our layers.

Cope glanced at the clock and cursed. "We need to get you going. And we'll call Quentin on the way, okay? I also need to sneak out, run to my car without Falco seeing, then drive my car here and pretend like we haven't been with each other for twelve hours."

"My acting will be flawless," I promised.

He was up and moving around now, tugging a white shirt over his chest and raking a hand through his messy, sexed-up hair. Before those walls of his went back up—before he was nothing but good humor and charm again—I needed to tell him something too.

"Every time I go surfing, since the day we met, I think about your dad when I paddle out."

He paused in his motions. "You think about my dad?"

"I never told you because, well, I was always worried I would make you upset. If I was only adding to your grief by bringing it up, making you remember," I said. "I didn't know if it was right."

His brow creased. "Can I ask, what do you think about?"

I let out a long breath. "Your sister used to show me old videos of your dad. Old pictures. It gave me a good sense of his style, how he approached the water. He was so fun to watch, Cope. He was really joyful on his board. Like it was a super fun party he loved getting invited to."

"Yeah," he said. "God, I haven't thought about that in a while. Billie and I loved watching him, the way he moved, like he was dancing with the waves."

"He always looked delighted."

"He did," he said softly. "He was delighted. I forget that a lot, actually."

I fiddled with my new braid, tugging it over one shoulder. "I picture him like that. Out there, surfing, having a good time while I'm paddling toward the next set. Or waiting during a break. I can see him really clearly, and it makes me feel safe."

I wasn't sure what to expect of his reaction. And certainly didn't expect the dazzling smile that blazed across his face. "My dad would have *adored* you. He'd be so stoked that you were surfing the gnarliest waves on the coast today too."

He said *gnarliest waves* in an exaggerated surfer-boy accent that made me laugh. This wasn't the first time Cope told me that his dad and I would have gotten along.

But this time felt different.

"Then I better go do him proud then, yeah?"

Cope walked over to me and cupped the back of my head, kissing my forehead. "Who's going to win today, sunshine?"

Everything that happened in the past day—joy, ecstasy, trepidation, purpose—expanded in my ribcage, filling my lungs with clean, precious air.

"I am," I said.

33

COPE

Serena's heat was up in fifteen minutes, and I was actively working not to have a stress-induced heart attack.

I was going to watch her surf today, on waves so wild and aggressive they'd attracted spectators for miles. Drones and camera crews were situated everywhere, lenses trained on the heavy slabs of water tossing surfers around like popcorn in a skillet. People were here to see wipeouts, and there'd already been plenty.

The woman about to paddle out to surf those monsters on purpose stood a few feet in front of me in her black wet suit, hair still in the uneven braid I'd given her this morning. Next to her, in a straight line, stood Dora, Prue, and Kalei.

Dora held Serena's hand, and all three women were speaking to her in low tones, pointing things out on the water as she scanned the horizon with focus. Meanwhile, I kept scanning the beach for the Lattimore brothers, who'd sworn they would be here for a giant, splashy press conference.

They weren't. And neither were their podiums or huge banners. I recognized two members of the marketing team, who had greeted Serena politely when she arrived. But other than that, Aerial was conspicuously absent. I peered through crowds of vendors and tourists but still didn't spot them.

Tiny alarm bells went off in my head.

This was made worse by the parking lot this morning. I had absolutely clocked the same black SUV and license plate that had been following us. I couldn't discern the features of the men in the front seat, but they were of the beefy-and-scary variety.

I'd sent a quick message to Quentin since he hadn't answered his phone when we tried him on the drive over. That alone had me feeling on edge.

My phone finally buzzed with a message from him: *Sorry, can't talk right now. Tail is bad news. No word yet from Joey about Catalina. Stay safe, will call later.*

I slid my hands into my pockets in a pointless attempt at settling my nerves. It didn't work. I was all jacked up on anxiety and paranoia.

A loudspeaker creaked on. *"Calling next heat, Serena Swift. Five-minute warning."*

She held out her arms and let Dora tug on her lifejacket. She pulled on her helmet, and Prue checked it for her. Serena's eyes slid to mine, and I didn't miss the intention. She was trying to show me her safety protocols and the community that took care of her.

Dora held her shoulders. "You can do this. I know you can."

Prue and Kalei wrapped her in a group hug from behind, and Serena laughed, looking powerful and strong. The sun sparkled off the gold in her hair and highlighted the scar on her cheek. Like my father's joy, it was also easy for me to forget what it was like watching a person do the very thing they loved the most—hobby, career, vocation. Whatever you wanted to call it, the confidence, the sense of purpose, was so obvious it tightened my throat.

In the past when I stood on this beach as her boyfriend and then husband, I was always planted at the intersection of apprehension and appreciation. I was stuck in the middle, unable to fully accept either emotion: the fear that was natural and the admiration too.

I can see him really clearly, and it makes me feel safe.

Awareness tickled at the back of my neck. My focus wandered to the waves, waves my father had once called *priceless*. I blinked, and knew I was only projecting the comforting image Serena had given me. But I saw him out there—a flash of delight and movement—before he disappeared.

Once, on this very same beach, we had a picnic together as a family, and he'd taken short breaks to surf. He'd taught himself how to do a handstand on his board—although not well—and fell off so many times trying to impress us that my sister and I had stomach aches from laughing.

For my father, life was never *not* fun, but that didn't mean he ignored the injustice in this world or a call for help from someone in need.

"Serena Swift, your heat is up."

She flashed me a pretty smile over her shoulder.

"Remember. It's mathematically impossible for you to suck," I said.

She winked, and my heart skipped a beat. Then she picked up her board and ran toward the waves as the crowd cheered.

Dora didn't hesitate to drag me next to her. "It's weird seeing you here in a suit. You really stand out, you know."

"That's part of the whole security package," I said with a shrug. "I'm trying to give off the whole *I've got a special set of skills* vibe with my choice in tie."

She chuckled to herself. Cupped her hands around her mouth and yelled Serena's name.

Both Prue and Kalei were beaming at me with cheesy grins.

"Hey there," I said. "You got something to say?"

Prue looped an arm around her wife's shoulders. "We're happy to have you back, is all."

"I'm not... *back,* per se," I said, though I'd had my head buried between Serena's thighs not twelve hours earlier.

"It's a thing they're doing right now," Dora added in between wolf-whistles. "Pretending like they hate working together and that they'll never date again."

"That's so cute," Kalei said.

I rolled my eyes up to the sky. "It's not cute. I'm a highly trained professional, and I'm not here to gossip about my non-existent relationship with my client."

All three women stared me down until I sheepishly said, "Okay, I thought I was pulling it off."

"You two are so obvious they can see your relationship status from space," Kalei said. "Just accept it. We all have."

I shook my head but grinned at them both. "I missed you guys."

"Same here," Prue said. "Now let's watch your girl kick major ass."

The distraction had been nice, but as their attention turned to the water, I felt myself start to panic. Dora touched me lightly on the arm.

"I know it's hard," she said gently.

I nodded but didn't answer. My eyes were still on the sand. Next to me, Prue said, "I get scared when I watch Kalei surf. And vice versa. Watching the love of your life put themselves in danger isn't exactly pleasant."

I had promised, though, and Serena and I were somehow, against all odds, slowly rebuilding what we'd lost.

I needed to follow through with my promises.

Behind me came a rousing cheer, and Kalei grabbed my arm. "But when you don't watch, you miss out on moments like this."

The excitement in her voice drew my attention up. Suddenly I was watching Serena surf, live, for the very first time. I broke out in a cold sweat before my brain caught up with what I was seeing. She was paddling along the lip of a classic Wedge wave—sharply pointed, probably thirty feet high, and coming in hot like a speeding train.

"Go, go, go," Dora was chanting.

She pushed up on her board, body low and strong. Her arms reached for balance as she whipped down the face, hurtling through the water, sliding under a short barrel that shot her out clean.

Spray flew behind her, fingers catching in the wave as it kept pushing her for another few seconds. She was incredible.

She was *magnificent*.

As the momentum slowed, she dropped down to her board and straddled it. She faced the audience, and I swear to god she smiled right at me.

It hooked me right in the heart.

I couldn't believe I'd denied myself the pleasure of Serena's talent, had denied myself the pleasure of having this warrior woman smile at me like I was her everything.

Another set was rolling in fast, tall and choppy. She swam beneath the first wave then paddled fast to catch the second. She was balanced so high in the air my stomach bottomed out as her board tipped over. Suddenly she was racing across another wall of water in that same strong and balanced position. The wave curled behind her, forcing her forward. She caught a path up the end of the swell, hit the ledge fast and reached down, holding her board as she jumped it in the air and spun all the way around.

She landed perfectly with a spray of water like a fin behind her. The audience went wild.

"Damn," Dora said. "Now I need to buy her a whole cake."

I stepped forward in the sand, compelled to keep watching her now.

'Serena,' I wanted to say, 'You are a masterpiece.'

Was this how my mother could withstand watching my father compete for all those years? Through the filter of fear beat a pride that made me want to drop to one knee and beg her to marry me all over again.

She had about four minutes left, time to catch a final wave if she got lucky on the incoming set. Her score from the first two was coming in on the digital board behind us.

She was in the lead. And she appeared loose out there, calm. People were calling her name, and as I scanned the audience, there were so many women there I recognized as surfers. There was even a group of little girls jumping up and down with small signs. All of this I used to miss—the adrenaline, the community, the connection.

All of us watching a woman attempt to fly and actually succeed.

Behind her, I could see the shape of the wave forming with another, smaller one right behind it. This happened at The Wedge often, two waves colliding to form a swell known for its danger. The sheer force of it knocked surfers right off their boards.

Serena either wasn't aware of the combo or wasn't afraid.

Kalei said, "Oh shit."

"No," I whispered.

I took another step forward, heart in my throat. She was paddling hard, but the second she pushed up, it was obvious the wave was unpredictable. She wobbled, almost losing her footing before taking a spray of water to the face.

For one long, bittersweet moment, it seemed like she had it.

The second wave cut through the first like a butcher knife, right where Serena was. They collided around her as I swallowed bile.

"Oh my god," Dora said—and the alarm in *her* voice stopped my heart. The audience was hushed as the third wave in that set knocked into Serena.

She hung suspended in the air, arms and legs outstretched, *reaching* toward me.

Then she went headfirst into the churning fury of the sea.

I was vaguely aware of Dora calling my name. Just as I was vaguely aware of ditching my shoes, socks, and jacket. I ripped the tie clear from my body and tore my shirt off as I sprinted toward the waves that held Serena beneath the water.

Rescue crews on jet skis were already on their way, but I didn't have time to fucking wait. The two-wave monster finally reached the shore and was instantly sucked back into the ocean.

Serena didn't surface.

My arms pumped, legs burning as I hit the water going full speed. I didn't even register the icy shock of the Pacific Ocean or the strength of the tide. I ran through it like a battering ram, endlessly searching for her arms, her head. A light blue object flew out of the spray.

It was her surfboard.

The water was at my waist when I started swimming, grateful for a father who had taught his children how to handle themselves in the ocean. Some things in this world were simple muscle memory, and I could feel his presence now as my arms worked as hard as they ever had.

There was a break in sets so the first wave that approached was small. I did what my dad trained me to do—

made my body as streamlined as possible and dove beneath it, searching for the pocket of calm beneath the roar.

My skin burned from the water, and my lungs screamed for air. When I surfaced, I heard rescue crews calling her name. *Serena. Serena. Serena.* I spit out water and shoved the wet hair from my eyes.

Where the *hell* was she?

I remembered her apnea training, how upset it had made me. But now I could have wept with gratitude. Wherever she was, she had lungs that could keep her alive for whole minutes at a time.

Because at least a minute had passed, and she hadn't appeared.

Another wave, slightly larger than the last, rose up in front of me. I dove beneath it and surfaced with eyes streaming. I paddled in place, turning in circles, calling her name in a hoarse voice.

And like a miracle, her head broke through the water twenty feet away from me.

❧ 34 ❧

SERENA

I stared down from the top of a wave three-stories high.

A nanosecond later it felt like a herd of elephants stampeded into me. My board flew backwards. I wasn't on it. I went ice-cold with terror. Reached for my husband, standing on the beach.

All hell broke loose.

The ability to think clearly vanished. It was only thanks to years of dedicated apnea training that I managed to plug my nose and take the fullest inhale I could before I was sucked, face-first, into a churning maelstrom.

I got picked up in the barrel, whipped around like a rag doll, then forced deep below by the next wave. And although being deep in the ocean wasn't exactly *good*, I could just make out the faint light of the sun which meant I knew which way was *up*.

The water was still churning, yanking at my arms and legs, and I knew I'd only surface to another wave holding me down.

I sank further and tried not to panic, harnessing my adrenaline like my brother said. Holding tight to it like a rope that would lead me to sweet freedom. The distinct burn in my lungs told me it had probably been just under a minute, but I wasn't naive enough to risk much longer than that. I'd taken a deep breath but nowhere near what I was able to do in training. I guessed I had a minute of air left, maybe less. I started to count, if only to give my screaming muscles and lungs something to focus on. *Sixty... Fifty-nine... Fifty-eight...*

There was no anger about my parents keeping me focused this time.

I thought about Cope instead, flooding my brain with endorphins and joyful memories. I prepared this seriously to give myself a fighting chance on a wipeout this bad.

I wanted a fighting chance for *him*, for the true love that had stormed back into my life in a bodyguard's suit and the same charming grin.

Forty-five... Forty-four... Forty-three...

The water had gone still, and my body was throwing up all the signs of passing the point of no return, oxygen-wise. I yanked the cord on my life vest to help me get to the surface and stretched my arms toward the light. My lungs begged for fresh air as I kicked and kicked, and when my head broke through, I gulped in the most precious and delicious oxygen I'd ever tasted.

I whipped around, coughing up water, searching for rogue waves and the sound of jet skis. I raised my arms up as high as I could, yelled *"Help!"* The two skis saw me but were far away. I must have drifted under the water farther than I realized.

"Serena."

I would recognize my husband's ragged growl of emotion anywhere, even in the middle of a wipeout. I turned around to see his powerful arms swimming toward me, and I fully believed I was delirious from lack of oxygen.

The look of agony and ecstasy on his face indicated my rescuer was all too real.

I had never known a relief so powerful in my entire life.

"*Cope?*" I yelled. I coughed up even more water.

He collided with me, strong arms wrapping around my waist and holding me up. I clung to his neck in unadulterated elation, panting and coughing too much to speak.

"Are you okay?" He pulled back to check me over. The fear there broke my heart.

I managed to nod and say, "We have... Cope, the jet skis."

He spun around immediately, one arm waving. We could see the skis moving towards us, but a big wave was cresting near them, pushing them back and forcing them farther away. Every time they tried to get around, they got stuck in the same churning whirlpool that The Wedge was known for.

A sick feeling was growing in my stomach, and I knew the reason.

I could feel it.

It was in the way the hair stood up on my arms, the tingling sensation in my legs, the tug of the tides beneath us. As Cope yelled himself hoarse, I turned my head to the left and froze with fear.

"Cope," I whispered. He didn't hear me. "Cope, look at me."

I tugged him around and grabbed him by the cheeks, keeping his eyes on my face.

"What is it?" he asked.

"There's another wave coming. *Do not look at it*, look at me."

He obeyed, though I could tell it cost him, could tell he wanted to see the monster we were facing. Except I knew from Caleb's training about the danger of panic, how important it was for both people to stay calm.

I could do that for us, I knew I could. But I couldn't have Cope seeing the slowly forming, building-high wall of water approaching us.

"The skis won't make it in time so we're going to dive beneath it, okay? Your dad taught you how to do that, right?"

"Yeah, but—" His voice shook. "Is it bad?"

I gripped his face harder. "I *will not* let anything happen to you, Cope McDaniels. Do you trust me?"

"Yes," he said, breathing jagged, mouth inches from mine. "Yes, of course. Always."

He must have heard the roar. His eyes widened. I slid off my life vest since it wouldn't let us sink and grabbed hold of Cope's hand.

"On my count we are going to dive. I need you to kick as hard as you ever have, and I'm going to drag us down as deep as we can go." I chanced a glance at what was coming. We were quickly running out of time.

"Serena." His voice was a terrified plea.

"I know," I said. "I know. I'm scared too. But we're going to save each other, alright? You are going to take the biggest fucking breath of your life. Hold my hand. Do *not* let go. I'll bring us back to the surface when I think it's safe."

He was nodding at everything, staring at me like we were never going to see each other again. He grabbed my face and kissed me—it was hard, brutal, passionate. "I love you so much, sunshine."

The wave was mere seconds from hitting us. Already our bodies were rising, getting dragged toward a force of nature we weren't meant to tangle with. I wanted to press *pause,* kiss Cope forever, tell him over and over that I loved him to the moon and back. That I'd never stopped loving him, not for an hour, not for a day.

But we needed to survive first.

"Big breath," I coached. I squeezed his hand and inhaled with him, thankful for all the times he did breathing exercises with me. The roar was getting louder. With my fingers, I counted down: *three... two... one.*

We dove beneath the foam together.

I didn't give myself time to think or give in to fear. I swam, holding Cope, with everything I had in me, with every bit of strength and drop of energy. After this, I was going to bake Dora a hundred cakes for all those tortuous training sessions she used to make me do, walking on the floor of the pool while carrying heavy weights.

Cope's hand stayed in mine as we swam and swam. I tilted my face up, caught the fading light. *Up*, thank god. The tail end of the wave shoved us forward but didn't drag us with it. The roll of water passed us by, and I tugged him with me toward the light, toward air, toward our future.

The closer we got, the more I heard the jet skis. We broke the surface together, coughing and sputtering as our rescue arrived on a red-and-white jet ski. Two divers reached down and yanked us onto the long flat board behind it. He pressed a loop of rope into our hands.

"*Hold on tight*," he yelled. Before I realized what was happening, we were dragged off, going a million miles an hour toward the safety of the shore.

We turned to one another with matching weak but euphoric grins. It was too loud to really talk, and we were still coughing up buckets of water, but we didn't break eye contact once, not even as we reached the shore. I dimly registered the sound of the crowd pushing in and medics calling for space.

The only thing I cared about was telling the truth.

I tapped his ear. He dipped his head to my mouth.

I whispered, "I love you too."

35
COPE

Serena and I sat on the back of an ambulance, parked right on the beach with blankets wrapped around our shoulders. A kind paramedic pressed a stethoscope to my back as I inhaled and exhaled. He was working extremely patiently as Dora, Prue, and Kalei kept an anxious vigil off to the side.

Everything hurt. *Everything.*

"Once more," he said. I did it again, expanding my sore lungs. Serena caught my eye. I couldn't control the smile that spread across my face.

Neither could she.

We had exchanged a dozen or more of these love-sick grins since getting hauled out of the ocean on a jet ski. A single loop kept playing in my head:

Serena had saved my life.

And she still loved me.

"The good news is I don't hear any fluid in your lungs," the paramedic said. "The bad news is that as soon as the adrenaline wears off, you're going to feel like you were hit by a car."

I chuckled, then winced at the pull in my rib cage. "Thanks for that good news-bad news combo. I'm Cope, by the way."

"I'm Serena," my wife said. "And I think I'm already experiencing that *hit by a car* feeling."

The paramedic grinned, shaking our hands. He was a tall Black man with square-rimmed glasses, about my age. "My name is Trevor. Nice to meet you both."

"Is it normal to feel like my lungs were used as a punching bag by the ocean?" I asked.

"Unfortunately," he said, handing us ice packs before writing something down on a notepad. "You both went through the earth's spin cycle, basically."

"Yay," Serena said.

Trevor cracked another grin. "Having a sense of humor about it will help. Because it's going to be terrible. Not your first wipeout though, right?"

"No, but my worst by far," she said. "Did you see it happen?"

He grimaced. "I did. Until the hold down, the audience was going wild for you, though. You were the strongest competitor out there today. I'm no expert, but I do staff a lot of these events. You did great." He looked at me. "Both of you."

I shrugged. "I only showed up for the last five minutes. I don't deserve any credit."

He laughed as he handed Serena a piece of paper. "Nothing fancy here. Ice, heat, pain relievers, and *rest*." He glanced over at Dora. "That means no training, no surfing, no swimming."

Dora held up her hands. "The only thing on her schedule is to eat the cake I promised I would bake her." She paused. "Also, can we hug her now?"

"Go for it," Trevor said. "Gently."

Serena opened her arms, and all three women latched themselves to her, talking over one another. They'd called the competition a half hour ago. Serena had placed third overall but probably would have won if she'd stuck that final wave and hadn't wiped out.

When they called it, though, we were both still being examined—she was holding a bag of ice on her shoulder as Trevor checked her for sprains. I'd cast a curious look her way as they read the results, sure she'd be disappointed. Instead, she seemed ecstatic.

"That's fucking awesome," she'd said as she smiled.

"Do you see a lot of wipeouts in your job?" I asked Trevor.

"Some," he said, leaning an arm against the ambulance door. "This was the first one where a surfer was rescued so dramatically by her..." He waved his arm in my direction.

"Protection agent," I said carefully.

"Really?" He didn't sound convinced.

"We have really good professional chemistry." But I smiled at him, and he laughed, shaking his head.

"Say no more."

I shifted and felt a corresponding *zap* of pain. He touched my arm, searched my face. "What hurt? Are you okay?"

"Just like..." I indicated all of me. "In here. Everywhere."

"Make sure you see your doctor if any of it gets worse. If you hear a ringing in your ears or have muscle weakness, that kind of thing, okay?"

"I will, thanks," I said. For some reason, Serena's uncomfortable question from last night came back to me. *Are all of your clients Bond villains?* Between the thoughtful attention of Serena's friends, checking her gear, and the paramedics patching us up with compassion, it painted a grim comparison of the people I worked for.

"Can I ask you a personal question?"

"Sure, what's up?"

I rubbed my hand across my jaw. "Why did you decide to become a paramedic?"

"Easy," he said. "I really wanted to help people. Sounds corny, but it's the truth. And I believe that in emergency situations, people deserve someone who's kind and calm. A person who treats them like a human being and not just a body with symptoms. It's the toughest job I've ever done, but I always feel useful at the end of the day. Like I did the right thing."

A memory of my father floated up, a random sunny Sunday morning when I was probably eleven or twelve. He was making us breakfast, singing along to the radio, before we were heading out to help do a beach cleanup with some other surfers. I had wanted to sleep in, fuck around with my friends, and I definitely didn't want to pick up trash all day. Partway through my complaining, he'd slid a plate of pancakes across the counter, stopping me mid-sentence.

On this planet, our actions have more impact than our words. So we always have to do the right thing.

I leaned forward. "Could I talk to you sometime about your job?"

"Being a bodyguard isn't working out for you?"

I noted where I was sitting, in a vehicle full of life-saving medical supplies and devices. Thought about Arnold Sheffield, a man with totally gross levels of privilege and wealth, complaining about his $75 cup of coffee.

"You know, I'm starting to think it's not," I said. "Having someone to call would be nice."

He scribbled his number down on that same white pad and handed it to me. "Don't hesitate, honestly. We always need more good people out here."

Another person grabbed him, mentioning something about dehydration, and he hurried off toward the beach. Not a second later, Dora was hugging me, binding my arms against my side. "Honestly, Dora, this isn't really that gentle?"

"You're such a brave fool." She stepped back, covertly wiping her eye before lifting her chin. "Try not to do that again."

"I wish I could promise not to be a fool around Serena, but that's a promise I can't make."

She pursed her lips. "If you won't listen to me, maybe your mother can talk some sense into you."

I turned around in my seat, and there she was, looking equal parts amused, scared, and grateful. I'd asked Dora to call her, still gasping, as we were pulled onto the beach. The last thing that woman needed was to see video of her son being rescued on some breaking news segment. Not after the hostage incident. And not after my father's drowning either.

I opened my arms to her, only grimacing slightly. She came in for a hug. She was only shaking a little bit, but I held her extra tight until she finally went still.

"Were you terrified?" she asked softly.

"Out of my mind with it."

Terrified couldn't really describe the sudden realization that I was stranded in the middle of the ocean with Serena and a thirty-foot wave charging towards us. The fear was like an icy, endless well, and it was only Serena's level-headed composure that had gotten me through it. I'd barely had time to process that her sheer strength and expert training had saved us both.

I was prepared to thank her for that for the rest of my life.

"So really bad wipeout, huh?" she said as she stepped back, eyes shining but voice steady.

I grinned. "Dad would be proud."

She squeezed my hand. "Dad would be proud of everything you did today." She opened her right arm to Dora, hugging her close. They gazed at each other like old friends. "It's good to see you, Theodora."

"You too, Helen. I've missed the whole McDaniels family," she said with a wry grin. "And your mother's right, Cope. Your dad was always first in that water whenever anyone called for help. And his wipeout prescription was pretty similar to what Trevor said, except it also included first stopping for California burritos from Taco Surf Shack."

I still had a crystal-clear memory of my dad teasing Billie while eating that exact burrito with an ice pack on his knee. That one hurt. Had my throat closing with the sharp ache of missing him.

"He wasn't wrong about his burrito choices," I finally said.

My mom peeked at Serena, who was still turned away and watching videos of the event with Prue, Kalei, and a few other friends. "You forgot to mention who your new client was."

I gave her a sheepish grin. "Does 'my bad' suffice?"

"No, it does not."

"What about 'I've been so busy'?"

"Try again."

"'I'm sorry'?"

She smiled. "That's better." She studied me with an expression of maternal wisdom. "Are things... okay between you two?"

"Getting there. I hope."

She sighed, dropped her voice low. "I always thought your breakup was more of a pause than an ending. Couples, especially those as young as you both were, sometimes need space to grow. To branch out, to figure out who they are without a partner. Your father and I met when we were twenty-one, and even though it's exhilarating to be in that young-love stage, it was also when we had most our issues."

I laughed beneath my breath. "That is a truth we are both

now learning." I glanced over at Serena before looking back at my mom. "I watched her for the very first time today."

I didn't have to explain more. She understood.

"It changes everything, doesn't it?" she said kindly.

I nodded, remembered her surfing across that wave like she had wings. *Serena, you are a masterpiece.*

"Surfers really *live* the life they've been given. It attracts those with wild and unruly spirits and a hunger for adventure. It's why I fell in love with your father. And it's why I've *always* loved Serena." She rested her hand on my shoulder. "They teach us a lot about living fully in the moment, no matter what we're doing."

I mulled that over. I'd certainly felt that way since taking this assignment, but that was absolutely the Serena Effect and not the role I played as her paid security. The four years without her had flown by in a mixture of heartache, yearning, and being really bored with a job I believed was my birthright.

Maybe I was wrong about all of it.

"Helen?" Serena's eyes went wide when she realized my mom was here.

Then my mom was hugging her. It took a second for Serena to hug her back, like she wasn't sure she was real. But my mother held her close, and Serena relaxed into the embrace with a shy smile.

"I was worried about you when Dora called and wanted to make sure you were okay."

"Oh, thank you." Serena's smile widened. "You didn't have to do that."

"Of course, I did," she said.

The unspoken words hung between them. Serena didn't have a lot of people in her life who worried about her. I knew it meant something that my mom had come without judgment or expectation.

"It's so good to see you," Serena said.

"And you," my mother replied. "You were flawless out there today. Queen of The Wedge."

Serena grinned. "Thanks, Helen. That means a lot."

Dora reappeared by the ambulance. "You've both been cleared to go. Want me to give you a ride back home?" She didn't even hesitate to include me in that destination which was good. I wouldn't have left Serena's side for anything.

"Please," Serena said. "Trevor wasn't joking about that whole hit-by-a-car thing."

"Your brother is meeting us there by the way," Dora said. "Called in backup for food and other provisions."

I slid off the back of the ambulance and held my hand out for Serena. She took it, hopping down gingerly, and the electricity that sparked between just that casual contact rippled through my entire body.

"My brother is extremely good at provisions," she said. "And I'm about to fall asleep on my feet."

I felt it too, a deep exhaustion yawning ahead of me. I shook my head and grabbed my jacket and tie from where Prue had collected my shed clothing on the beach. Checked my phone, but no messages from Quentin.

Everything okay? Any updates? I texted.

As we started walking through the crowd with my mom and Dora on either side of us, people were making room, clapping for Serena, waving ecstatically. Still no David or Marty, and not a single Aerial employee came running over to see if their brand ambassador was okay after her massive wipeout.

It was concerning, but my brain was also getting fuzzier and fuzzier as the adrenaline drained away.

"Serena?" All four of us turned at the voice—it was Rosa Hernández, the reporter from two days ago. There was a camera guy next to her, and she was holding a microphone. "Oh my god, are you okay? We were all so scared for you."

Serena brushed a few strands of hair from her forehead. "My body has certainly felt better, but yeah. I'm okay."

Rosa peered over her shoulder like she was confused. "This is a weird coincidence, but we were scheduled to cover a press conference with the Lattimore brothers today," she said. "You haven't seen them, right? Because it's looking like they blew off my interview."

Serena shot me a covert glance. "That is weird, actually. I saw them yesterday, and they said they'd be here."

I peered toward the parking lot, squinting my eyes against the sun. Didn't see the SUV anymore.

"Well, do *you* feel up for a couple questions?" Rosa asked. "Especially since it seemed like you had more to say at Trestles before you were interrupted."

Understanding dawned on Serena's face. "I sure did have a lot to say."

Rosa nodded and spoke quickly to her camera crew. Then faced us with a camera-ready smile. "Serena Swift, you had an absolutely incredible day today, which culminated in a two-wave hold down and a dramatic rescue. How are you feeling?"

Serena shrugged but grinned. "Honestly? Like I was run over by a couple trucks the size of a thirty-foot wave."

"Everyone on the beach was watching with bated breath," Rosa said. "We are *so* happy to see you okay and standing up. How do you feel about coming in third?"

"I feel proud of myself," she said. "And proud of the women I competed with today. I'm in awe of their talent."

Rosa touched her earpiece and tilted the mic back toward Serena. "Is there anything you want to say about what today means to you? Or to Aerial?"

Serena drew herself up to her full height. The wind caught

her long hair, tangling it behind her shoulders, making her seem even more like an ocean goddess. "I won't speak for Aerial, but I will speak for myself, as a woman competing in an extreme sport dominated by men. I just survived a brutal two-wave hold down in pursuit of excellence, for a sport I've dedicated more than a decade of my life to. I wasn't here today for men's approval or their amusement. Unlike the messages that are pervasive in this industry, women surfers are not objects *or* sex symbols. We're elite-level athletes asking to be treated equally and for our blood, sweat, and tears to be taken seriously. And whether we deserve to be surfing the same big waves as everyone else isn't up for debate."

My heart soared for the woman in front of me—comfortable in her skin, bold with her words, strong in her voice. There was no wavering or diminishing. She was telling the truth, and it deserved to be heard.

Rosa's face was surprised and then approving. "I have to say I agree. You've always been a role model, and we're all very excited to see you getting a larger spotlight."

Serena's eyebrows shot up. "Oh, well, thank you."

The reporter brought the microphone back down to her side, ending the interview, and the camera man stepped back.

"I'm so sorry about the other day," Rosa said. "I was hoping I'd get a chance to talk to you without David and Marty around. My mom and my sister surf, and you are their favorite athlete."

"It's really okay," Serena said warmly. "I appreciate getting the do-over. And tell your mom and sister to come to my spot in La Jolla. We can surf together."

"They will—and I'm not joking here—literally die with happiness when I tell them this."

Serena grinned as Dora started leading her away toward the parking lot. "Thank you again for the opportunity."

The reporter smiled. "Thanks for always speaking up."

I followed behind Serena, Dora, and my mom as they stepped gingerly through the sand. I saw Dora wrap an arm around Serena's shoulders and squeeze.

"I'm so proud of you, kid."

"I was only doing my best *you* impression," she teased back.

Dora laughed as she led us to my car. "After everything that happened today, I think I'm going to have to bake you two cakes."

36

COPE

Caleb had, indeed, brought the provisions.

Serena's brother showed up right after Dora had left, driven back to her house by my mother. Both women had given us long hugs with suspiciously wet eyes and strict instructions on rest. The second they left, Caleb arrived, fully dressed in his white Coast Guard uniform, having come straight from base.

He took one look at us standing on the front porch—wobbling and exhausted—and said, "Ouch. *Wipeoutville. Population: You*, huh?"

Serena tried to punch Caleb in the arm but ended up yawning instead. He laughed, following us inside with his arms full of groceries and supplies.

"I can only stay for a minute, but I went out and got everything we tend to use after a big rescue job." He set the bags down and walked into the living room, where he immediately began making up the old yellow couch, pulling out the bed inside. As he grabbed sheets and pillows, I turned toward an extremely sleepy Serena. We hadn't had a moment to ourselves to discuss what had happened between us—the danger, the rescue, saying *I love you*—and I couldn't resist lifting the messy curls from her forehead to plant a kiss there.

"You need to sleep," I said softly.

"So do you." She could barely keep her eyes open. Neither could I, but my unease with Aerial was a steady thrum that, while severely muted, had me wondering if the two of us were safe right now. "Have you heard from Quentin?"

I shook my head as Caleb came back into the room. He grabbed his sister by the shoulders and gently propelled her to a couch bed that I remembered as being seriously lumpy but now looked like paradise.

"Dora said the paramedics said nothing broken, no water in the lungs, right?" Caleb asked.

Serena nodded, crawling under the covers. I busied myself unpacking what Caleb had brought for us—three different kinds of over-the-counter painkillers. Heating pads. Ice. Epsom salts.

"It was a bad one," Serena was saying. "Prue said I was two minutes under."

Caleb whistled low beneath his breath. "I'm sorry, sis. That is a truly frightening amount of time to be under the water like that." He twisted at the waist to look at me. "How are you feeling, Cope?"

"Like a tank used me for target practice."

He gave me a half smile. "Sounds about right. Can I ask when the last time you went swimming in the ocean was?"

I hesitated. "When I was fifteen."

He nodded, serious. "Then that was an extraordinary act of courage, buddy. Not a lot of people can swim through the waves at The Wedge."

"I didn't really have a choice in the matter," I said.

There was full understanding in his expression. I would gladly paddle out into a tsunami if Serena was in trouble, and he got that. He'd do the same. And routinely did the same for absolute strangers who needed his help.

I pulled out two Styrofoam containers that smelled like heaven and looked at Caleb for an explanation.

"Oh, that's California burritos from the Taco Surf Shack," he said with a grin.

I went still. "Did Dora mention this to you?"

"Uh, no," he said. "I just always think burritos are a solid choice after a casual brush with death."

I chuckled, thinking of my dad. "I tend to agree."

My phone buzzed a few times in my pocket.

"I need to take a call outside," I said.

Serena peeked around Caleb's shoulder, quizzical, but her brother's presence made it impossible to say anything. I stepped onto the porch, trying to tap into the agent instincts basically embedded in my DNA at this point. But things were quiet, peaceful. Birds were singing, neighbors were mowing their lawns, the sun was shining.

When I checked my phone, I had two missed calls from Marilyn.

Shit.

I didn't return them, knowing I'd pay for it later, and dialed my best friend instead.

Hi, you've reached Quentin Abernathy with the San Diego Times...

Sometimes, when he had a strong lead on a story, he'd ignore calls for hours, surfacing later like a deep-sea diver when he was done.

Or the beefy-and-scary dudes I saw in the SUV had gotten to him.

But a text came through ten seconds later. *Talking with a source. Will call, I promise.*

I let out a huge sigh of relief, feeling marginally better. I considered calling Falco, to keep an extra eye on the house, but then decided against it. I still couldn't tell him the truth about Aerial, and once I revealed the wipeout story, he'd be suspicious immediately. I wouldn't have risked my life so substantially for one of our regular clients. And I wasn't ready to unburden myself of *every* secret just yet.

Everything—from Quentin's source to the escalating threats—gave me the feeling that things would be coming to a head soon. Hopefully in a good way. I just needed a little more time, a few more days, and then everyone at my job could know the truth.

Besides, after what had transpired between me and Serena in the ocean, I was confident we'd protect each other, no matter what.

I walked the perimeter of the house to put my fretful mind at ease. My muscles groaned with every step. I felt sluggish, and heavy exhaustion swarmed my nerves.

Back inside, Caleb was organizing supplies on the counter and pouring two large glasses of water with ice. He nodded at the now sleeping form of his sister in the other room.

"Already out cold," he whispered. He pointed at the porch, and I followed him there, resting against the door for support.

"It's normal to feel like you want to sleep for a year," he said, touching my arm. "It's your body's healing response to the fear and trauma and, honestly, the tremendous amount of physical exertion you both just went through. Let yourself rest, and you'll start feeling a lot better."

I ran a hand through my hair and asked Caleb a question I was worried about. "Did I put Serena in greater risk? Swimming out there like that when there was already a rescue effort in place?"

He shook his head. "Generally, we believe the less bodies there are in the water, the better. And certainly Good Samaritans, as noble as their intentions are, have complicated rescue efforts in the past. But you didn't keep those skis from getting to Serena on time. That was the bad luck of a nasty set."

"But in the end, she had to save me," I said. "I wouldn't have been strong enough to survive that wave if she hadn't talked me through it and held us beneath the water until we were safe."

He leaned against the banister and crossed his arms. "Would anything have stopped you from going in there? Because nothing would have stopped me if I had been in your position. You were acting on a human instinct as old as time. One that I know you and your family are deeply familiar with."

The empathy on his face just about did me in. Nothing would have stopped my dad either, nothing *did* stop my dad, and he paid the ultimate price for it. The person he'd rescued that day was a man named Victor, a bodysurfer who'd gotten dragged into the riptides. And while my father had been able to push Victor to shore, an undercurrent trapped him before his friends could help. He drowned.

My father knew Victor from the small, dedicated group of people who happened to surf, swim, and bodysurf that section of the beach every morning. He knew that Victor's girlfriend was pregnant and due to have their baby in a few months.

Victor and Diana still sent us pictures of their daughter, now thirteen, who shares the name Cope with me.

"You're right," I admitted. "I couldn't have stopped even if I tried."

"Because you've got a good heart, Cope," he said. "And that's why I trust you with my sister. She doesn't need *anyone* to protect her on those waves, as you now know." His throat worked, making his voice hoarse. "But being on your own out there, facing that kind of wave, trust me. I've done it before, and the terror can freeze you in place if you're not careful. I believe Serena saved your life. And I believe having you there saved hers."

He dropped his hat back on his head and began walking back to the car. "I'll check on you both later. But try not to get into any trouble for at least a few hours? You two have had enough excitement for one day."

I managed a weak smile before hurrying back inside and locking the door. I barely made it through a routine check of locks and windows before I collapsed on the couch bed. Serena was curled on her side, hair obscuring her face, totally vulnerable.

I will not let anything happen to you, Cope McDaniels. Do you trust me?

I crawled under the covers, setting my phone right beside me. Then I pulled Serena against my chest and wrapped both arms around her, resting my nose in her hair. She let out a relaxed sigh and murmured something I couldn't hear.

"What's that, sunshine?" I whispered.

She snuggled closer. "I knew you would come for me. I just knew it."

37

SERENA

When I finally woke up, it was in total disorientation.

The only sounds I could hear were Cope's steady breaths paired with his heartbeat. As tempted as I was to pull the covers back up and sleep for another three hours cuddled against his warm chest, I was concerned about the sounds my stomach was making. I was *starving* and dimly remembered that Caleb had brought over burritos and salty snacks and enough dessert to last us through the weekend.

Rubbing my eyes, I sat up and immediately regretted it. My chest felt like a horse had stomped on it and every muscle ached down to the ends of my toes. Breathing out slowly, I untangled my limbs from Cope's heavy ones and crept across the floor in my bare feet.

I flicked on a few low lights in the hallway and kitchen, not wanting to disturb Cope too much. I found the containers with our food and almost fainted dead away with hunger when I smelled it. Grabbing a skillet, I placed it quietly on the stove just as I heard the rhythmic buzzing of Cope's phone. I'd stirred a few times to the sound during our nap but had fallen back to sleep before realizing what it was.

As I washed my hands in the sink, I peered at my reflection in the kitchen window and winced at the pinch in my shoulders.

A man moved across the yard, right in front of the window.

My hands stopped. The soap clattered into the sink as the water ran.

Another man appeared. Giant. Hulking. Both walking toward the back door that led right into the kitchen.

I thought I'd known true fear today, peering up at the wave about to crash over our heads without mercy. The sight of those two men froze my tongue, halted my heart, hushed my breathing.

"Cope," I said, but it was only a whisper. It was like my throat stopped working. The door to my left was locked. I could see it was locked. There was a scraping sound, like a tool being used.

The doorknob started to turn.

I screamed Cope's name as the men outside kicked open the door and were suddenly *in* my kitchen *in* my house. They wore face masks, dressed all in black, and the slightly bigger one had his hand over my mouth and my back against the wall in seconds.

A sharp fear left a metallic taste in the back of my throat.

"*Shhh*," he said. "Do not fucking scream again, do you understand? This doesn't need to be that hard. You know who sent us, and you know what they want. Give me those files or whatever that lady gave to you, and we'll be out of your hair."

Aerial.

If we hadn't experienced such a traumatic wipeout, we would probably have been with Quentin right now or looking for Catalina or anything that hadn't made us sitting ducks for their escalating threats to finally reach us. Instead, Cope and I had fallen dead asleep in an unprotected house.

The other guard stood menacingly to his left, like they expected me to cave in and give it up. To cave and let this company continue to lie about their sins because they had money and power.

I refused to do that. Beneath the pulse of fear, I remembered I was a woman who defied gravity, a woman with saltwater in her veins and the tides in her heart. I'd stared down a thirty-foot wave today and *survived*.

I snatched the skillet balanced on the stove and smacked the guy in the face. He yelled, grabbing his nose in pain, and let me go. I made a break for it, but the second guard grabbed me around the waist with hands the size of Frisbees. Cope had taught me a thing or two about self-defense when we were together. I pitched my elbow back into whatever body part was behind me while kicking my feet.

My attacks were met with a wall of unmoving muscle. I screamed as he hauled me upright, wrapping a meaty arm across my chest to hold me still.

Then two more things happened.

The guard holding me removed a small knife from his pocket.

And Cope appeared.

He leaned against the half-wall separating the kitchen from the living room, his arms crossed over his chest. The expression on his face could only be described as *lethal*. He was nothing but thick muscle and corded power. Everything about his body radiated a perilous confidence.

I knew his casual demeanor lulled people into a false sense of security, even as I knew those sharp eyes were busy calculating every move. Only I would have noticed the sweat on his brow and the tiny tremble in his fingers.

His blue eyes met and held mine, like he knew I needed

them to stay calm. I thought about being with him in the ocean, the way I harnessed his focus so we could live and not get swallowed up by panic. He trusted me to see us through the danger.

I trusted him to do the same now.

Cope arched an eyebrow and said, "What are you doing attacking my wife?"

The guy I hit with the skillet stood back up, blood streaming from his nose. "Just give us the files so we can get out of here, okay? It's not going to do you any good to fight them on this. Last time I checked, they always win." He cracked his knuckles. "Is it somewhere in the house? Or on a laptop?"

"This is kind of awkward," Cope said. "But we don't have any *files*. And I don't know what the hell you're talking about. You've also broken into our home." He paused. "You can let go of her now, by the way."

The guy's arm clamped down harder, but my husband's measured gaze kept my panic at bay.

Skillet Guy said, "Do you think we're stupid?"

"Yes, I do." Cope said calmly.

The guy holding me held the knife up—not against my body but close enough for me to see how sharp it was. "I don't care if you think I'm stupid. I do care that we've been told to do whatever it takes to get the information back. Do I need to use her to do the convincing?"

"I wouldn't do that," Cope warned.

"Give us the drive, or I start using this knife," the guy said.

I could feel my terror, begging to be released. But Cope kept staring at me with more love than I thought possible to convey. And as the knife danced near my skin, he went totally still, the way apex predators do in the jungle before they pounce.

"If you harm her in any way, I will make it my mission to turn your life into a shrieking hell of human misery," he said. "How about that for an answer?"

The other guy sighed like we were a giant pain in his ass. "I guess I'll beat it out of you then."

The guy ran past me at full speed, and Cope side-stepped him like they were partnered on a waltz. Cope punched him so hard in the jaw he stumbled back, dazed. Snarling, he lashed out at Cope, who was studying him the way a cat studies an especially tasty mouse.

The man holding me started to drag us farther back into the kitchen. "Maybe *you* can tell me where the info is while they're distracted. How does that sound?"

I went limp in his arms, scratched at his wrists, anything to slow down his progress. Cope landed a nasty hit in the other guy's stomach, causing him to bend over, clutching his side.

"I *told you* we don't have jack shit," Cope said. "And now I'm just fucking pissed off." His next punch sent the guy sprawling to the floor. He kicked him in the ribs. "And I'm *still* going to turn your life into a shrieking hell of human misery."

The guy curled into a ball, coughing and wheezing. Then Cope turned around and stalked toward us. I realized how much he restrained his strength and skill around me. Because he wasn't holding back now.

The arm around my chest loosened—out of fear or shock, I'd never know. But I jammed my elbows back into the guy's chest, catching him off guard, and dropped out of his hold just as Cope reached us. The guy made a scared, sloppy attempt at fighting back, but Cope had his knee in the man's groin a second later. And then he did it again. Grabbing his shirt, Cope lifted him up and against the wall with a hand around his throat.

"If you come near my wife again, I will hunt you to the ends of the earth. You got it?" Cope said with a snarl.

The guy managed a strained nod, gasping. Cope released him. Punched him across the face so forcefully I swore he spun before falling to the ground.

Slowly, my husband turned to face me with a heaving chest and a fierceness in his gaze. If we hadn't already been married, I would have eagerly agreed to do it on the spot.

"Did they hurt you?" he asked hoarsely.

"No, I'm fine," I said. "Did they hurt you?"

He shook his head, reaching for me just as a car came squealing down my driveway. When he wrapped his arms around me, I pressed my cheek to his chest. He held me there for a few comforting seconds as we caught our breath.

"You were incredible," I said. "You saved me."

Cope's lips landed on the top of my head, and he hugged me even tighter. "I'll do just that every day of my life if it's required of me." I looked up, propped my chin on his chest. Saw him smile. "And consider it a *thank you* for saving *my* life, earlier."

We'd survived big waves and multiple attackers, so why hold back now? I pressed onto my tiptoes and kissed him. "I love you so much."

His eyes searched mine like I was a miracle in the flesh. "I love you so much too."

Footsteps crunched across my driveway, and Cope reluctantly released me. When he pulled open the front door, I was shocked to see Falco standing there, looking serious and determined.

"Are you two okay?" he asked. He stormed into the kitchen and cursed when he saw our sprawled-out attackers.

"We're fine, and you have excellent timing," Cope said. To me, he explained, "I called for backup as soon as I heard you scream."

I heard another car come speeding down our driveway. Terrified, I yanked open the curtains and sighed when I recognized the jeep.

"Did you call Quentin too?"

"No, I did not," Cope murmured.

He took a second to help Falco restrain Skillet Guy. My other agent flashed us a wary look.

"When do you plan on filling me in on whatever's going on?" he asked Cope.

Cope winced. "As soon as I can. I promise. Thank you for coming. I would call for more backup while you stay at the property, since I'm not sure who else might come for Serena, and I won't be here to help you."

Falco nodded, sitting back on his heels. "Fine by me. But you know that Marilyn—"

"Is probably going to fire me, yeah," Cope said grimly, although he didn't seem that upset about this. "I'm taking Serena, and I'll call you as soon as I can with the full story. You got this?"

Falco shrugged next to the man wiggling on the ground with his hands tied. "Sure."

Quentin's beat-up Jeep careened to a stop in my driveway. We ducked out onto the porch as he was rolling his window down with that mischievous smile.

"I thought y'all were kidnapped or dead," he called up. "But since you're not, get in. I got good news."

Still out of breath, we jogged down the steps and into the car.

"We're neither," I said, pulling down my seatbelt. "We were actually taking a nap. Well, we *were*..."

"I just knocked out the two guys who've been following us around," Cope blurted. "They're in the kitchen, and Falco is tying them up."

"And we both survived a massive wipeout at The Wedge earlier today," I said.

"*Both* of you?"

Cope's grin was sly. "It's a long story—we'll tell you all about it. You've got that look on your face when you're about to break a story wide open."

"I've got *three* factory inspectors willing to speak on the record about being bribed to lie for years. Plus one very brave employee." He held up a slip of paper between his fingers. "And this right here is the address where Catalina Flores has been hiding."

"Holy shit." I grabbed it from him as he drove out of my driveway. "Where are we going?"

"She finally responded to one of my messages on social media, once I was able to convince her of my intentions and connection to you, Serena," Quentin said, casually breaking the speed limit. "And she's staying at her sister's house about ten minutes from here."

He glanced in the rearview mirror at Cope sitting in the back. "Do either of you wanna tell me about the two men who just attacked you in your home?"

Cope scrubbed a hand down his face. His knuckles were already bruising. "I'm pretty sure they were the two guys who've been following us. I don't think they're anything more than local muscle getting hired out to do shady or violent things. They had a knife but no guns, thank god. Makes me think they've done this before and had an easy time getting whatever they needed based on intimidation."

"They were there for the files, right?" Quentin asked.

Cope's jaw tightened. "The drive was all they wanted, and neither Lattimore brother was at the event today, which makes me think they're holed up somewhere trying to figure out how to plug this information leak. You've got everything you need for the story, now?"

"Catalina's the key missing piece," Quentin said, turning right into a small residential neighborhood. "All three inspectors confirmed bribe payments for the past five years—bribes to look the other way and pretend they were upholding the high standards Aerial is famous for. The employee willing to speak out told me the whole thing's a fucking mess, but Aerial uses a system of intimidation and bribes to keep them quiet too."

My stomach churned with nausea as Quentin slowed the car down, creeping to a stop in front of a ranch-style house with bright blue shutters. "She knows we're coming, but she's definitely scared."

We exited the car. Quentin at least appeared professional, with his leather bag and button-up shirt. But I was just now realizing that Cope and I wore the same clothing we'd fallen asleep in, and one look at my hair told me it was a snarled mess.

The neighborhood was quiet, nothing louder than bird song. The curtains in the house were closed, and the grass was a little high. At the front door, I looked to Cope for one last shot of bravery and then raised my hand to knock.

It opened wide before I could do it. The same woman who bumped into me outside of Aerial five days ago stood in the doorway with relief on her face.

"Thank god it's *you*," she said.

38

SERENA

Catalina served us glasses of ruby-red hibiscus tea that I sipped gratefully. Next to me on the couch, Cope was a solid, comforting presence. He didn't let go of my hand once, only pausing to stroke his thumb across my pulse point every few minutes.

Quentin sat in a chair, and Catalina pulled one up next to him with a shaky exhale. There were dark thumbprints beneath her eyes and lines around her mouth.

"We're *so* glad to see you're safe," I said. "We were worried Aerial had gotten to you. Did you plan to stay at your sister's house?"

She nodded her head. "My parents still live in Oaxaca, so my younger sister stays there with them in the summer for a few weeks, visiting family. With her gone, this was the best place for me to stay out of sight for a few days." She wrung her hands together. "I'm so sorry I made you worry about me. I couldn't reach out until now. Once things were a go on our end, we were all scrambling to hide our tracks. I didn't want to lead them to your location if they were tracking me online."

Quentin's forehead creased. "Who's *we?*"

Gripping the glass between her hands, she leaned over with a resolute look. "There's a core group of six of us at Aerial—three lawyers, including me, two people who work in operations and human resources, and one of the product engineers. We all started at the company within a year of each other, so we happened to grow close. It was at a dinner party I hosted here one night when I mentioned I was noticing things in their arbitration files that didn't match up with what the company was supposedly promoting to the public."

"The factory conditions, you mean?" Quentin asked.

"Yes, and the violation of environmental regulations, the injuries, the illness," Catalina continued. "All of us had signed non-disclosure agreements that guaranteed our silence and confidentiality. But between the six of us, we could more safely share what we were starting to find. Connections with sketchy lawyers and politicians. Hidden budget items and money trails. Complaints from employees not addressed or destroyed."

She regarded me and Cope. "They keep their staff and departments in strict silos, everyone holding a piece of the puzzle but never seeing the finished product."

Quentin leaned back in his chair, hands on his head. "That's the first rule of the game if you're wanting to keep your employees in the dark. That and generate obsessive brand loyalty."

She was nodding faster now. "Yes. *Yes.* That was the other thing. You've met the Lattimores and the other directors. They're nice and unassuming and claim to love the environment as much as our consumers do. It doesn't line up with what they're doing behind the scenes, and *that,* more than anything else, had us doubting ourselves for a long time before we decided to come up with a plan to get the information out. We *hoped* the leak wouldn't get tied back to us. We now know they've been searching our work computers. And I didn't realize they'd put those cameras up on the perimeter of the building the day I passed the information to Serena. We were careful but not careful enough, I guess."

"Well, it's not your job to be careful. It's their job not to hurt people and lie about it," Quentin said firmly. "There's no instruction manual here, and you and your colleagues are doing something very brave and courageous. You made the choices you had to make to stay safe."

She gave him a smile of gratitude. "Thank you for that. I think all six of us have been replaying everything in our minds and only coming up with the mistakes that we made."

"I've been an investigative reporter for a lot of years, and you're not the first whistleblower who's come to my paper wanting us to print their story. It's near impossible to get out unscathed. You're going toe-to-toe with the ones in power. There's a reason why they have it, and there's usually a compelling reason they want to keep it."

"Like maintaining a pristine reputation right as you're being celebrated as the first sustainable company to sponsor the Olympics," Cope said.

She sipped her tea and nodded. "Everyone at the office was excited about the news but tense the past few weeks," she admitted. "Plus, Serena starting as our new ambassador meant there was a lot of pressure to get things right. No mistakes."

My conflicting emotions every time I was in those offices made a lot more sense now—feeling both welcomed and uneasy, listened to and ignored. The force of their long-standing values always pushed back, whispered that what I was seeing couldn't possibly be true.

"Were they always like this?" I asked. "Was the whole story a lie from the beginning?"

She bit her bottom lip. "Not that I can tell. The six of us

have tried to pinpoint when Aerial abandoned their sustainable practices, and the closest we can get is five to ten years ago."

Quentin glanced at us. "Lines up with some of the sources I'm talking to."

"I think they were honest back then," Catalina said. "And doing the right thing. They were pioneers for a long time. But it *is* more expensive for a company to pay people fair wages, protect them from harm, and ensure they're having the smallest impact on the planet as possible." She shrugged, looking sad. "I don't know—maybe they saw that they could inflate their profit margin by keeping the lie but using the same awful practices widely used by other companies."

Her fingers curled into tight fists. "It's *infuriating*. The more we uncovered and the more positive, happy press they received, the angrier we all felt. Especially since I don't believe everyone who works there is *in* on it. A lot of people work there because they stand by those values and want to see it reflected in a company that could lead the way for others."

I leaned forward slightly but kept my hand in Cope's. "You were all angry?"

"There are no words to express how angry," she said. "Going to work, putting a fake smile on my face, feeling like I was complicit in their actions. I was lucky the six of us had each other. We inspired each other to be brave and actually *do* something about it."

Cope squeezed my hand lightly. I was in awe of Catalina's courage and the incredible risk these employees had taken. And I thought surfing big waves was dangerous. This was on another level entirely. And her anger hadn't limited her ability to take action.

It had guided her towards it.

"It means a lot that you entrusted me with this information," I said. "Although I still don't know why. But I really hope I did what you needed me to do."

Her dark eyes brightened. "Serena, we chose you on purpose. We knew you'd be at that meeting, and we organized me bumping into you. The rest was a big risk. I knew you might not plug in a random flash drive dropped in your purse by a stranger. But it was our first usable idea to bypass our NDAs. And plain good luck that you're friends with a reporter."

"Because I was their new ambassador?" I asked.

"Because of who you are," she said simply.

My cheeks warmed at the sincerity in her tone. Cope squeezed my hand again.

"You have a platform, and you use it," she continued. "You've never smiled politely and gotten on your board while ignoring the problems that affect your sport. You don't stay in your lane, and the community is better for it." She caught my gaze and held it. "I know the detractors are usually louder, but a *lot* of people admire you. And not just for the fact that you're an incredible athlete. But for living your values."

I thought about Dora, gazing down at me and saying *there's always another way*. And the many, many times I railed against flaws in an industry that still benefited me because of the way that I looked.

It had always been infuriating to witness the way other surfers, the media, and plenty of fans echoed the manipulations of my parents. They also believed girls and women should be pretty, polite, and agreeable. As if I only existed to entertain them. As if upholding the lie of that existence was more important than standing up for what was right.

But *standing up* wasn't exactly the same as taking action.

"Thank you for saying that," I said. My throat was tight with emotion. "That honestly means more to me than I can say. Until Aerial, I was *stuck* in that anger phase you were talking about earlier. It's past time that I do even more."

I smiled in response to the excitement on her face. "Wait, what are you planning Serena?"

"I don't know yet," I said, feeling suddenly shy. Although the thoughts filling my head were so numerous, they could no longer be easily slotted away. "But I've got some ideas. And a lot of really, really awesome people in my life who have their own ideas too on how to increase equality to our sport."

"It's definitely needed," she said. "I mean, look at Aerial. They're a perfect example of how deep the problem can be and how power and money can still hide it."

Money. Those ideas in my head gave a standing ovation at Catalina's words.

"You're absolutely right," I said. My phone started ringing, startling all four of us. When I saw who was calling, my heart stopped. "It's Marty Lattimore." I showed them the screen.

Quentin held his hand out, and I tossed the phone to him. He ignored the call then shut my phone off. "I'm guessing someone told them that you beat up a couple of his guys in your kitchen."

Catalina's eyes widened. "You what?"

"Cope handled it," I said, looking sideways at the handsome bodyguard next to me, gripping my hand like he was never letting go.

"I think I impressed them with my fighting skills and witty rejoinders," he said.

"You told them you were going to turn their lives into a shrieking hell."

His mouth twitched at the end. "Some people would think that was funny."

Catalina pressed her hands to her cheeks. "If I had known they were going to come after you like that..."

I touched her knee. "There's no way you could have

known, and we're all okay. I think it's the next part that's going to bring its own challenges though."

Turning to Catalina, Quentin said softly, "This is where you and your coworkers come in. My editor is ready to run this story forty-eight hours from now, as long as my sources check out. But she's ready to make it a major headline, above the fold. So we need to talk about what you're comfortable with. And I've got plenty of connections because of prior stories, so whatever protection you or your coworkers need, I'm happy to provide it."

"I feel safer with six of us stepping forward, and the sources you found," Catalina said. "But talking to other lawyers is probably smart."

Quentin smiled. "I'll make it happen." Then he took out his notepad and tape recorder. "Are you ready to blow this story wide open?"

Her eyes darted to mine, and I gave her a reassuring nod.

"I'm ready," she said.

39

COPE

Before reality and its obstacles could set in, there was one last thing I needed to do.

Serena and I were in the back seat of a taxi on the way to La Jolla Cove, holding a thick blanket I'd stolen from Quent's Jeep. She was curled against my side, and I was stroking my fingers through her hair, listening to the sounds of her breathing and the steady rumble of the tires on the freeway.

I'd called Falco, who handled Aerial's men, made the requisite reports with the police, and was staking out the house until we returned. I was already dreading the conversation we needed to have about the many secrets I'd been keeping from him.

The conversation awaiting me with Marilyn was going to be even harder.

When we'd finally left Catalina's house, she and Quentin had started the process of unraveling Aerial's many lies, and calls were already being made to her coworkers. She seemed comfortable and at ease with him, and he was taking the time to be careful with her story.

She'd also taken *great* pity on me and Serena by ordering us takeout from the pizza place down the street—and didn't poke fun when we each ate one large pizza. Between the massive wipeout and fighting off two Hulk-sized attackers, we were ravenous.

She and Serena had shared a long and emotional hug before we left—there was so much left to uncover and do, and they both had their own tough decisions to make, but seeing the connection already forming between them was moving enough.

The cabdriver dropped us off at our location, and as I paid him, Serena stood on the low wall, hair blowing in the breeze, silhouetted in the moonlight. This was the location of our second date, where I'd once contemplated the foolish notion that I could walk away from this wild, passionate goddess instead of falling helplessly in love with her.

The waves were inky black and reflected the stars above. The full moon hung low and luminescent in the sky, turning the sand below us silver.

I walked her to the farthest end of the wall, which dipped down below the rocks, jutting out into the cove. It protected us from the sea breeze and any onlookers, although it was empty of people this time of night. I smoothed down the thick blanket and we sat facing each other, just like we had on that sunny day, all of twenty-two years old.

The ocean waves pounded an ancient rhythm in the background.

"Do you remember what happened here, sunshine?" I asked.

A brilliant smile slid up her face. "Our first kiss."

I gave in to the pressing urge I'd had since the jet skis dragged us onto the beach. I gripped her cheeks and crashed our lips together. She reacted immediately, sighing against me, fingers clutching at my shirt.

She opened for me, deepened the kiss. I smoothed my hand across her hair, and we stayed like that for a moment, finally able to touch and comfort each other after one of the hardest days of our lives. Finally feeling grounded, I sat back but didn't put much distance between our bodies. Our knees touched, and I kept my hand interlaced with hers. Even now, after a day of non-stop fear, my fingers shook as I reached for my wallet.

I opened it and slid out a thin gold band. I placed it on the blanket, directly between us.

"I've been carrying this around with me for 1,510 days," I said. "Wearing it hurt too much. Getting rid of it was never, ever an option. And falling out of love with you wasn't an option either."

Serena stared at me as she fished her wallet from her bag. Opened it and removed the matching gold band we'd had made.

She placed it on top of mine.

The sight of them together in the moonlight—the understanding that she'd clung to this symbol with the same devotion—had me light-headed with hope.

"It never felt real to me that we were only together for two years," she said. "Just twenty-four months. All that we did together, all that we *were* to each other, seems like an epic and endless amount of time. Not fleeting or temporary. Maybe..." She bit her lip, inhaled a big breath. "Maybe that's why I wasn't surprised when I walked into that room and learned you were my bodyguard. Because it's only ever been you, Cope."

I leaned in for another kiss. This one sweeter. Softer. But I knew this conversation couldn't end here—like Serena had said, talking about our best memories wasn't the same as true reconciliation.

And being in love had never really been the problem.

I cleared my throat and gathered my remaining shreds of courage. "I had a gun pointed at my head for forty-eight hours," I said, voice rough. Her face shifted as she understood what I was sharing. "It was me, Jake the other guard, and Gary, the boss I thought was really nice but was actually super shitty. They kept us in that office with our hands tied behind our backs. No food or water."

She moved even closer, gripped my wrists.

"There was a rotating cast of young, amateur kidnappers who hadn't expected to take a hostage during their fumbled kidnapping attempt. Certainly not three. Although it was obvious from their body language that Jake and I were expendable in their eyes. Just bodies to dispose of if we got in the way or became a burden." I smiled a little. "I wasn't chatty or overly familiar. I made myself as small and quiet as possible. I didn't want to be an aggravation or call attention to myself. It was the only way I could conceive of getting out of there alive. I kept my head down and dozed when I could and thought about you every second."

Her hand moved to cup my cheek.

"I still can't describe the heartbreak of believing I was never going to see you again. That I had gone to work on a Tuesday and would never hold you, kiss you, hear your laughter." I cleared my throat. "Talking about it afterward wasn't an option for me because it was like staring into a dark chasm. Joking about it, acting like everyone else was overreacting, was just easier." Regret flooded through me. "As was making our problems at that time about your surfing career instead. All of it was easier for me than acceptance."

I turned my head and kissed her palm, breathing in the familiar smell of her skin.

"Losing my father taught me a lot about mortality at a young age," I said. "But I always thought his death was supposed to *mean* something, that the universe was telling me

I had to spend the rest of my life protecting others, even if I was damaging my relationships. Even if it meant not trusting the woman that I loved to do the job she spent her whole life preparing for."

Her eyes filled with sympathy. "Cope—"

I shook my head, needing to go on. "Suddenly, facing my *own* mortality, all of those hard-and-fast ideas were scrambled and knocked loose. Because if I had died that day, there would be no grander message other than the fact that I'd been the victim of a random and tragic accident." Emotion rose in my chest. "Like my dad. Before, it was easier to hold tight to this role I thought I was meant to play. And not have to accept that his loss was, and still is, unfathomable. There is no larger context or symbol. He died in an accident, and it was the worst thing that has ever happened to me."

She was gently wiping at the few tears on my cheeks.

"In the end, it was easier to argue than to listen to you. Easier to beg you to quit than accept your choices. Easier to leave than to work through a complicated knot of issues."

I didn't expect Serena to kiss me, but she did. Wrapping her arms around my neck and pressing our bodies close.

"Thank you for telling me," she said. "Everything about you is good-hearted and noble and strong. I know your dad would be so proud of you. For all of it." She kissed my forehead. "I don't want to push you, ever again, to do something you're not ready to do, okay? I trust you to tell me when it's the right time."

"And I never want to go back to the way things were at the end," I said. "Where we don't listen to each other. Where we don't hear each other."

"I can agree to all of that," she said, smile tugging at her lips.

We kissed again, and this one had the jagged edge of grief and the metallic taste of fear to it. Like those forty-eight hours when we both experienced our own nightmare, separated and believing we might never see each other again.

I pulled back on a ragged breath and stared up at the gorgeous warrior who never ceased to amaze me. "I watched you surf today. I *saw* you. All of you. Serena, you are a work of art. You are elegance, you are *magnificent*. I've never been prouder of you, prouder to love you and to be loved by you."

Her eyes filled with unshed tears. "I was hoping you got to see. I wanted you to." She paused. "I want you to feel comfortable sharing about your dad with me. And I want you to feel that you can be scared for me and that I won't fight with you about it." Her fingers gently played with my hair. "I know you trust me. I know you understand what I can do. But I won't leave you out of any part of my training or safety preparations anymore. I want you to be in *all* the parts of my life, even the messy and scary parts."

"Do you mean that?" I whispered.

"Every word."

"Good." I kissed a clear path up her throat. "Because I meant all of it too."

The final threads of that knot in my chest broke apart, leaving nothing but dazzling love for the woman wrapped in my arms, surrounded by starlight and waves she could dance on.

I asked the only question that mattered now.

"Will you marry me again, Serena?"

The beaming smile that lit up her face was more beautiful than the moon that hung above our heads. "Yes."

I felt for the rings next to me, holding them between us. "Will you be my wife again?"

"Yes." She sighed, kissing across my face. "And I never stopped being your wife because I never stopped loving you."

I slid the ring down her finger as the ocean crashed behind us. The sight of the gold band stole my breath away.

"Will you be my husband again, Cope?" she whispered.

I fisted my hands in her hair and stared deeply into her eyes. "Always, sunshine. Forever."

When she slid on the ring, I flexed my fingers and gazed at the gold in wonder, astonished at the power Serena held over my heart, my body, my mind.

Everything in my life felt right again.

Everything was finally whole.

I kissed my ex-bodyguard and new husband with an ecstatic, joyful sigh, pouring our years of love and yearning into a moment I wanted to stay cocooned in forever.

We had survived four years apart, two monster waves, and a powerful company hunting us down. And it didn't feel physically possible for me to love another more than I loved this man.

My hands gripped his face as he licked his tongue into my mouth, drinking me in. His fingers slid over mine, our new-old rings clicking together, and the sound sent me back to the morning after our Vegas wedding. Hoarse, dehydrated, and starving, we'd stayed in bed well past breakfast, watching the sunlight glint off the cheap bands we'd bought from the Elvis sisters.

But we'd worn them with pride. And apparently had both kept them.

Cope lifted my shirt off and removed my bra, letting the night air caress my bare skin. I was straddling him on the bench, hidden by the rocks as his mouth moved down my neck and across my collarbone. His palms roamed across every inch of my bare skin, up to cup my breasts.

"Can we have a big wedding?" I asked, tilting my head back to give him more access.

"I was just about to ask you the same thing." His hot mouth descended on my nipples, pulling and licking. I reached past him to pull his shirt off, needing to feel those muscles flexing beneath me. He wrapped his arms tighter, lifting me until I was straddling right over his cock. Then he slid his hands inside my shorts, palming my ass, rocking me slowly against his body. I knew how sore we both were, and our movements were as intense as they were delicate, each caress dirty and tender and *just* right.

"I want to wear a pretty white dress." I sighed, smiling as he scraped his teeth along my neck.

I kissed him again and enjoyed the sexy growl that came from his throat. "Perfect," he said, mouth at my ear. "The first moment we're alone that day I'll have my hand between your legs so I can watch you come in it."

I shivered at the image he painted, and then that image was coming true. Together, we worked my shorts and underwear off, and then I was brazenly naked right here by the beach. It was illicit and sinfully forbidden. I *loved* it. As he kissed me until my head spun, those skilled fingers of his slid inside my sex, curling and stroking.

"What else?" he asked, staring up at me as I rode his hand.

"Dancing?"

"All night and into the morning if you want," he said.

Whatever Cope was doing with his fingers was a kind of advanced magic. Sparks of ecstasy fluttered up from between my legs, filling my whole body.

"Cake?" My nails scratched down his chest, twisting in his chest hair.

His mouth teased across my nipples again, his tongue flicking until I cried out. He stroked deeper, reaching some place inside me that had my muscles shaking with pleasure.

"We'll have a cake for every guest," he whispered. "Fifty cakes, a hundred cakes."

I kissed him. "Flowers?"

"I'll buy you every flower in this damn city, sunshine."

He slowly worked his fingers free from my body, but the look in his eye told me we were nowhere near done. He gripped the back of my neck with one hand and nipped my lip. Then he sucked his fingers into his mouth with a husky, satisfied groan. I crashed our mouths back together, tasting myself on his tongue, our movements growing frenzied.

"I need to taste you, and I don't care who sees." We fell backward onto the bench, and then Cope's strong hands were around my waist, dragging me up his chest to sit on his face.

"*Oh*." I sighed, shocked at the new sensation of his tongue licking between my folds. My hands found the rocks above us, and I held on tight as I rode his mouth as decadently as I pleased. When I looked down, his blue eyes watched me with a possession that set my skin on fire.

But it was a fire without the agony of the past few days, of wondering if we could embrace our love without hurting each other again. Here was my confident and sexy husband, on his back for me to enjoy, giving me the pleasure he knew I desired.

His fingers held my hips still so he could circle his tongue around my clit, and I gasped so loudly I was grateful for those waves behind us, covering up the sounds I couldn't suppress. I'd been close before this moment, and now Cope had me balanced on a razor's edge, working his tongue as I rolled my hips, encouraging him to never stop.

"I'm prepared to give you everything," I said, the words coming out on a long moan. His fingers tightened on my skin.

"All of me... *yes, like that*..." I moved my hips faster, keeping steady on the rocks, and Cope flattened his tongue against that bundle of nerves. "Oh god... *oh god*..."

My orgasm shocked me, hitting so hard and fast only my husband's hands kept me upright as I sobbed against the rocks, feeling it everywhere. I was limp with pleasure and fluttery with aftershocks as he pulled me back down his body. I straddled the thick erection that strained through his shorts. I kissed him breathlessly as I reached down, fisting him roughly just to watch his reaction.

"All of me," I said. "I want you to have it."

"Please put me out of my misery," he groaned. "I need you right now."

I lowered myself carefully, taking every single inch as he filled me, stretched me. We shared an anguished moan, faces close, and then I started moving. Cope's cock nudged and teased along my inner walls, a delicious drag and stroke as I rode him slowly. I stayed pressed against his chest, and his hands held the back of my neck, my hair.

His eyes locked on mine in the most intimate moment of my entire life.

"I'm giving you all of me too," he whispered against my lips. "And I will give you my mouth, my tongue, my fingers. I'll make you come until you can't stand and then I'll do it again. I will love every inch of your body, and I'll always let you know it."

"*Yes, Cope*," I moaned, taking him harder and faster now, unable to stop seeking the delicious friction. Beneath the ocean waves, the only sounds were our heavy breathing, Cope's raspy voice, and our bodies slapping together.

"I will cook you bacon every morning." His half-grin at my words had my toes curling. "And surprise you with road trips and bring you coffee when we're camping in the middle of the woods, and *I'm so close, so*..."

His hands left my hair but only to grab my waist and lift me up and down, setting a faster pace that had us both shuddering.

"I will braid all of this hair and help you breathe and hold you when you sleep," he whispered at my ear. "You will always feel safe with me, sunshine. That's a promise I intend to keep forever."

There wasn't time for coherent speech after that, only a dual seeking of release. I planted my hands on his broad chest and sat all the way up, the wind tugging at my hair and the breeze embracing my feverish skin. My nails bit into his skin. His fingers bruised my hips, lifting me up and down. I kept our eyes locked as I fucked my husband, the love of my life and the man I would do anything to protect.

His face was a mask of ecstasy, and despite our sore and tired muscles, that man worked me skillfully on his thick cock, panting my name until he took mercy on me and touched his thumb to my clit.

I threw my head back and cried out through a second, more powerful climax that had me shuddering and shaking. Lowering my face to his, I let Cope thrust into me hard and deep. Let him kiss me as he groaned, "I love you so much."

Watched him come like a revelation as I said, "I love you too."

After, I lay with my ear pressed to his heart. The steady rhythm soothed me as his fingers played with my hair and the waves curled against the sand. They were a force of nature that always returned, no matter the season or the weather, an endless reunion with their home.

An answer to all questions.

"I always hoped we'd find each other again," I whispered.

His lips brushed the crown of my head. I felt his ribs expand on a breath that matched my own.

"I always knew we would," he said.

❧ 41 ❧

COPE

Three days later

I sat in my office at Banks Executive Security and prepared to get fired.

I had a meeting with Marilyn starting in just ten minutes. This was our second in three days—in the first one, I confessed every detail that I'd withheld from my boss and Falco from the moment I'd been given the assignment.

Through a mixture of guilt and regret, I informed them of my marriage, the whistleblower files, and the escalating threats by the company we'd contracted with. My admission was made more dramatic by the article about Aerial— reported on by Quentin, of course—that had broken that very morning.

Marilyn had managed to conceal her emotions throughout the meeting, but she did send me home without any idea of what my fate would be. Although I could guess.

I spent the past two days stewing in that guilt and regret —and talking to Serena about my own reckless behavior and dissatisfaction with this career. I was just beginning to get an idea of what I needed to do next. There was something freeing about giving in to the clues and warning signs your subconscious shared with you.

But first, I needed to atone for my many sins.

Checking my watch, I picked up this morning's *San Diego Times*. The giant, front-page headline read: *Fall from Grace*.

The byline was Quentin's—it was a follow-up story to the first one.

As more employees step forward, the first paragraph read, *a beloved company must answer for more than a decade of fraud allegations and wide-scale abuse.*

Right in the middle was a picture of Catalina with the five other employees she'd worked with to expose Aerial's misdeeds. The FTC was currently investigating Marty, David, and their board members on claims of defrauding consumers and investors as the heinous practices at their factories were finally being revealed.

The brothers had yet to provide a comment.

Catalina had been right in her early assumptions: It wasn't that the Lattimores had always intended to lie and cheat their way into sustainability. It was that they'd given in when they decided that money was more important and remaining ethical was too hard. Foster Hemmings, the city's slimiest councilmember, had helped the brothers create a culture of threats and bribery among their employees. And while it still wasn't clear who at the top of law enforcement had been protecting them, the message was obvious: Maintaining this company's reputation benefited a lot of powerful people.

Thanks in large part to Quentin's respectful reporting, the media hadn't targeted Catalina or Serena. They checked in on each other every day. Catalina was still the real hero of this story, and Quentin was already planning to write profiles on her and her co-conspirators. He also planned stories on the people who worked in Aerial's factories and had experienced their horrific conditions, putting a spotlight on the pervasive problems our society preferred to ignore.

I folded the paper just as I recognized the sounds of Falco's footsteps. I leaned way past my desk as he walked by.

"Hey, Falco?" I called.

A moment passed, and then he appeared in the doorway. "What is it?"

I motioned with my hand for him to come inside. He did, shutting the door behind him and standing right in front of it.

I cleared my throat and made sure he was looking at me. "I'm really, really sorry."

"Uh, what?"

I held my hands out. "I'm sorry. I didn't get a chance to grab you after the meeting the other day, but I wanted to apologize for keeping the details of my relationship with Serena from you. And, more importantly, hiding the whistle-blower situation. It was reckless. It was *stupid*. And it put you in danger."

Falco nodded but stayed quiet, as usual.

"I know I've been a shitty partner this past year," I added. "Hopefully your next partner cares the way that you do. Works hard and takes their job seriously, like you do. You deserve it."

Falco glanced down then said, "I appreciate it. I like you, Cope." He paused. "I do not like working with you."

I smiled at his honesty. "That's fair. I've been an asshole. But I like you too. If it's any consolation, I'm pretty sure I'm about to get fired in a minute."

He shrugged. "Yeah, you're getting fired. Probably for the best, though."

I let out a long sigh. "I think you're right."

My desk phone rang—Marilyn's receptionist instructing

me she was ready for our meeting. I stood, rounded my desk, and followed Falco outside my office.

"You can still call me if you ever need help," I said. "I mean that."

I turned toward the elevators, assuming the conversation was done. But he said my name, drawing my attention.

"You should have told me that our client was your wife," he said.

"I should have," I replied.

He glanced down at my wedding ring, and I followed his gaze, feeling the usual bolt of joy that happened whenever I got to remember Serena and I were together again.

"Congratulations, though."

"Um, what?" I asked.

"Congratulations," he said. "On getting back together with her." At my shocked face, he lifted a shoulder and said, "I'm a romantic."

And then he left, walking stiffly back down the hallway on his way to his next assignment. With a confused smile, I made my way to Marilyn's office, feeling slightly lighter even though I was dreading this conversation the most.

I knocked on the open door.

"Come in," she said. She wore an inscrutable expression and a navy-blue power suit.

I sat down gingerly and winced as my hips screamed in pain. Although three days had passed, my body had not let me forget swimming through giant waves, fighting off two men, then having passionate sex with my wife on an outcropping of rocks. Technically, per doctor's orders, we were meant to be resting in bed. We'd stayed in bed.

Nothing we did there was *restful*. Serena and I had reached for each other every night and every morning, having sex that put our honeymoon to shame.

Marilyn sat down across from me with a look filled with delicate disappointment.

"Good morning," I said.

She arched her brow and opened a file. "Good morning. Now that I've been fully briefed on the actual situation at Aerial and the secret relationship with your *wife*, Serena Swift, shall I read off some of the protocols you so carelessly abandoned?"

I grimaced. Nodded. This was the atonement part, and I needed to accept what I'd done.

She flipped through papers and said, "You did not inform your superiors that you had a previous romantic relationship with the client. Romantic as in, *was married to* just four years ago. You repeatedly lied to your partner and kept pertinent details from him that compromised his own personal safety. *And,* while your best friend from college was fully briefed on an active whistleblower situation, you ultimately failed to inform *anyone* here of what was going on." She stared at me. "Does that about cover it?"

"Yes, ma'am," I said.

"Do not *yes, ma'am* me, Copeland," she said. "You cannot interject respect this late in the game. And I'm sure you're aware that I called you here this morning to inform you that you are fired."

The words landed heavily in the room—and hit me harder than I expected.

"I am aware that I am being fired," I said. "I take responsibility for all of it. There is no excuse except my own stupidity."

She let me hang there for a minute, simmering in my own discomfort. Then she stood up, rounded the desk, and perched on the corner right by me. "Your actions affected this company, our many clients, and *my* reputation. You left me no choice—you understand that, right?"

I felt like absolute shit. "I do."

She examined me for a second before crossing her arms. "Explain to me again why you thought keeping the whistle-blower information from me was a smart idea?"

I weighed my words carefully. "It was not a choice I made lightly. At the time, Quentin and I were extremely cautious of how vengeful Aerial could be and unsure of how far their reach extended. We were getting threats, being followed. They clearly wanted to scare us. We'd both seen whistle-blower situations end in a much more dangerous and violent fashion. At the time, with the information that I had, I believed I was protecting you and Falco. I wouldn't make that choice again knowing what I do now, but that was my reasoning."

"This is a firm of highly trained private security officials with years of experience diffusing situations like the one you found yourself in," she said. "But you thought you and your friend could do a better job?"

My face got hot. "It was short-sighted and the wrong decision to make."

The elephant in the room, of course, was the truth of what we hadn't addressed: my distraction and preoccupation with Serena, which colored every single thought and choice I made during those intense, heady days.

As if reading my thoughts, Marilyn pointed at my left hand. "I'd ask if you considered yourself professionally compromised by your past relationship with Ms. Swift, but the wedding ring you can't stop touching answers that question for me."

I winced, rubbed my forehead. "I was extremely compromised the whole time."

She sighed with deep frustration. "I can't fault you for thinking you were protecting us in the end, for making some rash decisions in the heat of the moment without the full picture. The issue is that your beliefs *always* outweigh your ability to make the smart and right decision. As evidenced by the chain of mistakes you made. Mistakes that could have gotten you and others around you hurt if you hadn't gotten so lucky."

"You are absolutely right," I agreed. "I'm sorry for all of it. For breaking the rules, for putting people at risk, for disrespecting you and this company. Your mentorship has meant a lot to me these past four years, and I am truly sorry for insulting a work relationship I value. I know an apology doesn't mean anything without action behind it, so if there's something else I can do, please say the word."

Marilyn glanced down at her hands with a rare moment of indecision. She peeked at the door, which was closed, and then sat in the chair right next to mine. She had never done that before—she was either behind a desk or perched above me but never at my level.

"There is something that you can do," she said. She pulled at a loose thread on her jacket before looking up at me. "I am not one for overly emotional sentiment, but I'm going to share something with you I don't tell many people."

The look in her eyes elicited a strange response in my chest.

"I know you've met my husband many times. I love him very much. But five years before we got together, I had a boyfriend who I also loved very much. He died, in a car accident." She said the words flatly, but I recognized that tone. I used that tone. "To say it was a shock is a gross understatement. It was random. It had no grander meaning. And it destroyed me."

It was like a fist, closing around my throat. I spent an inordinate amount of time obsessing over my final moments with my father. They were pedestrian and, thankfully, happy.

He was walking down our driveway barefoot, holding his board over his head and smiling at me.

When I get back, we'll do pancakes okay? Love you, bud.

I'd said *love you too*. I didn't do what I should have done— beg him to come back.

Tell him not to go.

It was brutal and unforgiving, that cycle.

"I have observed, over these years, you believing this job is some kind of referendum on your father's death," she said —gently. Very gently. "I had a similar experience with that kind of magical thinking in those terrible years. I constructed steps and patterns I had to follow, became oddly superstitious, enforced ideas on what the accident *meant* and how I had to live life a certain way because of it." She paused. "Does any of that sound familiar to you?"

I nodded. "Yes." My voice was hoarse. "I think it's why I also..." I shrugged, uncomfortable. "Tend to shut down when tough things happen. Shut people out that I love. Make everything about jokes or having a sense of humor. It's like building a wall. It's why I didn't want to admit that I wasn't happy here. That I was distracted and bored."

"It's time for a new career. That's what I want you to do," she said softly. "Much as your skillsets align with it, I don't think your heart does."

"Did Marilyn Banks just say *heart*?" I asked with a smile.

She returned it, holding up a finger. "Once a year, *once*, I allow myself a few moments of sentimentality. You are the recipient."

Guilt surged through me. "Again, I really don't feel like I'm deserving of it."

"Well." She sighed. "It just so happens that I quite enjoy seeing companies that exploit their employees pay for their crimes. Publicly. I'm not pleased with how you got to that outcome, but I'm pleased with the outcome."

"I understand," I said. I was never going to find an equilibrium between us, but then again, I'd been the one who'd fucked up big time.

She stood up and gave me a short nod. "I never said it before, but allow me to tell you how sorry that I am that your father was taken from you and that nothing will bring him back. I am so very sorry that he died."

This was the part that would never be easy. Because this job would never bring him back.

No job would.

It took me a few seconds before I could speak again. "And I'm so sorry about losing your boyfriend. Thank you for the advice. It was very much needed and appreciated."

She made her way back behind the desk, and I recognized our brief moment was over. But I was still grateful. "Do you want us to set up security at Serena's house until the Aerial situation is under control?"

I sighed, scrubbing a hand down my face. "Yeah, actually, that would help me sleep better at night. If you can spare it."

"I can spare it," she said. "I know Serena was able to terminate her contract immediately as their ambassador. But they'd already paid for the first month of private security. There's no reason not to make sure the two of you aren't targeted again."

"Thank you," I said. "For everything, Marilyn."

With my hand on the doorknob, about to leave, I turned to my boss one last time.

"You really didn't know that Serena was my wife the entire time?" I asked, curious.

"I most certainly did not know," she said. "An extremely rare mistake was made on our end. And on Aerial's. Your personal connection was missed while cross-referencing our standard background checks. Trust me, the person here who made the mistake has already been spoken to."

I cocked my head. "The whole thing was because of a mistake?"

Her brow arched. "Your reunion was made possible by a clerical error."

I shook my head with a laugh, staring down at the wedding ring I'd carried in my wallet for four years. I knew the real reason Serena had come back into my life—and it wasn't due to something as random as an *error*.

It was our destiny.

Even when apart, the universe had tangled us back together again—although that didn't mean we didn't need to put in the hard work to make sure our love flourished. That kind of intimacy and understanding required more courage than I imagined.

And I'd learned that courage came in all forms and expressions—like my father, who loved fully and lived for joy. Or my mother and sister, who lived each day with gratitude and hope.

Catalina and Quentin's courage came in the form of fearless action and fighting for justice.

And Serena? My wife was the most courageous person I knew. She lived her life boldly, went flying down big waves with a smile on her face. Stood up for what she believed in no matter the cost.

She would always be my most beautiful risk.

It was all worth it.

EPILOGUE

SERENA

One year later

Cope spun slowly on his barstool, looking much too handsome in his fitted linen suit. And the lascivious grin on his face had me blushing beneath my makeup.

He gripped my stool and dragged me until our legs entwined. He picked up his strawberry margarita and tapped it against my own glass.

"Cheers, sunshine," he said, taking a long drink with mischief in his dark blue eyes.

I arched an eyebrow. "You look like you're getting one of your ideas."

"Who, me?"

I wrapped my fingers in his lapels and pulled him close. "Is it dirty?"

"I guess that depends." His smile was on the sinful side of charming.

And he'd already made a dozen filthy promises about what he was planning to do to me in my pretty white dress.

"I'm listening," I said.

He brushed a stray curl from my shoulder. "What if we just did it?"

I fought a smile but lost. We'd both been giddy all day. "Oh, yeah? Did what, exactly?"

"Got hitched at the chapel next door." Cope kissed my neck, and I shivered.

"Tell me why you want to?" My eyes closed in anticipation.

His mouth hovered at my ear, breath tickling my skin. "Because I want you to be my *wife*," he said, echoing his exact words five years ago. "I want you for my forever. I want to be yours. I want you to be mine, Serena."

I hummed a little. "Can I think about it?"

He started laughing, tickling my sides as I tried to swat him away. "Such a tease."

"Last time I checked, you liked it."

His next kiss was firmer, harder. Hotter. "I do like it."

We'd abandoned all nods to tradition this morning, and my husband had absolutely seen me before the ceremony. While stepping into the shower, I'd crooked my finger, and he'd eagerly joined me beneath the steam—lifting me up and fucking me against the glass in a fast, dirty quickie that put a giant smile on both of our faces.

Somebody wolf-whistled in the back, and we broke apart, laughing. The bartender placed two more margaritas in front of us.

"From some Serena Swift fans down at the bar," she said with a wink. Delighted, I turned around to wave at a group of young women who clapped and cheered.

"*Congratulations*," one of them yelled.

"Thank you for the drinks," I called back.

Cope kissed the ball of my shoulder. "It feels incredible to be married, again, to a very popular, incredibly talented professional surfer," he said.

I squeezed his hand. "You're still the only fan that I need."

"I'm your number one fan, sunshine," he promised. "Forever."

He was on the beach most mornings now when I surfed with the ever-growing community of women who made that spot so special. He always watched. He always cheered. And he was there when I ran out of the water to jump into his arms after an especially good wave, squealing as he'd spin me around. Reminding me that I was a *masterpiece*.

He drank coffee with Dora or talked with Catalina, who was now a regular. He even ran on the beach with Caleb sometimes, making sure to wink at me when he jogged past.

My career had taken off over the past year with wins, international tours, and even a brand-new sponsor: *Betty's*. They were a women-run digital media company for the surf industry dedicated to inclusivity and diversity at every level. And they were the first partner Kalei, Prue, and I had turned to when we were looking for early supporters of the Surf Equity Community Fund.

The community fund was the culmination of all those sparkly ideas I'd had when I was working with Aerial. Run and managed by local surfers in San Diego, it provided the financial backing for surfers to train, travel, and compete at elite events. It leveled the playing field and removed the need to attract splashy corporate sponsors. And it raised the profile—and amplified the voices—of athletes often ignored and silenced.

Every month, my friends and I gathered in Dora's living room to work and learn alongside other women, Black and brown surfers, indigenous surfers, queer and gender nonconforming people—all of us dedicated to creating structural change from the ground up.

We discovered that we were all angry at the way things were. And we were all using it to make things better.

I crossed my legs beneath my white dress and slipped my hand into the pocket where I'd hidden a surprise for Cope. I stole a sip of his margarita, and we shared a sweet and salty kiss.

"I brought you a gift," I said. "In honor of taking the plunge a second time."

"You did?"

I removed a crinkled Polaroid picture. "Behold: the only photographic evidence of our first wedding at the Blue Suede Shoes Elvis Chapel in Las Vegas."

Cope's eyes widened—and then he started laughing. "Oh my god. I forgot I wore that pin-striped suit and *sandals*."

"I happen to think you look very dashing."

Loretta and Frankie were committed to the lost art of the Polaroid camera, and they took this picture for us *on the house*, they said. In it, I was beaming in my short sequined dress, holding pink carnations. Cope was sloppily kissing my cheek. There was no mistaking we looked young, drunk, and head-over-heels for each other.

"We're framing this as soon as we get home," he said. "I love it. I love *you*."

"I love you," I said. "*So* much." We said those three words a lot, making up for lost time.

Cope touched the picture tenderly. "Can you believe that a year ago I was standing in the parking lot outside of Aerial, waiting to see you again?"

I cupped his cheek. "My husband the bodyguard."

"*Ex*-bodyguard," he said, teasing. "I'm married to a professional surfer, and you're one step closer to being married to a paramedic."

"A true hero now," I said and meant every word. Trevor had helped Cope figure out how to go back to school for a new career that protected people, that saved lives and offered comfort in a crisis. He was currently halfway through an intensive paramedic training program.

As it turns out, Cope was an absolute natural. His big heart had a lot to do with that. Although last week, his instructors had praised his bedside manner and ability to make people feel safe. Being funny and chatty now came in handy.

"Your father would be so proud of you," I said.

He swallowed thickly. "He really would. I wish he was here today, sunshine. I felt him, though, all during the ceremony."

"Me too," I said softly. "Would he be one of the wedding guests dancing until dawn?"

"Oh, *absolutely*," he said. "If there was anything he loved more than surfing, it was going *wild* on a wedding dance floor."

I laughed because I could picture it perfectly. And ached because his absence was truly felt.

Cope tucked a strand of my hair back into place. "I really get it now. I get the way that you feel about surfing, like all you want to do is dream about it, talk about it. Do it."

"You have a calling now," I said, so happy for him I could burst.

He shook his head like he couldn't believe it. "I wouldn't have been brave enough to do it if Aerial hadn't happened. And we're not even the only happy ending from that story, either."

"We sure aren't," I said. "I still think it's amazing that so much good came from a situation that was so incredibly awful."

In the end, Marty, David, and most of their board had

been charged with fraud, among other criminal acts. But the majority of Aerial's staff—lead by Catalina—were staying to rebuild a company that actually vowed to protect people and the planet. And Quentin, with the months he dedicated to telling this story until justice was served, was now one of the most respected journalists in his field.

From outside the bar came a rousing cheer—a cheer that sounded like our names. Cope and I shared a look of pure excitement. Kissing my wrist, he said, "I think it might be time."

"Are you nervous?"

"Not at all," he said. "How about you?"

"This feels like the easiest thing I've ever done," I said.

He stood, pulling me with him, then bent me backwards for a Hollywood-style kiss that had the wolf-whistles starting up again. I gave in to our passion, gave in to the heady euphoria of our second chance. This new chapter of ours wasn't a resuming of our relationship. There was no pressing *play* despite our long pause. We'd not only changed and grown, but our dynamics had expanded to fit that growth, allowing for new vulnerabilities and honesty.

It was a beautiful blend of our fresh start, combined with the spontaneity of our young love.

"We should probably get to it then," Cope said.

"I'm so ready."

He hauled me up, twirled me around. I'd ditched the heels for sandals right away, given I was planning on dancing until dawn.

We walked through the bar hand in hand and stepped out onto a patio overlooking the turquoise ocean. Fairy lights twinkled against the sunset, and the community that loved us —our friends and our found family—let out another rousing cheer.

"Aren't you glad everyone was here this time?" I whispered at Cope, who had tears in his eyes.

"Second best decision we ever made," he whispered back. "The first being that spontaneous trip to Vegas."

We gazed out over the patio where our guests had enjoyed a happy hour after our wedding ceremony on the beach. And Cope and I had enjoyed a special thirty minutes alone together so we could drink strawberry margaritas before a night of dancing.

Caleb stood in the middle of the crowd with a microphone and a cheesy grin. "Ladies and gentlemen, I am so proud to introduce our newly married couple, for the *second* time, Serena Swift and Cope McDaniels."

We laughed with silly joy as everyone clapped and cheered. My brother had officiated the ceremony. Quentin had *finally* gotten to be Cope's best man. Dora, like we suspected, had bawled through the ceremony after walking me down the aisle.

Like he promised, every table was full of tiny cakes for each guest and a sea of pink flowers.

We walked slowly to the middle for our first dance: "Can't Help Falling in Love" by Elvis Presley, of course. We beamed at each other as our memories became entangled with this present moment, as we slow danced to Elvis Presley five years after being married in a Vegas wedding chapel where this song played in the background.

I wrapped my arms around Cope, and he held me so close we were barely swaying. An ocean breeze shimmered over my skin, and I knew, just beyond us, the waves broke against the sand, calling to those of us with wild spirits.

Calling us home.

Cope flashed me that lopsided grin. "Are we the *fools rushing in* in this scenario?"

"I think so," I said as we danced beneath the lights.

"There's nothing wrong with a little spontaneity. As long as we do it together."

He kissed my forehead and squeezed me tight. "You are my forever, sunshine."

"And you're mine," I whispered back.

Our past and our present coalesced as we danced, our future bold and bright and filled with new memories to be made. I blinked, and Cope was twenty-two, kissing me over coffee. And then twenty-four, marrying me in front of a stranger dressed as Elvis.

And then a year ago, as my protector, running toward me through the waves when I needed him the most.

Cope had returned to me, over and over again, as steady as the tides.

Our love story was always meant to be.

WANT MORE COPE AND SERENA?

What would a second wedding be without a second wedding night? Check out this steamy bonus epilogue that picks up right after Serena and Cope's wedding festivities end and the honeymoon begins.
TAP HERE: To check out this bonus scene!

If you are having any trouble tapping on the extra scene please type "twsspub.com/bonus/ootb" into your phone or computer browser.

DID YOU ENJOY OUT OF THE BLUE?

I've got another bodyguard romance in KU called FREE FALL!

Fifteen years as a bodyguard and Elijah Knight has never been tempted to break the rules. This close to the promotion of a lifetime, the last thing he needs is Luke Beaumont. The very definition of temptation. And the man he's just been ordered to protect at any cost.

Check out FREE FALL on Amazon

BONUS EPILOGUE

COPE

The woman at the hotel front desk beamed at us as soon as we stepped up to check in.

"Let me guess," she said. "You two lovebirds are here for our honeymoon suite?"

"Hell yeah, we are," I said, squeezing Serena's hand. "And we'll take the biggest bottle of champagne that you have, thanks."

My wife arched her eyebrow. "Two, actually. Two bottles."

The woman nodded. "Absolutely. That won't be a problem at all. Give me just a second to make sure your suite is ready to go."

As soon as she was out of earshot, I looped my arm around Serena and tugged her against my side. Dropped a kiss on top of her hair, which was tangled and messy due to our enthusiastic dancing.

"*Two* bottles?" I murmured.

She looked up at me with a sexy smirk. I brushed a few

curls from her eyes. "One for us to drink. One for you to lick off my naked body."

I instantly got hard. I'd also been hard for a lot of our wedding. "That's fairly presumptuous, sunshine."

"This is our *second* honeymoon," she said. "Please, we're not amateurs."

The woman returned with our key card. "Room 1015 on the tenth floor. The elevators are just over there. Your room is ready, and we'll be providing complimentary room service whenever you ring us in the morning." She glanced at her watch. "Well, technically it's three in the morning so..."

"We'll aim for noon," Serena said with a wink. And began dragging me to the elevators with clear purpose in her stride. I waved to the woman, said *"thanks for the champagne,"* and then my wife was shoving me toward the elevator doors. Our last wedding night had started off with a bang—literally— when I'd fingered Serena to a quick orgasm as we rode to our room. A memory so hot it was all I could think about as I cupped her cheeks and kissed her, licking into her mouth, opening wide.

"Ten floors, huh?" I whispered.

"I might have done that on purpose when I booked it," she said. There was a *ding,* and we practically sprinted inside.

Only to be followed by a herd of late-night partiers coming in from the street of bars near the hotel. Laughing softly, I pulled Serena against my chest for a sweet, tender hug as we rode the elevator with a bunch of boozy people loudly re-hashing their evening. We didn't stop smiling at each other the whole way. We'd both been floating on cloud nine since our pre-wedding quickie in the shower that morning. My cheeks ached from happiness. My ribcage ached from laughing. And my heart was full to the brim with a gratitude so intense it took my breath away. One year, almost to the day, since I'd sat in Marilyn's office and opened a file that contained Serena's picture—the woman I'd spent four long years pining for. And now we'd gotten married, again, in front of our favorite people in the entire world. Lived together in our blue beach house. And I was well on my way to embarking on a career that *actually* helped and protected people.

"I love you," I mouthed, kissing the tip of Serena's nose. She pressed up onto her toes and kissed me full on the lips. The partiers clapped and whistled until we started laughing and broke apart.

The doors opened on the tenth floor, and we spilled out from the crowded elevator, both blushing.

"Not the ride I expected, to be honest," I said.

We reached the honeymoon suite, and I pressed Serena against the door. She bit her lip. "I've got plenty of ideas to make up for it."

Holding her gaze, I swiped the card and followed her inside. Flicking on the lights, we paused as we took in the space—we'd splurged on a room with a view of the ocean, a hot tub in the bathroom, a fireplace. The bed was huge, and I was going to get a lot of joy out of fucking my wife on it in every position imaginable.

"This room is—" I stopped mid-speech. Serena had slipped into the bathroom when I was busy staring at the bed and had returned in pale pink lingerie that made my knees weak.

"Incredible," I finished. "*Jesus Christ*, Serena."

"Do you like it?" she purred. She placed her palm on my chest and shoved me hard against the door. I was still in my linen suit from the ceremony, but that didn't stop her from dropping to her knees and sliding down my zipper.

"I love it," I said, lifting up her chin. I pressed on her mouth. "I love you. More than anything in this world, do you understand?"

Her smile was slow and alluring. "I love you to the moon and back, Cope."

And then she slipped my cock free and took it between her lips. I speared my fingers into her curls. Twisted. And let my head fall back against the door. It was always *so fucking good* between us, but there was something wild and edgy about this second-round honeymoon. We needed each other so badly we'd gone ahead and gotten married *twice*.

"*God*, that feels good," I groaned, loving the wet sounds of her mouth on my skin. I looked down at the goddess on her knees who was taking me deep. "That's perfect, sunshine. Just like that."

She hummed her pleasure and closed her eyes. I flexed my hips and pushed between her lips. She moaned even louder. I spotted a silver bucket with two bottles of champagne and my mind filled with images from our last wedding night—the sweet taste of the alcohol dripping down her skin. How indulgent it felt to lap it up.

"Up," I said, grabbing her elbow. "I've got another idea."

She wiped her mouth. "Better than that one?"

I bent and scooped her into my arms. Kissed her. "There will be plenty of time tonight for me to fuck that smart mouth of yours. But I owe you champagne first."

Her eyes heated. I tossed her onto the bed, grabbed the champagne, and popped it open with little ceremony. The cork flew across the room. Serena watched from the bed, propped on her elbows. As bubbles fizzed out, I held the bottle up and sipped the liquid spilling down my hand.

"Tastes almost as good as you do," I said. She smirked, crooked her finger. I walked to her warm and willing body, covered in the pink lace bra and underwear I planned on ripping in two. "Now?" I asked.

"I won't stop until my new husband is satisfied," she teased.

We watched together as I carefully—and gently—tipped some of the bubbles across her stomach. She gasped, shivered. I placed the bottle on the nightstand and dipped my mouth to her skin. Her fingers landed in my hair as I licked up every single drop from the hollow by her hips, along the muscles of her stomach, up her rib cage. Serena tossed her lacy bra, and I tipped the bottle again—this time sucking and drinking from her collarbone. The space between her breasts. I lapped along her nipples as she writhed, panting, on the bed.

"Do you care about these?" I asked, gripping the lacy fabric of her underwear in my fist.

"Not at all."

I tore them easily and followed the trail of champagne down her beautiful body. Spread those strong, powerful legs of hers and buried my face against her pussy. She didn't seem to be in the mood for slow—and frankly, neither was I—so I flattened my tongue against her clit in small, fast circles. She arched against the bed and yanked on my hair. Sighed my name over and over as I licked her faster and faster. She sat up and planted her palms behind her, rolling her body against my tongue, urging me on. Her thighs tightened against my ears as I palmed her breasts.

"Oh *fuck*, I'm so close already," she moaned as her head fell back. I sped up my tongue, increased the pressure. She was thrusting up against my mouth. I could feel her shaking.

"Wait," she said, tapping my shoulders. I sat back on my heels, still out of breath. She placed her heel in the center of my chest and pushed hard. I fell backwards against the floor with a satisfied grin and then lost the ability to form thoughts as a very naked Serena straddled my hips.

"Do you care about this?" she asked, fingers in my button-down shirt.

"Not at all," I repeated.

"Good." She ripped it open, buttons flying, and raked her nails down my chest. I hissed and groaned, grabbing her waist as she placed my cock at her slick, hot entrance. Eyes locked together, she slammed down, taking every inch. Shuddered and sighed as she started to move. Not slow at all. Planting her palms on my chest, Serena rode me with a fury while I watched, enthralled. Her first orgasm hit her almost immediately, and the sight had me itching to propose marriage all over again.

I didn't give her a chance to catch her breath. I lifted her off of me and hauled her back on her hands and knees. I draped my body over hers and bit down on her ear.

"Is my new wife satisfied?"

"Not yet," she taunted.

"Good," I growled. "Because I'm not done with you yet."

Kneeling behind her, I lined up again and thrust back inside, fucking into her from behind. She threw her head back, and I reached for her hair, burying my fingers in the strands as I bore down. The room filled with our heavy breathing, our moans, our whispered endearments. When I slipped my hand between her legs and touched her clit, she exploded again in seconds. I fucked her through her aftershocks, through her internal walls clamping down, and my own orgasm detonated at the base of my spine. I lost myself in the sensation, in the total euphoria, head back and Serena's name on my lips.

We collapsed on the floor—her, naked and sticky with champagne. Me, partially clothed with a torn shirt. I pulled her into me and kissed her forehead with a giant grin on my face.

"See?" she panted. "We're basically experts in honeymoon sex."

"We're experts in all sex, I think," I said.

"Very true." She propped her chin on my chest, and her

smile was dazzling. "Shame we couldn't recreate our infamous elevator ride, but there's always tomorrow."

I patted down her snarled hair, tucking it behind her ear. "You are insatiable, sunshine."

"Give me a minute, and I'll be ready for shower sex next."

I pretended to think. "I can make that happen." I rolled her onto her back and kissed her deeply. Kissed up and down her throat and along her jaw. "Plus, we have to fuck in the closet. And on the bed..."

"And in the morning," she said with a happy sigh. She kissed my palm.

"It is almost morning," I pointed out. "We didn't quite dance until dawn, but I think 2:00 am is commendable."

"I don't want to be separated from you ever again," she said softly. "But I *would* recreate our wedding ceremony a dozen more times."

"Maybe we could do a vow renewal at Blue Suede Shoes. Give Frankie and Loretta a call and have them plan it."

She laughed and hugged me close. "That's a perfect idea." Her eyes searched mine as her fingers trailed across my lips. I kissed them. "You're my forever, Cope McDaniels. No matter what."

"And you're mine, Serena Swift," I promised. "Now let's get started on that shower sex."

A NOTE FROM THE AUTHOR

Dear reader,

Thank you for reading *Out of the Blue*. I fell head-over-heels for Serena and Cope and I hope that you did too!

This was, by far, one of the hardest books I've ever written. It took three full drafts until I finally understood how to delicately pull apart the complexities of Serena and Cope's marriage and then bring them together again in a way that resolved the issues that broke them apart. I peeked at the first draft just the other day and it's not even remotely the same as the book you just read. And while I fretted and stressed over the journey these two took me on, I was *overjoyed* while writing their epilogue, because I felt like I finally unlocked the vulnerabilities that made both characters so relatable – and so compelling.

My favorite scene to write (and rewrite) was the wipe-out scene, with Cope attempting to rescue Serena like we all knew he would, and Serena saving both of their lives in the end. I held that scene clear in my mind from the time I started outlining this book in October until final rewrites in

April. It was a scene that played in my mind like a movie and gave me goosebumps every time.

Other favorites: Cope's opening chapter, when he opens the folder and sees Serena's face, their cheeseburger-and-Pacifico date, their Vegas reminiscing, Serena being a bad-ass on the water, their found families, the first time Serena calls Cope her *husband* and not her *ex*. The interview with Chase when Serena stands up for what's right. When she makes Cope bacon in the morning and then he braids her hair. Okay, I'm just naming all of the scenes now – I love this book!

I've been fascinated with surfers for a long time (hello, Blue Crush!) but especially so after writing my first novel *Riptide* – the hero, Finn Travis, makes a quick cameo in this book. An immense amount of research went into big wave surfing and the stories and struggles of women surfers. The discrimination that Serena experiences is, unfortunately, not fictional. And while Serena was able to share her personal experiences as a woman, other marginalized groups, ethnicities, and identities have spoken out about their own negative experiences, from racism, to lack of equal pay, to being locked out of competitions and other opportunities. While I was grateful to learn about so many rad big wave surfers during this time, I was especially inspired by the big wave surfer Maya Gabeira, a Brazilian surfer who was recorded as surfing the biggest wave ever by a woman in Nazare, Portugal. The wave was 73-feet high.

There are so many amazing organizations and collectives doing the justice work that Serena and her friends commit to at the end of the book. A few that I recommend following to learn more: *Surf Equity,, Textured Waves, Queer Surf Club* and the *All Are We Water Collective. Black Girls Surf*

For the most part, the many beaches and locations I mention as big wave surf spots are real, although the actual surf competitions held at Trestles Beach, The Wedge and

Huntington do not line up in a three-week period and I had some fun shrinking down San Diego to allow Serena and Cope to get around quickly and without traffic. Any other fictional details around surfing and logistics are purely of my imagination.

This was truly a story of my heart – one of grief and heartbreak, understanding and growth, fear and love. It's a story about those with wild spirits, about using the gift of your anger to make real change, of allowing yourself to make hard choices. And, most of all, a story of how true love returns to us like the tides, over and over again.

Thank you for celebrating their love story – and I hope you all get to take a spontaneous trip to Las Vegas someday. And if you see the Elvis Presley sisters at their wedding chapel, tell them Serena and Cope say hi.

Love,
Kathryn

ACKNOWLEDGMENTS

This book would not have been possible without the following incredible people:

Faith, my best friend and developmental editor, who emotionally supported me through these tough-as-hell drafts and my endless text messages asking why I was writing another suspense novel again when they were so damn hard. I honestly could not do it without you, your brilliant ideas and your assistance with those *ah-ha* moments.

Jessica Snyder, who remains exquisitely talented in providing developmental edits that kick my butt and line edits that also close up every single remaining plot hole, no matter how microscopic. Also, Walter thanks you for the Christmas (dog) cookies.

Jodi, Julia and Bronwyn, my beta readers, who worked incredibly hard to help me put the finishing touches on this book, from scene corrections and mischaracterizations to subtle conflict adjustments that made the whole book ten times better. I literally do not know how you do it every time, but the draft they receive comes out a totally better book after they've worked their magic.

Rose Camara, who offered her insight, feedback and wisdom for the character of Marilyn Banks as well as helping to ensure Serena was able to stand up for other people while being mindful of taking up space. Any mistakes in this text are my own.

Lizette Baez, who offered her insight, feedback and wisdom for the character of Catalina Flores – and also helped in ensuring Serena was coming from a place of allyship during some of the tougher conversations she had in this book. Any mistakes in this text are my own.

The Hippie Chicks and their awe-inspiring support and enthusiasm; Lucy, Stephanie, and LJ for their authorly support and kind words when I needed them; Joyce and Tammy for their virtual hugs and compassion; Tim, Rick and Dan who turned all of my work into a real book and put it out in the world! And Lucy and I got to go on the best writer's retreat ever in the Poconos (peanut butter whiskey was involved), and that's where I first majorly outlined *Out of the Blue*. It holds an extra special place in my heart because of our time there together.

Finally – my husband, Rob, who is my forever. Our love story was definitely meant to be. And if you wanted to get married again on a spontaneous trip to Vegas, I'm down for our next road trip in the van! Walter can be the ring-bearer.

ABOUT KATHRYN

Kathryn Nolan (she/they) is an Amazon Top 25 bestselling author. Her steamy romance novels are known for their slow-burn sexual tension, memorable characters, and big, hopeful feelings.

Kathryn is a bisexual bookworm and femme cutie with big Leo energy. They love to spend their free time hiking, camping and traveling. When not on the road, they live in their hometown of Philly with their cute husband and giant-eared rescue pup, Walter.

Sign up for Kathryn's weekly newsletter to see what she's writing, what she's reading/watching and get all her travel stories (plus an abundance of Walter photos!):

https://www.authorkathrynnolan.com/join-my-newsletter

BOOKS BY KATHRYN

FREE FALL

Fifteen years as a bodyguard and Elijah Knight has never been tempted to break the rules. His pristine reputation is the reason why he's about to secure the promotion of a lifetime. So the last person he needs anywhere near him is Luke Beaumont, the very definition of temptation. And the man he's just been ordered to protect at any cost.

STRICTLY PROFESSIONAL

Edward Cavendish III and Roxy Quinn couldn't be more different. He's a polite, wealthy hotelier from England. She's a scowling, bad-ass tattoo artist. But when a night of heartbreak brings them together, their chemistry – and connection – is electrifying. Seeing each other romantically is not an option – until they meet again under *strictly professional* circumstances.

NOT THE MARRYING KIND

Fiona plans to be married to her soul mate by the time she turns 30. Unfortunately, she agrees to plan a benefit concert with Max, a cocky bad boy who swears he will never settle down. But when romantic sparks fly between these two friends, will they let their rules get in the way of true love?

BOHEMIAN

Shy, nerdy Calvin inherits his grandfather's bookstore in funky Big Sur, but has no idea whether to sell the bookstore – or take on the challenge of keeping the store's literary legacy alive. When a bohemian-style photo shoot brings famous super model Lucia Bell to Big Sur, sparks fly between these two total opposites.

LANDSLIDE

Gabe Shaw has the perfect life in Big Sur. He's the third-generation-owner (and bartender) at The Bar, the only place in this funky small town where the quirky locals can drink in peace. A hopeless romantic, Gabe's only lacking one thing: his soul mate. And when a sudden storm traps a sexy, funny make-up artist named Josie in Big Sur, one night of searing passion turns into much more. Too bad Josie doesn't believe in falling in love.

RIPTIDE

Avery Dacosta is an ambitious property developer, intent on building a luxury hotel on Playa Vieja's last untouched beach. And she has no time for Finn Travis, the laid-back, hippie surfer who decides to protest this hotel – and her workplace – every day. Unfortunately, Finn's not only the most aggravating man she's ever met – but sexy as hell. Can these two enemies-turned-lovers ever find a middle ground?

SEXY SHORTS (VOLUME 1)

A sweet, dirty collection of fourteen sexy short stories.

BEHIND THE VEIL (CODEX Book #1)

Private detective Delilah Barrett is entirely unprepared for her new assignment: hunt down a stolen rare manuscript that's hidden within Philadelphia's glamorous high society. The only catch? Delilah must go undercover as a fake married couple with her new partner Henry Finch -- a devastatingly handsome librarian. But as the danger intensifies...so does the temptation to let their fake desire become real.

UNDER THE ROSE (CODEX Book #2)

To infiltrate a secret society, private detective Freya Evandale and FBI agent Sam Byrne must go undercover as a pair of thieves in a dangerous world of shifting alliances. But can these lifelong rivals close the case...without falling in love?

IN THE CLEAR (CODEX Book #3)

While chasing a famous book thief in London, two private detectives work together while dodging danger at every turn. But can aloof, serious Abe and charming, mysterious Sloane resist their instant attraction to one another? Or will passionate temptation risk this case – and their careers?

WILD OPEN HEARTS

Luna's cheerful, hippie reputation is ruined when her billion-dollar company is caught in a scandal. And only a burly, dog-rescuing biker can help her. As these opposites give in to their electrifying attraction – will their differences keep them apart? Or will they learn to trust their wild hearts?

ON THE ROPES

Former pro boxer Dean Knox-Morelli is shocked when his new neighbor is Tabitha Tyler – his childhood friend and the woman he's had a secret crush on for years. But when flirty filmmaker Tabitha tries to tempt Dean into a sexy, summer fling, will he finally get the girl? Or will she only pack her bags and leave him heartbroken?

OUT OF THE BLUE

When famous surfer Serena Swift is provided a bodyguard by her new corporate sponsor, she's pissed to find it's her ex-husband, Cope McDaniels, tasked with keeping her safe. But these two ex-lovers soon find themselves in the midst of corporate espionage, and the only thing more dangerous than the secrets they uncover is letting the simmering sparks of their second-chance-attraction burst into flames.

RIVAL RADIO

Popular radio host Daria Stone despises her romance-obsessed adversary, Dr. Theo Chadwick. But when these workplace rivals are forced to share an on-air timeslot to save their radio station, will their sparks burn everything to the ground? Or can they play nice and save the day...without falling in love?

OFF THE MARK

When dirt bike racer Charlie needs a reputation fix before the biggest race of her career, she asks her friend Rowan – cocky ex-baseball player and flirty playboy – to fake date her for the cameras. But what happens when Charlie falls for the one man she knows will break her heart?

KEEP YOU BOTH

In this spicy, MFF novella, a blizzard traps wedding planner Paige Presley in a cabin over New Year's Eve weekend with the couple she's planning a wedding for. The only problem? She's secretly in love with them both.

www.ingramcontent.com/pod-product-compliance
Lightning Source LLC
Chambersburg PA
CBHW060516160726
47991CB00001B/51